ABOUT T

Emily Grimoire is the author of *Impractical Magic*. She was born and raised in Hartford, Connecticut. After graduating with a degree in History from the prestigious Smith College, she found solace from the hustle and bustle of everyday life in her storytelling. In addition to her writing, Emily is known for her philanthropy and dedication to various charitable causes. She serves on the boards of several cultural institutions and volunteers as a docent at a local whaling museum. Despite her success, Emily remains devoted to her ungrateful daughter and a granddaughter who turned out much better than expected.

JINGLE SPELLS

EMILY GRIMOIRE

avon.

Avon

a division of HarperCollins*Publishers* Ltd

1 London Bridge Street

London SE1 9GF

www.harpercollins.co.uk

HarperCollins*Publishers*

Macken House, 39/40 Mayor Street Upper,

Dublin 1, D01 C9W8

This paperback edition 2025

1

First published in Great Britain

by HarperCollins*Publishers* 2025

Copyright © Emily Grimoire 2025

Emily Grimoire asserts the moral right to be identified

as the author of this work

A catalogue record of this book is available from the British Library

ISBN: 978-0-00-876576-7

Printed and bound in the UK using 100% Renewable Electricity

by CPI Group (UK) Ltd

Also by Emily Grimoire

Impractical Magic

"Don't be cross, uncle!" said the nephew.

"What else can I be," returned the uncle, "when I live in such a world of fools as this? Merry Christmas!"

— CHARLES DICKENS, *A CHRISTMAS CAROL*

CHAPTER 1
BLUE CHRISTMAS

The greased-up pompadours of the Elvis dancers glinted in the December sunshine. In Tokyo's Yoyogi Park, seven men grooved and jived in a loose circle as an almost-but-not-quite-right cover of "C'mon Everybody" blared through a nearby speaker. Ostensibly the men were dancing together, but in truth each was lost in a rockabilly fantasia of his own. Hips swiveled and elbows pumped for an audience of lovesick girls who existed only in the dancers' minds. Occasionally one of them would burst into the center of the circle for a bit of anachronistic breakdancing.

Although no live teenyboppers were screaming for their Japanese Elvises (Elvi?), a modest crowd had gathered to watch, nonetheless. Delighted tourists snapped photos and videos to entertain the folks back home. Meanwhile locals looked on with a sort of knowing amusement; the "rock 'n' roller-zoku," as the men were known, have been a constant presence in the park for decades.

Meanwhile Delilah Melrose stood apart from it all: frowning, miserable, lost in her own thoughts.

Or rather, just one thought: *Papa would have loved this.*

When the song ended, the dancers gathered in a clump near the speaker. They whispered to one another, clearly planning something.

What could this be, wondered the crowd, *perhaps some special event?*

Soon the rock 'n' roller-zoku traded their leather jackets for red coats lined with white fur. They draped strings of battery-powered twinkle lights around their necks. One brave soul even pinned a floppy Santa hat to the top of his pompadour.

Oh yes, thought the crowd. *A lovely Christmas show!*

Oh no, thought Delilah. *A goddamn Christmas show.*

Delilah had deliberately, naively, chosen to visit East Asia in December, hoping to skip the holidays. She didn't realize that going to Tokyo to avoid Christmas is like going to Los Angeles to avoid smog. She'd traveled thousands of miles to avoid the holly-jolly and found herself positively soaking in it.

As the opening notes of "Santa Claus is Back in Town" echoed across the park, Delilah turned and fled towards Harajuku Station.

Roughly wiping at her eyes with the back of her hand, she muttered, "Fucking Christmas . . ."

Delilah's misguided decision to visit Tokyo in December had been made in the worst possible way—in the middle of an argument.

She was the eldest of three sisters: Scarlett was second, and Luna third. All three were witches, as was their mother, and as were all the women in their small New England town of Oak

Haven. The Melrose family was something of a "first among equals" in the town: their lineage dated all the way back to the town founders, who'd fled Salem back in the seventeenth century.

The girls' idyllic childhood had come to an abrupt and horrific end with the death of their father when Delilah was nineteen, Scarlett eighteen, and Luna sixteen. Each daughter had responded to the tragedy in her own way. Scarlett fled to the West Coast, swearing off magic and trying to blend in with the normies of San Francisco. Luna did the exact opposite: she focused obsessively on her magical studies, drifting from coven to coven like an excessively curious tumbleweed.

And Delilah? Delilah was the eldest. Responsible. Reliable. She didn't wander and study and perfect her witchcraft like Luna, and she didn't run away and date boys and feign "normality" like Scarlett. No. Delilah stayed.

She'd devoted the decade after Papa's death to managing the Melrose family business: Oak Haven's Stargazer Inn. She worked, and behaved herself, and stood glumly behind the reservation desk as her twenties passed her by.

When Scarlett finally did return to Oak Haven, she offered to assume her share of the burden in caring for the inn. Which meant Delilah suddenly found herself a free agent for the first time in her life. With great excitement, she'd packed a bag. The only question was, where to go?

Travel is quite different for Oak Haven witches than for average people. The women of Oak Haven have the ability to create and move through portals: a wall in one place can become a door to any other. For an Oak Haven witch, traveling from the Stargazer Hotel to, say, a Marriott in Sydney was merely a question of the right incantation and a pristine level of mental focus.

Gifted with the ability to go anywhere, baby sister Luna had ravenously gone everywhere. And in all the places she visited, she sought out magical communities with interesting ways of working and thinking and practicing their craft. It had been an adventurous life . . . but also rather a lonely one. So when Delilah asked to come along, Luna was delighted to have a companion.

They visited a coven on Mongolia's Eastern Steppes, where they studied a remarkable form of nature magic that could bend the very air to their will. They visited the fairy chimneys of Cappadocia, Turkey, where the witches cure disease and extend life nearly to infinity. They practiced telekinesis with the Warlpiri in the Great Sandy Desert of Australia. Luna was over the moon: at last, she had a companion in learning about all the mysteries of the magical world.

As it turned out, what Delilah mainly learned was that she hated sleeping in yurts.

And she wasn't so interested in finding out the mysteries of the magical world. She was more keen on finding eight-hundred-thread-count sheets and a bartender who could make a decent Manhattan.

To her credit, Delilah's patience with her sister's vagrant lifestyle stretched for nearly eight months. But when her little sister proposed a lengthy stay with a cadre of reindeer-herding witches in Siberia, Delilah put her foot down in the firmest possible of ways.

"I've had it! Enough 'roughing it' in some forgotten corner of the planet. I swear to you, I won't milk another goddamn yak, no matter what you say!"

"But Del," Luna explained patiently, "there aren't any yaks in Siberia."

"Don't pretend you don't understand what I mean."

"I know, we do *rough it*, a bit."

"A bit!" Delilah exclaimed. "*A bit*?! Compared to you, Luna, the Donner Party roughed it, *a bit*."

"That's a cheap shot. We're visiting the places where truly powerful magic still exists. The forgotten, overlooked places. And it's so important that we study and understand these practices before the modern world wipes them away completely."

"Luna! I've been trapped behind a desk *for my whole life*. The modern world is exactly what I want!"

"Well . . . okay . . ." Her sister thought for a moment. "Actually, there is a coven of powerful mind readers I've been meaning to visit in New York City."

"*New York City?* Okay, now you're talking."

"They live in the subway tunnels under Times Square. Is that the sort of thing you're after?"

"Subway tunnels." Delilah sighed miserably. "No, baby sister of mine, that's not *the sort of thing I'm after*. I'm after stuffing myself with duck confit at La Tour d'Argent. I'm after dancing down Bourbon Street in a second-line parade. I'm after singing karaoke in Shibuya. Doesn't *any* of that sound appealing to you?"

"I guess." Luna shrugged. "But not more appealing than what we accomplished last month."

"We stood on a dirt road in Middle of Nowhere, Australia, and learned to levitate rocks."

"You were so good at it, though! Telekinesis isn't a natural part of an Oak Haven witch's toolkit, but you were amazing!"

"I don't care, Luna."

"C'mon, of course you do! Telekinesis is very cool."

Delilah lifted an eyebrow. "It ain't cooler than duck confit, sweetheart."

And so it was that the sisters went their separate ways. Luna, to her appointment with the Siberian witches, and Delilah, to her date with decadence.

She did indeed find that second-line parade, and she did consume her weight in duck confit. With those two boxes checked, it was on to Tokyo, where Delilah had arrived just yesterday. She'd stepped through a portal inside the colorful street art in Paris's La Pointe Poulmarch and emerged in an octopus vendor's stall in the Tsukiji Outer Market.

As she wandered aimlessly across the city, she was shocked by the holiday light displays and the Christmas cake stands on every corner. Despite the loveliness of Tokyo at Christmas (or, really, *because* of it), Delilah began to worry she'd made a serious miscalculation.

Eventually she'd found herself in Yoyogi Park.

While he was alive, Papa Melrose had devoutly loved three things: his family, Christmas, and Elvis. For Delilah, the rock 'n' roller-zoku presented quite a personal, though unintentional, punch in the face.

Determined to salvage the trip, she'd abandoned the park and headed for Karaoke Kan Shibuya. At the bar, she downed a large sake and performed a Bonnie Tyler two-shot of "It's a Heartache" followed by "Total Eclipse of the Heart." The crowd ate her up; in fact, she wasn't allowed to pay for a single drink the rest of the night. One chap liked her so well he'd followed her back to her hotel like a lost puppy.

He was still snoring beside her when she awoke this morning.

Haruto? Delilah thought. *No, that's not his name. Hiroshi? Haruki?*

She sighed. *Oh dear.*

Once she'd gotten her bedmate dressed and out the door (his name was in fact Haruto, she'd had it right the first time), Delilah pulled on her fuzzy hotel robe, poured herself some room-service coffee, and pulled back the window shades. Gazing out at splashy Shinjuku City below, Delilah was aghast at what she saw.

The Christmas of it all. The Christmas was absolutely blinding.

And yet . . . despite how foreign Tokyo was to a Yankee like Delilah, even so there was something oddly familiar about it all. It took Delilah a while, sitting by the window with her coffee, to figure out why. A quick query to her phone revealed that Christians comprise *maybe* three percent of Japan's population; interestingly that was roughly the same percentage to be found in Delilah's witch-dominated—which is to say pagan— hometown. And once the traditional *reason for the season* is cut loose from its theological moorings, well. All bets were off. With no Christ Child to bring solemnity to the proceedings, Christmas quickly spun off its axis into rock 'n' roller-zoku Santas and a strange devotion to fried chicken.

Delilah was still mulling the cultural connection she'd found when a huge crash emanated from the bathroom. It was the sound of multiple haircare products hitting porcelain, followed by a hearty "Oh for crying out loud!"

Delilah wasn't startled by the racket. She was barely even surprised by it. With a deep sigh, she hauled herself to standing and moped over to the bathroom door. "What do *you* want?"

There behind the glass shower door stood her sister, sopping wet in blue jeans and a grey Stanford University

7

sweatshirt. Scarlett grinned widely. "Finally! There you are! This is the seventh damn bathroom I've checked in this hotel."

"It took you *seven tries* to locate my room?" tsked Delilah. "Still lousy at locator spells, I see. And why are you wet?"

"I was never lousy! It's not my fault that . . . *ugh!*" Scarlett freed herself from the pile of shampoo bottles and climbed out of the shower. "You've got way too many haircare products—it's ridiculous. Anyhow, it's not my fault that the locator spell was invented long before people could live fifty stories in mid-air. The spell gave me your latitude and longitude but not your *altitude*, which is a bit of a challenge in a building of this—ooh, is that a bidet? How class!"

Delilah frowned. "It's very simple to adjust the spell for altitude, if you just . . . You know what, no. I'm not doing Spell 101 with you. Get out of my shower and go home."

"Cut me some slack." Scarlett yanked a towel off the rack and tried to dry herself off. "I'm having a hell of a day. I've been all over this hotel looking for you. I've blundered into *at least* two close encounters of the infidelity kind, then a poor chap nearly opened his jugular when he saw me behind him in the shaving mirror. And—"

"None of which explains why you're wet."

"*And* . . . I'm getting to that . . . a Belgian woman was trying to enjoy a relaxing bubble bath when I was suddenly *in the tub* with her. Which made her, shall we say, rather the opposite of relaxed. In fact, we should probably get going because I'm pretty sure she's summoning the authorities as we speak."

"I'm not going anywhere with you."

"We need you at home, Del."

"I'm busy. Go handle it yourself."

"Haven't you seen my texts?"

"I assumed it was obvious that I'm ignoring your texts, Scar."

"But I used the little police-car-light emoji! Everybody knows to *always* respond to the police-car-light emoji! Why haven't you texted me back?"

"Oh ho." Delilah rolled her eyes at her sister's obvious hypocrisy. "You don't like being ghosted, eh? Well, little sister, I've only been ignoring you for a few weeks. Imagine what it's like to be ignored for ten years."

"Ah." Scarlett gave up on the towel, dropping it by her feet. "I'm still not forgiven, I see. Okay. And when does the statute of limitations run out, exactly?"

"Um, not sure. Check back around 2035."

"Sis . . ." Scarlett reached out to take her sister's hands. "We need you. We—hang on a second, where's Luna? Isn't she traveling with you? What, does she have her own room?"

"No, Luna is . . ." Delilah jerked her hands away. "Well, in fact I don't know where Luna is."

"What the hell? Why not?"

Del just shrugged. "Haven't spoken."

"Did you have a fight with our baby sister? Cripes, Del, who fights with *Luna*? Picking a fight with Luna is like picking a fight with one of those adorable pink salamanders with the . . ." Scarlett put her hands atop her head and wiggled her fingers. "One of those . . . what the hell are they called . . ."

"Axolotls, dum dum. And it wasn't a fight, we just went separate ways. Look, when I agreed to travel with her, I thought I was going to see the world. Like, the whole world. Not just witch covens. But all Luna wants to do is study. Her last idea was us going to New York City, which sounded great until I found out we were going to spend the whole time in the damn subway tunnels! If I go New York, I want to . . . I don't even know. I want to see *Hamilton* or whatever."

Scarlett made a face. "*Hamilton* is so 2016. People aren't still into *Hamilton*."

"Well whatever! What are people into?"

"I don't know . . . the new version of *Cabaret*, I guess?"

Now it was Delilah's turn to make a face. "*Cabaret*? Again?"

"Never stops being relevant, unfortunately. Look, Del, I don't have time for Broadway recaps, okay? The hotel needs you. Oak Haven needs you. And—"

"I told you, I'm not interested."

"Mama needs you."

Delilah met her sister's eyes. "I'm sorry to hear that. But I worked that reservation desk for ten years, while everybody around me got to run around and live their lives and get into all kinds of mischief. It's my turn now."

"Listen—"

"No, I won't hear it." Delilah turned away, gazing at herself in the bathroom mirror. "I mean, just look at me. I got old behind that desk."

"You're not old." Scarlett gingerly moved closer, standing beside her sister, the two of them framed in the too-bright neon light of the hotel bathroom. "You can't be happy out here on your own, Del. Come on. I mean . . . *Tokyo*?"

"Why not *Tokyo*? Luna traipses all over the world; nobody ever says a thing about it."

"Yeah," Scarlett said gently. "That's Luna. That's not you. What are you trying to prove, staying so far away for so long?" She slipped one arm around her sister's waist, squeezing her in an affectionate side-hug. "And at Christmas, no less?"

"I hate Christmas. I don't believe in Christmas."

"I know you don't, kid. But Christmas believes in you."

Delilah sighed, staring at her sister in the mirror. "I'm sorry. Really, I am. But I won't go home. There is nothing you can say that will make me return to Oak Haven right now. Absolutely nothing in the world that would—"

"The magicians are back."

Delilah spun around to face Scarlett directly. "What?"

Scarlett nodded. "And it's worse this time."

"I'll pack my things."

CHAPTER 2
CHRISTMAS IN THE DRUNK TANK

Jasper Hopkins was a man of solemn routine.

Every morning when he arrived for work at the county clerk's office, his ritual was the same. First, he'd locate an EV space to plug in his little Nissan Leaf. He'd gather up the wool car coat he carried (even on summer's hottest day), along with his insulated travel mug of super-hot Earl Grey (again, weather be damned) and his vintage leather attaché case. The case had been gifted to him by his grandfather upon Jasper's graduation from college and, like the coat and the tea, he never left home without it, despite the vast majority of the clerk's office having gone digital.

Once his belongings were organized, Jasper would lock his car and proceed along the buckling sidewalk and through a garden of modest government buildings—the county courthouse, the tax assessor's office, the parks and recreation department, and so on—before arriving at his destination.

There, every morning, Jasper would pause on the weathered granite steps and tilt his head back to admire the way the morning light caught the worn cornices of the clerk's office. The red-brick facade had darkened with age, its original color muted to a deep oxblood that spoke of nearly two hundred New England winters. Four Ionic columns flanked the entrance, their fluting still crisp despite the peeling white paint.

The building needed care, yes, but it had bones. Character. Not like the institutional nightmare of the interior. The offices themselves were a fluorescent-lit purgatory of drop ceilings and mud-colored carpet installed by 1980s bureaucrats in the name of "modernization." The building was forever stuck in a sort of design time loop: glorious early nineteenth century outside and nausea-inducing late twentieth century inside.

Alas, Jasper's beloved workplace was currently marred by numerous unwelcome additions: oversized wreaths clung to the columns, and a pair of Christmas trees stood sentinel on either side of the entrance. A horrible tinsel garland had been draped with bureaucratic efficiency across the entryway.

Echhh, he thought. *Goddamn Christmas.*

After many years of practice, Jasper was mostly able to put the so-called holiday out of his mind . . . But not when the building he loved was so determined to remind him of it.

He sighed, clutching his Earl Grey. *One more minute.* One more minute to drink in the symmetry of the twelve-over-twelve windows, the delicate branching of the cast-iron railings. Then with a sigh, he'd venture inside. The scene of a great crime, where progress had murdered beauty.

From behind the lobby's expansive reception desk, Deputy Clerk Toby Hearthstone observed Jasper's entrance with a wry smile. He reached out with one hand to mischievously turn up the volume on Mariah Carey's Christmas album, which he knew Jasper detested.

"G'morning, Jasper. You catch the game last night?"

"Don't be ridiculous," he said testily. "You know I didn't.

Anyway, the Patriots weren't the original Massachusetts football team. They were predated by the Boston Bulldogs, who were both founded and disbanded in 1929."

Toby blinked several times. "Excuse me? Since when do *you* know football trivia?"

"I, uh . . ." Jasper honestly didn't know. "I must've read it somewhere."

"Huh. Funky shit, dude. Hey, don't forget, we're closing early for the office party. Anita made rum balls. Aaaand I hear she's scheming to get you under the mistletoe."

Jasper grimaced. "Death first."

"Hoo boy." Toby chuckled. "Well, you brought in your Secret Santa gift at least . . . right?"

"Again, Toby, you know very well that I did not." Jasper marched by the front desk without pausing. "Eight years working here and I have never attended that ghastly event. I certainly won't start now."

"Aw, c'mon!" Toby called to Jasper's back in a tone half pleading and half joking. "Anita made her famous rum balls! And I hear Maureen and Dylan are gonna take a whack at singing 'Fairytale of New York' this year."

"Is that so?" Jasper spun around. "With the original lyrics? Or are they tidying up all the naughty words?"

"Well . . . it *is* an office party . . . and some of the language is pretty rough, so . . ."

"Listen, friend. Shane MacGowan wrote about particular types of characters who lived in a particular time and place. Do we agree with everything they say? No, we definitely don't. But he was a damn poet and that's *his* work whether it's comfortable to us or not. One does not put trousers on Michelangelo's *David*, and one does not *fix* Shane MacGowan."

"You're getting a little intense over a Christmas song,

Jasper." The deputy's words echoed off the cold stone floor. "And you're pretty full of yourself for a charity case. Maybe as a New Year's resolution you should work on your attitude?"

"Deal with it." Jasper marched on toward the stairwell, rolling his eyes.

Toby's remark about him being a *charity case* was a cheap shot about the fact that only part of Jasper's salary was paid by the county. The half of his job that involved fishing licenses and property deeds—the tedious, clerking part of the job—*that* was deemed worthy of taxpayer funding. But the good half of his job —the archival research, the historical preservation—*that* had to be underwritten by an anonymous donor. Every Christmas, a generous check arrived to fund Jasper's study of county history. Every Christmas, Jasper tried to discover out who his benefactor was . . . and every Christmas he was forced to accept that he couldn't figure it out and likely never would. All he could do was hope that whoever it was didn't die anytime soon.

He strode to the back of the building where the stairwell was flanked by twin elevators, yet another sacrilegious modernization. Yes, of course he respected the need for accessibility. Jasper took a back seat to no one in his love for local government or in his belief that it should belong to everyone. He understood that the elevators were a key part of making the clerk's office available to every citizen.

But personally? He detested *any* changes to the building he loved, even the good and necessary ones.

Fortunately he didn't need to confront the elevator very often. Jasper's domain was archives and records, just a short jog down to the basement. He was reaching for the stairwell door when he noticed a woman standing at the building directory, her finger trailing down the list of offices. Even in his rush to escape the Christmas music floating down the corridor, he couldn't help but notice her red-rimmed eyes and the way she kept dabbing at her nose with a crumpled tissue.

Jasper yanked open the door, took one step through . . . and stopped. With a quiet sigh, he turned back.

"Can I help you, miss?"

"What?" The woman startled, then tried to compose herself. "Oh, I . . . My mother passed last week, and I have all these papers, but . . . I'm not sure where to . . ." She gestured helplessly at the directory.

Jasper's expression softened. He'd seen that lost look far too many times. Given that nothing is certain but death and taxes, Jasper could never understand why the bureaucracy of death had to be so damned complicated.

He gave the woman's arm a gentle squeeze. "Fourth floor, probate," he told her quietly. "When you exit the elevator, you'll see a receptionist. Ask for Anita, she's the chief probate clerk. She'll need the death certificate. And did Mom have a will? Anita will also need that."

"Ohh, okay. Thanks very much. Yeah, I've got all that stuff here, I'm pretty sure. To be honest I haven't been able to understand what everybody wants from me at all. Everything is just so . . ." She sighed. "Anyway . . . you think Anita will be helpful?"

He chuckled. "Not one fiber of my being suspects Anita will be helpful, no. Especially if the rum balls have already come out. Still, though, she's the probate clerk, so she's your woman. I wish you the very best." Jasper patted the mourner on the shoulder and headed for the basement stairs.

"Thank you, sir," she called. "And Merry Christmas."

"*Ugh*." The door slammed behind him.

Jasper descended the stairs, each step taking him deeper into history. The stairwell walls displayed a gallery of his archivist ancestors—his spiritual family. And, in a real sense, his *chosen* family, given that he made the effort to salvage the portraits from a dumpster during yet another "modernization redesign" in 2018.

He remembered that day with perfect clarity: standing in the parking lot, watching maintenance workers cart out the "outdated decor" and toss it in piles. The second he spotted that gilt frame poking out from beneath a stack of broken venetian blinds, Jasper was in motion: stripping off his wool coat, rolling up his sleeves, and climbing into the trash container. The maintenance crew had watched in bewilderment as he'd excavated each portrait, carefully wiping away all the coffee grounds and plaster dust.

Now the portraits formed a perfect timeline on the basement stairs. More recent photos showed archivists from the 1980s, their faces illuminated by the sickly glow of the first IBM computers to infiltrate the archives division. Jasper touched one of these frames lightly whenever he passed it—a silent acknowledgment of the moment when efficiency had first trumped personality, when typed ledgers had given way to databases. The technology was useful, he had to admit, but something had been lost when they'd started reducing human lives to ones and zeros.

Then came the Sixties and early Seventies crew, who looked like they'd wandered in from a folk music festival. The Fifties bunch were all sharp angles and Don Draper haircuts, while the

1920s portraits showed a fascinating mix of old and new—men in starched collars and women in bobbed hair, all of them gathered around massive ledger books with the same reverent expressions Jasper himself wore when handling original documents.

The faces kept marching backward through time, clothes evolving in reverse like a fashion documentary being rewound, until photography gave way to paintings and sketches. The oldest portrait of them all hung at the bottom of the stairs: a hand-drawn portrait from the turn of the eighteenth century, showing a woman with sharp eyes and an expression that suggested she'd brook no nonsense when it came to proper procedures. Sometimes, alone in the archives, Jasper would pause beneath her portrait and imagine her approving nod or, on bad days, her stern disappointment. She must have been extraordinary, he thought, to have claimed that role in an age when even a basic education for women wasn't guaranteed.

Jasper's domain had mercifully escaped the modernization plague that infected the floors above. Oh, various committees had tried—for example, a line of atrocious fluorescent lights hung from the ceiling. But Jasper never used them. Instead, he relied on the original wall sconces and a collection of carefully placed desk lamps, creating pools of warm light between the towering shelves. The effect was rather like a Victorian gentleman's study. The air itself felt different down here: cooler, quieter, thick with the musty perfume of aging paper and leather bindings.

His desk was placed in a strategic corner position, allowing him to monitor both the main aisle and the research table where the rare visitor would work. The desk itself was a monument to controlled chaos: seven different projects spread out in precise arrays, each one marked with color-coded tabs. A lineup of German mechanical pencils stood at attention in a wooden holder. *A place for everything*, as his grandmother always said, *and everything in its place.* Which is why the messy pile of papers dumped in his inbox looked like meatballs dropped on a white tablecloth.

"Savages." His colleagues treated the archives division like some sort of paper-eating monster's lair. Just toss the documents down the stairs and run away, leaving Jasper to maintain order on their behalf.

Jasper hung up his coat, put away his case, and took a restorative swig on his still-warm tea. Rolling up his sleeves, he attacked the pile with the precision of a surgeon, sorting each document into its proper category. A property deed for the new subdivision in Litchfield. No fewer than *three* divorce decrees (apparently Jasper wasn't the only person immune to Christmas cheer). A stack of business licenses for a parade of food trucks and home-based crafting enterprises.

And then, at the bottom of the pile, something strange: a liquor license for a business he'd never heard of: J&J, Incorporated.

There was nothing particularly off about the license itself, but the name was unfamiliar . . . and that was the odd bit. To obtain a liquor license, firms had to leap through a complex series of bureaucratic hoops, applications, and committee meetings. Inevitably, by the time the formal approval hit Jasper's desk, the business owners were regulars at the clerk's office and well known to everyone in the building. And yet, Jasper was certain he'd never heard of J&J, Incorporated. Not once.

Then he saw the address, and his jaw dropped low: 278 West 113th Street.

What?

Jasper knew the county roads the way parents knew their children's faces. And this . . . this was impossible. The county's northwest corner was nothing but protected forest land, all hills and hollows and the occasional startled deer. There was certainly no grid of numbered streets. There was no 112th street anywhere in the county, nor was there 114th. There was no west side, no east side. How could West 113th Street possibly exist?

"What nonsense is this?" He reached for his phone, punching in the number for the Liquor Control Board. After sitting on hold for a while, Jasper was informed by a cheerful recording that the office had closed early for holiday festivities. *Of course,* he thought, annoyed. *Because why work when you can Christmas.*

He tried Zoning and Planning, the transportation department, and the tax assessor's office. Nothing but voicemails and Christmas Muzak. Next he tried the mayor's office; when someone picked up, Jasper momentarily hoped that maybe he was getting somewhere. But then the very drunk voice of the lieutenant mayor's third assistant slurred, "Helllloooooo, North Pole . . . hahaha, I said *pole*, do you get it?"

Jasper slammed down the heavy old phone.

He held the license up to the light. The paper was real. The signatures seemed legit. But the address had to be fiction. May as well be a building permit for a summer home in Narnia.

He drummed his fingers on the desk, the mystery vexing him. Like that feeling of having something stuck in his teeth that he couldn't remove. He glanced at his watch, then at the license, then back at his watch. He had questions. But everyone who might have answers was busy playing Secret Santa. Maybe tomorrow he could interrogate his hungover colleagues about this. For now, the mysterious J&J, Incorporated had to wait.

Or did it?

Jasper reached for his coat. He was already halfway up the stairs when he realized what he was doing. The lobby was empty—everyone else was upstairs singing butchered versions of classic songs and scarfing down Anita's rum balls. No one would miss him. No one would even know he'd gone.

The northwest corner wasn't that far. If there was a new business with a brand-new liquor license, surely it wouldn't be hard to find. *And really, what else am I to do? Go eat rum balls with Anita?* He shuddered and reached for his key fob. At least he had a legitimate excuse to avoid the mistletoe.

CHAPTER 3
FELIZ NAVI DON'T

The portal spat Delilah and Scarlett out into Room 301 of the Stargazer Inn. They collapsed in an undignified heap in the back of the closet.

"*For crying out loud, Scarlett!*" Delilah complained. "What kind of landing was that?"

"Oh, stop moaning. I got us here, didn't I?"

Delilah untangled herself from her sister and stepped out into the (fortunately unoccupied) room. Instantly she was struck by the scent: gingerbread and mulled wine, with just a hint of peppermint around the edges. It was the smell of Christmas at the inn. It was also the smell of Papa.

Why won't they change that stupid scent spell? she thought bitterly. *Make the air smell like . . . I don't know, cranberries or cloves or something. Why do they insist on filling our noses with his memory every year?*

She put down her case and straightened her blazer, hoping to maintain some basic level of dignity. "Scar, you really need to review the fundamentals of portal travel. See if you can get an eight-year-old to explain them to you."

"Blah blah blah, Grumpus McCrankypants over here. Would it kill you to admit you're a tiny bit happy to be home?"

"That would be false. But I'm here. You got what you wanted. Tell me what's going on with the magicians."

"In a minute. C'mere, you've got to see this—" Scarlett moved to the window and pulled back the curtains. "Mama's gone full Clark Griswold this year."

Delilah was horrified by the scene below. Twinkling lights wrapped every tree trunk and branch, creating a glimmering canopy. A collection of enchanted reindeer, crafted from branches and twigs, pranced around the shrubbery. One even had a glowing red nose, because of course. Even the old stone fountain was under a spell; instead of water, it sprayed streams of tiny golden lights, like an explosion at a sparkler factory. The sparkles formed themselves into patterns of stars and bells and wreaths as they dissolved into the air.

"Good grief . . . Santa's elves seriously got into the Red Bull."

"You're such a *Grinch*. You could be a tiny bit impressed, at least. Mama's had Nate hard at work helping out for weeks."

"Aw, good old Nate." Delilah couldn't help but smile at the mention of their childhood buddy and Scarlett's true love. "I've missed him. How's everything going with you two, anyway? Engaged yet?"

"No, not yet," Scarlett muttered, "and I really don't want to discuss it. C'mon . . ." She grabbed her sister's arm, yanking her toward the door. "Let's go downstairs—everyone's dying to see you."

"*Everyone* meaning Mama, who must be furious that I skipped Thanksgiving? Or *everyone* meaning Zahir, who I'm sure is annoyed that I haven't been around to help him in the kitchen? *Everyone* meaning the other witches in town, who all want to know why I'm not married yet? Or *everyone* meaning the outraged guests whose reservations you've bungled because you weren't paying attention when I taught you how to use the computer?"

"All of the above, obviously. But I only bungled a few reservations. Now, cheer up and come with me."

As they crossed the third-floor hallway, Delilah was hit with a memory so vivid it nearly knocked her sideways: she and her sisters as little kids, racing down this very corridor on Christmas Eve. Papa's voice calling after them . . . "Girls! Girls, wait! Did you know that the tradition of enchanted evergreen actually dates back to pre-Christian Germanic tribes? The druids believed—" Then Mama's laughter, cutting him off. "Edward, darling, they don't need a lecture on etymology. They need to get to bed before You Know Who arrives." But Papa was already deep into professor mode. He'd yanked a leather-bound tome from his study shelves and was standing in the hallway, waving it around. "But, Kelly, it's fascinating! The linguistic evolution from the Old English '*grēne garlēac*' to our modern 'garland' tells us about how magic adapted to—"

That's when toddler Luna had sneezed, and she must've been thinking about candles at the time because she accidentally set the stairway garland on fire. Mama quickly put it out while Papa beamed proudly and announced, "Great job, Luna! Burning the garland is *precisely* what the Saxons did! We'll make you a pagan queen yet!"

Delilah blinked hard as she forced the image back down the memory hole. "Scarlett. Will you please just tell me what's happening with the magicians?"

"Patience, grasshopper. There's lots of time to talk about those goons. Let's say hi to everybody first."

Delilah followed her sister down the staircase into the lobby, which was decked out in enough holiday regalia to make

25

Father Christmas blush. In the far corner, a string quartet had been enchanted to pluck out Christmas carols *without* the help of human musicians. "God Rest Ye Merry, Gentlemen" currently filled the air. A massive Fraser fir dominated the corner by the stairs, its branches already laden with antique ornaments. Delilah could hear the ornaments bickering with each other as they moved themselves around, all jockeying for optimal positions on the tree. ("People can see me better from this branch!" "Hey! You're blocking my light!")

Perched atop a tall, rickety ladder near the reservation desk was Nate, who was carefully attaching a long rope of evergreen garland along the crown molding. He had little metal clips clenched between his teeth, and he frowned as he concentrated on getting the spacing just right.

"Babe, be careful up there!" Scarlett called up to him. "Why don't you let me just . . ." She wiggled her fingers, suggesting a spell.

"Don't you dare," he replied through the clips. "I've got a system."

Delilah rolled her eyes. "Why are you letting him do that the hard way? One quick spell and the garland would be perfect. Is your magic that bad?"

"Oh, stop picking on me." Scarlett's face softened as she watched her true love at work. "It makes him happy. Men need projects. Especially Oak Haven men. They all marry witches who can fix almost anything with a quick spell and then spend the next thirty years not knowing what the hell to do with themselves. You gotta kind of . . . you know. You gotta let them *do stuff*. Besides, sometimes the hard way is the right way."

"Said no witch ever," Delilah replied. But it was true, there was something touching about Nate's dedication to getting the garland to hang *just so*.

The magical string quartet brought "God Rest Ye Merry, Gentlemen" to a dramatic finish, paused, and began to play the song again.

"Don't they know anything else?" asked Delilah.

"I've had some trouble with the spell," Scarlett admitted. "For some reason they can only play that one and 'Grandma Got Run Over by a Reindeer.'"

"Ah. So. 'God Rest Ye Merry' it is, then."

Her sister nodded. "We've been resting our merry asses for four days."

"I can fix the spell for you—it's very simple."

"Oh, Del! I'd love you forever if you could."

"That's all it takes, eh?"

The sound of raised voices drew the sisters' attention to the dining room. Through the open doors, they could see their mother, Kelly Melrose, presiding over a gathering of Oak Haven's most prominent witches. The women were all talking over one another, arms waving and complaints flying.

"We'd never do something so tacky," declared Jerusha, who was one of the elders. "I won't have it!"

"Tacky?!" shot back a younger witch called Candace. "How dare you?"

Delilah nudged her sister. "What's that about?"

"Planning meeting for the holiday pageant."

"I thought Mama swore she was done with it, that she'd never agree to organize it again."

Scarlett shrugged. "Doesn't she say that every year?"

Like many small towns, the annual children's pageant was a highlight of every Christmas season. But *unlike* many small towns—indeed, perhaps unlike *any* other—the pageant did not concern itself with the birth of a chubby-cheeked son of the Almighty. No, the Oak Haven Holiday Pageant was a pagan affair, recreating the battle between the Holly King, representing winter, versus the Oak King, representing summer. And given that this was *Oak* Haven, this was a very big deal. Indeed, there were few deals any bigger.

"The children absolutely cannot wear last year's costumes," Jerusha shouted. "Last year they looked like they'd been wrapped in bathrobes!"

"Well, excuse me for suggesting we be practical," Candace shot back. "Some of us remember that this pageant is supposed to focus on the eternal battle between light and darkness. It's not a showcase for a gaggle of six-year-olds dressed like Liberace!"

"Don't you lecture me about the pageant! I was organizing this pageant before you were even—"

Mama Melrose raised one hand, putting an end to the argument with just two sharp words. "*Ladies, please!*"

"Sorry, Kelly," muttered Jerusha.

"Sorry, ma'am," Candace echoed.

"Honestly, I don't know what to do with you. Of all people, I would expect you two to maintain some level of— *Oh! It's my girls!*" Mama's eyes lit up at the sight of her daughters. She rose gracefully from her seat, abandoning the bickering witches to join her children in the lobby.

"Darling, you're home at last!" She embraced Delilah but quickly pulled back with concern. "You've lost weight—you're skin and bones. And my gods, what on earth have you done to your beautiful hair? Is this what passes for fashion in Outer Mongolia?"

Funny what a year away can do, Delilah thought. Her mother's critiques, which had been endlessly irritating before, now just made her smile. In fact, if Mama *hadn't* complained about her haircut, Delilah would've felt a little disappointed.

"Hello to you too, Mama. Good to know some things never change."

"Things *do* change," Kelly protested. "Such as you, missing Thanksgiving this year! I hear you were too busy eating foie gras over in gay Paree to join your family."

"Duck confit, actually. I'm here now, okay? What's going on with the magicians?"

But the witches' voices were rising again. Conversation had turned in the direction of choreography, and some feelings were about to be bruised. "The dance of the holly sprites must be completely redone," Candace announced. "They look like sugar-rushed toddlers playing Ring Around the Rosie!"

"There's no need to be rude," sniffed Belinda Chatterjee, who happened to be the pageant's choreographer. "The children and I do the best we can, you know."

"They're supposed to be pagan manifestations of mortality and darkness, not the touring company of *Frozen*!"

"How dare you, Candace!"

"All right." Mama Melrose clapped her hands. "My meeting seems to be spinning out of control. Delilah, we'll speak later." She briskly returned to the dining room. "Candace! I must insist you *let it go*, as it were. No more attacks on Belinda's previous work, inadequate as it may have been."

"*Hey*!" Belinda protested.

Delilah turned to her younger sister. "Please, Scarlett, I'm begging you. What have the magicians done?"

"It's, ah . . . it's kind of hard to explain. You need to see it for yourself."

"Well, fine, let's go have a look."

From the kitchen came a huge crash of pots hitting the tile floor, blended with Zahir's voice raised in frustration. "Dammit to blazes!"

Long ago, Zahir's parents had been co-head chefs at the Stargazer; as a consequence, Zahir had grown up at the hotel, practically a brother to the Melrose sisters. These days *he* was the head chef, *plus* he had recently opened a pub in town, and the complexities of organizing it all had clearly pushed him to the edge of sanity.

"Scarlett, for crying out loud!" He burst through the kitchen doors and stormed over. "My presence is required for the dinner rush at the pub, but somebody also has to prepare for tomorrow's breakfast meeting of the Yuletide Planning Commission! And on top of all that, I also—"

"Psst!" Scarlett gave him a nudge. "Look who's back."

Zahir stopped short, arching an eyebrow. "Oh hello, Delilah. Your hair looks weird."

She turned to her sister. "What's everybody's problem with my hair?"

"And hey," Zahir continued, "thanks *so much* for all the help you've *not* given me these past months."

"Yeahhhh, I knew that one was coming." Delilah grinned. Her mother wasn't the only one for whom a verbal jab was a form of affection. "Nice to see you, too, Z."

"Scarlett!" He turned his ire on the younger sister. "You *must* hire me some help immediately."

"I have done," Scarlett said truthfully. "And you fire them all within a few hours."

"Well, maybe hire someone competent for a change. Because I cannot be in two places at once!"

"Buuuuut . . . couldn't you, though?" Scarlett asked. "We could take another whack at the doppelgänger spell."

"Don't you dare! The last ones were drooling nightmare creatures from the galley of the damned." Zahir stomped back toward the kitchen, calling over his shoulder, "They needed a recipe to make ice!"

Scarlett turned to her sister with a wicked grin. "I talked him into letting me try a 'Sorcerer's Apprentice' spell. I ended up with a dozen Zahir clones dancing around the kitchen like broomsticks in *Fantasia*. It wasn't especially productive, but man, it was funny."

"NOT! FUNNY!" Zahir's voice boomed from behind the swinging doors.

Delilah's head was starting to spin. It was too much. Too many voices, too many childhood memories, too much everything. She needed air. But as she turned to escape, a commotion from above caught her attention. The ladder beneath Nate had begun to wobble precariously. He'd lost control of the garland; his balance was off. Nate was going over.

From her inside coat pocket, Delilah removed a simple wand, carved from the branch of an ancient yew tree. She raised the wand toward Nate, her eyes closed for concentration. Just as Nate began to fall, an invisible force caught him in mid-air and gently lowered him to the floor, while the ladder clattered down beside him.

A hush fell over the lobby. Even the argumentative ornaments went quiet.

"God, Del! Thanks so much!" Nate jogged across the room to wrap Delilah in a grateful bear hug. "I'm so glad you were here for that!"

"Holy shit!" Scarlett exclaimed. "Thank you! Since when can you do that?"

But Delilah only shrugged. "It's nothing. Something I picked up with Luna, when we were in Australia. Just a goofy magic trick."

"Um, sis? Telekinesis is super impressive. It's not some goofy—"

A harsh voice cut Scarlett off. A deeply *unimpressed* voice. The voice of Kelly Melrose. "What in the name of all the goddesses in creation is *that thing* in your hand?"

The *thing* in Delilah's hand was, of course, a wand. In Oak Haven, a wand was a very unwelcome *thing*, indeed.

The power of Oak Haven witches sprang from a grove of oak trees that sits at the top of a hill, just above their little village. Oak Haven's young witches grew up playing hide-and-seek among the trees, drinking water from the same stream that feeds the grove itself. Magic became part of their bones, their blood, their very souls. As a result, no sacred objects were required. No wands or cauldrons or herbs were ever necessary for Oak Haven's particular brand of magic.

But when Delilah and Luna visited a coven in the Dartry Mountains of Ireland, a warlock had presented Del with a wand anyway. It had been carved from a branch of Eó Ruis, one of his people's Guardian Trees. She thanked him but explained that no, wands were not for her. The warlock demurred. "This is yours," he'd said. "It has always been yours. It's been waiting for you here."

Alas, Kelly Melrose was taking a rather different view.

"I ask again: what is *that thing*?"

Delilah sighed. She'd known this particular moment was coming; she'd just hoped to be home for more than ten minutes before it arrived. "It's a wand, Mama."

"The witches of Oak Haven do not use *props*. What, are you a prop comic now? Are you Carrot Top?"

Nate nudged Scarlett, whispering, "Your mom knows who Carrot Top is?!"

"It was a gift, Mama. And yes, of course I know that wands

32

are not typically a part of our practice. But I've been surprised to discover that the wand actually does help focus whatever I'm—"

"We do not use wands! Our magic thrums in our flesh and blood—leaning on some foreign object is an insult to your foremothers! Weak men with gout use walking sticks, and weak witches use wands."

Scarlett tried to intervene. "Mama, it's not a big deal. You're acting like she came home with a face tattoo or something."

"I would have preferred it," Kelly snapped. "And *not a big deal*? Betraying your ancestry with some phallic shortcut? Not a big deal? Delilah, I insist you put that cursed thing away immediately."

"Mama, come on . . ."

"We do not use wands in Oak Haven!" She turned sharply away and marched back toward her meeting. "Do not let me see you with it again."

"I need some air," Delilah announced. Between her mother's constant judgment and her father's inescapable memory, it was all too much. Before anyone could stop her, Delilah was heading out the front door. She heard Scarlett call out, but Delilah didn't turn back. Whatever was happening in town, whatever crisis had brought her home, it had to be better than drowning in her family.

CHAPTER 4
WE FOUR KINGS (OF THE HARDWARE STORE ARE)

The moment Jasper turned the key in the ignition, George Michael's voice filled the car with his doleful tenor: *"Last Christmas, I—"*

"Nope." He jabbed the radio off. "You did nothing of the kind, Georgie my boy."

Connecting his phone to the car, he scrolled to his personally curated playlist: *That Old Man Bach Sure Slaps*. The magnificent precision of the Brandenburg Concertos was just the thing to help him work through this mystery in a rational way.

Back in his office, that liquor license was still sitting on his desk, mocking everything he thought he knew about the northwest corner of the county. Come on, *278 West 113th Street*? He'd personally cataloged every road in that region. The very idea that he might have missed so much? No. No way.

Absolutely not.

Naturally his GPS selected this moment to go on the fritz, insisting there was nothing but protected forest ahead for miles. But Jasper didn't need technology to do his job, thanks very

35

much. He had his own mental map of the region, carefully constructed over years of meticulous research.

As the forest grew more dense, the naked branches wove a skeletal tunnel overhead. Jasper drove on, and drove on, and drove some more . . . and in time he began to wonder if he'd made a mistake.

That liquor license was probably just a clerical error, right? God knows typing mistakes are a dime a dozen in my line of work. Maybe they just got the zip code wrong? They could've meant New Windsor, I guess? They have numbered streets there . . .

Yes, that must be it.

This is nonsense. I should turn around, head back to the party, maybe even risk one of Anita's—

The trees suddenly parted, revealing a covered bridge spanning a frozen creek. The bridge's barn-red sides and mansard roof spoke of mid-nineteenth-century construction, though to Jasper's keen eye, the exposed structural elements suggested at least one renovation, perhaps around the 1920s. The craftsmanship was actually rather extraordinary.

Jasper parked and got out, his hands shaking slightly as he approached the bridge. He knew every historical structure in the county. He'd written papers about them. He'd given lectures to the local chapter of Daughters of the American Revolution. How could he not know about this bridge?

The mortise and tenon joints were properly maintained, showing none of the separation one usually encountered in structures this age. Even the roofing material appeared to be original, though how it had survived so long in New England was beyond him. He ran his hand along one of the vertical posts, appreciating the quality of the wood.

"What else have I missed?" he whispered, equal parts wonderstruck and horrified.

Back in the car, he drove slowly across the bridge and found himself transported into what could only be described as the bastard child of a Norman Rockwell painting and one of those year-round Christmas shops.

The homes were textbook examples of nineteenth-century domestic architecture: Greek Revival, Italianate, and Second Empire styles all maintaining their original details with impossible fidelity. However, while the construction looked perfect, the (garish, to Jasper's eye) house colors were worth a strongly worded letter to the County Preservation Society: sage green with cream trim, dusty blue with white colonettes, warm yellow clapboard with forest green shutters. This was wrong. All wrong. Not just the historically dubious color choices but the existence of the houses themselves. Jasper had never seen them before; of this he was unshakably sure. An entire town that he'd never visited or even heard of? It couldn't exist. He'd have known about these homes. Hell, he'd have written his dissertation on them.

He drove past a row of Greek Revival townhouses that had coordinated their twinkling displays into what looked like a Busby Berkeley production number, with lights dancing in synchronization across their identical porticos. A particularly lovely Carpenter Gothic cottage had what appeared to be a small army of animatronic reindeer prancing along its widow's walk. A bit further down the street, an eighteenth-century saltbox home boasted a collection of elvish ice sculptures that somehow hadn't melted despite the afternoon sun. (*Must be some new synthetic material,* Jasper told himself firmly.)

Most outrageous of all, across from the town green sat an otherwise stately Victorian mansion festooned with twinkling lights on literally every surface; it resembled a landing strip for absurdly festive aircraft. (*Incredible how the colored lights are so bright, even in the daytime,* Jasper thought. He couldn't help but be impressed, despite his distaste. *The things they manage with LEDs these days . . .*)

Jasper pulled over to snap a photo of the absurd building with his phone. But when he looked at the image, there was nothing but a sort of speckled grey mess. He took another photo, and another. All the same. They looked like a test pattern on an old television, back in the days before twenty-four-hour programming.

So my phone is broken, now, on top of everything else. Fantastic.

He sighed, locked the car, and decided to take a look around.

Main Street was everything that New England towns were advertised to be, from the brick buildings with their cast-iron storefronts to the gazebo on the town green. But if Jasper hoped this little field trip would be a break from the holidays, he'd severely miscalculated. Christmas had mounted a full-scale invasion. Garlands and ornaments adorned every lamppost and doorway, while the shop windows competed to create the most elaborate holiday displays.

On one side was Spellbound Books, its windows featuring some sort of winter wonderland theme. Down the street was All Who Wander, a travel agency whose facade maintained its original 1880s pressed-tin details. Henrietta's Music Store, with what appeared to be a viola in the window, *playing itself*.

He took a steadying breath of crisp December air. Time to get some answers. After all, he was a professional. He had multiple degrees. He'd written his master's thesis on New England architectural preservation, for crying out loud. And yet somehow he'd apparently overlooked an entire town? Didn't speak well for his graduate program, that's for sure.

All those college loans couldn't have been for nothing. There had to be a logical explanation . . . right?

Across the street, an elderly man was sweeping the sidewalk in front of a hardware store, whistling "We Three Kings" with impressive accuracy. *Perfect,* thought Jasper as he approached. *Nothing like a longtime resident for gathering intel.*

"Excuse me, sir?" Jasper adopted his most professional demeanor despite the existential uncertainty gathering in his belly. "This may seem like an odd question but could you tell me how long this town has been here?"

The old man looked up and his mouth curled into an enormous grin. "Well, well! Ahoy there, stranger! C'mon over. My name's Earl but you can call me Twelve!" Then the man turned toward the store's porch entrance, bellowing, "Hey, Earls! Come see what the cat dragged in!"

Jasper barely had enough time to wonder why the man was shouting his own name *and in plural* before another gentleman emerged from the store, looking older than the first. And another, older still. And a fourth, who may as well have been Father Time himself. They all grinned (a bit wickedly?) at the new arrival.

Oh dear, Jasper thought. *I should have risked the rum balls.*

"Coffee with a little something extra?" The youngest of the old men held out a steaming mug to Jasper. "Best thing for a December afternoon."

"Oh no, I couldn't . . ." But somehow Jasper found himself settled into a rocking chair in the center of the store, warm mug in hand. His first sip was a surprise: not just coffee, but coffee with rum. (Apparently there'd be no avoiding rum today.)

Jasper opened his mouth to object but quickly thought the

better of it. *If you want the information,* he told himself, *you better accept the hospitality.* In any case, far more surprising than the booze was the hospitality itself. Jasper had grown up not far from here, and he knew the classic Yankee response to strangers: cold shoulders and colder silence. Instead, he was on the receiving end of grins and backslaps and spiked coffee. It was like *Steel Magnolias* but with men.

"So tell me . . ." Jasper took a second, more cautious sip. "Are you . . . um, are you all named Earl?"

"Yes, indeed," said the eldest of the old. "I'm Earl the Ninth, but everyone calls me Nine. This here is my son, the Earl the Tenth, aka Ten, then that there is *his* son Eleven, and of course the young scalawag over in the corner is my great-grandson, Twelve."

Twelve laughed. "Be fair, the actual young scalawag is my boy, Nate."

"Sure, but my great-great grandson ain't here at the moment, which makes *you*, at age sixty-one, the young scalawag currently in the room."

"Your names are Nine through Twelve . . ." repeated Jasper slowly. "But your great-great grandson is . . . *Nate*? So he . . . what, he didn't want to be Thirteen?"

"Can ya blame him?" said Twelve with a wink. "Say, how's your grog, there? Can I get you a warm-up?"

"No no, I'm good. Tell me, is everyone in your town this welcoming to strangers?"

The Earls exchanged glances.

"Well. We believe in hospitality, I suppose you could say," said Ten.

Nine nodded. "Seems only right, given our history."

"What history is that, exactly?" Jasper tried to keep his tone casual, professional. But inside, his archivist's heart was racing.

An entire town's worth of untapped historical records? The academic papers practically wrote themselves. The ladies at Daughters of the American Revolution were going to flip their perfectly coiffed wigs.

"Well now—" Eleven settled back in his chair "—that's quite a tale. Goes back to Salem—the true Salem, mind you, not that tourist trap they've got going now."

"That's right." Nine picked up the thread. "You see, back in the bad old days, when the witch trials started, the true witches of Salem had a choice to make. They either—"

Jasper nearly choked on his coffee. "I'm sorry—did you say *true* witches?"

"Yes, *true* witches," Nine shot back.

Twelve chuckled. "Try and keep up, Jasper."

"Anyway, they could've stayed, fought the witchfinders. And that idea was discussed at the time, or so I'm told. But instead, they picked up and ran. Founded their own town, **Oak** Haven. So, they saved themselves. Which was good, cause **wouldn't** any of us be here if they hadn't. But unfortunately, **they did leave** the innocent gals to their fates."

"Weren't even witches, those girls that got hanged," Ten added softly. "Bridget Bishop, Sarah Good, Alice Parker, all the rest. Poor things, just in the wrong place at the wrong time."

"That memory is the burden we carry here in Oak Haven." Nine nodded. "It's the *original sin*, if you like, that we all live with."

"Sorry but, uh . . ." Jasper took a gulp from his mug for courage. "I'm still stuck back on the *witches are real* part of this story. How do you expect me to believe—"

"Tell me, Jasper. Have you tried to take a picture of anything since you arrived?"

"Um. Yeah."

Nine winked. "And how'd that go?"

"Have any trouble locating Oak Haven with the GPS on your car?" asked Ten.

"Or," added Eleven, "have you tried looking us up on the, uh, the Wiki-whatchamacallit?"

"Or Yelp," offered Twelve, a bit mockingly. "Checked us out on Yelp, have you?"

Jasper's mind raced. The missing street records, the unlikely architecture, that violin in the window . . . "Are you saying there's some kind of . . . *spell*? What, like there's some magical fairy dust protecting the town from *auslanders*? Am I in *Brigadoon* all of a sudden?"

"*There* he is." Twelve grinned. "There's our grouchy little archivist."

Eleven smiled too. "Good of you to join us, Jasper."

"What does that even mean?"

"The forgetting spell keeps us hidden from the outside world," explained Nine patiently. "Outsiders who visit Oak Haven forget the town as soon as they leave. And the spell has been updated for this here digital age—no selfies, no satellite images, no Google Street View."

"But . . ." Jasper's hand trembled slightly as he set down his mug. "None of this is possible. You do understand that, right? That this is impossible? I mean, I'm the county archivist! I should know about this place. I should have records, documentation . . ."

"Records are just paper." Eleven's eyes twinkled. "Paper burns. Paper gets lost. *Paper forgets*."

"Never! Paper absolutely never—"

"And *people* forget," interrupted Twelve. "Every outsider who visits Oak Haven? Ziiiip! They go all smooth-brained, the minute they leave town."

"Which is why," Nine continued, "we take in the folks who need forgetting. Oak Haven takes refugees, runaways . . . even retired pirates."

"I'm sorry . . ." Jasper picked up the mug and drained it. His professional composure was hanging by a thread. "*Pirates*?"

"Oh sure!" Nine gestured at his boys. "Me and the boys here are all descended from the Great Sea Wolf, Earl of Anglia, Terror of Tortuga. Reformed himself, married a witch, opened this very hardware store. We've been helping folks start fresh ever since."

"Let me get this straight. Oak Haven is a magical sanctuary town, protected by spells, founded by Salem witches trying to make up for abandoning their innocent neighbors?"

"That's about the size of it."

"So tell us . . ." Twelve leaned forward like he was ready to start a conspiracy of two. "What are *you* running from, Jasper?"

"Nothing." He frowned. "Unless you consider me a refugee from an office Christmas party. But I still don't understand. If secrecy is so important to you all, why are you just . . . telling me all this? You do understand that I'm a representative of the county government, right? Aren't I the last person you'd want to be so candid with?"

The Earls burst out laughing. Nine actually slapped his knee. "Oh, that's a good one!"

"What's so funny?"

"Well—" Eleven wiped a tear from his eye "—seems a bit late to worry about government oversight. Considering this is your sixth visit in as many weeks."

The empty mug slipped from Jasper's suddenly numb fingers. "*My what*?!"

CHAPTER 5
HAPPY CHRISTMAS (WAR IS COMING)

Delilah stepped out onto the inn's front porch, and immediately part of her wished she hadn't. The winter air was crisp and clean, the snow pristine and untouched, and *every single goddamned thing* was decorated for the holidays. She felt as though she were under the sway of some powerful Christmas bully, smashing her face into every bit of tinsel on Earth.

But despite her best efforts to maintain a proper Grinchian attitude, the simple beauty of her home still managed to take her breath away. It seemed like just yesterday she'd been in Perth, watching Aboriginal witches paint the sunset with their fingertips. Mere months ago, she'd wandered through an enchanted Bangkok market, where the merchandise floated from stall to stall without any visible means of support. She'd seen the Northern Lights dance a waltz over Iceland, watched Romanian witches race their enchanted Dacia sportscars through the mountains, and attended a rave in Sao Paolo where the DJ was a particularly musical ghost.

But none of those wonders had prepared her for the simple magic of coming home.

Even when excessively Christmas-ed, the Stargazer Inn radiated a kind of power that no amount of globetrotting could replicate. The kind of power that came from generations of witches living and loving and arguing and reconciling under one roof. The kind of power that made you feel like you belonged here, even when you were dead set on not belonging anywhere at all.

The inn sat about a mile from downtown, where properties spread out into gracious lawns and prehistoric trees. The old stone wall that lined both sides of the road dated back to the turn of the eighteenth century, when the first witches had arrived. Delilah had seen a lot of impressive stonework in her travels—the Great Wall of China, Angkor Wat, those mysterious ruins in the Belize River Valley that the local witches refused to explain—but there was something about these humble New England walls that caught Delilah's heart. Maybe it was knowing that her ancestors had placed each stone, powered by nothing but pure determination to make a home.

The windows of neighboring houses glowed with the warm light of carefully placed candles. Garlands of evergreen draped elegantly along rooflines, and tasteful wreaths adorned every door. The kind of restrained holiday decorating that spoke of old money and good taste and—

Oh, who was she kidding.

The Chatterjees had transformed their formal boxwood garden into the Island of Misfit Toys, with their gnomes dressed as Charlie-in-the-Box, the Doll for Sally, and the Bird that Swims. The Friedmans' house, just down the way, was surrounded by a small army of inflatable dreidels that spun in perfect synchronization. Meanwhile the Adebayos had unleashed what could only be described as a fusion Christmas —their animatronic Santa wore traditional Nigerian formal attire, and his sleigh was pulled by a team of enchanted zebras who appeared deeply confused about the whole snow situation.

It was exactly the sort of cheerful holiday chaos Papa would have loved.

The thought stabbed through her like an icicle. Edward Melrose had been the one who brought Christmas to Oak Haven in the first place. Before him, the witches had focused solely on celebrating the winter solstice—none of this business with mangers and reindeer and jolly old elves. But Papa, raised in a typical human family in Bedford, Massachusetts, had refused to give up his beloved holiday traditions just because he'd married a pagan. Instead, he'd infected the entire town with his enthusiasm for the secular pleasures of the season. Under his influence, the entire town eventually gave itself over to the many nonreligious delights of the holiday: to fanciful decorated trees and elaborately wrapped presents, to wassailing and cookie making, to Bing Crosby and Jolly Old St Nick.

For Delilah, every single Christmas decoration was on some level a reminder of Papa. And every single one jabbed her in the heart just a little.

Worst of all, she was clearly the only one who felt this way.

The first Christmas after Papa's death had been very grim indeed. Scarlett had run off to San Francisco by that point, so it was only Delilah, Luna, and Mama that year. And since they had the hotel to run, there had been no time for sleeping till four or drinking at noon or any of those so-called self-care measures that people go on about. They had no choice but to set their jaws and keep going.

The Melrose women had hated every minute of the holiday that year, and they'd done so together, as a team. They decorated only the most minimal amount possible. They'd steered well clear of the pageant and the snowman-building

47

contest and all the rest. And holiday carolers would inspire nothing but irritated glances and rolled eyes. The only song they could tolerate that year was Otis Redding's version of "White Christmas"; the natural anguish in his voice made it clear Otis had no expectation that *his* days would be merry or bright, and he certainly wouldn't judge if *your* days weren't, either.

In time, her family somehow forgave Christmas. Not immediately, that's for sure. But over the next few years, the joy of the holiday gradually crept back inside the Stargazer Inn. The decorations returned, and the Yuletide feasting . . . and the carols.

Ugh, the carols.

As if summoned by her thoughts, music drifted through the winter air. Delilah's eyes landed on the source: a line of enchanted snowmen positioned at intervals along the stone wall. Each had the traditional coal eyes and carrot nose, each wore a jaunty scarf, and each was lip-syncing Donny Hathaway's "This Christmas" with surprising soul. The snowmen were created by a collaborative spell of all the witches along the road. As you walked past one snowman, the next would pick up the song, creating an endless, inescapable chain of melody.

Delilah just shook her head and started down the path toward town. She heard the inn's front door thrown open and slammed shut behind her. "Del, wait!"

She spun around on one heel to see Scarlett, chasing after her as usual.

"Sorry about the wand thing," Scarlett said as she caught up. "Personally I think it's groovy. Some sexy warlock, offering you his sharp stick? Love it. But you know how Mama is."

Rather than evaluate the sexiness level of Irish warlocks—

which was surprisingly high, but she didn't feel like getting into it at the moment—Delilah changed the subject entirely. "I hate these fucking snowmen, Scar."

"Oh stop, they're adorable."

"They're an imposition, is what they are. *Someone else* picked the music, which means *someone else* is controlling my environment. Trying to control *my* mood. And I can't escape it." *Just like I can't escape the memories,* she thought. The way Papa used to jokingly conduct the snowmen as they walked past, using a candy cane as his baton . . .

"Ah, I see!" Scarlett's voice broke through her brooding. "As it happens, the decorating committee agrees with you; they put a new spin on it this year. Watch." She pressed her fingertips to her forehead, squinting in concentration, then snapped her fingers. Instantly, the snowmen switched to "Christmas Wrapping" by the Waitresses.

"You're kidding." Delilah sighed. "The snowmen take requests now?"

"Hey, it's fun when it's fun! Although, things did get a little weird for a while, when all the neighbors were arguing about which songs to play. Mrs. Chatterjee kept overriding everyone else's selections with the Mariah Carey one until finally Mama had to step in."

"Whatever," Delilah cut in. "Can we talk about the magicians now?"

"Oh yeah. So let's see, you and Luna left right after last Thanksgiving, right? It was quiet around here for most of the year. Then about a month ago, a massive convoy of trucks arrived in Oak Haven. Nobody I talked to had ever seen anything like it. Just eighteen-wheeler after eighteen-wheeler rolling through the streets. I lost count of how many. Naturally, the witches were all kinds of freaked out. There was a whole town meeting where everybody argued about the 'juggernaut jamboree.' But the weird thing was, the trucks didn't stop in town. They just drove on through. So . . . it was weird but, on the other hand, no big deal? Or so we thought? About a week later we woke up to, um . . ."

"To what?"

Scarlett put her hands on each side of Delilah's head and turned it toward the center of town. Then she tilted her sister's head up. And up. And up some more.

Holy shit.

For over two hundred years, the tallest structures in Oak Haven had involved the occasional Victorian turret. But now, over the tree line, loomed a behemoth. Fifty stories of glass and steel thrust up from the earth like some dark version of Jack's beanstalk. Its sides spread out in a series of swooping curves that suggested both tacky Vegas fever dream and Brutalist concrete nightmare. Its massive footprint dwarfed the entire Oak Haven downtown, like Godzilla looming over a smattering of dollhouses. One good stomp from this monster, and they'd all be so many broken candy canes in the rubble.

Giant neon signs promised SLOTS! SHOWS! CELEBRITIES! Searchlights swept the sky in lazy circles, as if the building was casually marking its territory: *Mine now, mine. All of this is mine.*

"You're telling me they built that overnight."

"More or less, yep."

"And you let them?"

Scarlett made a face. "We didn't know! How were we supposed to know?"

"My gods!" Delilah shouted. "The noise? The clamoring and hammering and all the heavy equipment?"

"That's what I'm saying, Del. There was none of that. They seem to have trucked in some supplies and then assembled everything, instantly, with no sound, no workers, and no effort that we could perceive."

"But how? How is that possible? How do a bunch of dum dums who yank rabbits from hats at children's parties accomplish a feat like this? What, you're telling me they pulled infinite scarves out their sleeves and turned them into a hotel?"

"And casino, don't forget the casino."

"A casino? Did they put a McDonald's in while they were at it?"

"Wimpys."

"Wimpys? What the hell, Scar? I didn't even know that was a thing anymore. A Wimpys in Oak Haven—good grief!"

"Ah ha, well," Scarlett sighed. "This is where things get tricky. It is not *in* Oak Haven, strictly speaking. It's a few yards beyond our perimeter."

"So . . . it's not influenced by our magic."

"Exactly. I think we can officially abandon the idea that magicians aren't every bit as powerful as we are. Or, you know . . ." Scarlett gestured helplessly up at the glittering tower. "More."

Delilah felt a hot flush of shame. While she'd been off collecting passport stamps and exotic magic tricks, this . . . this *thing* had sprouted up like some kind of corporate *kaiju*, threatening to swallow everything her ancestors had built. She'd been swanning around the world with Luna when she should have been here, protecting her home.

But what could anyone have done against something like this? The witches of Oak Haven were capable, yes, but their magic was intimate, personal—enchanted snowmen and floating ornaments, protection spells woven into stone walls. This hotel seemed to present a different kind of power entirely. The kind that came with lawyers and permits and

51

environmental impact studies. The kind of power that could crush a small town.

Delilah stared up at the casino. The building's endless rows of windows stared down at her with the impassive menace of a thousand eyes.

"There are who knows how many guests up there, in those rooms, gazing at us. At Oak Haven. They are looking at us from up high and just beyond our range—a vantage point that is *not* influenced by the forgetting spell."

"Del, you know how I was complaining before, about the locator spell that doesn't consider altitude? Well. Here we are, altitude fucks us yet again. But that's not even the worst bit."

"That's pretty bad! Our anonymity is completely blown. People must be looking out the windows: 'Oh, look, Tyler! What an adorable little town. Won't our followers just eat that up?' 'You're so right, Chloe! Think of the content we could generate.' How long do you reckon before we end up a trending topic? Those magicians are trying to wipe us out, Scar, pure and simple. Last year they infiltrated the town to get us from the inside out. This time, it's a full-frontal assault from the outside in. They're trying to—"

"Okay, you're ranting, sis. I agree with everything you're saying. But I'm telling you: it's not the worst bit."

"Well, what is?"

"Let's go into town, because I think you need to see for yourself. But I have to tell you, I just . . . I don't know . . ." Scarlett's voice trailed off and, for the first time, Delilah could see the worry in her sister's eyes. "I can't figure how we're going to fix this one."

Delilah grabbed her sister by both shoulders. "They won't beat us. This is our town, built by our mothers and fathers, and *their* mothers and fathers, and *their* mothers and fathers before them, going back hundreds of years. In Oak Haven, magicians do not win. Got it?"

Scarlett impulsively threw her arms around her sister and squeezed her tight. "I'm so glad you're home, Del."

"Okay, okay, cut it out. Come on." Delilah pulled back, wrapping one arm around her sister's. "Let's go fuck their shit up." But first she paused, put one hand to her forehead for a moment, then snapped her fingers. Suddenly the headbanging snowmen were belting out "Back in Black." The sisters marched toward town like twin storms while AC/DC's thunder rolled down the perfect New England street.

CHAPTER 6
LAST CHRISTMAS (I GAVE YOU AMNESIA)

Jasper stared into his coffee mug, hoping it might contain a few answers along with the rum.

No such luck.

"Six times," he said slowly. "You're certain? I've been here six times?"

"No, we've *met you* six times. Who knows how many other times you've driven through town. But yeah," said Nine, "we're certain. As certain as we are that you'll forget this conversation, same as all the others."

"If it helps," Ten offered, "you do mix it up a bit each time we see you. First time you visited, you got so angry about Oak Haven being off the map that you threatened to call the U.S. Department of Defense to report a glitch in the Global Positioning System."

"The time after that, you were hopping mad at the National Registry of Historic Places," added Eleven.

"You do have a tendency to get worked up, Mr. Hopkins," Twelve said. "That's why we started adding rum to your coffee."

"But hang on . . ." Jasper's mind was spinning from all the

questions he wanted to ask. "When exactly does this forgetting happen? The second I leave town?"

"Like stepping from light into shadow," Ten confirmed. "When you cross that town line, Oak Haven becomes nothing but a weird feeling you can't quite place. Like déjà vu, but backwards."

"Sure, the French call it *jamais vu*. The feeling that something familiar should be recognized but isn't."

"Look at the brain on this kid!" Twelve clapped his hands.

"Is it all at once? Or gradual?" Jasper pressed. "And is it complete? Do I forget everything?"

Nine stroked his beard thoughtfully. "Not everyone forgets the same way. Sometimes visitors retain tiny fragments: a smell, a tune they can't place. Nothing useful, mind you. Likely that's why we get the occasional repeat visitor such as yourself. Curious souls who keep wandering back, who can't quite shake us."

"How does it work, though? What's the mechanism?"

"The spell fills your noggin with trivia," Twelve explained. "Crowds out the real memories with random facts. You'll suddenly know which sea creature has three hearts, or which horse won the Grand National three times."

"So . . . hang on." Jasper blinked. "The spell doesn't erase memories, it buries them?"

"More like it interferes with the recording and organization," Nine corrected. "It fills up your head with useless stuff so there's no room for what the witches don't want anyone remembering. You know how it's impossible to find anything useful in a junk drawer? Kinda like that."

"This town is turning my mind into a junk drawer," Jasper repeated unhappily. "That's . . . not great to hear. Is anyone immune?"

"The witches, of course," said Ten. "They designed the spell that way. And those of us born here build up a certain tolerance. We can leave for short trips—a few hours, maybe a day or so—before it kicks in."

Twelve nodded. "I managed an entire long weekend one time. Of course, then I got overconfident, stayed away too long and forgot where I live, even forgot my own name. Nate had to come looking. Eventually he tracked me down in a Macaroni Grill at Atlanta International Airport. So . . . not really worth it, if I'm honest."

"But if you're somebody like me . . . if you don't have magic, and you *weren't* born here . . ." Jasper's voice trailed off.

Nine raised his glass in something between a toast and a condolence. "Junk drawer."

Jasper's hand crept to his jacket pocket, where a crumpled piece of cardboard had been bothering him all week. He hadn't been able to bring himself to throw it away, even though he couldn't read the water-damaged writing. Now he pulled it out, smoothing the wrinkles. It was a postcard, showing a quaint New England town square. The message side was a mess of bleeding ink, but he could barely make out his own handwriting: "Dear Future Jasper . . ."

"That's from visit four, I think," Ten said. "You bought a whole rack of postcards over at Spellbound Books. Mailed them to yourself, your boss, the Library of Congress . . ."

"Oh! Well, maybe somebody got one! Maybe—"

"Guaranteed that none of them arrived legible," said Nine. "The forgetting spell's thorough like that. It's not just your brain, it'll put a whammy on your writing, too."

"And your camera," added Ten.

"And your electronic devices," Eleven chimed in. "Ohh ho, remember that, boys, back in the Eighties? The witches had to revise the spell to cover emails and such?" The old men all chuckled. "The whole zeroes-and-ones thing was new to our gals, and the spell kinda backfired at first. For three days, that '*You've got mail*!' voice got stuck in everybody's head like a bad pop song. *You've got mail, you've got mail* . . . over and over."

"I have to go." Jasper stood so abruptly his chair rocked backward. "I'm going to leave myself a voicemail."

"What did I *just* say?" said Eleven. "Stubborn kid, ain't he?"

"Hey, maybe hire yourself a singing telegram," suggested Ten. "That'd at least be a new one."

"How about if you tattoo the details on your arm," offered Twelve. "You could kinda *Memento*-yourself."

"*Memento*-himself?" Ten stared at his grandson. "The hell does that mean?"

"It's a movie," Twelve explained. "Fella has no short-term memory, so he starts tattooing information on himself. His body *becomes* his memory, if you will."

"Huh." Ten shook his head thoughtfully. "How come we've never tried that around here?"

"Come on," said Eleven. "You know tattoos about Oak Haven would never stick."

"True," Twelve agreed. "Or they'd all transform into pictures of mermaids. Or infinity symbols—whatever the kids get nowadays. Anyway, *Memento*, good flick. It stars . . . um . . . ohhh, what's his name. That Australian fella."

"Hugh Jackman," Eleven offered.

"Chris Hemsworth," said Ten.

"Wrong," Twelve demurred. "No, it's um . . . the other one."

"*Liam* Hemsworth!" cried Nine.

"Russell Crowe."

"Mel Gibson."

"No, no, and definitely no. He's um . . . Guy . . ."

"Yeah," Ten said, "you made it clear he was a guy."

"No, I didn't say he's *a* guy, I said he *is* Guy."

"Twelve, what are you talking about?!"

Jasper sighed deeply. "Guy Pearce. The actor's name is Guy Pearce."

"That's it!" Twelve clapped his hands, delighted. "Guy Pearce!"

Nine frowned, muttering to himself. "Who in the blazes is Guy Pearce . . ."

As if beyond his ability to control it, Jasper kept speaking. "Guy Pearce got his big break in *Priscilla, Queen of the Desert*, soon followed by 1997's *L.A. Confidential*. As a young actor he appeared in more than four hundred episodes of the soap opera, *Neighbours*, only to return as the same character in 2022. He was actually born in England but moved to Victoria in—" He stopped abruptly. "What is happening? Why in the name of the National Archives do I know *any* of this?"

Twelve smiled. "Told ya. Junk drawer."

"Oh! That must be why I knew random football trivia this morning. I can't beat the spell, can I? It's hopeless."

Eleven gave Jasper a friendly slap on the back. "For *you*, maybe it's hopeless. For us, it's a privacy dream come true. Or at least, *it used to be*. Speaking of which, c'mon lads, it's about time we got outside."

Ten checked his watch. "Yeah. It's almost time."

"Time for what?" Jasper asked helplessly. "What is it *now*?"

"The current show," said Nine grimly. "Though you might want to brace yourself. May get ugly."

The men arranged themselves along the store's front porch and stared out into town. Jasper followed their upward gazes and felt his knees go weak.

Just beyond the tree line, a massive casino tower thrust up

59

from the earth like the world's largest middle finger, its mirrored surface reflecting the winter sun with smug superiority. It was the kind of Vegas brutalism that would make Frank Lloyd Wright wish he'd gone into accounting instead.

"That's what all the paperwork's been about," Nine explained. "The environmental studies, the zoning variances, and um, what brings you here this time?"

"A liquor license." Jasper squinted up at the monstrosity. "But how did *this mess* pass an environmental impact study? I mean, who are they kidding?"

Eleven shrugged. "These are some powerful people we're talking about."

"Look, I know powerful, okay? Powerful is, like, somebody's son-in-law plays golf with a committee chairman. There's powerful and then there's . . . whatever the hell that is. Nobody is politically connected enough to sneak something like this by county government. I mean, what are they, wizards?"

"Funny you should say that—"

"Also? I can't get my head around the address . . . West 113th Street? Where are the other hundred and twelve?"

The Earls shared a dark look. "Just their idea of a joke," said Ten. "West 113th Street was Harry Houdini's address in New York."

"Harry Houdini? Why would anybody even *know* his address, much less—"

"Magicians," all four Earls said in unison.

"Smug little shits," Twelve added.

"This isn't the first time they've tried to take Oak Haven for themselves."

"Far from it," said Nine. "They've had it in for this town for a very long time. Fight's been going on so long, nobody even remembers how it started."

"Okay, hang on." Jasper put both hands to his head, which was starting to ache quite a lot. "First you tell me I'm supposed to believe in witches. Now you're telling me that *witches* have some longstanding feud with *magicians*."

"Oh sure," Nine began, "it's an old, old thing. Nobody even remembers how it started. My dad told me witches and magicians were on opposite sides of the Civil War, but I'm not even sure that's the first—"

But Jasper had stopped listening. Two women were coming down the street, and one of them . . .

Oh, Jasper thought. *Oh dear.*

She moved like a lightning storm trapped in a human body, all barely contained power and imminent destruction. Her dark hair was cut in a sharp bob that managed to look both elegant and vaguely dangerous, like a switchblade at a garden party. She wore a blazer that probably cost more than Jasper's car, but she walked like someone spoiling for a fight.

Jasper suddenly realized he'd forgotten to breathe.

"Delilah!" called Nine. "Welcome home, stranger!"

The old men all called out warm hellos, but the woman—Delilah—barely acknowledged their greeting. Her attention was fixed on the casino tower with an expression that suggested she was calculating how to disassemble it, one brick at a time. And something about her presence suggested she'd probably succeed.

Her companion touched her arm. "Del, wait. The hardware store is the perfect place for you to learn what's been happening."

"Learn what, exactly?" Delilah's voice crackled with irritation. "Listen, Scarlett, unless they're selling industrial-grade wrecking balls, I don't see how—"

61

Nine cleared his throat. "Ladies? Perhaps I could introduce our friend Jasper? He's the county archivist."

"Delightful," Delilah said flatly. "Fascinating. But right now, I'm focused on that monstrosity up there."

"About that," said Twelve, grinning. "Hold that thought. Company's coming."

The sound hit them first: the distinctive wheeze of air brakes presaged the arrival of the most garish tour bus Jasper had ever seen. Its sides were painted with dancing rabbits emerging from top hats, accompanied by the words "HAVEN OF HORRORS TOUR: WHERE EVIL NEVER DIES!" in a font that appeared to be bleeding glitter.

A woman's voice crackled through speakers mounted on the bus's exterior: "Ladies and gentlemen, we're now entering the heart of darkness itself—Oak Haven! Imagine, if you dare, a town where the infamous Salem witches might still practice their dark arts . . . if our brave forefathers hadn't put a stop to their reign of terror!"

Delilah gasped. "What the fuck is happening right now?"

"Steady on," Scarlett said quietly.

"That's right, folks," the guide continued as the bus slowed to a crawl. "Every 'resident' you see is actually a trained actor, helping us recreate the spine-chilling atmosphere of colonial witch hysteria!"

The bus lurched to a stop, wheezing like an asthmatic dragon. A woman emerged from the bus, wearing a top hat, tails, and round reflective sunglasses that made her look like a steampunk John Lennon. A small group of tourists filed out behind their guide.

"And here we have one of our most popular photo opportunities," she announced with a theatrical flourish. "The authentic colonial hardware store, still operated by the same family of . . .retired pirates! Note the inappropriate Christmas decorations, showing how the witches corrupted even the most sacred of holidays, mocking our ancestors with their pagan ways! C'mon, folks, say hello to the witches and their pirate companions—if you dare!"

The tourists swarmed the porch, firing questions at the group. Jasper glanced around and could see that the two women looked ready to murder the visitors with their bare hands. The Earls, on the other hand, seemed to be having the time of their very long lives.

"Is it true pirates and witches were allies?" someone asked.

"Oh sure." Nine nodded sagely. "Who do you think gave Blackbeard his famous beard? Magical hair tonic, that was."

"Did you really make people walk the plank?"

"Only on Tuesdays," replied Ten. "Wednesdays were for keelhauling, and Thursdays we just threw people to the kraken."

"You don't look like a real witch," a young boy called out to Scarlett.

"I *am* a real witch," Scarlett replied. "And *not* a 'reenactor,' no matter what your guide says."

The boy's mother smiled happily. "That's exactly what a good reenactor *would* say. Always staying in character! Very good."

"Is it true that witches can't cross moving water?" called out a man in a HORROR HAVEN T-shirt.

"I think that's vampires," Scarlett replied.

"Can you turn people into newts?"

"Why would we want to?"

"Do you actually float?"

"Only after a really big lunch."

Delilah rounded on her sister. "Don't play games with these people."

"What difference does it make?" Scarlett shrugged. "It doesn't matter what we say."

"Well, it should!"

"She's right," Jasper heard himself say. *And not just because she's the most remarkable creature I've ever seen.* "You can't just make up history. Facts are facts."

"Ehhh, reckon we may as well enjoy ourselves," Twelve said with a grin. "None of them will remember it anyway. On the upside, Jasper, *you* won't remember how much this bothered you."

Jasper's attention drifted back to Delilah, and he realized with a start that he wouldn't remember her tomorrow, either.

"Barely a dozen tourists in that big bus of yours?" Delilah took a step forward, and her challenging voice carried across the porch. "Wow. Business is really booming, huh?"

The tour guide's smile turned sharp. "Just warming up, honey. Not all of us can coast on inherited family magic forever. Some of us actually have to earn our power."

"Is that what you call it? Stealing a few cheap tricks and pretending it makes you special?"

"At least we're honest about what we do." The guide adjusted her top hat with deliberate precision. "We don't hide behind some fake New England facade. Face it—your kind's time is over. These days, people want magic they can understand. Magic they can buy tickets to."

"*Are they fighting?*" The young boy whispered to his mother. "Is this part of the show?"

"Shh, of course it is," his mother replied. But she instinctively pulled her son closer, just in case.

"You wouldn't recognize real magic if I turned you into a

toad." Delilah stomped down from the porch to confront the magician face to face. "Which, by the way, I could do. Without smoke or mirrors or whatever sad little mechanism you've got hidden up your sleeve."

"Ohh, could you?" The guide's expression was pure venom now. "Go ahead then, let's see what you've got. All that power, and what do you do with it? Run a shitty bed-and-breakfast that barely breaks even. At least *we're* building something."

Scarlett nudged Jasper. "Sorry about my sister," she told him quietly. "She's not great with . . . well, people in general. But especially people in top hats who insult our family business."

"A B&B?" Jasper tried to sound interested, but he was preoccupied memorizing every detail of Delilah's profile. The fierce tilt of her chin. The crackle in the air around her, like static electricity with a grudge.

"The Stargazer Inn." Scarlett nodded. "Been in our family for generations. Speaking of family . . ." She turned to the Earls with a grin. "How are my future fathers-in-law, grandfathers-in-law, and such like?"

"We're all very well," Nine replied. "Though we wish Nate would hurry up and make an honest woman of you."

"You know him," Scarlett laughed. "Everything in his own sweet time. Hey, Del," she called to her sister. "Maybe let's chill out a bit, okay?"

All the while, Jasper kept his gaze locked on Delilah. As she stalked down to the bus, it was apparent she wouldn't be *chilling out* anytime soon. "You're not building anything except bullshit," she lectured the guide. "You're selling lies to tourists who don't know any better. Of course, none of them are able to post about their 'authentic witch-town experience' online. Having some technical difficulties with those Instagram influencers?"

"Technical difficulties are *temporary*. Unlike, say, an entire town trapped in the past because they're too scared to join the modern world. Tell me, does it bother you, knowing you'll end up like Salem? Just another sad little footnote in someone else's story?" The tour guide turned away from Delilah's withering stare to her charges. "Don't forget, folks—after the tour, join us back at the Houdini Hotel and Casino for our spectacular 'Burn the Witch' revue, featuring death-defying illusions that will have you believing in *actual* magic!"

"I'll show you some actual magic—" Delilah removed her wand from her coat and pointed it toward the sky.

"Del!" Scarlett shouted. "Not now!"

Jasper looked worriedly from one sister to the other. *What the hell is going on?!*

"They want to see some magic, right?" Delilah said. "Let's show them."

"Del, dammit! Not now! *Come on*!"

Delilah glanced up at the porch, and Jasper could feel her rage even at a distance. He made a mental note to never, ever be the cause of an expression like that. But after a moment, Delilah seemed to take in her sister's panicked expression, and she slowly lowered her arm. "Fine. But this isn't over."

"Whatever you say, darling." The tour guide plastered her smile back on. "Let's get back on the bus, everybody. And when we return, be sure to visit our gift shop for authentic replicas of witch-hunter weaponry!" She stared meaningfully at Del. "You never know when you might need some."

Delilah marched back up to the porch, her hands still crackling with barely contained power. But she was looking at Jasper now, really looking at him, as though seeing him for the first time.

"They said you're a historian of some sort? So you must know what actually happened in Salem?" she asked quietly.

He nodded but then frowned slightly. "Well, in fact . . . I knew what I thought happened. But the Earls here explained to me about the founding of Oak Haven, so clearly the official story didn't include everything."

"But you understand why we can't let that tour group turn our history into a sideshow attraction. We can't let them make it into something it wasn't—you get that, right?"

"I do, of course. Your ancestors' decision to abandon the other women, while painful, is also what makes your town what it is today." Jasper surprised himself by reaching for her hand. More surprising—she let him take it. "But there has to be a better way to fight off that tour bus than giving them exactly the magic show they want."

"I suppose you have a point, Mr. Archivist."

"Please," he managed through suddenly dry lips, "call me Jasper."

"All right, Jasper." The ghost of a smile played at the corners of her mouth.

"Ohmigod, look at them!" one of the tourists squeaked happily. "Are they doing a meet-cute? Are they, like, Phoebe and Cooper on *Charmed*?"

The tour guide herded the visitors back on their bus, making one final snippy comment about "actors who take themselves too seriously." The bus pulled away, its garish paint job catching the winter sun. And high above, the casino's mirrored windows reflected it all: the bus, the hardware store, and the town beyond.

The Earls surrounded Delilah, forcing hugs on her as they welcomed her home and demanded the details on her travels.

Jasper moved off to the side, a little uncomfortable as a

spectator to the reunion. He thought about the postcard he'd been carrying around in his pocket, about all his previous failed attempts to remember this place. About how many times he must have discovered Oak Haven, only to lose it again.

About how he couldn't bear the thought of forgetting her.

He pulled out his phone, his fingers moving before his brain could catch up. The phone rang five times and went to voicemail.

"Hi, Toby? Yeah, it's Jasper. Listen . . . I won't be in tomorrow. Or the next day. Or . . . actually, I'm not sure when I'll be back. I need to do some research. In-depth research. The kind that requires . . ." He glanced at Delilah again, then up at the looming casino. "The kind that requires a longer stay."

CHAPTER 7

WALKING IN A WARDED WONDERLAND

"I can't *believe* you . . ." Delilah was still fuming as she and Scarlett made their way to the casino. "I should've shown that nitwit what real magic looks like. But no-o-o, no. You made me let that hack in the hat off the hook."

"Whatever you say, Dr. Seuss." Scarlett matched her sister's furious pace, but every crunch of gravel sounded like a tiny accusation. *You should've done something.* "I get that you're mad. But putting some kind of magical whammy on a total stranger would not have defused the situation."

"Who said I *wanted* to defuse *anything*?"

"We need a plan, Del. We can't just pop off without thinking it through."

"Since when? That's your whole brand, isn't it, Scarlett? Shoot first, ask questions later?"

"I'm maturing," Scarlett insisted. "I've evolved."

"Yeah, right."

As the sisters made their way out of town, the winter forest closed around them like a fretful parent. These trees were here when the first witches fled Salem, when Oak Haven was nothing but desperate women and raw magic and pure determination to survive. They'd be here long after the Melrose sisters had come and gone.

"They're just *magicians*," Delilah muttered. "Just small-time, silk-scarf-wielding nobodies." But even she could hear the doubt in her own voice.

"Time to bury that myth. I know, our whole lives it's been *witches are real; magicians are fake*. But they built a forty-story hotel in a week, Del. And I still don't know how. I didn't see a bulldozer. Or an excavator. Not a single dump truck, not one. Nothing. Just poof, and it was there. And I mean, just look around. Where did all the trees go?"

The clear-cut zone around the casino was like a gaping wound in the forest, raw and wrong. Even the trees at the edge of witch territory seemed to shrink away from it.

"I don't know if witches have been simply wrong about magicians all these years," Scarlett continued, "or if they've been lying to us young folks, or—"

Delilah whirled around to face her sister. "You take that back. Witches don't lie."

Scarlett made a huffing sound, and her breath was visible in the winter air. "Everybody lies, Del, come on."

Delilah's expression went as dark as the shadows between the trees. "I don't. Truth is truth, period." She returned to stalking down the road like a hungry apex predator. She passed the old stone wall that marked the edge of witch territory . . . and kept going.

Her sister followed, a mischievous smile playing on her face. "Now you sound like that historian guy. Hey, he's pretty cute, yeah? You and he certainly seemed to hit it off."

"Oh, don't start."

"What? I'm just saying. It's not every day we get a handsome nerd traipsing through town."

"I agreed with him because he was the only one talking sense. Which at that moment, just happened to align with my completely justified rage."

"Uh-huh. And the way he kept looking at you like you were the *Mona Lisa* come to life had nothing to do with—"

"I swear, Scar, if you don't stop? I will turn *you* into a toad."

They rounded a bend in the road and there it was: the casino erupted from the winter landscape like some fever-dream merger of Hogwarts and a Kardashian bathroom, its mirrored surfaces reflecting and distorting the winter sunset.

The main tower reached toward the sky like a bully's middle finger to good taste, but the entrance was where the worst aesthetic crimes could be seen. Where the Excalibur Hotel in Vegas had princess turrets at the front, this monstrosity sported a lineup of giant top hats, each one rotating slowly while puffs of smoke emerged. Mechanical white rabbits popped out of the hats at regular intervals, their red eyes glowing with demonic intensity.

A fountain danced in front of the main entrance, with jets of rainbow-colored liquid spelling out "MAGIC IS REAL" in Comic Sans.

"Oof, look over there. Is that . . ." Scarlett squinted. "Is that a topiary rabbit being sawed in half?"

Sure enough, the landscaping featured a series of sculpted shrubs depicting various magic tricks. A rabbit emerging from a hat, a prone woman levitating above a platform, and yes—a rabbit being bisected while somehow maintaining a cheerful expression. Like Edward Scissorhands had a mental breakdown at a birthday party.

"Never give magicians a landscaping budget," Delilah

muttered. She squared her shoulders and marched toward the entrance.

"Del, wait. Hang on a sec, there's something you don't—"

But Delilah wasn't listening. *Someone* was about to receive a rather substantial piece of her mind about both their terrible taste and their acts of botanical cruelty.

She stomped straight at the golden awning and suddenly bounced off thin air like a bluebird hitting a plate-glass window.

"Ow! What the—" She pressed one hand against the invisible barrier. Little sparks of angry magic crackled around her fingers.

"I tried to warn you!" Scarlett steadied her sister. "They've got the whole place warded beyond belief. Belinda tried to sneak in and ended up with her eyebrows singed off."

"Really?" Delilah pushed against the invisible wall, letting her own magic probe at the barrier. The wards snapped back like rubber bands made of pure spite. "What kind of protection spell is this?"

"The nasty kind. We tried everything. Counter-spells, enchanted lockpicks, even that old trick with the mirror and the sage bundle that Jerusha swears by. Nothing has worked so far."

Delilah pulled her hand back. Wisps of blue smoke curled from her fingertips where they'd touched the ward. "Okay, new plan. Let's make a quick circle around the building, look for weak spots. Maybe if we—"

"Shh!" Scarlett yanked her behind one of the larger shrubs as two gardeners approached, pushing a cart of pruning tools.

"—brilliant plan really," the older gardener was saying. "The bosses are gonna be so pleased when they get here."

"Wait, is that why we're out here at this hour?" demanded his companion. As they passed some shrubs, he deadheaded a topiary dove with perhaps more violence than necessary. "To impress some stupid *bosses*?"

"Listen, young one. The top brass has some powerful magic. You don't mess with those boys. And if they want the topiaries spruced up in time for tomorrow's meeting, then that's what we're gonna do."

From the safety of their shrub, Scarlett turned to her sister, eyes wide. She mouthed, "*Meeting. Tomorrow,*" and waggled her eyebrows.

"*NO,*" Delilah mouthed back silently. "*Don't even think about it.*"

"And this game they're running, with the tours," continued the older gardener. "I'm telling you, it's genius. By the solstice, those broads won't know what's real anymore. The boss says that will totally—"

Delilah shifted position, the better to hear the men, and promptly lost her balance, taking down both herself and Scarlett in a spectacular crash of limbs and cursing. They tumbled out from behind the shrub in a decidedly un-stealthy heap.

The gardeners stared. The witches stared back. For a moment, nobody moved.

Then the older gardener reached for something in his pocket that definitely wasn't pruning shears.

"Run?" suggested Scarlett.

"Run," agreed Delilah.

As they sprinted back toward town, Delilah could have sworn she heard the topiary rabbits laughing.

They didn't stop running until they reached Main Street, where Delilah finally slowed to catch her breath. "Well," she managed between gasps, "that was . . ."

"Graceful?" offered Scarlett. "Elegant? A testament to the legendary poise of the Melrose women?"

"I was going to say 'informative' but sure, mock me if you like."

"Del, you fell out of a bush."

"It was a tactical surprise exit from concealment."

"You landed on my chest, elbows first."

"Tactical surprise ribcage."

They walked the rest of the way to the Stargazer in companionable silence, though Delilah could practically hear her sister crafting the most embarrassing possible version of events to share with Nate later. At least the running had warmed them up. December in Oak Haven had always been cold, as if the weather itself was trying to justify all those cozy Christmas traditions Papa had loved so much.

Delilah pushed the thought away, trying to focus instead on their discoveries: the magical wards, the gardeners' cryptic conversation, and the terrible rotating top hats.

"Oh ho ho, what have we here?" Scarlett muttered.

"What?" Del looked around, trying to figure out what Scarlett was—oh. A little electric car was parked in front of the hotel. "So? Whose car is that?"

Scarlett snorted. "Come on. Can't you guess?"

They found Jasper in the lobby, attempting to check in while simultaneously babbling nonstop about the many intriguing architectural features of the building. Mama was on the far side of the reservation desk, enduring the newcomer's enthusiasm with the kind of forced patience she usually reserved for drunk wedding guests.

"The neo-Gothic elements are fascinating . . ." He was clearly oblivious to Mama's expression; her smile was becoming increasingly wooden. "Though the Victorian influences in the wooden detailing suggest—"

"There's gonna be a meeting!" Scarlett burst into the lobby and marched up to the desk. "Mama, we overheard some gardeners talking. We couldn't get the details, but the magicians are gathering here tomorrow. The big ones, apparently. Or, big enough to merit sending landscapers out to make everything perfect."

Delilah was right behind, nodding vigorously. "All those lies they're telling? I don't know why exactly, but they aren't doing it by accident. There's some sort of plan and—"

"Girls! I'm so happy to see you!" Her mother's relief at the interruption was palpable. "Perfect timing. Why don't you show our enthusiastic new guest to his room while I check on . . . um . . . *something* in my office?"

"I, ah . . . well." Jasper glanced at Delilah, then down at his shoes, then he adjusted his glasses, somehow making them more crooked than before. "That is, I was hoping to document the . . . that is . . . um. You have leaves in your hair," he blurted suddenly.

Delilah's hand flew to her head. Sure enough, evidence of their *tactical surprise exit* from the shrubbery remained. Perfect.

"Botanical research," she said with all the dignity she could muster while picking bits of hedge out of her hair. "Very important witch business. Nothing you need to document."

"Though if you're interested in documentation," Scarlett chimed in with her usual mischievous helpfulness, "I'm sure Del would be happy to show you around the hotel. The architecture is fascinating, especially in the evening. By candlelight. Just the two of you—"

A little growl escaped from Delilah's throat. "Don't you have a boyfriend to torment?"

"Don't you have a room to assign our historian friend here?"

Jasper looked between the sisters like he was watching a tennis match played with live grenades. "I don't want to impose . . ."

"You're not," said Scarlett, just as Delilah said, "You are."

Mama watched this exchange with barely concealed amusement. She hadn't seen her eldest so flustered by a man since . . . maybe ever.

"Room 301," Delilah found herself saying, just to make everyone stop looking at her with those bemused expressions. "Best view of the gardens. Not that you'll be able to document them, what with the forgetting spell and all, but . . ." She shrugged. "At least you'll enjoy them while you're here."

"Thank you." He smiled, and something warm and uncomfortable fluttered in Delilah's chest. "I look forward to forgetting them thoroughly."

Their fingers brushed as she handed over the key, and they both jumped in surprise. "Oh! I'm so sorry," he said quickly. "Static electricity . . . so annoying this time of year. I apologize."

"No no . . ." A little flush appeared on Delilah's cheeks. "I'm pretty sure I'm the one who shocked you."

"Oh, I'm quite certain it was my fault," Jasper argued.

"*Ooh, I'm sorry I shocked you,*" Scarlett said teasingly. "*No no, I'm sorry I shocked you . . . No I'm sorry . . .*"

"Shut up, dear sister." Delilah backed away from the reservation desk. "Mama, you said something about your office?"

"Yes." Her mother's eyes were twinkling in a way Delilah absolutely did not like. "I found something rather interesting in

76

the old records. Come along, girls. Mr. Hopkins, you're most welcome at our inn. Breakfast begins at seven-thirty."

As the sisters followed their mother, Delilah found herself glancing back at the new arrival. Jasper had his notebook out again. He was sketching the lobby's architectural details as though he could make his memories permanent through sheer force of documentation. He'd fail, of course. More than that, he seemed to know he'd fail. And something about his dedication to preserving what he knew he was doomed to forget made Delilah's heart race in a way she was absolutely not ready to examine.

Mama's office still smelled exactly as it had when Delilah was small: the scents of ripening persimmons and old books and distant campfires, with maybe just a soupcon of nonspecific disapproval. The piles of books, the hotel ledgers, the mysterious old parchments written in symbols that didn't make any sense . . . It was all as it was when Delilah had left.

Her mother's voice cut through any moment of nostalgia that may have been brewing. "Girls, look at this letter I've found. I came across it while looking for the Christmas pudding recipe." Her tone was perfectly casual, as though stumbling on centuries-old documents while researching side dishes was an everyday occurrence. Which, at the Stargazer, it basically was.

"Please tell me it has instructions for blowing up a hotel," Delilah muttered. "Because otherwise it's not anything we need."

"Hardly. It's from Agnes Bartlett. She worked at the county clerk's office when it was established right after the

Revolutionary War. She was one of the town founders, which really was a big enough role to play, if you think about it. However, she also took a job with the county, specifically to make sure that Oak Haven never ended up in any official archives. In the course of things, she ended up creating their original filing system. Which has always amused me, that those pencil pushers at the clerk's office have no idea their entire bureaucracy is based on magic. Anyway, listen to this:

"My most worthy successor, I put quill to paper with grave disquiet regarding the nature of truth and remembrance. Though scant years have passed since our deliverance from Salem, already I perceive our tale taking new shape, like clay upon the potter's wheel, molded to please the hand that shapes it. We who fled now cast ourselves as martyrs most pure, turning blind eyes to the darker shadows of our history. The young ones speak of their mothers' flight as though 'twere ordained by fate itself, as though no other path lay before them."

"What other path, though?" Delilah interrupted. "What, were they supposed to stay and get hanged? They had to get out of there."

"But maybe they should have brought the accused women along," Scarlett suggested. "Instead of abandoning them?"

"*Maybe* . . . but maybe not. Maybe there wasn't enough time. Maybe they tried and the women didn't want to leave home. We don't know what was happening; we weren't there."

"*Girls!*" Her mother's other eyebrow joined the first. "Might I continue?"

"Sorry."

"But truth is not a dress pattern, to be adjusted for a better fit. If we blind ourselves to the weight of our choices, how then shall we guide those who follow to choose more wisely? Thus have I

commenced to create certain protections, certain safeguards against the dimming of our common memory . . ."

The letter went on, but Delilah was stuck on that phrase: the weight of our choices. What choices? The witches didn't have a choice; they fled Salem because they had to. Because staying meant death. Because . . .

She realized her sister was watching her with an odd expression. "Why are you making that face?"

"Nothing." Scarlett shifted uncomfortably. "Just . . . I dunno, I guess I'm still stuck on those other women? The ones who were wrongly accused? I mean, why *didn't* our ancestors just bring them along? What would've been the harm?"

"Because they weren't—" Delilah stopped. She was going to say they weren't *real witches*, but she immediately realized that didn't exactly excuse leaving them behind to get murdered. "I don't know why."

"Me neither."

Mama lowered her reading glasses. "I suspect that may be the point of this letter. Perhaps there are things we don't know because long ago, we decided not to know them."

From the lobby came the sound of Jasper dropping what was probably his notebook. There was a shuffle of papers, a muffled curse, and the distinct sound of someone trying very hard to maintain professional dignity while crawling under a table to chase a ballpoint pen.

Delilah smiled before she could stop herself. *Jasper Hopkins. Now, there was someone who would never decide not to know something.*

She turned back to see her mother and sister watching her with identically smug expressions. "Oh, shut up," she said to both of them. "What about the rest of the letter? All that philosophy is fine, but does Agnes say anything about magical

79

protection? Like, say, how to prevent a tacky casino from destroying our town?"

"Nothing, I'm afraid," said Mama. "I don't think errant casinos were top of mind in colonial times."

Outside, snow began to fall. Delilah went to the window to look. Real snow this time, not the enchanted flurries that sometimes decorated Oak Haven's winter nights. Through the office window, they could see the casino's lights reflecting off the flakes, turning them strange colors that nature never intended.

Delilah thought about weight of choices, and about the things people tell themselves to sleep at night. She thought about her father, about Christmas, about all the things this visit home was forcing her to remember. And she thought about a county archivist who believed in preserving everything, even the hard parts. Even the parts that hurt.

From the lobby came the sound of Jasper realizing that the lobby baseboards were original to the building's construction in 1832, when the witches had turned the remains of an old barn into the Stargazer Inn. His cry of joy would have been goofy if it wasn't so . . . what was the word? *Genuine.* That was it. The man was genuinely, unabashedly excited about historical woodwork.

"Adorable," she said without thinking.

"Oh, big sis." Scarlett joined her sister at the window. "You are in so much trouble."

CHAPTER 8
MINT LEAVES AND FRUIT CLEAVES AND INFINITE DIYAS

Back at his apartment, Jasper's sock drawer was arranged by color, pattern, and thickness. His spice rack was alphabetized by name and cross-referenced by type of cuisine. He had an alarm on his phone, notifying him to change his toothbrush every ninety days. (A wholly unnecessary alarm, as it happened, because he changed it every eighty-five days with no reminder required.) And yet here he was, standing in a strange hotel room in an even stranger town, with nothing but the clothes on his back and eighteen dollars in his wallet.

"This is fine," he told his reflection in the bathroom mirror. "This is reasonable. People spontaneously abandon their lives to stay in magical hotels all the time."

His reflection gazed back skeptically.

"What's more, the county clerk's office will barely notice I'm gone. They'll be relieved, most likely."

His reflection allowed that this much was probably true. And what did he have to lose, really? It wasn't as if there was anyone waiting for him back in that little apartment.

The guest room was amazing, of course. Dominating the

space was a four-poster bed with hand-carved acanthus leaves that had been enchanted to slowly unfurl and curl back up again. A Yuletide wreath of evergreen hung above the fireplace, tiny golden lights dancing among its branches like captive stars. The walls were lined with bookshelves, all overstuffed with leather-bound treasures that could easily occupy Jasper for weeks.

On the other hand, his phone was at twelve percent battery and dying fast. His dress shirt was not the freshest. And he had absolutely no explanation for why he'd decided to stay, beyond the way Delilah Melrose's eyes had flashed when she'd threatened to turn that top-hat lady into a newt.

His stomach growled, reminding Jasper that he hadn't eaten since this morning. Hadn't he seen a dining room off to the side of the hotel reservation desk? Yes, he was certain he had.

Good plan, he thought. *Let's hunt for food. Far preferable to standing here, contemplating why I've done this crazy thing in the first place.*

The hallway was decorated for both Christmas and what appeared to be a significantly more ancient holiday. Silver and gold garlands shared space with bundles of wheat and ivy wreaths that definitely pre-dated Christianity. Guarding the hallway was the carved stone bust of a severe-looking man with a long beard. Was it Roman? Greek? Jasper wasn't certain. All he knew for sure was that statue seemed to glare at him when he paused to study it. And then— *Wait, did that thing just blink at me?*

Jasper decided to be on his way.

The air was scented with a complicated potpourri of holiday smells, along with something else . . . Was that fresh bread? He followed his nose down to the first floor. The dining room was empty, but peeking into the kitchen, Jasper saw a harried-looking man in chef's whites. He was simultaneously kneading three different kinds of dough while muttering under his breath.

"Oh!" The chef looked up. "You must be the newcomer that the gals were talking about. I'd shake your hand but . . ." He gestured at his flour-covered fingers. "I'm Zahir. And you're just in time to witness my annual descent into madness. Well, no, on second thoughts, you can't *descend* to a place you already live in. My annual in-depth exploration of madness, how about that?"

"I don't mean to interrupt—"

"Nonsense. Sit. You're hungry, a cook can always tell. I'll make you something. Just bear with me one sec." He glanced around the kitchen conspiratorially. "And don't tell Kelly I'm using the dried pasta. I'm way behind here, and I am NOT hand-rolling noodles until three in the morning just because it's Saturnalia."

"Saturnalia? You mean . . . no, you can't mean *Saturnalia*. The Roman festival?"

"The very same. You've picked a wonderful time to visit, actually. Oak Haven comes to a complete halt for three days of all sorts of shenanigans. Poetry readings at Spellbound Books, live music at the pub every night. Oh, and a weaving competition at the yarn store, Sometimes a Great Notion. And it all kicks off with a massive feast here at the hotel, which *supposedly* the witches prepare but let's not kid ourselves. It's me. Don't rat me out, though."

"Your secret's safe. Why all the skullduggery, though?"

"Ah yes. Well." Zahir kept working as he talked. Kneading, rolling, punching multiple batches of dough. "Historically, a big aspect of Saturnalia was this sort of social inversion: servants being waited on by their masters, et cetera, et cetera. Our interpretation of that here in Oak Haven means no magic is allowed for the whole five days. Tomorrow at midnight, there's a ceremony where the witches willingly put their powers into containment. And then for the remainder of Saturnalia, witches use no magic whatsoever, and the town's non-magical residents get to lord it over them."

"Oh, wait!" Jasper exclaimed. "That grouchy-looking stone bust upstairs. That's the god Saturn, isn't it?"

"None other."

"He was, um. He was glaring at me? Possibly? Am I nuts?"

"You are not. He's permanently pissed off that Kelly only brings him out of storage for one week every year. However, if you balance a coin on his head, he will smile for you. So give that a shot maybe."

"Huh . . . not sure if I want to see that or not."

"Understandable. Anyway, yeah so every year there's this feast. Trouble is, the Melroses can't so much as make ice without assistance. Which means all the prep has to be done for them in advance. And I do mean alllllll the prep. It's not just *mise en place,* it's *mise en every goddamn thing.* Every pinch of salt has to be measured. Takes me days."

"So here you are, doing all this cooking? Isn't that . . . I mean, it's not my place to judge, but isn't that—"

"Cheating?" Zahir grinned. "Absolutely. We are absolutely cheating. Having me do all the prep totally defeats the purpose. But trust me, you don't want to go anywhere near a Melrose-cooked meal that wasn't carefully plotted in advance. Like . . . take a look at this." He reached for a well-worn cookbook on a nearby shelf, its spine cracked and pages stained. "This old thing has saved more lives than penicillin around here. *Grandma Doralee Patinkin's Holiday Cookbook: A Jewish Family's Celebrations.*

84

Kelly swears by it, though between you and me, I think it's only because she has some sort of a past with the author's son. Anyway, my point is, before we put this little cheat code into action? We had dozens of food-poisoning incidents, and I can't count how many times this kitchen has burned down."

"Okay . . ." Jasper paused a moment to try and process all this, while Zahir attacked his dough. "So let me get this straight . . . The entire town celebrates an ancient pagan festival, the observation of which routinely leads to illness, fires, and general catastrophe, all while drowning in Christmas decorations?"

"Welcome to Oak Haven's holiday mayhem." Zahir grinned. "Originally the witches were hardcore pagans, full stop. Which, I mean, fair enough, given that it was Christians who'd chased them out of Salem in the first place. But then Kelly married Edward Melrose and, well . . ." He gestured at a nearby window: outside, an enchanted snowman was enthusiastically lip-syncing "All I Want for Christmas Is You" while a stone gargoyle wearing a Santa hat clapped along.

"So Delilah's father brought the holidays to Oak Haven?"

"More like he infected the place with them. The man never met a tradition he didn't want to adopt. Look—" Zahir pointed to various decorations around the kitchen. "See that Diwali lamp display? The Chatterjees brought that over. And over there, that's an image of Lady Fatima Zahra, the Prophet's daughter, whose birthday falls around this time. Edward's theory was that they are all celebrations of light over darkness, and all worth celebrating. Of course, some people think that's—"

"Culturally incoherent?" Jasper suggested.

"I was going to say 'bonkers,' but sure, Professor, get fancy with it." Zahir plopped the dough into a collection of proving trays and went to work on yet another batch.

"And it all works out?"

"Mostly—sure! Overall, the town gets incredibly excited about the whole thing. Of course, there's the occasional grumpus who isn't quite so keen . . ." Zahir's eyes took on a mischievous glint. *"All the witches in Oak Haven loved Christmas a lot,"* he declaimed. *"But Delilah, who lived at the Stargazer Inn? Did NOT."*

"She's not a fan."

"Del's complicated. She was really close to her dad, you know? When we lost him . . . well. Sometimes the people who love the hardest also break the hardest." He attacked his dough with renewed vigor. "But don't tell her I said that. She'd probably turn me into something with substantially fewer limbs."

"Zahir!" Kelly Melrose's voice preceded her into the kitchen. "We've come to help!"

"Oh no."

"Oh yes!" She swept in like a great ship arriving in port, with her daughters following close behind. Scarlett looked eager to assist; Delilah looked like she was being dragged to her own execution. "We thought we should lend a hand with the preparation before tomorrow."

"Kelly, please no . . ." Zahir's tone carried a bit of PTSD around the edges. "Remember the potato incident?"

"Those poor potatoes," murmured Scarlett.

"They died with honor," Delilah added. Then she noticed Jasper. "Oh. Hey, you."

"Uh. Hey, you," Jasper agreed awkwardly.

Kelly regally waved away Zahir's concern. "How hard can cooking be? Normals do it every day." She picked up an onion with one hand and a large knife with the other, regarding both with theatrical suspicion. "Though I must say, whoever invented the concept of chiffonade was clearly disturbed. Chiffonade sounds like a place to keep one's undergarments."

"You're thinking of a chifforobe." Zahir gingerly removed the deadly weapon from Kelly's hand. "And you don't chiffonade an onion, that's a technique for leafy greens."

"Well, there you go! I've learned something already—how charming!"

"Mama." Scarlett took the onion away, too. "Maybe we should start with something simpler?"

"Absolutely not. I refuse to be defeated by an allium. Ooh, wait, though, how about *these* beauties?" She reached for a bowl of large, dark red orbs. "What can we do with these?"

"Pomegranates," Zahir said with the desperate calm of a man about to witness culinary war crimes. "Actually, though, that's a fairly safe job for—I mean *good*, it's a *good* job for you. A fun job. You and Scarlett can remove the arils."

"The what?!"

"The seeds, Mama," Scarlett whispered. "The tasty bits."

"Oh I see, of course, yes. Which knife shall I use?"

"Uhh." Zahir chuckled uncomfortably as he handed her a wooden spoon. "I'll cut them open for you, then you tap them. Knock those seeds right out for me, okay? I mean, after all, what can go wrong?"

Scarlett's eyebrows did a little dance. "I'm excited to find out."

"Right," Zahir sighed. "Delightful. Okay, so while you two do that, Delilah could you work on the mint for me? See the pile, on that work table in the corner?"

Delilah's eyes widened. "That's one big pile of mint you got there, pal."

He shrugged. "It's one big dinner. No stems, please."

"And no magic," warned her mother. "Mr. Hopkins, perhaps you can assist Delilah in that task."

Delilah glared at her mother. If looks could kill, Kelly would have been a small pile of ash on Zahir's immaculate kitchen floor.

Zahir glanced at Jasper sympathetically. "Let me set these ladies up with some pomegranates and then I'll get something together for you to eat, okay? Haven't forgotten, I promise."

Delilah plonked herself down on a stool beside the mountain of mint stems. "Leave it to the Romans to invent a tradition that involves epic levels of mint deforestation."

"Did you know—" Jasper carefully sat down on a stool beside her "—Saturnalia's roots likely go back even further than Rome? There's evidence of similar winter solstice celebrations in—" He caught himself. "Sorry. I tend to . . ."

"Go full Nutty Professor?" Delilah was picking her own mint leaves with the kind of focused precision usually reserved for bomb disposal. "Don't apologize. It's . . . I mean, it's interesting. I like to know the real history, not the sanitized version."

Their fingers brushed as they reached for the same stem. Jasper felt himself flush a little and tried to change the subject. "Speaking of history," he ventured, "that tour guide seemed determined to write her own version of it."

"Yeah, well. Nothing says 'authentic witch experience' like cartoon villains in pointy hats, right?"

"Interestingly, the association between witches and pointed hats didn't emerge until—" He noted her raised eyebrow. "Right. Sorry again. Not the point."

"No, but it's kind of exactly the point." She told him about visiting the casino, and the conversation she and Scarlett had overheard. "Scarlett is of course all excited about this big

88

meeting the magicians are apparently having. But I keep thinking about what the men said about the tours, and us not knowing what's real. It's like they're deliberately spreading different versions of everything."

"Creating uncertainty about what's true and what isn't . . ." Jasper's hands stilled over the mint. "Why, though? What's the endgame? You know that saying, *cui bono*? Who benefits?"

Their conversation was interrupted by an ominous squelching sound, followed by Kelly's voice from the far side of the kitchen: "Darling, is pomegranate supposed to stain *quite* this dramatically?"

Red juice sprayed across the kitchen in a Freddy Krueger–esque arc.

"Mama!" Scarlett dove for cover. "That's not how you—"

"Well how else am I supposed to—" Kelly gestured with the spoon, sending another spray of juice across the kitchen. "Everything is so *sticky*. And heavy. It's so ridiculous to do this the hard way."

"Annnnd that's the whole point of Saturnalia," Delilah said, attacking her mint with renewed vigor. "We're supposed to remember what it's like to live without magic. To honor the non-magical members of our community who—" She stopped abruptly, realizing everyone was staring at her. "What? Zahir's not the only one who gets to share backstory."

"I'll help clean up," Scarlett offered, but Zahir cut her off.

"No! No more help. You're officially banned from my kitchen until after the banquet. Except . . ." He glanced at the mint-picking operation. "You two can stay. You cuties can rip mint until sunrise if you like. The rest of you, out."

On her way into exile, Kelly swept past the "two cuties" at the mint table and paused. She gazed from Delilah to Jasper and back, one eyebrow arched so high it may as well have been in the air over her head. "You aren't employing your wand on that mint, are you, Delilah?"

"Oh my gods, Mama," Delilah groaned. "Can you maybe *not* talk to me like I'm a child? No, I'm not using a wand, or any magic at all for that matter, as you can obviously see just from observing what we're doing."

"Good. And there's no need to be snotty, I was just checking. Because *we do not. Use wands. In Oak Haven.* Come along, Scarlett, I believe the decorations in the dining room need adjusting."

Scarlett just sighed, saying, "Sorry, Del, you know how she gets . . ." as she followed her mother out.

A silence settled over the kitchen as Delilah and Jasper went back to work. He could see the embarrassment all over Delilah's face, and he chewed his lip for a moment, trying to imagine if there was anything he could say that might make this awkward moment even slightly better.

Finally, he repeated Kelly's command, but in his best Christopher Walken voice. "We do NAHHT. Youse WAH-nds. In oakHAVEn."

Caught off guard, Delilah snorted. "Wow. I would not have expected someone who looks like you to have a respectable Walken impression in his quiver."

"I have many. LAYers. So, anyway, let's get back to my question from before. *Cui bono?*"

"Who benefits?" Delilah considered this. "Well, whatever the magicians are doing is for *their own* benefit, rest assured. Why, though, I don't know."

"Something about the almighty dollar? Do you get repeat customers, if you tell completely confusing stories?"

"Sure, tourists just love that . . ."

Jasper grinned, taking on the persona of a Yelp reviewer.

"Did the Oak Haven witch tour, and the guide confused the shit out of me. Five stars, totally recommend."

A crash from the dining room interrupted her revelation. "Everything's fine!" Kelly's voice rang out.

"Should we . . ." Jasper gestured vaguely toward the noise.

"Absolutely not." Delilah returned to her mint with renewed focus. "Trust me, when my mother starts 'helping,' that's when you run. Of course, all *you* have to do to forget her reign of terror is just go home."

The words hung in the air between them like frost.

"Right. I'm a human Etch-a-Sketch, basically. One good shake and . . ." He gestured like he was wiping a slate clean. "I wonder if that explains the magicians' behavior? Seems like it would be tough to really grow a tourist trap if your visitors can't remember where they've been."

Their eyes met and something electric crackled in the air. Jasper watched her with that same focused intensity he'd given the molding in the lobby, like he was trying to memorize every detail before it slipped away.

"What?" She made a face. "Why are you looking at me like that?"

"Professional habit. You're a significant historical feature."

"Excuse me?"

"I mean . . ." He fumbled with the mint. "Not in an artifact way. More in a . . . uh. You know what? I'm going to stop talking now."

"Probably smart." But she was smiling that reluctant smile again, the one that made his chest do complicated things.

"Del!" Scarlett's head appeared around the doorframe, her hair dusted with what appeared to be Roman tinsel. "Quick question about load-bearing walls . . ."

"No." Delilah didn't look up from her mint massacre. "Whatever Mama's planning, the answer is no."

"She says she's been inspired by the Chatterjees' Diwali celebrations? Something about how if *one* festival of lights is beautiful, then surely multiple would be better? So she's conjuring more chandeliers. Like, a lot more, and uh, they're all ghee-powered? She's calling it her 'Infinite Diyas Project.'"

"Her *what*." Delilah slowly turned to face her sister.

"Yeah, she's gone a bit . . . recursive with it? Each new chandelier spawns two more, and each of those spawns two more? And uh, I could really use some backup in here."

"*Oh fine*, I'm coming." She turned to Jasper. "Sorry about, uh . . ." She made a vague gesture, encompassing everything from the mint pile to Zahir's frenzy to her mother's apparent determination to bring the ceiling down.

"No worries," he said. "Like you say, I won't remember any of it anyhow."

Something flickered across Delilah's face, and for a moment she looked like she might say something else. But then came the sound of crashing crystal in the dining room. She stood, looking exasperated, and stalked out of the kitchen.

Jasper was left alone with his mint and a nagging feeling that he'd said exactly the wrong thing.

Pausing his work to take in the newcomer's troubled expression, Zahir advised, "Don't take it too hard, buddy. Del is a tricky one."

"Sure." Jasper stared at his pile of meticulously separated leaves. They offered no insights. "I don't suppose you have any advice about falling for someone you're destined to forget?"

"Plenty," Zahir said. "So here goes: *Don't.*"

CHAPTER 9
RIGHT THIS VERY MINUTE

It was the final morning of magic in Oak Haven. Delilah sat at breakfast with her sister and gazed around with thinly disguised annoyance.

A key selling point of the Stargazer Inn experience was the hotel's enchanted dining room. It could be transformed into any sort of venue imaginable, from a twelfth-century banquet hall to a space-station cafeteria and anything in between. Today, the dining room looked like something out of one of Papa's beloved Christmas movies: all twinkling lights and "snow" that sparkled as it fell from the enchanted ceiling but conveniently disappeared before ruining anyone's breakfast. Tiny elves in pointed hats, looking like escapees from a Rankin & Bass TV special, skated between tables delivering coffee and syrup. It was a sight that would have made Edward Melrose beam with delight but was currently giving his eldest daughter a tension headache.

Delilah had talked Mama out of her Infinite Diyas project, but even she couldn't stop the Christmas.

At the Stargazer, a number of rooms were currently

occupied by the Injabere family. They were visiting for a holiday reunion with Daniel and Linda Injabere, a pair of Oak Haven's most recent arrivals. The extended Injabere family had claimed most of the tables by the window. Little Maya Injabere raced around the room, determined to catch an elf. The elderly matriarch, Ruth, held court at the center table. Delilah couldn't stop looking at the old woman, though she knew it was impolite. But Ruth Injabere was gazing at her great-grandchildren with the kind of joy that Delilah could feel all the way down to her toes. It was the same look Papa used to get, watching his girls discover some new Christmas wonder he'd arranged.

Stop that, Delilah told herself firmly. *No Papa thoughts before coffee.*

"Del?" Scarlett's voice pulled her back to their corner table. "Are you even listening to me?"

"Sorry, what were you saying about your completely insane plan to get us all killed?"

"It's not insane. Look, yesterday we learned there's going to be some big meeting of magician leadership at the casino. This could be our chance to—"

"To get captured? End up in some magician equivalent of Guantanamo?" Delilah watched one of the elves do a particularly elaborate figure-eight between tables. Papa would have loved that. He'd definitely have named all the elves by now, given them elaborate backstories grounded in his knowledge of Norse history.

No. Stop it. I am not doing this today.

"Listen," Scarlett interrupted her thoughts again. "You just got back to town. I've been obsessing over this kaiju-casino situation for weeks. This is the first chance we've had to really get our heads around what the hell the magicians are up to.

I'm not blowing this opportunity to dig up some real information."

Delilah shook her head. "Doesn't it seem a little convenient that we would *just happen* to be lurking outside, right when the gardeners *just happened* to show up? For all we know, the gardeners *wanted* us to overhear them. Maybe this whole thing is a trap."

"Oh, don't be ridiculous. How could they possibly have known that we'd even—"

"TRAP!"

Scarlett rolled her eyes. "Okay, Admiral Ackbar, whatever you say." A cranky silence fell over the table as the sisters poked at their waffles. "Well, well, look who's here." She nodded toward the buffet table, where Jasper was deep in conversation with Ruth Injabere.

He looked adorably rumpled, as though he'd spent the night obsessing over the history of his four-poster bed instead of sleeping in it.

". . . and it doesn't bother you, Mrs. Injabere?" Over the giggles of the Injabere children, the sisters could just make out their conversation. "You've arranged this big family reunion, everyone traveling from hundreds and even thousands of miles away, and the minute you leave, none of you will remember it?"

Ruth's laugh was as warm and nourishing as Zahir's fresh bread. "Young man, I'm eighty-six years old. Do you know how much I no longer remember? Honestly, I've already forgotten half of what I did yesterday! Details fade for all of us, no matter what. But that doesn't mean the experiences didn't matter. They may not be up here," she touched her head. "But in here?" She pressed one hand to her heart. "Here, they stay."

Something twisted in Delilah's chest, sharp and familiar. She'd spent ten years guarding the front desk of this hotel, watching other people make memories while she locked her own away.

"Hey, Jasper," Scarlett called out. "Come sit with us." She waved him over, ignoring her sister's attempts to kick her under the table.

Jasper nodded and came over, sliding into the chair beside Delilah. He'd barely set his plate down before he was pulling a notebook out of his back pocket.

"This room is fascinating," he said, gesturing at the enchanted ceiling. "Am I understanding correctly that a witch can transform the entire room into any size or design?"

"Good morning to you too," Scarlett interrupted cheerfully.

Jasper flushed. "Ah. Yes. Good morning." He glanced shyly at Delilah beside him. "Er, hello."

"Hey. Um, listen. Sorry I didn't come back to finish the mint," she said awkwardly. "The situation with Mama and the chandeliers was . . . uh . . . It took a while to sort out."

"No worries, I stayed for a while longer and helped Zahir. Pretty fun, actually."

"So!" Scarlett set down her coffee with a decisive gesture. "We're planning a heist. Want in?"

"We are *not* planning a heist," Delilah corrected.

"You're right," Scarlett admitted. "It's not technically a heist. I just always wanted to do a heist, and this is as close as I've gotten. Jasper, I presume you heard we have intel that a significant meeting of magicians is about to happen? I want to sneak in there, do the whole fly-on-the-wall thing, and learn what their plan truly is. So, actually, if you think about it, we'd be stealing *information* . . . which is kind of like a heist? A bit?"

Delilah groaned. "Why are you determined to turn a simple fact-finding mission into *Ocean's Eleven?*"

"Because it's awesome."

"Danny Ocean never had to deal with anti-witch wards," Jasper pointed out.

"See?" Delilah gestured triumphantly with her fork. "Even the historian thinks it's a bad idea."

"Actually, I think it's fascinating. Historically speaking, magical barriers have always had unexpected vulnerabilities that just need to be exposed to enable—" He caught the threat in Delilah's eyes. "Yes. Terrible idea. Very bad."

Nearby, Maya Injabere was conducting a very serious conversation with one of the elves. "But *who cares* if the other elves don't like your hat," she said with that special degree of seriousness only six-year-olds can muster. "I think your hat is very pretty."

Her mother hurried over. "Maya, honey, we talked about this. Let the elves do their jobs in peace."

"But, Mama, he's sad about his hat!"

Watching the mom shepherd the little girl back to the family table, Delilah felt that familiar ache. Papa would have helped the little girl start a support group for elves with self-esteem issues. Made them tiny motivational posters. Maybe an elf clinging to a tree branch with *Hang in There!* across the bottom in a cheerful font.

"So *anyway*," her sister's voice cut through the distracting thoughts. "I want to have a bit of sneak, see what I can learn from the proverbial horses' mouths."

"Or," Delilah countered, "we could focus on something slightly less likely to get us all captured. Like, why they're running these weird historical tours through town."

"Ah yes, the tours!" Jasper said. "I also want to know about those tours. Why are they spreading misinformation?"

"Exactly!" Delilah tried to ignore how his entire face lit up when she agreed with him. He looked like a golden retriever discovering that tennis balls exist. "Why bother making things up? The real history is plenty dramatic without embellishment."

"Unless . . ." Jasper's eyes took on a sneaky little gleam. "Unless the point isn't the content of the lies, but the act of lying itself."

Both sisters stared at him.

"Think about it—what did that tour guide say yesterday? About how witches corrupted Christmas traditions? I went for a walk earlier, and—"

Scarlett scoffed. "It's barely 9 a.m. What do you mean, *earlier*? There is no such thing as earlier than nine."

"There, I must disagree," Jasper grinned. "In fact, there is an entire buffet of hours that are earlier than nine, and some of them are delightful for strolling in new places. My point is, while I was out, I heard another guide telling a *completely different* version of that story."

"Different how?"

"According to that tour guide, the witches of Salem were actually secret Christians who helped spread holiday celebrations through New England."

"That's ridiculous. Everybody knows we were pagans until Papa—" Delilah stopped abruptly, the words catching in her throat. *Great.* Apparently she couldn't even get through one conversation without stumbling over another Papa-shaped landmine.

Scarlett frowned, and she reached for her sister's hand. "Hey, Del . . ."

But Delilah was already pushing back from the table. "You know what? Let's go see for ourselves."

"Del, it's okay . . ."

"*I'm fine.*" She managed a smile that was only slightly wobbly. "What do you think, Jasper? Shall we go have a look?"

"Uh . . ." He glanced regretfully at his completely untouched plate of food. But then he looked at Delilah and his expression turned resolute. "Let's do it. No time like the present, right?"

"Right." Scarlett forced herself not to grin at them. "Okay, Mulder and Scully. I'm gonna visit Louise Demain. See if she has any ideas about those wards."

"My gods, Scarlett, *don't* drag Louise Demain into this."

Jasper frowned. "Who's Louise Demain?"

"Time witch," Scarlett said with a twinkle in her eye. "Most powerful witch in Oak Haven, bar none."

"She's out of her damn mind," Delilah complained. "Picture Ursula from *The Little Mermaid* but written by H.P. Lovecraft. Nothing Louise has to offer is going to—"

"I'll be careful," Scarlett interrupted. "Look at me, Del, I'm being responsible! Making plans, gathering intelligence. Isn't that the younger sister you've always wanted?" She reached for a cloth napkin, wrapped a waffle in it, and held it out to Jasper. "Here, a bit of Belgium to go. Tours start every half hour. If you hurry, you can catch one by the bookstore."

CHAPTER 10
THE TWELVE LIES OF CHRISTMAS

The tour bus wheezed through Oak Haven like an asthmatic polar bear. Jasper and Delilah had claimed a seat near the back, partly to maintain a professional distance and partly because the stench of peppermint coming from the driver was giving them both a headache.

Their guide, who introduced herself as Esmerelda with the kind of theatrical flourish usually reserved for Vegas showgirls, kept up a nonstop flow of patter as the bus lurched around the town's narrow streets. "And here we see Oak Haven's historic town square . . ." Her voice crackled through the speakers, full of synthetic cheer. "Here, in 1492, the witches of Salem first established their underground railroad for magical refugees!"

Jasper's eye twitched. "Excuse me," he muttered, "did she say *fourteen*92?" He clicked his ballpoint pen and added this error to the running list he was keeping in his little notebook. He didn't have any particular use in mind for this *Lie List* (as he'd written at the top). It was just something to do to keep all the nonsense from melting his brain.

"And here's another fun fact: Oak Haven's witches were the

ones who taught Santa Claus the art of chimney-diving. Before meeting them, poor Mr. Claus had to use the front door like everyone else!"

A smattering of appreciative chuckles came from the handful of tourists. The bus was barely a quarter full, but what the crowd lacked in numbers they made up for in enthusiasm. "Oh my God," breathed a woman in a MAGIC IS REAL sweatshirt. "It all makes so much sense!"

"What is happening?" Delilah said through clenched teeth. "I thought this was a horror tour. I'm not crazy, right? It was a horror tour just yesterday? But apparently it's a Christmas tour now. What is she even talking about? And *what are you scribbling?*"

Jasper showed her the notebook and she grinned. "You missed a lie. Earlier she claimed George Washington consulted Oak Haven witches about whether to cross the Delaware on Christmas Eve."

"Ah yes." He nodded. "Noted."

"Did you know," Esmerelda continued, "that after the town was founded in 1885, Oak Haven's witches were the ones who first developed the concept of flying reindeer—"

"Oh, it's 1885 now," Jasper said in amazement. "A second ago the town was founded in 1492."

"—because before that, Santa's sleigh was pulled by enchanted moose!"

"Moose?" A tourist wearing at least four different kinds of holiday-themed accessories leaned forward eagerly. "Really?"

"No," Delilah and Jasper said in unison.

"Yes! But they were *very* unreliable and their attitude was terrible. The switch to reindeer happened after the Great Moose Mutiny of 1783."

"You know what . . ." Jasper tucked the notebook back into his jacket. "I give up."

They listened in shared horror as Esmerelda launched into a detailed explanation of how Oak Haven's witches had taught the Puritan colonists how to properly decorate a Christmas tree.

Enough. Jasper couldn't take it anymore.

"The Puritans *literally outlawed Christmas*," he shouted in frustration. "Christmas was *illegal* in the Massachusetts colony! Anyone who so much as hummed a carol was hit with a five-shilling fine!"

Every head on the bus swiveled to face him. "Shhhhh!" they said as one.

Jasper leaned forward, head in his hands. "I can't take this anymore . . ."

But then Delilah put her hand on his shoulder and gave him a little squeeze. And Jasper thought, *On the other hand, perhaps I can manage a bit longer.*

The bus rattled past Oak Haven's town hall, where a collection of enchanted snowmen were performing what appeared to be the entire score of "Jesus Christ Superstar."

"Now *that*—" Delilah pointed out the window "—I can explain. Mama went through an Andrew Lloyd Webber phase a while back, and the snowmen haven't been the same since."

"Well, let's see what Esmerelda has to say . . ."

"And here we see Oak Haven's famous musical snowmen!" Right on cue. "Created by George Gershwin himself during the winter of 1923!"

"You know, I could hex her hat," Delilah whispered playfully. "Just a small hex. Maybe make it play 'La Cucaracha' every time she tells a lie."

"That poor hat would sing itself into a coma."

As the bus turned the corner, Esmerelda began explaining

how Oak Haven's witches had helped Mark Twain to write "A Visit from St. Nicholas" using a magical quill pen that automatically generated rhyming couplets.

A tourist raised her hand. "But I thought ''Twas the Night Before Christmas' was written by Clement Clarke Moore?"

"Well yes." Esmerelda's toothless smile was unwavering. "That was a pseudonym of Samuel Clemens, which was itself the pseudonym of Mark Twain."

"She has that completely wrong and somehow also backasswards," Jasper whispered to Delilah.

"And it doesn't bother anyone but us."

"You notice that too." He clenched his jaw even tighter.

"It reminds me of this letter my mother was reading last night," Delilah murmured. "She came across it when looking up an old recipe for Zahir. It was a letter from the bad old days. This witch was worrying about how people were rewriting Oak Haven's history. And that they *wanted* it that way. Like, the truth didn't really matter if the lie was easier to live with."

"Such as the truth about the execution of innocent girls in Salem?" The words slipped out before Jasper could stop them, and when he saw the hurt look in Delilah's eyes, he would have given his whole soul just to take them back. "I'm so sorry, that was so out of line."

"No, you're right. That's precisely what Agnes was talking about. My ancestors told themselves a pretty story for so long, we started to forget it was a story."

"But you didn't, though," Jasper said carefully. "Not completely. That's the thing about stories. They always leave traces behind. The truth is still available if someone cares to go digging for it."

"Digging for the truth . . ." she said thoughtfully. As the bus rounded another corner, Delilah's shoulder touched his. Neither moved away. "Do you think that's what this is about, with the magicians?"

Jasper gazed out at a display where animatronic elves were performing synchronized swimming routines in what appeared to be a small swimming pool of eggnog. "Dear lady," he said with a chuckle, "I have no clue what any of this is about."

The bus wheezed to a stop in front of a Victorian mansion that looked like the love child of Liberace and Buddy the Elf. Every inch of the building was draped in lights, garlands, and tinsel. Mechanical angels pirouetted on the widow's walk while an entire herd of light-up reindeer pranced across the roof, led by what appeared to be a cyberpunk Rudolph whose LED nose strobed in time to that old song about the Dominick the Italian Christmas Donkey.

"A crime against architecture," Jasper said acidly. "Arguably, against human vision."

"Singular? Just *a* crime?" Delilah raised an eyebrow. "You're too kind."

Nevertheless, they steeled themselves and exited the bus. Standing on the sidewalk, the "Grandma" song was even more searing, and Jasper winced as the earworm made itself a nest deep inside his brain. Shooting a withering glance at the festival of kitsch that loomed before them, he thought, *This can't get any worse.*

Then Esmerelda the tour guide announced they were all going to enjoy a tour of Oak Haven's famous Christmas House.

Oh, he thought. *Never mind.*

"Have you ever been in there?" he asked Delilah. "And is it as terrible as I'm imagining"?"

"Not since I was a kid. And I'm certain it's far more terrible than you are imagining."

Jasper took a deep breath and steeled himself as the group

approached the front porch, which was framed by twinkling icicle lights and flanked by two towering nutcracker statues. But no sooner could Jasper think, *this is a bad mistake*, than Delilah slipped her hand into his, giving him a supportive squeeze.

On the other hand, he thought. *Maybe not so bad.*

Esmerelda threw open the heavy wooden door, releasing a blast of warm air that carried the scents of cloves and pine, which might've been lovely, were they not blended with the overpowering funk of cigarette smoke. Jasper's eyes darted around, seeking the source. He didn't need to look far. An elderly—nay, antediluvian—woman sat in a rocking chair by the door, a freestanding and overflowing ashtray beside her. Next to her chair stood a life-sized nutcracker, dressed in the typical military uniform. But instead of the usual ceremonial sword, this nutcracker gripped a curved obsidian blade, covered in arcane symbols that seemed to shift and change shape even as Jasper gazed at them. The blade was less a Christmas decoration and more something that belonged in a museum of ancient artifacts. Or torture devices.

Jasper shuddered. *That's not very* festive, *is it?*

As he gazed from the creepy sword to the creepier old lady and back, an odd wave of dizziness washed over him. *Must be all that cigarette smoke,* he told himself. *Right?*

The ancient lady peered at them through rheumy eyes and took a long drag on her cigarette. "Welcome to the North Pole," she croaked in a phlegmy rasp. "Now fuck off."

Esmerelda just breezed carelessly past. Whether she was totally oblivious to the woman or just unconcerned was unclear. "Right this way, everybody!" she trilled, and she guided the group deeper into the surreal Christmas explosion.

"Hey there, Myrna," Delilah said to the woman as they walked by. "Long time no see."

Myrna gave her the tiniest sneer of recognition and ejected a cloud of toxic smoke. "Fuck off," was her only reply.

The inside was more absurdly, more excessively overdecorated than out, with twinkling lights and tinsel exploding across every surface. An animatronic nutcracker army marched along the mantelpiece, while a trio of tree-shaped robots decorated with ornaments spun slowly in the center of the room, singing an off-key rendition of "Deck the Halls."

"Should I ask what Myrna's whole deal might be?" Jasper asked as they trailed behind the tour group.

"Fun fact," Delilah said, "*nobody* knows what Myrna's whole deal might be, not even my mother who makes it her business to know everybody. Is Myrna a witch? We don't really know. I mean, probably, given this house? But on the other hand, who can say? She never takes part in any events in Oak Haven, doesn't do Saturnalia, doesn't go to town meetings. Doesn't leave the house at all, as far as I'm aware. The mansion sits completely dark all year, and then on the first of December, boom, this happens. Suddenly the Christmas House is open to tours at all hours of the day and night. This, despite the fact that all Myrna does is stare and smoke and say rude things. And then, January 1st, it's back to dark and spooky. As kids we used to dare each other to go up and ring the doorbell. She never answered, which is probably just as well."

"Okay, but if she never goes out, who buys all the cigarettes?"

Delilah laughed. "The mysteries of Myrna are multiple and eternal."

They found themselves alone in a narrow room. Possibly former servants' quarters? No fewer than twelve Christmas trees were crowded inside, each decorated in a different "historical" style. Though Jasper strongly questioned the authenticity of the one labeled "Ancient Egyptian Solstice Tree."

One tree, tucked into the far corner of the room, caught Jasper's eye. Instead of ornaments, its branches held what appeared to be . . . offerings? Small carved figures, dried flowers, coins that gleamed too brightly in the twinkling lights. Miniature bottles of liquor and cartons of cigarettes. Folded-up pieces of paper, some with dollar bills sticking out. It looked like a shrine, not a Christmas display.

"So does Myrna worship the holidays," Jasper wondered aloud, "or is it the other way around?"

"Well well, aren't we philosophical," Delilah said teasingly. But if she had any thoughts about the tree/shrine, she didn't share them, opting to change the subject instead. "Hey, check out that one over there." She pointed to a tree claiming to represent "Medieval Yuletide Traditions." Its branches were laden with tiny plastic knights riding tiny plastic horses, all pursuing what appeared to be a tiny plastic Holy Grail. "I don't suppose you'd care to comment on the historical accuracy?"

"I believe my eye twitch speaks for itself."

The pair wandered from room to room, their revulsion giving way to a sort of giddy appreciation for the sheer commitment to chaos. One space was entirely devoted to Santa through the Ages, featuring dozens of representations: everything from a Stone Age Santa to an elegant Victorian Father Christmas figure, a Wall Street Santa representing the

1980s, and what appeared to be "Space Santa" complete with jet pack and ray gun.

Jasper caught Delilah unsuccessfully suppressing her grin at the sight of Disco Santa. "Enjoying yourself?"

"I am not," she insisted. "I'm conducting important research into American cultural decline as expressed via holiday decorating choices."

"Ah yes. Very serious business."

"Extremely serious. For example, this . . ." She gestured at Disco Santa's reflective platform shoes. "This is clearly a cry for help."

"How dare you," said Jasper in mock offense. "I own three pairs of those."

Delilah laughed. "You do not."

"I inherited them from my grandmother."

"Wow, you gotta invite me to the next Hopkins family reunion." She wrapped her arm around his and they walked on together. In the next room, they were surrounded by an army of animatronic choral singers, all swaying in slightly imperfect synchronization. Their painted-on smiles gleamed in the twinkling lights. Jasper couldn't decide if the effect was charming or deeply unsettling. Possibly both.

"You know what's funny?" Delilah's voice was soft. "I came in here expecting to hate everything about this. But it's actually kind of nice."

"*Nice*?" His eyebrows shot up. "Are you feeling all right? Should I check you for Christmas fever?"

"Oh hush." She gave him a reluctant, crooked sort of smile that made it impossible for Jasper to look away or move or really do anything but smile right back. "I just mean . . . it's . . . uh. Forget it. Never mind. Let's keep going—we've fallen behind the tour."

They drifted into what appeared a room-sized winter wonderland diorama. Tiny figures ice-skated on mirrors while miniature trains wove between villages and hot air balloons drifted up to the ceiling and then back down. The craftsmanship was extraordinary, Jasper had to admit; every tiny face painted with an identical expression of joy, each figure positioned just so in their perfect little world.

Soon he found himself gazing at Delilah instead of the display. But then he noticed her frown.

"What is it?" After a moment's hesitation, he touched her wrist gently.

She didn't pull away. "Look at them all," she said quietly. "All these little people, frozen in their perfect Christmas moments. Everyone so happy."

He nodded. "I think that's always been my complaint with this time of year. Everyone is supposed to be happy all the time. And if you aren't? If you're depressed or annoyed or just sick of it all? Well, you're failing Christmas. And worse, you're ruining it for everyone else."

"Yup, that's about right." Delilah gestured at a scene where tiny carolers gathered around a tiny tree. "Look at that. Only someone failing Christmas would *not* want to be a part of that scene. It's like, December rolls around and everybody's gotta strap on the identical Christmas outfit, whether it fits them or not. Actually . . ." She turned to look Jasper right in the eyes and his insides lurched. "You know what that reminds me of? This letter my mother found, from one of the first Oak Haven witches? Agnes, her name was. She wrote, *Truth isn't a dress pattern, to be adjusted for better fit.*"

"That's well put. Of course, if you can't adjust it . . ." Jasper's eyes brightened as an idea took shape, ". . . you can make people doubt the original pattern entirely . . ."

She frowned again. "You're talking about the magicians now."

"Well, this has been nagging at me all day. The tour guides are all telling different stories, right? Contradicting each other . . . heck, contradicting themselves, even. Maybe it's not about any one of their lies in particular. Maybe it's about all of them, collectively. Flooding the air with so much nonsense that people lose track of the truth. I mean, you heard the people on the tour. Esmerelda kept contradicting herself and everybody just ate it up, like they couldn't tell what the truth even was anymore. But . . . Oh, wait. No."

"No? You lost me."

"Well, I mean, *why* do that, though? What's the point? Sorry, I thought I had something for a second there, but no. There's no reason they'd do it." *Such a stupid thing to say,* he thought. *Christ, Jasper! Why can't you just shut up?* He wished, yet again, that he could pull his words out of the air and shove them back down his own throat.

But Delilah grabbed his arm in a burst of excitement. "That's actually brilliant. Horrible, but brilliant."

"Excuse me?"

"The forgetting spell. It's just as you said—the forgetting spell is *in the air!* It works by overwhelming visitors' brains with trivia. But what if you could overwhelm the spell instead? I mean, trivia is just another word for pointless little facts, right? What if you put out so many versions of 'facts'—just flood the air with so much gibberish that the spell itself gets overwhelmed. It shorts out, almost."

"Like a magical denial-of-service attack."

Delilah frowned. "I have no idea what that is. But sure, if you say so? Last time they attacked us, the magicians tried to become experts at trivia, so the spell wouldn't affect them. But this time, rather than *beat* the spell, maybe the game is to break the spell."

"Just blow it up."

She nodded. "Just blow it up. Do you think that would work?"

"Um, Delilah?" Jasper checked his watch. "I've known that witches exist for all of twenty-four hours. *You* tell *me* if it would work."

They had drifted closer together as they talked, drawn in by the thrill of shared realizations. Jasper could see the individual lights reflected in Delilah's eyes, like tiny sparkling stars caught in dark water.

I wonder what would happen if I kissed her right now?

But then from the next room came Esmerelda's screeching voice: "And now, folks, who's ready to hear the story of how the witches of Oak Haven's wrote 'Silent Night'?"

"Oh, for crying out loud . . ." As Delilah's eyes narrowed, the stars all fled.

Ah well, Jasper thought. *Wasn't meant to be, I guess.*

"It wasn't witches, it was Franz Gruber," he said wearily. "And it wasn't in Oak Haven, it was in Oberndorf. But you knew that, Delilah." He extended his elbow for her to take. "I don't suppose you'd like to join me in correcting some historical inaccuracies?"

"Oh yes, let's!" Her grin was positively wicked. "After all, what's the point of being a witch if I can't occasionally terrorize a tour guide?"

Behind them, the mechanical carolers launched into "The First Noel," their painted faces beaming with artificial joy. For once, Jasper didn't mind the excessive Christmas cheer. He and Delilah made their way back out to the tour bus, their heads bent together, co-conspirators in the best possible crime.

CHAPTER 11
IN THE BLEAK TOWN MEETING

"Wait, Scarlett. Say that again. Louise suggested we do *what*?"

Delilah, Scarlett, and Nate were crossing the town green, headed toward what promised to be the most contentious town meeting since the Great Garden Gnome Uprising of 2005.

Scarlett rolled her eyes. "In order to get past the magician wards protecting the casino, Louise said we need to gather the midnight tears of sleeping children."

"Please tell me you're joking."

"I wish." Scarlett wrapped her arms around herself, either against the December chill or the memory of her visit to the lair of the time witch. "She said they had to be gathered with, and I quote, 'a brush made from a mother's grief.' Whatever that means."

"It means Louise has officially lost what remained of her mind," Nate offered. "Okay, so what's Plan B, ward-removal-wise?"

"I didn't stick around for Plan B. Once she started talking about collecting children's dreams in mason jars, I realized Louise wasn't going to have any suggestions I wanted to hear."

Delilah fought off the urge to say she'd told her so. "Well, at least you tried. Meanwhile, Jasper and I might have figured out what the magicians are actually—"

"Ooh, speaking of your historian." Scarlett's grin was uncommonly wicked even for her. "Why isn't he with us? I would've thought he'd want to document every second of an authentic New England witch meeting."

"He's not *my* historian." Delilah focused very hard on not meeting her sister's eyes. "He's helping Zahir prep for tomorrow's feast."

"Oh, Jasper and Zahir are pals now, are they?"

Delilah shrugged. "Apparently they've bonded over a shared dedication to doing everything the hard way."

"*Uh-huh.*" Scarlett's knowing tone was deeply irritating. "And you left Jasper alone to chat with a guy who's known you since you were in diapers? A guy who knows every embarrassing story about you? It's a bold strategy, sis. Let's see if it pays off for ya. You know, as we speak, Z's probably telling him all about the time you accidentally turned the entire breakfast buffet into frogs."

"Can we focus?" But Delilah could feel her cheeks warming, and not from the winter air. "The point is, Jasper and I think we know what the magicians are up to. We were on this absolutely ridiculous Christmas house tour, and—"

"Hold that thought." Scarlett grabbed Delilah's and Nate's arms, yanking them both to a stop. "What fresh hell is this?"

Delilah followed her sister's gaze . . . and her heart sank. *Oh fantastic. Because this day wasn't messy enough already.*

Outside the town hall, two distinct crowds had formed on either side of the entrance. On the left, a tour group milled about, gawping at the sights, their HAVEN OF HORRORS T-shirts glowing eerily in the winter twilight. On the right stood a cluster of Oak Haven's witches, their faces set in such fierce expressions, the phrase "ready to rumble" was practically visible across their foreheads.

"Yikes," Nate said. "This is a bit too 'Sharks versus Jets' for my taste."

A man with a MAGIC IS REAL fanny pack made the questionable life choice of trying to get Louise Demain to "break character." "C'mon, lady! Give us a smile! You can't be grumpy *all* the time! I got a member of the Queen's Guard to smile one time—surely I can get a grin out of you."

Louise's eyes glowed with an unsettling purple light. "Hear me, meatsack. Your doom approaches posthaste. Your last coherent thought shall be the maddening recognition of your own inconsequence in the vast and indifferent cosmos. Your death will be as unmerciful as Time itself."

"Um." The tourist's smile wavered. "Just a quick selfie, then?"

Part of Delilah wanted to warn these people. Not about Louise specifically; anyone dumb enough to poke that particular bear deserved what they got. But about what was really going on here. About the damage they might be doing, treating Oak Haven like it was budget dinner theater.

Then again, they wouldn't remember what transpired here, anyway. None of them would. Just like Jasper wouldn't remember . . .

Nope. Not thinking about him right now.

The town hall doors burst open and Conrad Delmonico emerged, his cardigan somehow managing to radiate both authority and anxiety in equal measure.

"Ladies and gentlemen," he announced to the tourists, "I'm

afraid town hall is closed for a private event. If you could please return to your buses, I'm sure they'll take you back to your hotel. Or back to the airport. Or to perdition, frankly. Truth is, I don't care where you go next. But you know what they say: you don't have to go home but you can't—"

"But we paid for the Authentic WitchTown Experience!" a woman protested. "The hotel promised we could watch you guys perform a real town meeting!"

"I assure you," Conrad replied with impressive patience, "that whatever the hotel promised, we are not actually a living history museum, and—"

"That's exactly what a living history museum would say!"

Delilah felt a headache building behind her eyes. Reality in Oak Haven seemed to be getting slipperier by the hour.

"You know what?" Conrad's voice cracked slightly. "Everyone is welcome to join us! Yes, what a wonderful idea. Very authentic! Come right in!"

A cheer went up from the tourists. The witches, meanwhile, looked about ready to riot. Delilah couldn't blame them. How exactly were they supposed to discuss fighting back against a magician mafia who didn't technically exist, in front of people who thought *they* didn't technically exist?

Delilah's gaze drifted to the tree line, where the sun was sinking toward the horizon. In just a few hours, Saturnalia would begin. Every witch in Oak Haven would willingly give up their powers. The timing couldn't possibly be worse.

Inside, the town hall looked exactly as it had for Delilah's entire life, except now it was infested with tourists taking endless photos that would never come out. The wood-paneled walls still bore the scorch marks from the Great Pyromancy Debate of 1922, and the old folding chairs still creaked like they were auditioning for a horror movie.

Mama Melrose sat on the raised platform with the other elder witches, each wearing a carefully maintained expression of annoyed but dignified impatience. Delilah knew that look; she'd seen it directed at herself plenty of times.

"Young lady!" A tourist grabbed Delilah's arm. "Where do you burn the witch?"

"We don't," Delilah shot back. "And we never have, by the way. There may have been witch burnings in Europe, but not in America. That's a myth."

The woman's face fell. "Ah, nuts. Really? The casino told us someone would be put to the torch. I mean, we paid extra!"

Delilah grabbed the woman by the collar of her WITCHTOWN sweatshirt. "You *paid extra* for seats to an execution?!"

Nate swooped in to separate the two. "Okaay, let's not pursue this. Ma'am, why don't you join the other . . . uh . . . *audience members* in the back. Okay? Del, please don't kill the out-of-towners. C'mon, come sit with Scar and me."

Grumpily, Delilah slid into a seat beside her sister, wishing that Jasper were here to see all this. Not that she missed him or anything. She just . . . appreciated his academic perspective. On history. Nothing else.

"Order! Order!" Conrad's voice cracked as he tried to maintain control. "Now, before we begin, I must remind everyone that we have some, ah, visitors joining us this evening . . ."

"Visitors, my eye!" Polly called out. "More like colonial cosplayers with boundary issues."

A tourist in the back raised his hand. "Excuse me, is this *authentic* colonial sass?"

"Silence from the peanut gallery please! As I was saying," Conrad soldiered on, "we need to discuss certain . . .

community concerns . . . while being mindful of our audience."

Delilah watched her mother exchange meaningful glances with the other elders. How exactly were they supposed to discuss the magician problem with half the room treating this like a Renaissance faire?

"I would like to speak." Belinda Chatterjee stood, straightening her shoulders like a general preparing for battle. "It seems clear that our first—and for that matter, second, third, and fourth—order of business should be the upcoming holiday pageant. After all, we've been planning this for months."

Of course. Delilah groaned inwardly. Trust Belinda Chatterjee to prioritize her precious pageant over an actual crisis.

"Yes, about that." Scarlett rose, and Delilah felt her stomach clench. *Here we go.* "Given the current situation with . . . uh, our new *neighbors*, shall we say, maybe we should consider postponing the pageant? Along with the rest of the holiday festivities?"

The horrified gasp from the witches made the tourists lean forward eagerly, no doubt hoping for some authentic witch-versus-witch drama.

"Cancel Christmas?" Mrs. Chatterjee pressed one hand to her chest like Scarlett had suggested canceling oxygen.

"No no, not cancel. Postpone. Why don't we deal with our *neighbor issue* first, and then we can really focus on celebrating. It'll be better, actually, because we won't be under threat and we can really enjoy ourselves."

"Scarlett Melrose, what on earth is wrong with you," Polly called out. (This wasn't framed as a question. Ever since Nate had chosen Scarlett over her, Polly always seemed very clear

118

that there was quite a bit wrong with Scarlett.) "We haven't missed a celebration since the founding of Oak Haven! Not through war, not through plague, never!"

Murmurs of agreement rippled through the crowd. But Scarlett wasn't moved. "I know, the timing sucks. But we have intelligence suggesting that the magicians—er, I mean, our *neighbors*—are planning something big. Likely tomorrow. And if we're all powerl— if we're all *indisposed*—"

"You have intelligence, you say?" If dubiousness were an Olympic sport, Polly would've been covered in medals. "And where exactly did you get this intelligence, Scarlett? The same place you got the brilliant idea to handle the last crisis? How did that work out for you? Refresh my memory—how many months did you spend as a bird?"

Delilah felt something hot and fierce surge in her chest. How dare they? How *dare* they throw that in her sister's face? Yes, Scarlett had made mistakes. But she'd been trying to protect Oak Haven, and her plan had worked, by the way. Which was more than could be said for people who just wanted to stick their heads in the red-and-green sand and pretend everything was fine.

Before she knew what she was doing, Delilah was on her feet. "You know what? My sister's right."

Dozens of pairs of witchy eyebrows shot upward. Delilah never made a scene at town meetings. That had always been Scarlett's thing, jumping up to share opinions nobody asked for. Delilah was the sensible one. The reliable one. The one who—*oh gods, am I really doing this?*

Apparently, she was.

"Yes, mistakes were made in the past." The words felt strange in her mouth, like she was tasting them for the first time. "But at least Scarlett was trying to protect Oak Haven.

Which is more than I can say for people who just want to focus on their precious pageant while our entire town is being turned into some kind of . . . I dunno, magical Disneyworld!"

A tourist raised his hand. "Is this part of the show?"

"Oh shut up." Delilah turned her fiery gaze on the audience. "We're not your dinner theater, we're not your living history museum, and we're definitely not going to sit here planning party games while our enemies try to destroy us. Now, ladies, I've made a discovery about their plan that I really think you all ought to hear about. If you could just—"

Jerusha rose, her face flushed. "Now see here, young lady. Some of us understand the value of tradition. Of doing things the proper way, in the proper order. Our rituals have protected Oak Haven for centuries!"

"Protected us," Delilah continued, "or just made us comfortable? Maybe that's our whole problem. We're so caught up in our traditions that we can't see when they're being used against us."

"Ooh, this is so good!" the fanny-pack woman was stage-whispering excitedly. "If only Claudia Winkleman were here to host this episode!"

Delilah tried to ignore her, but her forbidden wand lay heavily in her coat. *I could shut that woman up for good with one stroke.* But her better angels prevailed, and she pressed on with her argument. "Please, all of you. Give me a moment to explain my theory about the forgetting spell."

"*Silence, child!* Remember you are in company!" Jerusha waved her arms. "We don't air our laundry in public."

"I apologize, Jerusha, you're right." Her mind raced, trying to sort out how to explain how the magicians wanted to destroy the forgetting spell without using the words *magicians*, *forgetting*, or

120

spell. "It has become very clear to me today that our . . . neighbors . . . intend to use our greatest strength against us. I'm sure you've noticed the . . . inaccuracies . . . being repeated by our visitors. I believe this is no accident. We need to understand the impact of—"

"Enough!" Up on the platform, Mama abruptly stood and silenced her daughter with one sharp clap of her hands. "Delilah, I agree that we have good reason to be concerned with regard to our neighbors. However, you are overlooking something important. We will be without certain abilities for the next few days. And given that, we are not currently in a strong position to pick a fight. Not with our neighbors or anyone."

The older witches all hmm'd and aha'd. But mixed in with the vague sounds of agreement, Scarlett let out a little gasp. "Oh, of course! Why didn't I think of it before?"

Delilah shot a confused glance at her sister but carried on with the debate. "Mama, I don't think we can afford to put this off. If you'd just hear me out, *please*! I have good reason to believe that the longer we wait, the worse things will get."

"*Not now*, Delilah. The situation with our neighbors will still be there once the festival is over."

"Yeah," Delilah replied, "and maybe that's exactly what they're counting on. That we're so worried about maintaining our perfect little snow globe, we won't notice it's being shaken apart!"

"Young lady!" Conrad interrupted. "Perhaps we could discuss this in a more . . . appropriate way? For our guests?"

Right. The tourists. Who were eating this up like it was the spiciest production of *The Crucible* since Winona Ryder made eyes at Daniel Day-Lewis.

Delilah closed her eyes for a moment. When she opened

them, she fixed Mrs. Chatterjee with her best impression of Mama's *we-will-discuss-this-later* stare.

"What I mean is . . . our *neighbors* have plans. And I'm trying to tell you, those plans involve destroying the single most important thing that has protected Oak Haven since its very founding. You know *the thing* I mean—I don't need to say it here. But if we just ignore what's clearly happening because we're too busy hanging holly and organizing pageants . . ." She took a deep breath. "Well. Then maybe we deserve what happens next."

She sat down hard, her heart pounding. Scarlett's hand found hers and squeezed it.

"That was incredible," her sister whispered.

"I think I'm gonna be sick," Delilah whispered back. "Is this what it feels like to be you? Just talking shit, without thinking about it first?"

"Pretty much. Fun, no?"

"*No.*" But she was smiling, just a little.

"Well, you did great, sis. You made a scene, which is normally my department, but more importantly, you figured out the answer to our problem."

Delilah turned to her sister, utterly baffled. "I what? No. No, I definitely didn't."

"Sure. You and Mama, and that little verbal tennis match just now? You found the answer."

"Scarlett, what are you talking about?"

"And, since you figured it out, that's tantamount to agreeing to help me."

"Is not."

"Is too."

Delilah sighed. "This is going to end badly, isn't it?"

"I mean . . . probably?"

"But we're doing it anyway?"

Scarlett grinned. "Definitely."

The meeting broke up in classic Oak Haven style, which is to say, with nothing resolved beyond everyone's commitment to being annoyed. The tourists drifted out in happy clusters, chattering about the "totally authentic colonial drama."

"Do you think they noticed that none of their photos came out?" Delilah muttered to her sister as they lingered in the back of the hall.

"They'll blame it on the lighting." Scarlett was staring off into space with an oddly focused expression. An expression that Delilah recognized from childhood, one that never led to anything good.

"Oh no." Delilah groaned. "I know that face. That's your 'I have a terrible idea' face."

"How dare you. It's my 'I have a *brilliant* idea that may blow up in my face' face." Scarlett glanced around to make sure nobody was in earshot. "Look, what if we're thinking about this all wrong? Everyone's so worried about the magicians catching us at our weakest during Saturnalia. But what if that's actually our advantage?"

"How exactly is being powerless an advantage?"

"That's what I realized when you and Mama were arguing," her sister said cheerfully. "Starting at midnight tonight, we won't have any powers."

"So?"

"If we don't have any powers, we technically aren't witches. And if we aren't witches . . ."

Delilah's stomach did that familiar drop it always did right before one of her sister's plans went spectacularly wrong. "If we aren't witches, then the wards can't keep us out of the casino."

Her sister's eyebrows did a little dance. "What do you say to a little double date? Me and Nate, you and your historian. Let's go see what the magicians are hiding in that nasty old skyscraper of theirs."

"Hey, you two . . ." Nate came over, his expression suggesting he'd also recognized Scarlett's plotting face. "Are you scheming? Should I be worried?"

"Absolutely," they replied in unison.

CHAPTER 12
O Holy Night

Jasper was up to his elbows in peeled mushrooms when Zahir burst through the kitchen doors. He had a wild look in his eyes. "No, no, *no*! Those cuts have to be *perfect*! If we leave this job for Kelly, we'll end up with blood-splattered mushrooms and a severed finger!"

Jasper set down his knife. "Who peels mushrooms, anyway?"

"People who love perfection. And anyone in my kitchen."

"But I thought the whole point of Saturnalia was for the witches to make this meal?"

"Oh sure, that's the *story* and we stick to it." Zahir set about organizing containers to hold the various elements of the mise en place. "Like I've already told you, we cheat. We cheat like grannies at cribbage. There's no other option, believe me. A few years back, Kelly tried to make an espagnole sauce and somehow created a small black hole. And that *despite* having given up her powers during the Saturnalia ritual. Like, I don't even know how she managed that one. But somehow I lost three whisks and a measuring cup to the Great Void."

"That seems unlikely."

"And yet." He tasted something from a nearby pot and clutched his chest like he'd been shot. "Oh sweet merciful Julia Child, no. This is off. Quick, hand me that shallot. No, the other shallot. The *pretty* shallot. This has to be *perfect*."

Jasper couldn't help but smile. There was something touching about the way Zahir fussed over every detail, determined to help his adoptive family maintain their dignity during their magic-free period.

"So all this prep is for them to . . . *pretend* to cook later?"

"Finally you're catching on. What, you think I'm going to let Delilah Melrose anywhere near an actual stove? The last time she tried to make pasta without magic, she somehow managed to turn the water *solid*. Not frozen. Solid. Like glass. I had to chisel it out of the pot."

"Seriously?"

"Oh ho!" Zahir went to the fridge and pulled out a container of perfectly diced mirepoix, every cube of carrot and celery precisely identical. "Suddenly we're interested in Delilah's culinary catastrophes, are we?"

"I just . . . it's professional curiosity."

"Sure, sure. Very professional. Like the way you keep staring at her like she invented sunshine? *That* kind of professional?"

Jasper flushed. *Whoops.* "Is it . . . uh . . . is it really that obvious?"

"Oh you know, only to anyone in possession of eyes. Listen, I need to say something to you . . ." Zahir was suddenly very still for the first time in days; something in his expression made Jasper nervous. ". . . and you may not like it."

"About Delilah?"

"Sort of. Also about Moses Injabere. You met some of his family, right? They're here for a reunion?"

"Sure, I saw a whole gaggle of Injaberes at breakfast. Which one was Moses?"

"None of them. He doesn't visit anymore. You see, he helped his parents move here a few years ago, and he stayed for a while, to help them settle in. One day he came into the hotel, looking for directions to the hardware store. One glance at those eyes and . . . Well, I was done for. You know? That big romantic moment that the movies say we're all supposed to get? Well, I got mine." Zahir went to the window and snipped some oregano from a potted plant. His hands were steady but his voice had an edge. "We were together for little while, and it was . . . everything. The kind of everything where you start planning a future. But Moses was a lawyer. Damn good one, too. Immigration cases, civil rights. That kind of annoying, *make the world a better place* type of lawyer. But Oak Haven doesn't exactly have a thriving legal community, you know? We don't really do *courts* around here . . . I mean, unless you count Louise Demain's occasional attempts to sue the concept of time." He shrugged. "Anyway, in the end, Moses left. Had to. And the minute he crossed the town line—"

"The forgetting spell," Jasper said quietly.

"You got it in one, Professor." He brought the oregano over to the counter and began portioning it out, wrapping each bit in damp paper towels. "I could have left with him. We did talk about it. Sometimes I still wonder what would have happened to me in the outside world. Hell, I watch *Top Chef* and know I could run circles around those nudnicks. But the Melroses are the only family I've got left. And this place . . . it's home. The only home I know. Plus I've got the pub to look after now, and my people, too." His eyes met Jasper's. "I have my people to look after."

Oh. I see. Suddenly Jasper understood this speech wasn't about Zahir's past, not really.

"So the thing is, yes, relationships with outsiders *do* work out from time to time. Like this couple in town: Dayo and Aphra? Me and Dayo run a pub downtown—I do all the food, and Dayo does pretty much everything else. Dayo is not a witch. But Aphra is. The two of them met at Burning Man a few years back, fell in love, and Dayo gave up everything to come live here. But that's the exception."

"You're saying it does happen, though. Relationships between Oak Haven witches and outsiders do work out sometimes?"

"I mean, yeah, I guess Aphra and Dayo are evidence that it does work out. But, again, that's the kind of crazy shit that happens at Burning Man. That's not normal. It's not what usually happens."

"Well, what would you reckon . . ." Jasper asked hopefully. "Maybe one time out of a hundred?"

"Try one out of a million."

"So you're telling me there's a chance."

Zahir sighed. "Look, I like you, man. You're a good guy—I can tell. But Delilah? She's basically my sister." He went to the fridge to fetch another container, this one filled with perfectly julienned parsnips and turnips. "And she's been through enough without some county clerk striding into her life, making her care, and then just . . ." He mimicked something disappearing into thin air.

"But I'd never want to do that!"

"I know. Nobody *wants* to. But here's the thing about Oak Haven: sooner or later, everybody has to choose. And I've watched enough people choose the outside world to know how that ends."

Jasper thought about his carefully arranged office in the basement at the county clerk's office. About his perfectly organized sweaters and his calendar of dental appointments stretching years into the future. About his parents in Hartford, his sister and her family in Providence . . . about how his entire life was out there, waiting for him to come home.

"I wouldn't hurt Delilah." But it sounded lame even to his own ears.

And Zahir could certainly recognize a weak sauce when he heard it. "You might, though. And if this goes too far? You definitely will. And then . . ." He sighed dramatically. "And then Nate and I will have to bury you in the woods, which is just such a hassle, you know? The shoveling, the alibis, the argument about whether we should've sprung for a better-quality tarp . . ." Then he smiled, slightly scarily.

Jasper thought, *oof*.

"I'm totally kidding, of course. Just a joke. Anyway, enough about that! We better get back to work. If we don't get these mushrooms taken care of, Kelly's going to try peeling them herself, and I am *not* explaining another missing finger to the paramedics."

At last, the men had completed every bit of prep Zahir could conceive of, and it was time to go. On their way out, the newly transformed dining room stopped Jasper in his tracks. "What the—" He gaped at the sheer impossibility before his very eyes. "This was a completely different room when I walked in here."

Where there had once been a typical bed-and-breakfast dining room, with heavy oak tables, colonial-style chairs, and walls adorned with New England memorabilia, there now stood a grand banquet hall that would make the Windsors blush. The ceiling soared some thirty feet overhead, supported by marble columns wrapped in evergreen garlands and twinkling lights. Crystal chandeliers bigger than bicycles dangled like frozen fireworks, each dripping with red and gold ornaments. Massive tables of polished mahogany stretched the length of the hall, enough to seat hundreds, each place set with gold-trimmed china and more silverware than Jasper knew how to use. At the far end of the hall was a small stage, dominated by an enormous glittering Christmas tree.

"But . . . this room is at least five times larger than the original," Jasper said. He took a cautious step forward onto what certainly looked like genuine Italian marble flooring. "The structure of the building shouldn't . . . I mean, how is this even physically possible?"

"Not a sci-fi guy, huh? Unfamiliar with rooms that are bigger on the inside?"

"Trust me, if I found myself standing in the TARDIS, I'd be just as baffled as I am right now."

"Kelly is one of the most powerful witches in town," Zahir said with a shrug. "Frankly the chandeliers are a little much, in my opinion, but . . ."

"Well . . ." Jasper ran his hand along one of the marble columns. "It's one hell of a trick."

Zahir's eyes widened in horror. He glanced around quickly as if expecting lightning to strike. "Don't ever, *ever* call it a 'magic trick' in front of the witches," he whispered urgently. "Not if you value your current physical form. *Magic tricks* are what those buffoons at the casino do. You call this a spell."

"But I thought the witches gave up their powers for Saturnalia?"

"They do, as of midnight. This—" Zahir gestured to the grandeur all around "—is Kelly's grand finale before surrendering her magic. Speaking of which, we need to get moving if we're going to see the ritual."

Jasper nodded, though part of him still believed this banquet hall must be an elaborate hallucination. But then again, nothing about his current situation made any sense whatsoever. Why should the dining room be different?

The path to the grove wound upward through winter-bare fields, strips of old snow hiding in the shadows of the stone walls. As Jasper and Zahir climbed, their shoes already regretting the muddy ground, the excited chatter of the crowd ahead gradually softened to something more reverent. The air felt different here—sharper, more alert, as though the atmosphere itself understood the significance of what was about to take place.

The oak grove emerged from the twilight like a cathedral built by nature itself. Ancient branches reached toward the darkening sky, their bare limbs black against deep purple. These trees had sheltered Oak Haven's first refugees, had witnessed countless rituals, had grown strong on centuries of magical energy. Even Jasper, who couldn't sense magic directly, felt something profound. For him it was like standing in the Sistine Chapel, or holding a document signed by Thomas Jefferson. It was history, but alive. Breathing.

The crowd moved with quiet purpose now; their footsteps hushed against the frozen ground. Here and there, witches reached out to brush their fingers against the rough bark of the oaks as they passed, like parishioners dipping their hands in holy water.

All this reverence made Scarlett's barely contained excitement all the more conspicuous as she bounded up behind them. She was practically vibrating with energy, and it wasn't the Saturnalia kind. "There you guys are!" She grabbed Jasper's arm, her voice far too loud for the solemn mood. "Hey, Jas. Ready for our casino adventure?"

Before he could answer, she raised her hands. "Wait. Hey, Nate, get your butt over here." She positioned her partner beside Jasper. Jasper turned to Nate, confused, but Nate's shrug indicated this was standard behavior where Scarlett was concerned.

"Last spell before the ritual," she said with a wink. She closed her eyes and raised both arms, her palms flat and fingers splayed. Golden light shimmered around both Jasper and Nate, and suddenly they were wearing perfectly tailored tuxedos.

"Can't have you boys looking like a coupla local yokel hobo types when we hit the poker tables."

"Um, I don't know if I'm comfortable with—" Jasper started, but then caught his reflection in a frozen puddle. "Oh. Actually, that's . . . huh."

"Not bad, right?" Scarlett circled him appraisingly. "I was worried you'd look like Ichabod Crane on prom night, but no. Very *Frank and Dino at the Sands*. Jasper, congratulations: you clean up surprisingly well for someone so spindly."

"I am not *spindly*!"

"Dude." Nate clapped him on the shoulder. "You're like an after-photo of Benedict Cumberbatch on hunger strike."

"Totally," Scarlett agreed. "You have 'haunted Victorian radiator' energy."

Jasper had to laugh. "Are you guys about finished?"

"Shhhh!" Several witches shot them disapproving looks, and Jasper felt himself flush. *Right. Solemn ritual.*

Ahead, a woman stood slightly apart from the others, her arms wrapped around herself despite the black velvet coat that pooled around her feet like ink. Even in the gathering darkness, Jasper could see there was something deliberate, even guarded, in her posture. Unlike Delilah and Scarlett, who treated their magic as casually as an old handbag, this woman carried her power with a kind of deliberate grace—something not casually given nor casually maintained.

Nate and Zahir immediately moved to join her, and the three friends embraced.

"This is Aphra," Scarlett said, her voice finally dropping to match the hushed atmosphere. "She owns the yarn store, Sometimes a Great Notion. We all grew up together. Come on, let me introduce you."

Zahir had wrapped Aphra in a bear hug. "You've got this," he was saying. "Just like every year."

"I know, I know." She managed a wobbly smile. "It's just . . . it's different for me, you know?"

"Sure." Nate squeezed her shoulder. "Of course we do. Oh hey, Aphra, this is Jasper Hopkins. He's um . . . he's applying for the job of town scarecrow."

"Oh good," Jasper chuckled. "I'm so glad *that's* continuing. Hello." He reached out to shake Aphra's hand. "Pleasure to meet you."

"Same." Aphra took Jasper's hand with both of hers. "This is quite a night for you to visit our little town. Hey, Scarlett." She reached out and the women hugged. "I guess we should get this over with, huh?"

"You're gonna be fine, my girl," Scarlett assured her.

Jasper tilted his head. "Everything okay?"

133

Scarlett and the guys all glanced at one another, unsure how to answer. But Aphra just laughed. "Oh, everybody is so polite round these parts, it's adorable. Jasper, they're all tiptoeing because when we were growing up together, I was raised as a boy. It was only later I came to know my true self. Which is all well and good, but on Saturnalia, when we give up our powers? Well, when you spend the first part of your life hiding what you can do . . . The act of *choosing* to give everything up, even temporarily . . ." She shrugged. "It hits different—let's put it that way."

"But you're your true self now," Nate said quietly. "That's not going away just because of a few days without magic."

"He's right." Zahir squeezed her shoulders. "Powers or no powers, you're still our Aphra."

Something clicked in Jasper's mind; his historian's instinct suddenly scattered facts into a pattern. He thought about all those historical records he'd encountered in all his studies; all the people who'd had to hide who they were for one reason for another. And it struck him suddenly how some of them might have found sanctuary here, in this strange little town that didn't appear on any map.

"Okay," Aphra said boldly. "C'mon, Scar. Let's get this done."

Scarlett wrapped her arm around Aphra's. "I got you. See you boys after."

The witches began arranging themselves in a loose circle around the grove's largest oak, its massive trunk wider than three people standing together. The oak trees seemed to be reaching toward each other overhead, their bare limbs intertwining like clasped hands. One by one, the witches moved forward to touch the oak. Each contact produced a subtle shimmer in the air, like heat waves rising from summer pavement. Threads of light began to weave between the women's hands, a web of golden energy that pulsed in time with some rhythm Jasper couldn't hear but somehow felt in his bones.

His eyes found Delilah in the crowd without trying; his vision seemed to have developed its own magnetic north where she was concerned. The golden light from the oak caught in her dark hair, making her look otherworldly, untouchable. She looked like just the sort of creature a man gives up everything for.

This is dangerous, he told himself firmly. *Never forget, this isn't your world.*

But then she glanced his way. Her eyelashes fluttered shyly, and she smiled a reluctant smile that made his chest ache, and his logic crumbled like old parchment.

The web of light grew brighter, climbing the massive oak like luminous ivy. Where it touched the bark, frost began to form—not the dull white of normal ice, but something that sparkled with captured magic. The effect spread from branch to branch until the entire tree glowed like a crystal sculpture touched by starlight. The other trees followed, one by one, their branches encasing themselves in magical ice until the whole grove blazed with captured power.

Zahir was standing beside him, and all of a sudden Jasper heard his breath catch.

"You okay?" Jasper whispered.

"Oh yeah." Zahir wiped his eyes quickly. "Just nice to remember that some things are worth staying for."

The web of light began to fade, leaving only the crystalline trees behind. For a moment, nobody moved. Nobody spoke. The only sound was the winter wind through ice-covered branches, like distant windchimes.

Then someone (probably Scarlett) let out a whoop that shattered the silence. Grins and hugs and laughter were everywhere. Someone started singing; it was something old, some tune Jasper didn't recognize. The crowd began moving back down the hill toward town as one, toward feasting and dancing and whatever chaos the first night of Saturnalia might bring.

But Jasper lingered there, gazing up at the frozen trees. The magic trapped in their branches cast strange shadows, making the oaks look both familiar and alien. Like his own world, but shifted just enough to make him question everything he thought he knew.

"Beautiful, isn't it?"

He turned to find Delilah beside him. She wasn't looking at the trees.

Dangerous, his mind whispered again. But in the moment, he couldn't remember why.

They walked down the hill together, trailing behind the celebrating crowd.

"So," Delilah said finally. "Saturnalia. What does your historian brain make of all this?"

"Well, technically speaking, the ancient Romans would have included a lot more gambling and public nudity." He caught her raised eyebrow. "But, ah, your version is . . . lovely?"

"Lovely?" She snorted. "Wow. Don't strain yourself with the enthusiasm there, Hopkins."

"No no, I just mean . . ." He gestured helplessly at the grove behind them. "It's hard to put words to. And it's very striking, seeing magic just . . . stop like that. Usually in historical accounts, the loss of magic is violent. Witch trials, persecution . . ." He winced. "Sorry, probably not the best example."

"No, it's okay." Her voice was quiet. "That's kind of the point, actually. We choose to give up our power. To remember what it feels like to be powerless. So we don't . . . I don't know. So we never become the ones doing the persecuting, I guess."

"Delilah. What's wrong?"

"Nothing. Everything." She kicked at a frozen clump of grass. "My sister's about to do something spectacularly stupid, and instead of stopping her, I'm going along with it. Meanwhile my other sister is off who-knows-where, presumably studying more of the same old pointless nonsense she always does. My mother's trying to hold the town together with tinsel and fruitcake, and I'm . . ." She threw up her hands. "I'm flirting with a county clerk who's just going to forget me anyway!"

From the look on her face, Jasper could tell that last statement was more earnest than she'd intended. Very sweet, though, and his stomach did a disconcerting little *flippy-floppy* thing. "I have to say, your version of flirting has an odd note of hostility around the edges."

"Yeah." She blushed a little. "Sorry. It's a **Melrose** trait, unfortunately."

Jasper stopped walking and faced her directly "I'm not going to forget you."

They both knew it was a lie. But it was a pretty sort of lie.

"You can't promise me that. Which is my whole point. Because this?" She gestured at the space between them. "You and me? *This* is temporary. Like Saturnalia. Like everything else in this town."

"It doesn't have to be." The words surprised him as much as her.

She turned to face him fully, and something in her expression made his heart stumble. "What are you saying?"

"I don't know." But he did know. He just wasn't ready to say

137

it out loud. "I just . . . maybe some things are worth remembering."

Behind them, the frozen grove glittered like a thousand captured stars. Ahead, the sounds of celebration drifted up from town: music and laughter and the promise of feasting. Of belonging.

Delilah took a step closer. "Jasper—"

"There you are!" Scarlett's voice shattered the moment like an icicle dropping from a tall roof. "Come on, you two! Casino's waiting."

"Scarlett, it's so late already. Shouldn't we wait until tomorrow?"

"Don't be ridiculous. Who knows when that big magician meeting is happening—it could be going on right now, for all we know. We could be missing it. Plus? Casinos don't have clocks *for a reason*. Shake a leg, Nate's waiting at the bottom of the hill." Scarlett turned and skipped down the path, singing "Viva Las Vegas" with Oak Haven substituted in the lyrics.

"Your sister," Jasper said carefully, "seems very excited about a plan that might get us in a fair amount of trouble."

"She gets like this when she's nervous. When we were kids, she once sang half the score of *Les Mis* while we were trying to smuggle a dragon's egg out of the inn's kitchen."

They stood awkwardly for a moment, the weight of their interrupted almost-something settling between them like frost.

"We should . . ." Jasper gestured vaguely downhill.

"Right." Delilah smoothed her coat, a gesture that seemed more about collecting herself than fixing her appearance. "Time to go spy on some magicians. You know, normal Saturday night stuff."

But neither of them moved.

"Delilah, listen. I—"

"Don't." She shook her head. "Not now. Not when we're about to do something monumentally stupid." She managed a crooked smile. "Let's save the monumentally stupid emotional conversations for after the monumentally stupid breaking and entering, okay?"

He wanted to argue, to finish what they'd started. But she was already walking away. He watched her go, thinking of that randy old joke about *I hate to see you go, but I love to watch you leave.* In truth, though, there wasn't any sense in which he loved seeing Delilah moving farther away from him than absolutely necessary. So after a moment, he followed.

Behind them, the crystalline grove continued to glitter, holding Oak Haven's magic in trust until the witches returned to claim it. Ahead, the casino's neon lights painted the winter sky in unnatural colors, like a challenge. Or maybe a warning.

CHAPTER 13
CHRISTMAS INFILTRATION

"This is the worst idea you've ever had." Delilah marched beside her sister down the road leading to the casino. But just because she was going along with Scarlett's crazy plan, that didn't mean she was going to let Scar off the hook. "And I'm including the time you tried to teach the Chatterjees' gnomes about dance battles."

"They were doing great until *someone*—" Scarlett shot her sister a meaningful look "—told them about popping and locking."

"It's not my fault gnomes have crappy knees."

The sisters marched along through the darkness, the casino's overdesigned neon entrance beckoning them onward. Nate and Jasper trailed behind like a pair of fretful ducklings. As they approached the town limits of Oak Haven, Scarlett paused. "Okay, everyone clear on the plan?"

"You mean the plan where we stroll on in and hope none of the magicians notice that we're the witches they've been feuding with for centuries?" Delilah asked. "Yeah, crystal."

"Actually . . ." Jasper raised his hand like a nervous student.

"I have a question. What happens when I forget everything about Oak Haven? Won't I be a bit confused about why I'm in a casino? Won't you three just be—" he suddenly locked eyes with Delilah but just as quickly looked away "—be, uh, strangers?"

"Don't worry," Nate assured him. "I'll keep an eye on you."

"Great, that's . . . But wait, how, though? Won't you forget everything too?"

"No, because I grew up here, so I've got that learned resistance on my side. Of course, I can't I stay away too long or . . ." He made a popping sound with his mouth. "Poof. Clean slate."

"Right." Scarlett nodded. "So, no dawdling. In and out— we'll be fine."

"Well," Jasper said weakly, "some of us will be fine."

Delilah found herself wanting to reach for Jasper's hand, to tell him they didn't have to go. But that would mean admitting she cared whether he remembered her or not. Which she absolutely did not. Probably. Maybe.

It's better this way, she told herself firmly. *It's already getting complicated with him. Best that he forget me now. Makes everything simpler.*

Then he smiled at her: an annoyingly endearing smile that plonked at her heartstrings like a ten-year-old at her first violin lesson. Suddenly she remembered why she'd spent so long avoiding interactions exactly like this one.

The casino loomed over them like the MGM Grand's most-hated cousin. The building's facade managed to combine the worst excesses of Sin City with the most aggressive aspects of holiday cheer. Giant rotating top hats sprouted mechanical rabbits while holographic doves circled overhead, trailing tinsel. Sequined Santas performed card tricks for an audience of animatronic reindeer. Even the fountain had gotten into the spirit, the multicolored water was now spelling out "DECK THE HALLS WITH ENDLESS WONDER" in a font that looked like it had been created by someone who'd had too much eggnog and access to too many exclamation points.

They were about twenty feet from the entrance when Jasper stopped dead in his tracks.

"I . . . Where am I?" His voice had gone oddly flat. "What's happening? Who are you people?"

The town line, Delilah thought. *We just crossed it.*

"Hey, buddy." Nate stepped in smoothly. "Remember me? I'm, um, a visiting archivist from uh, Schoharie County . . ."

Scarlett turned to her sister and mouthed, *Schoharie County, what the hell?!*

"We're helping these ladies with their research about Christmas traditions in casinos?"

"You . . . I . . . We are?" Jasper blinked several times. "That doesn't sound like something I'd—"

"For the clerk's office historical records," Delilah added quickly. "Very important documentation project."

"Oh! Yes, of course. Documentation. Of course." Jasper nodded in that eager way people have when they've got no idea what's happening but dread the idea of getting caught out. He pulled a small notebook from his pocket. "Should I be taking notes? That entrance shows a fascinating mix of neo-brutalist and—"

"Maybe later," Scarlett interrupted. "Come on!"

Inside the lobby, the shiny marble floor was overlaid with holiday-themed carpeting. On each side of the reservation desk stood enormous nutcrackers with magician's capes slung over their shoulders. Their painted-on smiles managed to look somehow festive and threatening at the same time, like Ted

Bundy at an office Christmas party. A group of middle-aged tourists in matching holiday sweaters, likely down from Maine or Vermont for a wild weekend of penny slots and all-you-can-eat prime rib, posed for photos in front of a massive Christmas tree. But all that kitsch took second place to the lobby's main spectacle: an Elvis impersonator in a gold spangly jumpsuit gyrated atop a platform beside the reservation desk. He warbled "Blue Christmas" along with an appallingly loud karaoke machine. A bundle of mistletoe hung conspicuously over his head.

The sisters stopped abruptly and stared up at Elvis. Papa's favorite, especially the Christmas albums. It was as though Time itself had frozen them to the spot.

After a verse or two, Scarlett squeezed her sister's arm. "I miss him too, you know."

Del tore her gaze away from Elvis and looked into her sister's eyes. "I'm sure you do. But . . . I don't know, it always seemed so much easier for you and Luna. Even Mama. I've never understand why that was."

"It's *not* easy for me, Del. It's not. More than a decade, and the sadness still jumps out at me sometimes. Like somebody hiding in the shadows in a bad horror movie. I mean, sometimes I can remember Papa and just feel happy. But other times, it's like . . ." She trailed off.

Delilah studied her sister as if for the first time. "I thought it was just me."

Scarlett smiled, a little sadly. "Mmm, maybe you *decided* it was just you. But on the other hand, I'm the one who left, remember? How could you know how I felt? Wasn't like I stuck around long enough to show anybody."

"We should talk about him more, Scar. It always felt like Mama wanted to box up all the memories and just move on."

"Ehh, I think that's just her trying to be the tough guy. You're right—we should talk about him more. But at this *particular* moment . . ." Scarlett gestured at the casino. "Maybe for now we focus on this?"

"Sure, let's do your plan." It was a bad plan, Delilah knew, but it felt good to be teaming up with Scarlett. She gave her younger sister a playful sock on the arm. "No time like the present to stroll right into a trap."

"Not a trap, Del."

Delilah snorted. "Reckon we're about to find out."

They moved together toward the casino proper: islands of slot machines and gaming tables stretching as far as the eye could see. Slot machines played "Let It Snow" when someone hit a winning combination; their electronic bells mixed with the constant drone to create a demented holiday Muzak. Grouchy blackjack dealers wore elf costumes complete with jingling bells that tinkled as they handled cards with a ruthless efficiency.

Scarlett nudged her sister, a big grin on her face. "Del, you remember the last time we were in a casino? You had a *very* different reaction to the hubbub compared to now! Back then, you just about shat yourself, if I remember correctly."

Much as she firmly believed they were standing in the middle of a huge mistake, Delilah had to grin at the memory. "Sure, but that was over a year ago. At the time I'd never been anywhere. I've seen some things since then."

"Oh, I remember," Nate piped up. "That was when you guys took a portal to Vegas! You were chasing that magician . . . that guy, uh, whatshisface."

"Maximillian the Magnificent." Scarlett nodded.

"*Maximillian*! That was him. With the ever-changing accents. That guy was hilarious."

Delilah frowned. "He was a spy, Nate. A filthy dirty rotten spy, bent on destroying our town."

"Funny dude, though, that's all I'm saying." He turned to Jasper, as if to justify himself a little bit. "Max had this great trick with a rabbit—it was very funny."

"Oh my gods, I'd almost forgotten about him!" Delilah whirled around to face her sister. "Is Quentin okay?"

"Totally," Scarlett said. "Ever since we rescued him, Quentin has been living in the back garden, happy as a—oh shit, look over there!" She pointed toward a cluster of intense-looking goths who whispered to one another before disappearing down a dark hallway. "Those have to be council members. Look at how they're dressed!"

"You can't possibly know that," Delilah objected. "Just because a gal wears lingerie as outerwear . . ."

"Yeah babe," Nate offered. "You're looking for the magicians' council but you could end up at a Siouxsie and the Banshees tribute show."

But her sister was already moving. "It's them, you guys." The other three had to hurry to catch up, dodging past a craps table where the dice had been replaced by tiny snow globes and the dealer was dressed as Frosty the Snowman.

The hallway grew darker and quieter with each step, and the casino's din faded to a distant hum. Scarlett moved like a heat-seeking missile, letting nothing distract her. Meanwhile Delilah kept stealing glances at Jasper, who was taking in their baffling surroundings with an academic's precision, despite having no clue what he was doing there.

"Fascinating implementation of capitalist Christmas aesthetics," he murmured, gamely scribbling away in his notebook. "Though the architectural integrity of the structure seems completely—"

"Shh!" Scarlett had stopped in front of a heavy black door. "I think this is it!"

"Why?" Delilah asked, but her sister was already reaching for the handle.

Scarlett pulled on the handle and the door flew open. The quartet found themselves blinking in sudden bright stage lights. They were standing in the wings of what appeared to be a 1970s game show, complete with furniture in avocado and mustard colors, a host in a spangled tuxedo and a studio audience full of people in ugly Christmas sweaters. A Herb Alpert-style theme song burbled away in the background.

"Perfect timing!" The host bounded over. "Our final round of contestants have arrived!"

"Our what?" Delilah managed, but she was already being hustled onto the stage. Somehow she found herself shoved onto a stool beside Jasper while Scarlett and Nate were settled onto stools across from them.

"Ladies and gentlemen," the host announced, "welcome to the Houdini Casino's Christmas edition of—" the audience joined in, shouting the answer along with the host "—Made! For! Each Other! That's right, folks, it's everybody's favorite romantic game, Made for Each Other, where we pose telling questions to charming young couples, to see if they are truly destined to last!"

Nate grabbed Scarlett's arm. "We're not doing this, are we? Why are we doing this?"

"Just play along," she said. "Be glad we didn't end up in a casino that has a live wrestling show. That happens sometimes, you know."

He made a face. "What do you know about live wrestling shows?"

Meanwhile Delilah squinted into the bright lights and

147

focused on not throwing up. She was on a stage. In front of many strangers. Expected to answer questions about someone who didn't even remember meeting her.

This was going to be a disaster.

Jasper's brows were knitted in bafflement. He leaned close and whispered, "*What* did you say we were researching? Because this is the strangest research trip I've ever—"

"First question!" the host's voice boomed through the excessive sound system. "Players, please write your answers on the provided whiteboards, and then we'll see how you did. Ready? The first question is, what is your partner's preferred coffee order?"

Delilah stared at the little whiteboard they'd given her, marker hovering uncertainly. This was ridiculous. She barely knew Jasper, and at the moment he didn't know her at all. She glanced over at her sister, radiating smug confidence in her superior knowledge of Nate.

Welp, Delilah thought, *the truth is what it is*. She wrote "Black" in her careful script and turned the board face down on her lap.

"All right, let's start with our first couple!" The host turned to Scarlett and Nate. "Sir, tell us: what is your lovely partner's absolute favorite coffee?"

Nate held up his board with a confident flourish: "Grande triple shot soy cappuccino with three and a half pumps of vanilla."

Scarlett's face fell as she revealed her answer: "Oat milk latte with cinnamon."

"Now hang on a sec," Nate protested. "He said favorite."

"Yeah, but that mess you wrote is only on holidays, it's not my daily order. Don't you know my everyday order by now?"

"Of course I know it! It's just that . . . Wait, when did you switch to oat milk?"

"Moving on!" the host cut in cheerfully. "Let's see what our other couple wrote!"

Delilah's stomach clenched as she turned her board around. Jasper revealed his answer and—

"Black and black!" the host called out gleefully. "We have a match!"

The crowd applauded. Delilah caught Jasper's eye and he gave her a shy, precise smile. For a moment she almost forgot that he'd forgotten her.

But Scarlett was glaring at them. "Those dum dums got lucky," she muttered.

"Next question," announced the host with oily game-show enthusiasm. "Name a movie that was an improvement on the book it was based on."

Oh, for crying out loud! Delilah thought. But she heard her sister crack her knuckles in excitement.

The marker squeaked against her whiteboard as Delilah wrote down the only logical answer.

"Let's check in with our leaders over here!" The host turned to Delilah and Jasper first this time. "What did your lovely partner write?"

She turned her board around just as Jasper revealed his answer: "The question is moot."

"No film," they said in unison, then stopped, staring at each other.

". . . is better . . ." Delilah continued hesitantly.

". . . than a novel," Jasper finished.

The audience broke into delighted applause. Someone actually shouted, "So cute!"

We're not cute, Delilah thought. *We're correct.*

"Oh come on!" Scarlett protested. She flipped her board around to reveal *Jaws* written in huge letters. "The movie was absolutely better! Even Peter Benchley said so!"

"*The Godfather*," Nate's board read. He shrugged apologetically at Scarlett. "I mean, Brando, Pacino . . ."

"How is this happening?" Scarlett demanded. "I've known you my whole life and those two goofballs literally just met!"

Well no, Delilah thought. *We didn't just meet. Except . . . we did. Except . . . we didn't*. Her head was starting to hurt.

"Moving right along!" The host was practically levitating with excitement; *Made For Each Other* didn't get many word-for-word answers. "For our next question: name a quotation or motto that your partner lives by."

Delilah scribbled without thinking: "The truth will set you free, but first it will make you miserable."

Her hand shook slightly as she looked at what she'd written. There was no way Jasper would—

He turned his board: "The truth will set you free, but first it will make you miserable."

The crowd went wild. Someone shouted, "Soulmates!"

"This is ridiculous," Scarlett announced from behind them. She revealed her board: "Not all who wander are lost."

"There's no place like home," read Nate's answer.

"Yikes," said a woman in the front row. "Those two are in deep shit."

As Scarlett and Nate bickered over their bad answers, Delilah glanced over at Jasper. She could see him trying to catalog this bizarre moment, to figure out where to store it in his well-ordered mental filing system. He glanced up and gave her an awkward little shrug, like he wasn't sure if he should apologize or not.

She smiled and shrugged back.

"Final question!" The host beamed at them all like a demented Christmas elf. "Ladies, tell us how your partner would complete this sentence: *The proper way to organize books is . . .*"

Oh no. This was a topic that had started wars. At the Oak Haven Library, two librarians came to blows over the merits of different organizational systems. They didn't speak to one another for years after.

But then she thought, *What do I have to lose?* Her marker was already moving: "Dewey decimal system with additional subcategorization by acquisition date and condition assessment."

The second after she revealed her answer, she wanted to die of shame. To sink through the floor and never emerge. Nobody would ever guess that level of—

Jasper's board came up: "Dewey decimal system, but with secondary categories that factor in acquisition date and condition assessment."

The audience erupted.

"Who even *are* you people?" Scarlett demanded. Her board read: "By color because it's pretty!"

Nate's answer was: "Alphabetically by author," and then he added verbally, "Because I'm not a monster?"

"But the rainbow shelves look so nice on Instagram!"

"Scar, the question was about what I think, not some dingbat influencer."

"And that's the game!" The host's voice cut through their bickering. "Thanks for joining us on another edition of *Made! For! Each Other!* Don't feel bad, you runners-up. Just remember: there's lots of fish in the sea, okay? As a consolation prize, I'll give you the name of a good lawyer, ha ha ha. Now, audience? Please congratulate our winners!"

Confetti rained down, the trumpet-heavy theme song blared, and the audience was on their feet. In the mayhem, Delilah caught Jasper's eye. Reflected in his face, she saw the same surprised delight that she was feeling. But then she remembered: this nonsense was all he'd take away from his Oak Haven adventure. He wouldn't remember the inn or the witches or walking arm in arm through the snow. He'd remember matching answers about the Dewey decimal system with some nerdy stranger. This moment was destined to become nothing but an amusing cocktail party anecdote: "Did I ever tell you about this time at a casino?"

Delilah and Jasper were taken off stage to collected their prize: a gift certificate for the casino's magic shop, because of course. They looked at one another, uncertain what to say. Much to their relief, Scarlett came bounding over and grabbed them both by the elbows. "C'mon!" She pointed to the far side of the stage, where a new group of well-dressed people were heading out of the theater. "Those are definitely council members. Come on!"

They followed at what they hoped was a discreet distance, though Delilah suspected they were about as stealthy as those mechanical rabbits out front.

Nate was muttering to himself, "I hope we stumble onto *The Gong Show* next time, I bet we could win *that* . . ."

The hall grew darker and quieter, with only the faint sound of "White Christmas" drifting up from the casino floor.

"This is it," Scarlett whispered excitedly. They found themselves before an unnecessarily tall door.

"Scar, c'mon." Nate sighed, clearly at the end of his infiltration enthusiasm. "Maybe we should quit while we're ahead?"

Delilah nodded. "We can't just crash through every scary door we come across, Scar. We should probably—"

"It's stuck!" Scarlett announced, yanking fruitlessly at the massive handle. "Everyone help!"

"I really don't think—" Jasper began.

"*Push!*" Scarlett threw her shoulder against the door.

Before Delilah could object, Nate was helping, then Jasper reluctantly joined in, and finally Delilah surrendered, adding her weight to the effort.

"On three!" Scarlett ordered. "One . . . two . . . *three!*"

They gave it everything they had: a united, unstoppable force straining against the immovable door. Then Delilah heard a soft *click* from the other side, like someone had just released a latch, and suddenly—

The door swung open effortlessly, inviting them in. Having committed their full momentum to the push, the four went tumbling forward, skidding across polished marble in a tangle of limbs and startled yelps. The least dignified entrance in the history of magical espionage.

"Aw, dammit," Scarlett muttered, "George Clooney would be so ashamed of me right now."

Meanwhile, Delilah found herself at the bottom of the pile, her face pressed uncomfortably against cold stone, with Jasper half on top of her and someone's elbow (Nate's?) digging into her ribs. *Well,* she thought, *this couldn't possibly get any worse.*

Then she looked up.

They were in a narrow chamber with what appeared to be an infinite ceiling, soaring upward into shadow. Delicate tendrils of light crawled up the walls like kudzu made of stars. At the far end of the room was a U-shaped table on a raised dais where sat what could only be the High Council of Magicians. Intricate carvings ran along the edge of the table—a riot of runes and symbols that made Delilah's eyes water if she looked at them too long.

The four had to crane their necks to peer up at the council members, who sat in high-backed chairs that probably weren't actually thrones but were certainly trying their best. Each magician wore formal evening wear in dark jewel tones that made them look like a murder of very well-dressed crows.

"Wow," Scarlett whispered. "They've gone full Evil Overlord with this throne room."

Jasper nodded. "Saruman's interior decorator has been keeping busy."

"Shut up, guys," Nate said between gritted teeth.

"Fuuuuck," Scarlett said, "I wish I had my magic right now."

A woman at the center of the table rose. She wore an elegantly cut suit in deep burgundy, and her long hair was twisted into a complicated knot that looked like it could turn into glittering silver snakes at any moment. "Good evening." Her cold smile unfurled slightly. "Welcome, witches of Oak Haven. We've been expecting you."

CHAPTER 14
YOU BETTER WATCH OUT

Jasper was desperately trying to keep up with what was going on around him. But he felt like he was alphabetizing books in the middle of an earthquake.

The chamber they'd tumbled into was scrambling his brain; the ceiling appeared to stretch upward into infinity, which was obviously impossible. Then there was the massive, U-shaped table towering over them. Its edges were carved with symbols that Jasper wanted to study but couldn't get a proper look at; his eyes would kind of slide off them, like they were rejecting the information. Again, impossible. Unless of course this was all a dream.

Ohhh, that's it, he assured himself. *This is a very elaborate, incredibly vivid dream. But why? Anita's rum balls, maybe? Or did Toby slip me one of those cannabis gummies he's always bragging about?*

But wait . . . had he even gone to the party? Hadn't he been adamant about avoiding it? The memory felt slippery, like he was grabbing at minnows in a stream. There was definitely something in his memory bank about a party, and mistletoe.

He'd made a sharp comment about the Pogues, and then . . . what?

Well, hardly matters now. He was clearly fast asleep, enjoying (if that was the word) the most intense dream of his life. *May as well just ride it out until I wake up.*

But enjoyment was challenging. The faux-throne room just got more menacing the more he looked around. There were shadows in the corners that seemed to move independently of the light, and the air held a metallic tang to it. Like blood in his mouth.

Dream or nightmare, he wondered suddenly. It wouldn't be the first time his subconscious had betrayed him.

At least he'd conjured up interesting company. The three people with him had seemed to know Jasper immediately and hadn't bothered to introduce themselves. And there was zero chance he'd ask (he'd never reveal himself to be *that* thoroughly confused). But from context clues and overheard conversation, he'd pieced together that the couple, the ones currently holding hands like their lives depended on it, were named Scarlett and Nate. And the woman beside him, his partner in that crazy game show, was Delilah.

Delilah. She had a razor-sharp bob and eyes that seemed to contain entire galaxies within them. She was easily the most fascinating woman he'd ever seen, in a dream or otherwise. Her posture suggested she might know seven different ways to kill a man with an olive pick, but somehow that just made her more appealing.

I've created her, he thought with a mixture of pride and disappointment. *My brain has conjured the perfect woman, and she can't possibly exist in real life. And even if by some miracle she did exist, someone like me would never have a chance with someone like her. No matter what that game show said.*

The council members on the dais stared down at them with expressions ranging from contempt to outright hostility. Their faces held the sort of cold disdain usually reserved for finding gum on the bottom of an expensive shoe. Whatever this dream-narrative was, Jasper was clearly cast as an unwelcome intruder.

"We desire to speak with the witches," the burgundy woman said. Her voice sliced through the room. "The others may go."

Witches? Jasper thought. *Who's a witch? Witches aren't real.*

But Nate seemed to understand the situation perfectly. He wrapped a protective arm around Scarlett and shook his head. "I'm not going anywhere."

Ah, they're the witches, apparently. Jasper, wanting to be part of the team despite having absolutely no clue what was happening, awkwardly extended his arm around Delilah's shoulders. "Neither am I," he declared with a confidence he absolutely did not feel.

Delilah turned to glare at him, and he immediately withdrew his arm, his face burning.

"How charming." The burgundy woman's voice dripped with venom. "The men are so protective. Odd, given that you witches hate men." She delivered this pronouncement with a smile that reminded Jasper of documentaries he'd seen about deep-sea predators: all teeth and no warmth.

"We do not!" Scarlett objected. "Oak Haven's magic is matrilineal but not because we hate men. It's just how our power is passed down. There are plenty of covens with male witches!"

"I can personally attest to that," Delilah chimed in. "I've just returned from traveling the world and I encountered plenty of men with remarkable powers. In fact, I had a particularly memorable time with some warlocks in northwestern Ireland."

The burgundy woman started to respond, but Scarlett held up one finger. "Hold please." She turned to Delilah, her eyes twinkling. "Memorable? You mean because he gave you the wand?"

"Wait," Nate sniggered. "*Who* gave Delilah his wand?"

"How memorable are we talking here? Do you mean, like, *memorable* memorable?"

Delilah's eyebrows performed a little dance that made Jasper's mouth go dry. "Memorable memorable," she confirmed.

"But what about the infamous Irish curse?" Scarlett pressed.

"I don't know what to tell you, sis. More like the Irish blessing where Conor the Warlock was concerned."

Conor the Warlock?! Jasper's ego deflated like a budget soufflé. Even in his own dream, he was being outdone by some magical Irishman. Presumably half Colin Farrell and half Thor. *And if she were real, what chance would I have then?*

"If you've quite finished—" the burgundy woman's voice sliced through their exchange like a scalpel through flesh "—I'll repeat myself. We shall speak only with witches. The others shall leave."

"And I'll repeat myself," Nate shot back. "I'm not going anywhere."

A chilling laugh drifted down from the council table, multiplied by the acoustics of the chamber until it sounded like the entire audience at a villain convention was mocking them. The hairs on Jasper's arms stood at attention, and he fought the urge to wake himself up. Because this was definitely veering into nightmare territory now.

"Very well," the woman said, and snapped her fingers.

A cloud of smoke exploded at Jasper's feet, acrid and thick. He coughed, his eyes watering as he tried desperately to wave it away.

When the smoke cleared and he could finally see again, the council chamber, the dais, and the witches were gone. He was standing next to Nate in the middle of the casino floor, surrounded by the cacophony of slot machines. One directly beside them was currently having a seizure, lights flashing and coins spilling onto the carpet.

"What the—" Jasper spun around, trying to get his bearings. "Where did they go? Where did *we* go?"

"Back to the casino," Nate replied grimly as his eyes scanned the crowd. "They didn't want us there for whatever they're planning to tell the girls."

"But . . ." Jasper gestured helplessly at the slots, the tourists, the general Vegas-meets-Christmas cacophony. "How did we get here?"

"It's magic, dude." Nate gave him a look that was equal parts pity and exasperation. "They're magicians. It's kind of their whole deal."

"Magic? What, like, pulling rabbits out of hats and stuff?"

"We all used to think that way. *Magicians are fakes, they're just performers,* blah blah blah. But as you can see—" Nate gestured at their surroundings. "We underestimated them."

"So, what do we do? Should we go back to the room and rescue the women?"

"*Rescue the women!*" Nate laughed. "Who do you think you are, Conor the Warlock? Nah, nothing we can do, except wait." He bent down to scoop up a fistful of coins that had spilled out of the slot machine, then clapped a hand on Jasper's shoulder. "C'mon, lemme buy you a beer."

The magicians' chamber seemed to contract, as if the walls themselves were breathing in. Whispers slithered through the darkness, too quiet for Delilah to make out but too deliberate to be random. Something cold brushed against Delilah's cheek, something unknowable that left a trail of ice along her skin.

She edged closer to her sister. "I really hate this 'separating the group' crap. Very 'horror movie 101'."

"Agreed," Scarlett whispered. "And I'm not really feeling like a final girl at the moment."

The woman in burgundy was still visible on the dais. Her colleagues had melted into shadow, leaving only the impression of forms sitting at the U-shaped table.

Any lingering doubts that magicians had nothing to offer but smoke and mirrors had evaporated along with Jasper and Nate. Even Mama, with all her power, couldn't teleport people with just a snap of her fingers.

"What did you do with them?" Delilah forced a belligerence into her voice that she absolutely didn't feel. In truth, her pulse was pounding so hard, she worried the entire room could hear it.

The burgundy woman's smile was the kind therapists reserve for patients with particularly embarrassing delusions. "They're perfectly safe. Simply enjoying our casino's amenities while we have a little . . . witch-to-magician chat."

A voice from the shadows hissed, "It'sssss about time," stretching the 's' into something serpentine that made Delilah's skin crawl.

"Oh my gods, are you *actually* doing the eerie whisper

thing?" Delilah crossed her arms, channeling her fear into what she hoped passed for contempt. "What's next on your Villain Clichés checklist? Any of you got long-haired cats on your laps?"

"What my sister means," Scarlett cut in, "is that we'd appreciate hearing exactly what you want with us. This casino, the tour guides spouting nonsense . . . What are you all playing at?"

"Impatient children," came another whisper from the shadows.

"'Twas ever thus," added another. "Rushing through their teeny meaningless lives, never understanding the true nature of the eternal cosmos."

That one talks like Louise Demain, Delilah thought, and she filed that away for later consideration. Assuming there was a later.

"You said you wanted to speak with us," she said as confidently as she was able. "Fine. Speak. What the hell are you doing, putting up this bootleg Bellagio directly in our backyard? And what about the ridiculous 'living museum' tours? They clearly don't make you any money—there aren't enough people on the buses. So what's the point?"

The burgundy woman leaned forward, her hair catching what little light existed in the chamber. "The point, my dear, is negotiation. We wanted your attention, to let you know we're serious. And now that you're here, we're offering you a deal."

"A deal," Scarlett repeated flatly.

"Indeed." The woman gestured expansively, as if presenting them with a magnificent gift. "We propose that the witches of Oak Haven allow us unfettered access to the magical powers of the oak grove. In exchange, we'll allow you to continue living in your little town. We'll even extend casino privileges. We know

161

how rarely Oak Haven witches get out, after all. You'll probably find it quite exciting."

Delilah blinked several times. "Let me get this straight. You want us to hand over the source of all our power, and in return, you'll . . . what? Allow us to exist? Toss us the occasional comped drink at the nickel slots?"

"You misunderstand," the woman said, though her tone suggested she understood perfectly well that Delilah understood perfectly well. "This is a question of sharing resources. Everyone wins."

"That's not sharing," Scarlett's voice was tight. "That's surrender."

"It's not a real offer," Delilah said. "It's Don Corleone's version of an offer."

Cold laughter echoed through the chamber. "Perhaps it is." A new voice from the shadows, deeper than the others and somehow older. "As they say, *it's a nice town you have here . . . shame if something happened to it.*"

More mocking laughter drifted down. The burgundy woman added, "Like it or not, you have two choices. Share the grove willingly, or we destroy your little town and leave you with nothing."

The temperature in the room seemed to drop several degrees. Something moved in Delilah's peripheral vision, but when she turned to look, there was nothing there. Just shadows playing tricks. Or shadows playing for real.

"Actually," Delilah said, surprising even herself with how steady her voice sounded, "there's a third option. We could just send you all packing. Like we've done *every other time* magicians have tried to take Oak Haven."

The burgundy woman's laughter sounded like icicles

breaking. "Oh, child. You think this is like those other times? We were just toying with you then. This is the big one."

"What do you even want our grove for?!" Delilah exclaimed. "Back when we thought you were just a bunch of sideshow entertainers, your obsession with us at least made a little sense. But look at this place! Look at you guys, with your burgundy robes, skittering around in the shadows like a bunch of Walmart Voldemorts. You built a fifty-story casino overnight! Surely you don't need the grove's power, not really. So what's it all for?"

"It is our obligation," the burgundy woman intoned. "We seek justice long denied."

"What are you talking about?" Delilah turned to her sister. "Scar, can you make that one make sense?"

"You're the ones who won't leave *us* alone," Scarlett pointed out. "You dummies want *justice*?! What about justice for Oak Haven? Or hell, justice for me personally? You kept me in a birdcage for a year—remember that bit?"

"This discussion is at an end," intoned the lead magician. "Take our offer back to your coven. Let all the witches discuss it. I suspect there are wiser ones than you. For your sake, I hope that there are."

"We're *not* giving you our grove."

"Then," said the deep voice from the darkness, "we take it. You have until sundown to accept our terms."

A single blink, and the sisters were standing outside the casino entrance, squinting in the sudden bright lights and noise. No smoke, no dramatic exit; just there one moment and here the next.

"Wow," Scarlett breathed. "Del, we're in deep shit."

"I know." Delilah scanned the surroundings for any sign of Jasper and Nate. "And honestly? I felt better when I thought this was about stealing our oak grove. I do not care for whatever honoring their ancestors might entail."

"Yeah, that's pretty dark. What does that even mean?"

"No clue. Do you see the guys? We should grab them and get out of here."

Whatever power these magicians had, it wasn't penny-ante stage tricks. This was old magic. The kind of magic that made Louise Demain seem downright stable by comparison. And Delilah had just told them, essentially, to go fuck themselves.

I suppose Tiny Tim said it best, she thought grimly, *God bless us, every one.*

As the quartet trudged back toward home, the sky was just beginning to lighten. The morning air was crisp and extremely cold, the kind that made your lungs feel scrubbed from the inside out. The casino's garish lights receded behind them like a bad hangover.

Jasper walked slightly behind the others, still trying to make sense of the incredibly vivid dream he'd had. Flashing lights and strange people . . . some sort of game show . . . an evil council meeting? His subconscious really had outdone itself this time.

I'm returning that Brandon Sanderson novel to the library, he thought, *the first chance I get.* But as he studied the backs of his three companions, he had another, different thought: *What am I doing here?*

The last thing he remembered with any certainty was . . . what? The county clerk's office. Right. And then there was that liquor license with the impossible address. And . . . after that, things got fuzzy. Like someone had smudged the ink on his mental ledger. Through the haze, a crystal-clear memory flashed through his mind: Delilah turning her whiteboard around to reveal the exact same opinion about the Dewey decimal system that he held. The synchronicity made his chest tighten.

Ahead of him, Scarlett and Nate were whispering intensely, their heads close together. Something about a "bullshit offer" and how "Mama was going to lose her mind."

Delilah hung back a bit, eventually falling into step beside him. She looked exhausted.

"You holding up okay?" she asked, her voice surprisingly gentle.

"I, uh . . ." Jasper adjusted his glasses. "This is going to sound completely insane, but am I dreaming right now?"

"Ummm, don't think so?"

"I had the most vivid dream that you and I were teammates on some ridiculous game show. And we kept giving the exact same answers to all these personal questions. Wild, right?"

Delilah's eyebrows shot up. "You believe that you dreamt that?"

"I know, I know. Too much late-night television, clearly." He laughed nervously. "Sorry, I don't usually share my bizarre dreams with strangers."

Something flickered across Delilah's face. Amusement? Concern? It was gone too quickly to read.

"That does sound like quite a dream," she said carefully.

"But the weirdest part is, I can't quite remember how I ended up here with all of you." He stopped suddenly, as if just realizing something crucial. "Good grief, where are my manners? We haven't even been properly introduced, have we?"

He extended his hand, as if clinging to a small bit of normalcy might anchor him somehow. "Jasper Hopkins, pleasure to meet you. I'm the archivist with the county. Which I guess is probably why I'm here? I don't really know," he admitted. "But I don't normally wander through forests at dawn, I promise. I'm usually quite boring."

Delilah took his hand, her grip firm and somehow reassuring.

"Delilah Melrose," she replied. "My family owns Stargazer Inn. I'm usually a little too boring to take strangers home, but something tells me you could use a room?"

"Well, I am exhausted," he said. "But I'm afraid I don't have a reservation."

She grinned. "Bah, we'll figure it out."

Ahead of them, the trees began to thin, revealing what appeared to be a picture-perfect New England town nestled in the valley below. The sight hit Jasper with a wave of déjà vu that left him slightly dizzy.

Have I been here before? he wondered. *It feels familiar, but I can't quite . . .*

"Home sweet home," Delilah murmured beside him, and there was something in her voice, a noticeable mixture of relief and dread, that made him want to comfort her. But he had no idea why she needed comforting or why he felt qualified to provide it.

"It's beautiful," he said instead. "Like something from a Christmas card."

"It won't be if those magicians get their way," Scarlett called back, having apparently overheard him. "Which is why we need to figure out how to stop them."

"Magicians?" Jasper echoed, blinking in confusion.

Nate gave him a look that was almost like pity. "Man, he's completely scrambled. That forgetting spell is brutal. Yeah dude, the magicians. You and I literally just discussed it, when we were having a beer at the casino. Remember? I was telling you about how these magicians keep trying to take over our town?"

Strike that, Jasper thought. *It's definitely pity.*

"Hey, Scar," Nate said to his companion. "I know he's supposed to forget Oak Haven the moment he leaves, but shouldn't he remember a conversation we had five minutes ago?"

Scarlett approached Jasper and peered into his eyes like a doctor performing a neurological exam. "You reckon all the shit that the magicians are doing is making everything worse?"

"Oak Haven?" Jasper repeated, increasingly wondering if he was in fact still asleep. "Is this still part of my dream?"

"You're not dreaming, Jasper," Delilah said gently. "But it's . . . complicated."

"A little sleep might help," Nate suggested. "Let's all meet back at the inn to talk strategy tomorrow. Obviously the town's going to reject that ridiculous excuse for an offer, but the question is, what do we do next?"

"Works for me," Scarlett agreed. "Not that I'll be able to sleep, but I can stare at the ceiling and catalog all my regrets for a few hours. That's always fun."

With that, he and Scarlett headed off down the main street, leaving Jasper alone with Delilah.

"C'mon, let me get you settled at the inn," she offered, not quite meeting his eyes.

"That's very kind, thanks." Suddenly he became painfully aware that he was just standing there, staring at her like an idiot. But he couldn't help it. The way the moonlight caught in her hair, turning the dark strands almost blue. The determined set of her jaw that suggested she was keeping about seventeen different emotions locked inside.

"What?" she asked, noticing his stare.

"Nothing, I just . . ." He cleared his throat. "I keep having this feeling that we've met before. Which is impossible, because I would definitely remember someone like you. But there's something about you . . ." He trailed off, unsure how to explain his unexplainable sense of connection.

Oh, fantastic job, Hopkins, he thought. *Very smooth. She's definitely not going to think you're a total creep now.*

But instead of backing away slowly, which would have been entirely reasonable, she said, "Yeah, well. There's something about you too."

For a moment, they just stood there, surrounded by the impossible perfection of a town Jasper was certain he'd never visited, yet somehow knew in his bones.

"Come on," Delilah said finally. She gently took his elbow and guided him in the direction of the inn. "I'll show you to a room with an actual bed, where no one will try to quiz you about your coffee preferences."

"That was part of the dream!" Jasper exclaimed. "Or, wait . . . was it? Did that happen? Oh God, I don't even know what's real anymore."

Delilah's laugh was warm and genuine. "Welcome to Oak Haven, Mr. Hopkins."

CHAPTER 15
SATURNALIA'S UPON US

Delilah awoke to the sound of little feet thundering down the hallway outside her room. The footsteps were followed by children's laughter, then the unmistakable clatter of something expensive hitting the floor.

"Maya Injabere! Elijah! What have I told you about running in the halls?" Their grandmother Ruth's voice was warm but steeped in authority. "There are people still sleeping! Or, there were before just now!"

"Elijah said he could beat me to the end of the hall," came a little girl's voice, "but he was *wrong*."

"You cheated!"

"Did not!"

"Did too!"

"Did not!"

"*Children*," said Ruth. "Go downstairs for breakfast. *Now*. Before you wake up every guest in the inn."

Delilah pulled her pillow over her head, but it was too late. Wide awake after maybe three hours of sleep, tops. Every time she'd closed her eyes, she'd see that woman in a red suit. Her

169

hair piled atop her head like some demented snake charmer. The council lurking in the shadows. All the while, their ultimatum still echoed: *Share the grove or we take everything.*

"*Share,*" she muttered into her pillow. "Share, my ass."

On top of all that, it was awfully strange to be back in her own bed after her Year of Yurts. The bookshelf still held her worn copies of Tolkien, Le Guin, and Butler—books that Papa had insisted every right-minded person should own. The ceiling still bore the glow-in-the-dark stars that he'd helped her arrange into constellations. Here in her room, it was like the past year had never happened. But even if the room wasn't any different, *she* was. Delilah could feel the changes inside; she just didn't know what they meant.

A soft knock at her door made her groan. "Go away. I'm hibernating until the apocalypse is over."

"Miss?" It was Ruth Injabere again. "I just wanted to apologize about the children. And I wanted to make sure they didn't wake you."

Delilah chuckled. Waking you up to discuss someone else having woken you up—such a grandmother move. "No worries. I should be up helping Mama anyway."

"Oh, you mean Mrs. Melrose?" She heard Ruth chuckle on the far side of the door. "Last time I saw her, she was trying to use magic to stir the pancake batter and then yelling at the bowl when nothing happened."

Mama forgetting the Saturnalia restrictions was no surprise. It's tricky when you're used to using magic for the smallest things and suddenly you can't. It's like a right-handed person suddenly trying to do everything with the left.

"I'll be right down," Delilah called back. "Just need to locate my will to live . . . I think it rolled under the bed."

"Check behind the nightstand," offered Ruth. "That's where all the important things hide."

After Ruth's footsteps retreated, Delilah dragged herself into the shower. Perhaps the water pressure could blast away some of her existential dread.

You have until sundown to accept our terms, she could hear the magician saying.

But Delilah knew there would be no accepting of terms. Whether they'd accept wasn't in question. No, the question was: *What happens when they don't?*

Forty minutes later, freshly showered and arguably more awake, Delilah made her way to the dining room. The inn was bustling with activity. Guests chatted over breakfast while staff darted around, overburdened with holiday-themed everything. Kelly had transformed the dining room yesterday, before giving up her powers, and it remained expanded to outrageous dimensions, the ceiling soaring and the walls stretched to accommodate the entire town for the Saturnalia feast.

Delilah spotted Jasper in a quiet corner, huddled over a very large mug of coffee and a plate of untouched eggs. He was still wearing his tuxedo from the night before. Scarlett was right, there *was* a sort of "haunted Victorian radiator" about him . . . but in the best possible way. Besides, who wouldn't look haunted if they woke up in a strange place with no memory of how they'd gotten there?

Poor guy, she thought. *This isn't fair to you at all.* Her heart did that stupid little stutter it had been doing since she first saw him at the hardware store. It was both infuriating and increasingly hard to ignore.

Get a grip, she thought. *Exactly ten seconds after he stepped out of Oak Haven, he completely forgot who you were. This is not worth getting worked up about. Later on he's going to go back to his real life and you aren't a part of it.*

But *later on* felt very far away.

Ruth Injabere sat across from Jasper, chatting away while her grandchildren shoveled pancakes into their mouths. Jasper's smile was polite but blank. Delilah could see the confusion in his eyes from all the way across the room. No surprise there. Ruth remembered having met Jasper yesterday. But Jasper couldn't say the same.

As Delilah approached, she caught the tail of Ruth's remarks. "It's all right, dear. Perhaps a bit too much celebrating after the ritual last night, eh? Overdid the eggnog, did we?"

"Um . . . right, yes!" Jasper seized on the explanation like a drowning man on a life preserver. "It must've been the eggnog."

"Morning, everybody." Delilah slid into the chair next to Jasper. "Mrs. Injabere, I see you've been keeping our archivist company."

"Good morning! Yes, such a lovely young man," Ruth said. "But perhaps I should leave you two in peace. Maya, Elijah, would you like some more pancakes?" Both kids nodded their syrup-smeared faces. "Wonderful, let's see what we can do. Come along, bring your plates." She shepherded the two kids away.

"How are you this morning?" Delilah asked carefully.

"Well . . . " Jasper looked around furtively and lowered his voice. "I'm not sure what's going on."

So sexy, she couldn't stop herself from thinking. What is so sexy about sneakiness?

"Maybe you can help me," he said. "I seem to be experiencing significant memory gaps. That lady thinks we've met before, but I have no memory of her. In fact, I'm not at all sure how I ended up here in the first place. The last thing I remember is being at my office, and then things start to get fuzzy . . . And I had an absolutely insane dream about a casino . . . Wait, you were there, actually! And. Then we were outside, I think? Uh. It was so . . . I don't know. I'm, uh . . ."

He leaned in closer, staring straight into Delilah's eyes and forcing her to consider how a man could look so petrified and so irresistible at the same time.

"The truth is, I think I might be having some sort of psychotic break?"

Guilt stabbed through her. "No no, Jasper, I swear, you're perfectly all right. The truth is . . . You *have* been here before. And Mrs. Injabere does know you. It's just that you can't remember meeting her."

"I—" He gazed around the room, utterly lost. "I don't think I'd forget all this."

"It's a spell. You're um . . . I'm sorry but you're under a spell." The stabbing sensation intensified. Delilah had never thought about the forgetting spell in quite this way before; she'd never questioned the ethics of the whole thing. The forgetting spell was such a good deal for the witches of Oak Haven . . . She'd never realized what a shit deal it was for everybody else.

"But that's—I mean, I'm sorry." Jasper adjusted his glasses. "But that's not a real explanation. Spells aren't real."

"Says the man sitting in a banquet hall that's several stories taller than the building it's housed in. You did notice that, right?"

He opened his mouth as if he was going to argue the point,

then closed it again when he looked up and realized he could barely see the ceiling. "Did I drink last night? I did, right? I must've had too much to drink and I'm still drunk. That would explain so much right now."

"No no, you're okay." Delilah surprised herself with how gentle her tone had become. "You're not drunk. Or hungover, or anything like that. You're just very *very* far outside your usual frame of reference."

"So if I'm under a spell, are you . . . a witch?" Jasper asked. It was clear that he had every intention of at least *sounding* like he was taking Delilah seriously. But he clearly thought he was talking to a madwoman.

"Yes, most of the women in Oak Haven are witches. Well, we're temporarily non-practicing at the moment, due to the holiday. And yes, I know it all sounds crazy but it would be great if you could suspend disbelief, just for a bit. Because we could really use your help. We have until sundown to figure out what to do about the magicians, and I haven't been able to get anyone to take it seriously."

"Magicians?" Jasper's eyebrows shot up. "Like . . . *pulling rabbits out of hats* magicians?"

"More like *threatening to enslave our town*, but yeah. Magicians."

"Right." Jasper's voice was faint. "Obviously."

Oof, she thought. *I have to start from the beginning now.* Delilah had never dealt with someone who'd been in Oak Haven, then left, and then returned . . . much less tried to *flirt* with someone who was in Oak Haven then left then returned. *He's basically living yesterday all over again but he doesn't remember a thing.* Like *Groundhog Day* but upside down.

But before she could explain the situation any further, Scarlett appeared. She slid into a chair across from them, looking like she'd slept even less than Delilah. Her hair was pulled into a messy ponytail and there were dark circles under her eyes.

"Morning, sunshine," Delilah greeted her. "You look like you're riding the Saturnalia struggle bus."

"Riding it?" Scarlett grumbled. "More like it ran me down and left me for dead. I forgot that my entire skincare routine is magic-based, and I don't even want to talk about haircare."

Nate joined Scarlett at the table. He was looking slightly less disheveled than his partner, but no less exhausted. "Hey, guys. We checked out the casino from a distance this morning. Place is crawling with magicians in fancy outfits, looking all smug and villainous. A lot of capes."

"Way too many capes," Scarlett added. "They're definitely preparing for something. And I don't think it involves taking 'no' for an answer tonight."

"Have some coffee, my darlings." Mama glided over, carrying a fresh carafe of coffee in one hand and mugs in the other. "You'll need your energy for the day's labors."

Kelly was looking improbably put-together for someone orchestrating a feast for hundreds. Only the slight flour dusting on her sleeves betrayed any kitchen activity whatsoever.

"Mama," Delilah began, "the magicians—"

"—are lurking about, being menacing and overdramatic. Yes, I gathered." Kelly poured coffee into the empty cups with precision. "That's not exactly breaking news, dear. Magicians have been menacing and overdramatic since top hats were invented."

"This is different," Scarlett insisted. "They gave us a deadline. Sundown tonight. That's when—"

"Darlings, tell me: what exactly do you propose we would do right now? Storm the casino with wooden spoons and strong

175

language? We won't have our powers back until after Saturnalia."

"Well . . . we could warn everyone," Delilah said. "Get the town prepared?"

"And cause a panic that would ruin a sacred tradition?" Kelly arched an eyebrow. "No, I think not. We can't give in to bullying. If those magicians think they can disrupt Saturnalia with vague threats, they clearly don't understand Oak Haven very well."

"But, Mama—" Scarlett tried again.

"The feast begins at six," Kelly interrupted. "There will be plenty of time to deal with the magicians later."

Delilah exchanged a look with her sister. Their mother's confidence felt misplaced, especially given the creep show they'd seen in the council chamber.

"Now," Kelly continued. "Caffeinate yourselves as necessary. I need all hands on deck, please. The feast preparations are catastrophically behind schedule, and I just caught Jerusha trying and failing to enchant the cranberry sauce. Now we have cranberries all over the ceiling."

"The thing is, Mama . . ." Delilah tried one more time.

"No arguments, Delilah. This feast is happening, no matter what. I've already taken precautions. Why do you think I hired Maximillian to perform tonight?"

"I was wondering about that," Scarlett said. "Isn't he the one who helped the magicians try and take over the town last year?"

"Of course—not that he remembers." Kelly smiled with the satisfaction of a chess player revealing a particularly clever move. "Keep your friends close and your enemies where you can watch them sparkle. Now, finish your coffees and meet me in the kitchen. All of you."

She departed in a cloud of subtle perfume and absolute authority. "And if anyone sees Candace," she called over her shoulder, "tell her those centerpieces need to be redone! They look like something the cat dragged in and vomited tinsel all over!"

A silence fell in her wake.

"Is she always like that?" Jasper asked.

"Yes," the sisters said together.

"So I guess we're—"

"Yep." Nate stood up. "Galley slaves until further notice."

"Wait," Delilah said as the others began to rise. "Hang on. I still don't think we should just wait for disaster to strike."

"Sure." Scarlett nodded. "But what can we do? Everybody in town is focused on this feast tonight. Mama does have a point: they're all salivating about coming here for dinner, and they aren't going to want to hear any bad news from the Melrose sisters."

"Although," Jasper offered hesitantly, "isn't that exactly what you want?"

Three pairs of eyes turned to him.

"I mean," he adjusted his glasses nervously, "from what I gather, your entire town will be in one place."

"You're right," Scarlett agreed. "Maximize our warning efficiency. But when? Mama's got the whole evening scheduled down to the minute. There's the welcome speech, the traditional toast, Maximillian's performance . . ."

Delilah brightened. "That's it! Everyone will be heckling the crap out of him anyway. We'll interrupt it."

"Mid-performance?" Nate asked. "Your mom will be furious."

"Better in trouble with Mama than attacked by magicians," Scarlett pointed out.

Nate made a face. "You sure about that?"

But Scarlett was already plotting. She turned to Jasper. "Could *you* do it? You're a neutral party here. People might actually listen to you. Del and I have a history of—"

"Shenanigans," Nate interrupted. "Hi-jinx. Tomfoolery."

"I was going to say, *unfortunate errors in judgment*. But okay. Point is, they may not take us seriously. But Jasper, you've got that whole professor vibe going." Scarlett gestured at his general . . . Jasperness. "You're an outsider. You're an authority."

"I don't know . . . How can I be an authority on anything? I barely know where I am."

"It's a great idea! Listen—" Delilah squeezed his arm in her enthusiasm, and Jasper's eyes widened in shock at her touch. It was an unpleasant reminder that he no longer knew her as well as she did him. "Listen," she began carefully. "I know none of this makes sense to you right now. But our whole town is facing something really dangerous, and we could use your help."

Jasper looked at her for a long moment. "Okay," he said finally. "But if I'm going to stand up in front of an entire town of witches, I'd like to at least understand what I'm talking about. Can you explain everything to me? The whole situation, from the beginning?"

"Absolutely." Delilah nodded. "But we better do it over a pile of potatoes, or Mama will hex the hell out of us once she gets her powers back."

As they made their way toward the kitchen, Delilah found herself watching Jasper. The way he took everything in, his expression one of anxiety and fascination in equal parts. The way he kept glancing at her when he thought she wasn't looking.

Focus, Delilah, she told herself sternly. *Crisis first, feelings later. If there is a later.*

But as she followed him into the kitchen, she couldn't help but think that even in the midst of impending doom, her heart had picked a spectacularly inconvenient time to remember it existed.

The kitchen was, as Delilah had expected, an utter madhouse.

Steam billowed from massive pots while three different timers beeped at different rates, each more insistently than the last. A mountain of potatoes sat beside an equally impressive pile of potato peels, looking like the Alps recreated in starch. There was a puddle of spilled hot sauce on the floor.

Jerusha stood atop a teetering stepladder, trying to wipe cranberry sauce off the ceiling. Her elegant hairdo was now polka-dotted with red.

"Oh for—" she muttered, stretching to reach a stubborn glob. "If I could just—" She pointed at the ceiling and snapped her fingers, then looked surprised when nothing happened. "Dammit!"

"You can stop your snapping," Candace muttered. She was arranging flowers at a nearby workstation, her otherwise immaculate appearance undermined a bit by the holly leaves stuck to her sweater.

"Amateurs." Zahir moved through the mayhem with resignation, quietly adjusting temperatures and rescuing sauces from the brink of separation. "You'd think after centuries of doing this, you'd remember how to function without magic for a few days."

"Easy for you to say," Jerusha shot back. "You've never had to live without it."

"Oh yes, the lifetime I've spent actually developing skills is *so much easier* than your charmed existence of pointing at things and snapping your fingers."

Across the kitchen, Kelly was attempting to truss a turkey, but the string kept slipping. "For heaven's sake," she muttered, trying again. "This would take two seconds if I could just—" She made a quick gesture, then looked annoyed when the string remained uncooperatively limp.

"Need a hand?" Delilah asked, approaching her mother.

"Pshh . . . I've been trussing poultry since before you were born," Kelly replied. "I just need to remember how to do it manually." She fumbled with the string again and cursed under her breath.

"Here." Delilah gently took the string from her mother's hands. "Let me."

Kelly surrendered. "Thank you, darling. I don't know what's wrong with me today. I keep reaching for magic that isn't there."

"Happens every year," Delilah reminded her, expertly looping the string around the turkey's legs.

Mama laid a gentle hand on the small of her daughter's back. "I want you to know—I do understand about the magicians."

Delilah looked up sharply. "So you believe us now?"

"I always believed you. I just don't think panicking is especially helpful. We handle this the way we've always handled magicians: calmly, strategically, and without letting them disrupt our lives." Kelly's eyes gleamed. "If those magicians want a fight, we'll give them one. But first, we feast."

On the far side of the kitchen, Jerusha had surrendered on the cranberry ceiling front and taken up berating Candace about the centerpieces. "Those pinecones should be pointing north-northwest to honor the winter solstice! Did you do them wrong? Or have they moved on their own?"

"They're pinecones, Jerusha," Candace shot back. "They don't have directional awareness!"

"Um, Mama?" Delilah ventured, returning to the more pressing crisis. "About Maximillian. Are you sure hiring him was a good idea? I mean, given his history with the town . . ."

"Of course it's a good idea," Kelly replied, inspecting Delilah's turkey-trussing with approval. "The forgetting spell wiped his memory of ever being our enemy. Now he's just a mediocre stage magician with a questionable accent. Plus, keeping him close lets us monitor the doings of his colleagues. Last time, he gathered information on us, but tonight, we turn the tables."

"You're using him as bait," Delilah realized.

"I prefer to think of it as strategic entertainment booking." Kelly smiled thinly. "Now, enough conspiracy theories. Scarlett, those napkins won't fold themselves."

As Kelly moved away to intervene in yet another holiday crisis, Scarlett nudged Delilah. "Mama's playing a dangerous game."

"When isn't she?" Delilah watched their mother effortlessly separate Jerusha and Candace, redirecting their energies to different tasks. "But I think she might be right about Maximillian. If he is working with the magicians again, tonight's performance would be the perfect cover for whatever they're planning."

"So what do we do?" Scarlett asked.

Delilah caught sight of Jasper across the kitchen, peeling potatoes with the precision of a surgeon. Despite everything, he was still here, still trying to help.

From across the kitchen came a crash, followed by Kelly's

voice rising above the chaos: "Who put turmeric in the figgy pudding? Zahir! Someone fetch Zahir to come fix this!"

Delilah and Scarlett shared a look.

"It's going to be a long day." Delilah sighed.

"May as well eat, drink, and be merry," her sister noted. "Isn't that what they say?"

After all, they were Melroses. And Melroses knew how to throw one hell of a party, even at the end of the world.

CHAPTER 16
NOW BRING US A FIGGY PUDDING

Delilah frowned at her reflection. She'd already changed outfits three times, and she still wasn't a hundred percent sold on her choice. First, she'd tried on a red dress, but it was way too "Dunder Mifflin Christmas Party." Next, a green jumpsuit that made her look like a deranged elf. Finally she'd tried a black cocktail dress that screamed "I'm mourning the holidays," which, okay—accurate. But perhaps not the vibe for tonight.

She'd finally settled on a midnight blue velvet number that Scarlett had conjured up before surrendering her powers. Simple, elegant, and made her feel like she belonged in one of those old movies where everyone spoke exclusively in witty one-liners and the telephones were always white.

"Come *on*, Del!" Scarlett's voice carried from the hallway. "Quit stalling. Saturnalia waits for no witch!"

"I'm not stalling! I'm having a fashion emergency."

The door burst open and Scarlett stormed in, a vision in emerald. "Oh stop it, you look perfect. Let's go!"

Delilah looked her sister up and down, then let out a whistle. "Look at you. Nate's going to lose his mind."

"For all the good it does me. Hang on, do you have that buttoned correctly?" Scarlett didn't wait for an answer, just reached for the back of her sister's dress. "Ugh, you messed this all up in the back. Let me fix it."

Delilah knew better than to argue; Scarlett had always been the most fashionable of the Melrose girls. If she said your dress needed fixing, all you could do was stand there and take it. "So what's going on with you two, anyway? I've been gone a year, I can't believe you aren't hitched by now. Unless you were waiting for me to come back, of course, which would be awfully sweet?"

"*Hardly*. No, the issue is, Nate doesn't want to get married until we can go on a proper honeymoon. Which we can't, of course, because of the forgetting spell."

"Weren't you all working on a forgetting-spell loophole when I left? Something with studying trivia?"

"Yeah well . . . Suck in your breath a little for me . . . ugh, *more*, Delilah, c'mon . . . *The trivia loophole* has not been effective thus far. And so, I wait. And wait. Okay, you're set. You look gorgeous, big sister. Now can we *please* get going? There's a praying mantis in a tuxedo downstairs who keeps nervously checking his watch."

"*Mean*. Jasper's just nervous because you asked him to address the whole damn town."

"Sure, *that's* what he's nervous about." Scarlett's eyes twinkled. "Not a certain witch he can't stop staring at."

"Oh shut up." But Delilah couldn't prevent the flush in her cheeks.

"He likes you. And you like him. Which makes total sense, since you're both huge nerds."

"You don't know that."

"That you're both huge nerds? Are you kidding? That man

184

has never met a filing cabinet he didn't want to marry and have little manila folder babies with. Trust me, *anyone* can see you're both huge nerds. Aliens can see it from space. Blind people can see it. The dead can see that—"

"Cut it out. I meant, you don't know that he likes me."

"Silly girl." Scarlett wrapped her arm around Delilah's. "He looks at you like you're the pen-and-pencil set he's been searching for all his life." She gently steered her sister toward the door. "Now, we have a feast to attend, a town to save, and a romance to kindle. ¡*Ándale!*"

They hurried down the hallway, but Delilah abruptly stopped. "Scar, I miss Luna. This doesn't feel right without her."

"Yeah . . . I know. I miss her too."

"I wonder what she's up to."

Scarlett shrugged. "Probably marking the holiday with a coven of telekinetic yak herders. Can we go now?"

"I just hope she's okay."

"She's fine, Del. Luna will turn up—she always does. She's probably just waiting to make the most dramatic entrance possible."

The sisters paused at the top of the grand staircase that swept down to the lobby. Below them, the inn hummed with activity. Staff hurried to and fro; Mama directed traffic. The oak banisters had been wrapped with evergreen garlands and twinkling lights. And there, at the bottom of the stairs, stood Jasper and Nate, deep in conversation. They were still in their casino-inspired tuxedos.

"*Look* at my guy," Scarlett whispered gleefully. "I'd never get Nate into a tux under normal circumstances."

Nate's face split into a wide grin as he caught sight of his girlfriend bounding down the stairs. "Hey, look at you! Best Christmas present ever!"

Then Jasper looked up.

When his eyes met Delilah's, something in the air shifted. And that insecure voice in Delilah's head? That voice that kept whispering *"Girl, better change your dress one more time"*? That voice fell silent. In the warmth of Jasper's gaze, the dress was perfect. She was perfect.

But as she descended the stairs, she thought, *Don't be an idiot, Del. To him, we've just met.*

"You look amazing," he said simply.

"Gosh, thanks," she replied, and then cursed herself internally. *Gosh?! Since when do I say* gosh? "You clean up pretty well yourself."

"Technically, I haven't changed since last night. Or this morning. However time works around here." He adjusted his glasses. "I mean, I don't actually own a tux. I don't know where this even came from."

"Fits you nicely," Delilah said.

"Another mystery. My proportions are all weird, nothing fits me . . . and yet this does. Plus, I'm still not sure why I'm at a magical banquet in a town that technically doesn't exist. But um . . . well, looking at you now? I'm certain that I wouldn't want to be anywhere else."

"That's . . . that's a very nice thing to say."

"It's the truth," he replied. "I thought I'd better tell you before I forget."

"Do you have your notes for the speech?"

Jasper patted his jacket pocket. "Right here. Though I'm still not convinced anyone's going to listen to the guy who just rolled into town yesterday. Or was it today? I've never been less certain of what actually happened to me or when."

"Trust me, a stern lecture from a visiting historian might be exactly what this town needs." She touched his arm gently. "You'll do fine. Just wait for my signal during Maximillian's act."

"What's the signal?"

"Swift kick under the table."

"Ah. Subtle."

"Melroses aren't known for their restraint."

"I'm getting that." His smile was warm, and for a moment, Delilah allowed herself to imagine how things might be different if they'd met under normal circumstances. If Oak Haven wasn't hidden, if Jasper wasn't going to forget her every time he went to work, if magicians weren't threatening to destroy everything she loved.

"Come on, you two!" Scarlett called from the doorway to the banquet hall. "They won't serve the boar until everyone's seated, and I've been starving myself all day for this!"

As they approached the entrance to the banquet hall, they were greeted by Aphra, stationed beside an enormous basket.

"Io, Saturnalia!" Aphra called out when they approached. She pronounced the traditional greeting with a clear "EE-oh" but, when shouted, it sounded remarkably like "YO, Saturnalia!"

She handed each of them a cone-shaped felt hat. "A pileus for each of you."

"Oh, Aphra, you've outdone yourself. They're beautiful." Delilah examined the intricate embroidery, with oak leaves, stars, and tiny symbols of protection stitched in golden thread.

"That's me and my crafting circle." Aphra beamed. "Every weekend since Thanksgiving they'd come by the shop to make hats and chew gum, and you know what they say . . ."

In unison, Delilah and Jasper offered, "You ran out of gum."

"Got that right."

"In Rome, these were worn by freed slaves," Jasper said, admiring the craftsmanship. "They symbolized liberty."

Aphra's eyes lit up. "Look at you! Someone's been doing their homework."

"Occupational hazard." Jasper placed the hat on his head. He should have looked ridiculous—a grown man in a tuxedo wearing a cone-shaped party hat—but somehow he made it work.

Just inside the hall, Jerusha and Candace were tending bar, but they seemed more focused on some sort of silent turf war, each trying to claim more counter space than the other. A line of thirsty guests had formed, all looking slightly apprehensive about their chances of receiving what they'd ordered.

Delilah swept past the line and around to the far side of the bar. She grabbed two bottles of champagne from the fridge and rejoined Jasper with a wink.

"Oh dear," he cried in mock alarm. "Delilah, what have you done?"

"Ah ha, the privileges of hosting are many. Let's find our table. Oh but first, grab a little plate and check out the pièce de résistance."

She ushered him over to a massive table beside the bar, an edible diorama stretched across its surface. The entire town of Oak Haven had been recreated in cheese, meat, bread, and various garnishes. Tiny houses made of aged cheddar with prosciutto roofs lined miniature streets. The town green was a bed of arugula dotted with cherry tomato "ornaments." A river of blue cheese wound through the center, crossed by a breadstick-covered bridge.

"I present to you," Delilah announced with a theatrical flourish, "the Oak Haven Charcuterie Tableau."

"My God," Jasper breathed, leaning in to examine the detail. "Is that . . . Is the town hall made of *brie*?"

"I'm told it's Gruyère, actually. Structural integrity issues with the brie."

Zahir appeared beside them, surveying his creation with a mixture of pride and embarrassment. "Behold my masterwork: Cholesterol Heights. Three days of work for something that will be run through by an army of hungry wolverines in approximately twenty minutes."

"You're a marvel," Jasper said.

"You are correct, my friend." Zahir clapped him on the back. "Thanks for all the help. Couldn't have done it without you."

"Wait, what?" Jasper turned to Delilah, confused. "Oh, you mean yesterday, with the potatoes?"

"I mean, sure? But I really mean the day before when you and I spent the entire afternoon on—ohhh, never mind," said Zahir knowingly. "Forgetting spell. Yes, Jasper you helped considerably. Far more than just a few potatoes."

"Well!" Jasper smiled. "Good on me, I guess!"

Delilah and Jasper made their way to their table, where Scarlett and Nate were already seated, along with all four Earls, all dressed in competitively ugly Christmas sweaters. They greeted Jasper like a long-lost friend.

"Io, Saturnalia!" shouted Ten.

"There's our favorite archivist!" Nine called out. "When are you coming around for some more grog?"

Delilah subtly shook her head, trying to signal the Earls to dial it back.

"I'm sorry," Jasper said, clearly uncomfortable. "I'm afraid I don't—"

"Course you don't," Twelve cut in smoothly. "We've only just met. Tonight. For the first time. Ever."

"Subtle, Dad," Nate muttered.

"What?" Twelve grinned. "I'm being hospitable to this new person who we've definitely never seen before."

"This is the weirdest form of gaslighting," Jasper said thoughtfully.

Delilah said, "How about let's eat. And drink! Look what I purloined from the bar."

The Earls applauded at the bottles of champagne. "That's our girl."

The feast began with servers bringing out platters of appetizers: Sticky Date and Bacon Rumaki that disappeared almost as soon as they hit the table; Chai-Spiced Latkes, a collaborative undertaking from the Chatterjee and Silverberg families; and finally the famous "Truce of '89" dumplings, half filled with traditional Chinese fillings, half with Italian ingredients, commemorating the legendary dispute between Mrs. Li and Mrs. Cattaneo that only ended when they realized they were basically making the same food in different shapes.

"The soup course arrives," Scarlett announced as bowls of vibrant red liquid were set before them. "Ah, 'Better Than Therapy' Borscht."

"It's certainly beautiful." Jasper studied the herbed sour cream stars floating on the surface, almost too delicate to touch with a spoon.

"Just wait till you taste it," Nate enthused. "Every year I tell myself I'm not going to cry, and every year I'm wrong."

"You cry over soup?"

"Don't knock it till you've wept in it."

As Delilah took her first spoonful, she had to agree with Nate's assessment. The borscht was silky, earthy, with a tart brightness that cut through the richness of the beets. It was perfect. Glancing around the table, she saw the same blissful expression all around.

With each course, the festive atmosphere intensified. By the time the main dishes arrived, all the pilei hats were listing at jaunty angles, and the volume in the hall had risen to a cheerful roar.

The centerpiece of the meal was a massive wild boar, roasted to perfection, surrounded by caramelized fruits and root vegetables. Everyone applauded when Kelly wheeled it in.

And then came Edward's Famous Five-Cheese Lasagna.

Delilah felt her breath catch when she saw it. Papa's signature dish, still included in the feast every year, still made exactly according to his recipe. She glanced at Scarlett, who gave her a small, sad smile.

"You okay?" Jasper asked quietly, noticing her expression.

"Yeah . . . This is my dad's lasagna. I don't know, I wish Mama didn't insist on dragging this out every year. It's hard to see it without him here to enjoy it."

"Oh sure, I understand that. Although, on the other hand, maybe it's also kind of a nice thing, too? That he's still part of the festivities? A tiny part of him, still joining in somehow?"

Delilah just blinked, saying a silent prayer no water would spill out of her eyes.

Jasper gently laid his hand over hers. "I'm not trying to tell you how to feel. But I think that's what traditions are supposed to do. Keep the people we love present, even when they're gone."

"That's a very non-Grinchy perspective from someone who claims to hate Christmas." She glanced at his hand, willing it not to move away from hers.

"You got me. I suppose I don't hate every aspect. Mostly I hate the pressure. All the expectation. Like, Christmas is always supposed to be perfect but somehow it never quite is. And every gift is supposed to be perfect but they never quite are, either. And after all that stress, the gifts are opened in twenty minutes. And then it's over, and that's somehow the worst part of all."

"*Oh totally*!" Delilah leaned forward, pleased to feel so understood. "That's exactly it. The build-up, the worry, and then it's all vaguely dissatisfying, and then it's over."

"Still, I have to say. *This* . . ." Jasper gestured around at the feast, the decorations, the smiling faces. "*This* is pretty amazing."

"True," she admitted. "I want to hate it on principle, but I can't."

"Delilah! Scarlett!" Mrs. Chatterjee approached their table, resplendent in a sari the color of a perfect snowy day. "Your mother has outdone herself! These Cardamom-Maple Roasted Brussels Sprouts are divine!"

"Oh, thank you," Delilah said with a perfectly straight face. "I'll be sure to pass along your compliments."

"Such talent in the kitchen," Mrs. Chatterjee continued. "She's a treasure! Io, Saturnalia, dears!"

"Io, Saturnalia," they chorused back.

Just then, Zahir passed by with a platter of Yorkshire puddings. Scarlett couldn't resist the opportunity to rub it in. "Oh, Zahir, Mrs. Chatterjee was just telling us what a marvelous job *Mama* did with those Brussels sprouts. You know Mama. And all her work. On the sprouts. That she did."

"Uh-huh." He rolled his eyes.

"Careful, buddy," Scarlett said to him. "Your face could freeze that way."

"My face has every reason to freeze that way," he shot back. But then Zahir shrugged good-naturedly and continued his rounds, ever the unsung hero of the Saturnalia banquet.

As the meal progressed, Delilah found herself relaxing despite the knowledge of what was to come. There was something about sitting beside Jasper, watching him interact with her community, that felt both strange and perfectly natural. He asked Nine about the history of piracy in New England, discussed the tools of architectural preservation with Nate, and even got Scarlett to admit that maybe, just maybe, the Dewey decimal system had some merits after all. And whenever there was a lull in conversation, she would catch him looking at her with that same expression from the staircase, like he was trying to memorize her.

"What?" she finally asked, after the fifth or sixth such glance.

"Nothing," he said quickly. Then: "Well. Okay. I keep feeling like I've known you longer than I have. Which I guess is true, right? I have known you longer . . . than I've known you. I don't know, this is a little trippy."

Before Delilah could respond, Scarlett broke out in a tipsy version of "The First Time Ever I Saw Your Face," except with the lyrics changed to the fifth time, then the fifteenth, then the fiftieth.

Delilah nudged Jasper. "What do you think?"

He grinned. "Adele has nothing to worry about."

The crowd gradually grew quiet. Kelly Melrose took her place on the makeshift stage at the far end of the banquet hall. She tapped a spoon against her glass, and the festive chatter died out.

"Before we begin the entertainment portion of our evening," Kelly said, her voice carrying easily across the vast hall, "I want to remind everyone why we're here. Yes, Saturnalia is about revelry." A knowing smile. "And believe me, there will be plenty. But let us never forget—we are here to exercise a muscle that, in all honesty, witches sometimes allow to go slack: humility. We are here to remind ourselves what it means to live without magic, to be dependent on one another. To be . . ." She paused thoughtfully, gazing out at the crowd. "To be human. Which, as our non-magical neighbors remind us daily, is quite an extraordinary thing to be."

A chorus of "hear, hear" rose from around the room.

"I'd like to propose a toast," Kelly continued, raising her glass. "To everyone here tonight, and to those who are not. To the ones we love who are far away—" here she glanced meaningfully at Delilah and Scarlett, clearly thinking of Luna "—and to those who are gone but never forgotten.

"To family, friends, and the bonds that sustain us through dark winters and bright celebrations alike. Io, Saturnalia!"

"Io, Saturnalia!" the room roared back, glasses clinking.

"And now," Kelly announced, "I am delighted to introduce our evening's entertainment. Please welcome, Maximillian the Magnificent!"

There was a puff of smoke on the stage, and when it cleared, a man in an aggressively sparkly tuxedo stood there, his cape fluttering despite the lack of wind.

"Look at that big faker," Scarlett whispered, less discreetly than she should have. "His teeth are so white, I gotta wear shades."

"Good evening, ladies and gentlemen and all magical beings!" he announced in an accent that wandered vaguely through Europe without landing on any specific country. "Maximillian the Magnificent is honored to perform for you on this most auspicious occasion!"

He launched into his first trick: a bog-standard card manipulation routine, enhanced with exaggerated gestures and a constant patter that did not distract from the fact that his fingers weren't nearly as nimble as he imagined they were.

"Is he always this . . . much?" Jasper whispered to Delilah.

"Oh yeah," she whispered back. "He lived here full-time for a while, about a year ago. Turned out, he was helping his magician buddies try to take over the town."

"But now he's . . . entertainment?"

"Mama hired him to keep an eye on him. Keep your enemies close and all that."

"Hmm." Jasper frowned.

"You think it's a bad idea?"

"What do I know, right?"

On stage, Maximillian had moved on to his second trick: pulling seemingly endless colorful scarves from his sleeve while simultaneously delivering terrible puns.

"Watch closely!" he declared. "For nothing is as it *seams*!"

"That doesn't even make sense," grumbled Jerusha from the bar.

"I've seen better tricks from my five-year-old niece!" someone else called out.

"Ah, but can your niece do . . . *this*?" Maximillian produced a white rabbit from his hat with a flourish that suggested he'd just invented nuclear fusion.

"Well, yeah," came a shout from one corner of the room. And: "Of course we can!" from another.

"Not today, you can't!" Maximillian shot back, surprisingly quick on his feet. "*Yo Saturnalia* and so on."

The audience roared with laughter.

"You got us there," Candace shouted from the bar.

"Indeed! And now—" Maximillian drew himself up to his full height "—for my next spectacular illusion, I shall require a volunteer from the audience!"

Jasper nodded. "Hey, maybe this is a good moment to—"

Before he could even finish, both Delilah and Scarlett delivered swift kicks to his shins.

"Ow!" he yelped. "Dammit!"

"Is that brave gentleman volunteering?" He pointed dramatically at Jasper. "Yes, you sir! The man in pain! Please, join me on stage!"

Jasper straightened his jacket with as much dignity as he could muster and approached the stage. "Actually," he began, "if Maximillian will indulge me ... I wanted to take this opportunity to introduce myself. I'm Jasper Hopkins, the chief archivist of this county. I've been asked to address some troubling developments ... literally, real estate developments ... right outside of Oak Haven."

But Maximillian wasn't having it. With the practiced ease of a performer used to handling hecklers, he smoothly cut Jasper off, placing an arm around his shoulders and steering him toward a large box: an upright coffin-like structure painted with mystical symbols.

"Ladies and gentlemen, what we have here is a most unusual volunteer! A man of history, of documentation. A perfect subject for ... THE CABINET OF FATE!"

"Yes of course," Jasper tried again. "But if I could just have a moment to address the crowd—"

"The magnificent Maximillian will make this gentleman vanish before your very eyes!" the magician continued, ignoring Jasper completely. "Prepare to be astounded!"

With a flurry of movements too quick to follow, Maximillian opened the cabinet, showed the audience that it was empty, and then, before Jasper could protest, shoved him inside and slammed the door.

Delilah sat up straighter, and a chill ran down her spine.

This wasn't part of the plan. Jasper was supposed to deliver his warning, not actually take part in some stupid magic trick. She glanced at Scarlett for reassurance, but her sister was staring at the stage.

Maximillian waved his hands over the cabinet, reciting nonsense in that same wandering accent. "Abracadabra! Hocus-pocus! Bibbidi-bobbidi-boo!" He paused, looking slightly embarrassed. "That last one was from a movie, but you get the idea."

He flung open the cabinet door with a dramatic flourish. "Behold! The volunteer has vanished!"

The cabinet was empty.

Scarlett whirled around to meet her sister's eyes. *What the hell?* they both mouthed. Delilah started to get up.

"For my next astounding feat—" Maximillian began, but he was interrupted by a sudden shift in the atmosphere, like pressure dropping before a storm. The candles fluttered, and the temperature seemed to plummet by several degrees. In a swirl of burgundy fabric, a woman appeared at the entrance to the hall. Her silver hair was twisted into an elegant knot, and her face held a kind of cold, terrifying beauty.

It was the magician from the casino, the one who had delivered the ultimatum.

Maximillian's expression faltered. "Ah, madame! I wasn't expecting—"

"Your performance is over," the woman said, her voice cutting through the suddenly silent room. With a casual gesture, she sent Maximillian flying off the stage.

"Ramona! What is the meaning of this?" Kelly stood, her voice steady despite the obvious threat. "You and your magician thugs not invited to our celebration."

Delilah and Scarlett made eye contact again, this time each mouthing "Ramona?!" at the other.

Mama is on a first-name basis with a powerful magician? Apparently? Delilah was struggling to take this in. *And here I thought the Mandy Patinkin thing was the weirdest connection Mama had.*

Wonders really never did cease where Kelly Melrose was concerned.

"Your deadline has passed." The burgundy woman, apparently Ramona, strode forward through the crowd and ascended the stage. "We magicians have come to claim what is rightfully ours."

"And what would that be?" Kelly asked.

"Everything. Starting with the grove."

Witches all over the banquet hall instinctively tried to summon their magic, gesturing wildly or muttering incantations under their breath. But of course, nothing happened. No magical shields formed, no counter-spells manifested. The realization spread through the room like a virus.

Then Delilah saw her mother, marching towards the stage to confront Ramona face-to-face. "Mama, don't!" She leaped to her feet, Scarlett mirroring her action on the other side of the table.

But it was too late. Kelly had already ascended, standing toe-to-toe with the burgundy woman.

"Our answer is this: we will never *give* you the grove, because the grove is not ours to give away. It belongs to the land itself. It belongs to the Earth. It cannot be given, nor can it be taken. It cannot be owned at all."

"How charming." Ramona's voice was practically drowning in condescension. "A witch who thinks she knows her history.

198

But all you know are lies." With a flick of her wrist, she sent Kelly stumbling backward toward the open cabinet.

"No!" Delilah shouted, finally reaching the stage, Scarlett right beside her. They lunged forward, trying to grab their mother, but an invisible force held them back.

"The time for negotiation has passed," Ramona announced. "Now we take what we want."

"Mama!" Scarlett cried.

Kelly's eyes locked with her daughters. There was fear there, yes, but also something else: resolve, and beneath that, something that looked almost like a plan. "Get Luna," she managed to say before the door slammed shut. "You three need each other."

Ramona smiled, but it was a cold, satisfied smile that made Delilah's blood run cold. "Let this be a lesson," she announced to the horrified crowd. "Magic belongs to those strong enough to wield it."

With a broad, arcing gesture, she enveloped herself and the cabinet in a massive burst of flame. When the smoke cleared, all that remained was a pile of ash and the echo of her laughter.

CHAPTER 17

PANIC! AT THE HOLIDAY INN

Jasper Hopkins had been in strange situations before. One time he'd gotten locked in the county records room over a long weekend because none of his colleagues thought to check on him before locking up. He'd survived on vending machine protein bars and bathroom tap water, and he'd passed the time finishing the cataloging of the county's property tax assessment records from the years 1873 to 1899. So really, who was the winner there?

But now Jasper found himself in a dim, quiet library after being shoved into what looked like a magician's coffin. This was definitely new territory.

"Hello?" he called out, his voice echoing slightly in the empty room. "Mr. Magnificent? Is this . . . part of the act?"

The only sound was the distant revelry of the Saturnalia banquet filtering through the walls. *Well,* he thought, *that's a relief anyway. Wherever I am, I'm still at the inn.* The notion of being somehow teleported far away from Delilah didn't sit well at all.

Jasper adjusted his glasses and took stock of his

surroundings. Books lined every wall, leather-bound tomes with gilt lettering catching the soft glow from the fire in the stone fireplace. A large wooden desk dominated one corner, its surface organized with the kind of meticulous precision that made Jasper's heart flutter. Everything was perfectly aligned, every pen and paper exactly where it should be, as if placed according to some internal geometry that only made sense to its owner.

Still, though. Something was off about this room. It took about five seconds for Jasper to grok what it was.

The architecture was different from the rest of the inn. Not just, *oh, a bit of a change in here*. No, it was jarringly different. Where the hotel featured Victorian craftsmanship, everywhere ornate moldings and decorative ceiling roses, this room was stark, almost severe. Simple exposed beams crisscrossed the ceiling, their rough-hewn edges speaking of a far, far earlier construction date. The dentil moldings where walls met ceiling were mathematically precise but devoid of ornament. Clean lines and unadorned symmetry that would have made even the most stern of Puritans nod in approval.

Puritans, he thought. *Yes, that's it exactly.* This room belonged to an entirely different era.

Jasper ran his fingers along the edge of a bookshelf, feeling the smooth wood worn by generations of hands. This wasn't a reproduction or some themed room designed to evoke the colonial era. This *was* the colonial era, somehow preserved within the walls of a Victorian inn.

"Well, that doesn't make a damn bit of sense," he said aloud. Though at this point, architectural anachronisms were the least of his concerns. He'd already accepted that he was in a mysterious town where witches temporarily surrendered their powers to celebrate an ancient Roman festival. A room that was over a century or so out of time was practically mundane by comparison.

His gaze drifted to the fireplace, where flames danced merrily in the grate. Above the stone mantel hung a portrait that made Jasper freeze.

"It can't be," he whispered.

The woman in the portrait stared back at him with keen, knowing eyes. She wore the simple, severe clothing of early American colonial gentry, her hair pulled back under a white cap, her expression one of unflinching determination. A quill pen rested in her right hand, poised above what appeared to be an open ledger.

Jasper knew that face. He knew it as well as his own reflection. A smaller version of this portrait hung on the wall of his archive office. She was his daily companion, her intense stare urging him toward greater precision and care in his work.

The first county archivist.

But what was her portrait doing here, in a hidden town that supposedly no one from the outside world remembered? The plaque at the bottom of the gilt frame read "Agnes Bartlett, Founder of Oak Haven Archives, 1693"".

"Agnes wasn't just the first county archivist," he murmured, putting pieces together. "She was a *witch*."

The implications sent his mind spinning. If Agnes had been from Oak Haven, if she had been a witch, then she must have been immune to the forgetting spell. She would have remembered this place even while working in the outside world. And if she had been the county clerk . . .

"She could have used that role to hide Oak Haven's existence from official records," he realized. "I wonder if that's why she took the job in the first place. To protect the town."

Jasper stepped closer to the portrait, searching for any

additional clues. The ledger in Agnes's painted hands was open to a page filled with elegant script, but the words were too small to read. On the desk beside her elbow sat a large piece of parchment, etched with symbols that momentarily appeared to be the Latin alphabet but, upon closer inspection, was absolutely not. It was no alphabet Jasper had ever seen before. *What language could that possibly be?*

"What were you up to, Agnes?" Jasper whispered.

A sudden commotion from outside caught his attention. The distant sounds of a festive party had transformed into something else entirely: raised voices, cries of alarm, the unmistakable soundtrack of panic.

Something was wrong.

Without a thought, Jasper bolted for the door. Agnes Bartlett would have to wait. Right now, Delilah might need help.

As he raced down the corridor, the cries grew louder, more frantic. By the time he reached the banquet hall doors, his heart was pounding not from exertion but from a cold, creeping dread. Whatever had happened in there, he was already too late.

The banquet hall was in chaos. Witches were frantically trying to summon powers they'd willingly surrendered, guests were crying out in confusion and fear, everyone talking over one another. In the midst of it all, Delilah and Scarlett stood frozen on the stage, staring in horror at a pile of ash where magician's coffin had been.

"What happened?" Jasper rushed toward them. "I was in the library, and I heard—" He stopped, taking in the scene, the panic, the expressions on their faces. "Where's your mother?"

"Gone," Delilah said, the single word containing all the fear and rage she couldn't express. "The magicians took her."

"Is it possible she's still in the building?" Jasper could see the exasperation on the women's faces, but he kept on anyway. "Maximillian just sent me to the library. Could she be somewhere in the inn? We don't know how powerful their magic even is, right? Maybe this was all just to scare everyone."

"That is a huge long shot," Scarlett said.

"Agreed," said Delilah. "On the other hand, we don't want to run around like a bunch of headless chickens only to find out later that she was locked in the walk-in freezer the whole time."

Her sister nodded. "Okay, you have a point. You two, turn this place upside down, just to make sure. I'm gonna track Luna down . . . oof, and I'm doing this without magic, somehow. Shit, how do I find somebody without a spell?"

"Maybe try using your phone?" Jasper offered.

Scarlett's eyes glittered with anger. "Are you being a dick right now?"

"No, my God!"

"Simmer down, sis," Delilah said. "He's just trying to help." She nudged Jasper and said, "Luna doesn't have a phone. She's probably the last holdout on Earth. Scar, last time I talked to her, she mentioned New York. Some mind-reading coven in the subway tunnels. Why don't you start asking around? Some witch in Oak Haven has got to know some witch in New York."

"Okay." Scarlett nodded anxiously. "Okay, sure. Sorry, Jasper. You two double-check that Mama isn't trapped here somewhere. I'm gonna find our kid sister." She nodded once more, as if convincing herself, then marched out of the banquet hall with purpose, calling out to anyone in earshot. "Who here has contacts in the Big Apple?"

Delilah was already moving to the back of the banquet hall. "Let's start with the kitchen. Maybe Zahir saw or heard something. He has an uncanny ability to know what's happening at the inn even when he's elbow-deep in béchamel."

The kitchen was a study in suspended animation. Several dishes sat mid-preparation on counters, as if their makers had simply walked away mid-task. A pot of something rich and aromatic bubbled unattended on the stove. The contrast between the cheerful feast preparations and the current crisis created a dissonance that made Jasper's skin prickle.

"Zahir?" Delilah called out, scanning the room. "Are you in here?"

A muffled thump came from the walk-in freezer, followed by a string of creative curses. The heavy metal door swung open, and Zahir emerged, clutching a tray of what appeared to be elaborately molded ice sculptures in the shape of various woodland creatures.

"*There* you are," he announced, as if Delilah was the one who'd gone missing. "Would someone please explain why half my kitchen staff just abandoned their stations? I've got crème brûlées waiting to be torched, a sauce that needs constant attention or it'll separate, and—" He finally registered their expressions. "What? What the hell happened?"

"The magicians took Mama," Delilah said, the words still feeling unreal as they left her mouth.

Zahir's face went slack. The tray of ice sculptures tilted dangerously before he caught himself. "What? How? When?"

"Just now," Jasper explained. "During Maximillian's performance. A woman in burgundy appeared and—"

"The one from the casino," Delilah interjected. "She shoved Mama into that magic cabinet and then both of them disappeared."

Zahir set the tray down with deliberate care. "What are we doing about it?"

"Scarlett's trying to locate Luna, bring her back to help," Delilah said. "We're checking the inn to make sure Mama isn't still here somewhere. You know, like Jasper was in the library."

"Sorry, what?" Zahir's eyes narrowed. "The library?"

"Yeah, Maximillian put me in the box first," Jasper explained, "and somehow zapped me to the other side of the building. So maybe . . ."

"Got it," Zahir said, already untying his apron. "I'll check the basement and the wine cellar. There are some storage areas down there that nobody's been in for decades." Zahir squeezed Delilah's arm gently. "We'll find her, Del."

Delilah turned to Jasper. "Let's check the guest rooms."

The upstairs hallways were eerily quiet; most guests were still milling around the banquet hall, trying to make sense of what had happened. Del and Jasper methodically checked each vacant room, calling Kelly's name, peeking in closets and bathrooms.

"Listen," Jasper began. "I feel like I should tell you something. When I was in the library? I saw that portrait of Agnes Bartlett."

"Who? Ohh, the hatchet-faced Puritan chick above the fireplace. Sure, yeah, she's some kind of distant relative of ours." Delilah shuddered. "We used to avoid the library as kids because of that face. Why does it matter?"

"Because," Jasper said urgently, "her portrait also hangs in my office. I pass it every day but I had no idea who she really was."

"So what?"

"So what?! A witch from Oak Haven held an official position in the outside world. Maybe she used her role to hide any official record of Oak Haven's existence."

Under different circumstances, Delilah might have found

207

his enthusiasm endearing. At the moment, though, he may as well have been telling her the weather in Melbourne. "But how does that help me *right now*?" she demanded, her voice tight with fear and anger.

"No, you're right." Jasper deflated slightly. "I don't know what it means, just that it seems significant. A connection between Oak Haven and the county going back to the beginning."

They continued their search in silence, moving from room to room with increasing urgency. On the third floor, they ran into Ruth Injabere and her grandchildren, who had just heard the news.

"We've been looking everywhere for you," Ruth said, her calm demeanor now taut with concern. "Is it true about Kelly?"

Delilah nodded, unable to find words that wouldn't break her apart to speak them.

"What can we do?" Ruth asked, already rolling up her sleeves metaphorically.

"We're checking the inn," Jasper explained. "There's a chance she might still be here somewhere."

"Maya, Elijah." Ruth turned to her grandchildren with the authority only a grandmother can wield. "Go get your parents and uncles. Tell them we need everyone checking the grounds outside. Quickly now. I'll take the south wing," Ruth said. "Daniel and Linda will organize search parties."

"Thank you," Delilah managed.

As Ruth hurried away, Delilah wilted against the wall. Something about talking to Ruth made the whole thing seem much too real. The momentum that had been carrying her along suddenly faltered. "I can't believe this is happening."

"We'll find your mother, I'm sure of it." Jasper stood beside her, close but not touching. He wanted to put his arms around her, tell her everything would be okay. But he wasn't certain that would be welcome . . . Hell, he wasn't sure any of it was true.

"That's what everyone keeps saying," Delilah said, a bitter edge creeping into her voice. "But what if we don't? What if she's just . . . gone? Like Papa?"

The rawness in her voice made Jasper ache. He'd been in Oak Haven for what felt like both minutes and years, but Delilah's pain reached through all the confusion and disorientation, anchoring him to something real and immediate.

"Your father," he said carefully. "Wait . . . is he . . . That's why you don't like Christmas. You said he loved it."

Delilah nodded, wrapping her arms around herself. "He brought Christmas to Oak Haven. Before him, it was all solstice celebrations and Saturnalia. But Papa couldn't imagine a winter without Christmas. After he died . . ." Her voice caught. "Everything just reminded me of him. Every decoration, every song, every tradition. It was unbearable."

"And now your mother . . ."

"I can't lose her too, Jasper." The confession emerged as barely a whisper. "I don't think I'd survive it. None of us would."

Jasper moved before he could overthink it, closing the distance between them. His hands found her shoulders, steadying her. "Listen to me. I'm new here, I know. Kelly Melrose is clearly a formidable woman. Not someone to be underestimated. And those magicians? They made a critical mistake."

"What's that?" Delilah asked, looking up at him.

"They left her daughters behind. You and Scarlett are already pretty formidable. I have to assume that once you've added your third sister into the mix, you're unstoppable."

A ghost of a smile touched Delilah's lips. "You're very convincing for someone who's only known me for a day. Or less."

"Or more," he whispered sweetly. "At the moment? It feels like more." Before he could stop himself, he was reaching out to stroke her cheek. This was unlike him, he knew, and utterly wrong. But he couldn't help himself; it was as if his hand belonged to some other, far less cautious man. To his shock, Delilah did not move away. She closed her eyes and leaned her cheek into his hand, like a lost kitten in need of petting.

Jasper's heart raced, sensing the sudden shift between them. He leaned into her, drawn by her marvelous scent and a deep desire he'd been trying so hard to push away. This was wrong. Her mother was missing, and he was only here by bizarre accident. Yet every atom of him ached for this connection, this brief escape from the madness around them.

"Jasper . . ." Delilah opened her eyes and tilted her chin upwards, her gaze locking on his. "Please kiss me."

Unable to deny her or himself, Jasper obliged. His lips met hers in a hungry, desperate kiss. Hands entangling in each other's hair, they clung to each other as if they could somehow stave off the world by sheer force of will.

Her lips were impossibly soft, her hands warm as they slid inside his jacket and up his back. Heat bloomed through his whole body and he deepened the kiss, tasting the sweetness of her mouth as her body leaned against his. He kissed her more deeply, and all the longing he'd felt for her suddenly spilled out beyond his control.

With a groan, Jasper lifted her onto the nearest piece of furniture—a solid oak writing desk that complained only mildly under the weight—never breaking the kiss. A lamp rocked precariously but neither of them cared. Their attention was consumed by each other. Delilah's hands clenched Jasper's chest, her body molding to his like a puzzle piece that had found its match at long last.

Caught in this swell, it was easy to believe that nothing else mattered. Not a missing mother, not a town under siege, not even their own highly tenuous connection to each other. But their sanctuary couldn't last forever. Reality crashed back in as voices echoed from downstairs. People calling out, organizing search teams. Jasper and Delilah broke apart, each retreating to the opposite side of the hallway.

"We shouldn't have done that," she declared. "Not with everything that's happening."

"No . . . no, of course not. We shouldn't have." But then he looked at Delilah. Her cheeks were flushed, the collar of her dress was pulled slightly to one side, and her chic hairdo was now a guilty-looking mess. And in that moment, he knew he never wanted to look at anyone else.

He also knew he couldn't lie to her. "I hope we do it again, though."

A small laugh escaped her, surprising them both. "I'll consider it." Then air seemed to shift again, and determination and focus returned to her voice. "We should check the attic. It's the last place in the inn we haven't looked."

The attic was accessed via a narrow staircase at the end of the third-floor hallway. The door creaked ominously as Delilah pushed it open, revealing a steep ascent into darkness.

"I don't suppose witches have invented electric lighting for their attics?" Jasper asked, peering up into the gloom.

"We're not big on changing lightbulbs when a simple illumination spell will—" Delilah caught herself, remembering. "Right. No magic until after Saturnalia. There should be a switch somewhere . . ."

After some fumbling along the wall, light flooded the stairwell. They climbed in silence, emerging into a vast space beneath the inn's sloped roof. Unlike the pristine organization of the rest of the hotel, the attic was a labyrinth of family history: old trunks, stacked furniture draped in sheets, boxes of books, and paintings leaned against the walls.

"Wow," Jasper breathed, the archivist in him immediately calculating how long it would take to catalog everything. "This is incredible."

"This is a mess," Delilah corrected, picking her way through the narrow paths between stacked belongings. "Mama?" she called. "Mama, are you up here?"

No response came except the settling of old wood and the whisper of dust motes disturbed by their movement.

"Look at these," Jasper said, carefully examining a stack of leather-bound books. "These look like journals. Family records, maybe?"

"Probably," Delilah said, only half listening as she continued searching. "The Melrose family has been keeping records since they arrived in Oak Haven. Half the attic is just documenting the other half."

"Your family history is extraordinary," Jasper said, carefully replacing a journal. "All this tangible connection to the past . . . it's remarkable."

"It's a lot of dusting, is what it is," Delilah replied, but her tone was softer now. She paused by a large object covered with a sheet. "This was Papa's desk. After he died, none of us could bear to see it empty, so we moved it up here."

Jasper joined her, standing close enough that their shoulders touched. "I'm sorry about your father. And we're going to free your mother."

Delilah nodded, swallowing hard. "I know. I just—"

A noise from the far corner of the attic cut her off—a soft thump, like something being knocked over. They both froze, straining to hear.

"Mama?"

Another sound, more distinct. The unmistakable shuffle of movement behind a large wardrobe near the back wall.

"There's someone here," Jasper said, instinctively stepping slightly in front of Delilah. He had no idea what he would or could do to protect her, he only knew he wanted to.

They moved cautiously toward the sound, stepping around piles of old holiday decorations and what appeared to be several generations of outgrown winter coats.

"Hello?" Delilah called, her voice steady despite the tremor in her hands. "Is someone there?"

The shuffling stopped. A moment of tense silence stretched between them and whatever, or whoever, was hiding in the shadows beyond the wardrobe.

Then, with a sudden movement that made them both start, a figure emerged from behind the looming piece of furniture.

But it wasn't Kelly Melrose.

CHAPTER 18

I'LL BE CLONE FOR CHRISTMAS

The figure stepped forward. The weak glow of a strand of Christmas lights—plugged in but only half working—illuminated his eerie, semi-transparent features. Delilah felt her jaw actually drop. Beside her, Jasper tensed and stepped partway in front of her—as though he could somehow protect a witch from whatever magical nonsense was about to unfold. It was an adorably pointless move that Delilah couldn't even take time to enjoy, due to the strange person standing before her.

It was Zahir.

Except it wasn't. Not really. Zahir was downstairs trying to salvage the Saturnalia feast while processing the fact that magicians had just kidnapped the closest thing he had to a mother.

This Zahir was . . . off. Like someone had taken the original and given him multiple runs through a poorly maintained photocopier. He seemed faded around the edges somehow. Ever so slightly transparent. And Zahir's usual tightly wound energy had been replaced by a lounge-lizard, *can't be bothered* sort of air.

"Well, well." Not-Zahir leaned against a massive plastic tub labeled X-MAS DÉCOR (PRE-1950). "This is awkward."

Jasper's hand, still half extended in that protective gesture, drifted down to Delilah's wrist. His touch sent a completely inappropriate tingle up her arm.

Get it together, Delilah.

"Who are you?" she demanded while trying not to think about how Jasper's fingers had somehow migrated from her wrist to her palm.

The figure executed an ironic little bow that the real Zahir would rather die than perform. "I'm Epsilon. Or Eps, for those who've earned the privilege of nickname usage."

"Epsilon?" Jasper repeated. "What, like the Greek alphabet?"

"Very good. We are Alpha, Beta, et cetera et cetera. I was the fifth clone off the magical assembly line."

"Oh my god," Delilah said, realizing. "Scarlett's kitchen doppelgängers. She was trying to help Zahir manage two kitchens at once. Here and the new pub he opened with Dayo. She said it went pretty badly."

"Picky picky picky," the clone said indignantly. "Original-recipe Zahir is such a little whiner. Nothing we did was good enough for him. Beta made him this *five-star* béchamel and Zahir said it tasted like cursed wallpaper paste." Eps sighed bitchily. "*Anyhoodle*, Scarlett did what every witch does when a little magical experiment goes wrong: immediately gave up and erased it. One minute we're failing at basic culinary tasks, the next we're being sucked back into the primordial magical soup. Except I wasn't quite ready for magical oblivion, thanks muchly. So I took off and hid up here." He plunked down on a stool-sized elephant made of wicker and hummed a little tune. "*Call me . . . irresponsible . . .*"

Something tiny and furry went streaking across the attic floor. Close at its little heels was a sleek black cat. With an impressive leap, the bigger furry thing pounced on the smaller, gave several violent shakes, and then trotted proudly to Eps. The cat deposited a dead mouse on the floor and curled up at Eps's feet.

"Excellent work, Poe." Eps didn't seem the least bit disturbed by this gruesome offering. "Another trophy for your collection."

"You have a cat," Delilah said, her voice pitching slightly higher than normal. Then she noticed a tabby lounging atop a decrepit box of tinsel. And another was curled up inside Papa's old Santa hat, the one with the battery-powered flashing lights. Yet another was perched on the attic windowsill, staring intently at nothing in particular.

Cats. Actual cats. In her attic.

The discovery sent a bizarre cascade of emotions through Delilah. First and strongest was the thrill of it—she'd always longed for a cat. This was followed by alarm—Mama would be furious, as she viewed witches with cats to be excessively clichéd, as bad if not worse than witches using wands. Next a sharp, painful stab of guilt—Mama wasn't around to be furious because she'd been kidnapped. And finally the most dreadful thought of all—*I'm not losing another parent. I can't go through that again.*

Quite the rollercoaster, and it left Delilah with nothing to say except, "Our attic is Cat Lady Central."

"Cat Gentleman Central, if you don't mind," Eps corrected. "And yes, there are a baker's dozen of them, at present. Of course, if you want to get technical about it, they're not literally cats so much as they are me. Parts of me."

"I'm sorry, what does that mean?" Jasper asked.

"What, are you new here? How do you think witches conjure things? They take pure magic and shape it into whatever they want. In this case, an army of me's. And when they get tired of us? Quick flick of the wrist and we're magic soup again."

Jasper turned to Delilah for confirmation, and she could only shrug. "That is basically correct. Not an especially generous explanation but—"

"Generous!" cried Epsilon. "She wanted to turn me into soup."

"*Back* into soup. You were soup before, and to soup you returned. . . .You know, actually," Delilah interrupted herself, "I'm not wild about the soup analogy, The point is, clones were made of magic, and all Scarlett did was return you to your original form."

"Well, I wanted to be me a little longer. Is that so wrong? I mean . . . look—" Epsilon stretched out his lanky body for inspection. "Can you blame me? Pretty great, am I right? Anyhow, given that I'm magic myself, I can reshape myself into other forms if necessary. The mice were destroying irreplaceable family artifacts." He gestured at the surrounding chaos of trunks, wardrobes, and stacked boxes. Basically anything that any Melrose had ever saved since the inn was built was up here. "Thought I should do something about it."

"So you turned parts of . . . yourself? I guess? Into cats." Jasper's voice had that particular tone he got when his brain was struggling to fit a new piece of information into an already overloaded framework.

"What would you have done?" Eps asked.

"Called an exterminator?" Jasper suggested.

"Yes, well, I didn't have that option, seeing as I was supposed to be reabsorbed into the collective magical essence, or whatever nonsense you ladies call it." Eps directed this last part at Delilah with a pointed look. "I wasn't ready for magical oblivion just yet."

"Let me get this straight," she said. "You're a piece of pure magic that Scarlett shaped into a duplicate Zahir, but you didn't want to go back to being just magic, so you've been living in our attic making cat versions of yourself to hunt mice?"

"*At last* we're all on board, yes."

"Wait," Jasper said slowly, "does every cat you create makes you . . . less?"

For the first time, Eps looked slightly uncomfortable. "I prefer to think of it as magical recycling."

Delilah stared at the clone, realizing why he was looking so translucent; it wasn't bad conjuring on Scarlett's part. "You're using yourself up."

"Well, that's a bit dramatic. I've merely repurposed some nonessential aspects of me for the greater good." Eps waved dismissively, a gesture that sent several nearby cats into alert mode, thinking it might be a game. "Now, are we going to discuss why you two look like you've seen a ghost? Besides me, I mean."

The events of the past hour came crashing back, and Delilah felt her knees go weak. Somehow, in the bizarre discovery of Eps and his feline army, she'd momentarily forgotten the horror of watching her mother vanish. She sank onto a nearby trunk, disturbing a Siamese that shot her a reproachful look.

"The magicians took my mother," she said, the words still not feeling real. "Right in the middle of the Saturnalia feast. You didn't hear *anything* going on downstairs?"

"Oh I see. Yes, there was some commotion earlier," Eps said with a shrug. "But generalized mayhem is pretty much par for the course with the Melroses, so I didn't think too much about it."

Jasper settled beside Delilah on the trunk. Their thighs touched, a warm line of contact that shouldn't have been as distracting as it was. "One minute we were watching a second-rate magic show, the next . . ." He gestured helplessly.

"Well, shit." Eps looked worried for the first time. "That's significantly more important than my Tom and Jerry situation."

Something in the clone's concerned look (an expression so familiar from the real Zahir) made Delilah's eyes sting. "We've searched the entire inn. No sign of her."

"And you came up here because . . . ?"

"Process of elimination." Jasper's hand found Delilah's almost unconsciously. She tried not to read too much into it. He was being supportive, that's all. Just because they'd shared one kiss (okay, one mind-blowing kiss) in a moment of weakness . . . "Also, we're avoiding the chaos downstairs."

"Mass panic?" Eps asked knowingly.

"All the women at the feast tried to fight magicians without actual magic," Delilah confirmed. "It went about as well as you'd expect."

"Ah yes, the Saturnalia catch-22." Eps nodded sagely. "Nothing like a self-imposed magical blackout during a crisis."

"How do you even know about Saturnalia?" Jasper asked, a slight frown creasing his forehead. "If you've been hiding up here for—"

"A month, give or take," Eps supplied. "But I know most of what the original Zahir knows. Well, not about cooking, apparently. Also it's pretty dull up here, so I've been reading. Your family keeps *everything*, Delilah. Really." He gestured to a frighteningly tall stack of books beside a pile of quilts that probably hadn't seen the light of day since the Taft administration. Next to this was a rustic side table—or actually, upon closer inspection, a repurposed steamer trunk—piled high with leather-bound volumes, loose papers, and scrapbooks. "Have you heard of that reality show, *Hoarders*? You should look into it."

A fluffy white cat with mismatched eyes—one blue, one green—was currently batting at a low-hanging glass icicle ornament that dangled precariously from a half-decorated artificial tree.

"Snowball, no!" Eps lunged forward with surprising speed, catching the antique ornament before it could shatter. "Show some respect. That's from 1932."

"You named them all?" Delilah asked, watching in awe as yet another cat threaded itself between her feet.

"They're cats, of course I named them—what am I, a monster? Oh, by the way, I found something you might want back." Eps retrieved an object from behind a stack of boxes. It was the old Christmas star that Papa had insisted on using every year, despite the fact that half its lights no longer worked. "Thought it might be significant. Your father had an entire journal devoted to Christmas traditions. Way too many of them involving this particular star."

Delilah's throat tightened unexpectedly. She'd forgotten about that star; how she and her sisters would fight about which one of them would be lifted onto Papa's shoulders to place it atop the tree. How Mama used to complain that the star was ugly and half broken, and how Papa insisted that Christmas stars, like real ones, didn't need to be perfect to guide you home.

"Keep it safe for me," she told Eps. " I don't know what I'd do with it right now."

"Your father and Christmas, huh," Jasper said quietly.

Delilah sighed sadly. "My father and Christmas. You know, he had a different ugly sweater for every day of December? Most of them played music. It was like if a Hallmark movie was a person."

"Sure, but maybe it was a little bit wonderful too," Jasper offered. "Just the idea of caring much about something. To share it so enthusiastically with the people you love."

Delilah blinked rapidly. "Yes, well. That was Papa." She looked into Jasper's beautiful worried eyes and wondered if being in the presence of a magical clone was kind of like being alone, and was it close *enough* to being alone that she could maybe kiss him again.

From downstairs, a voice pierced through the floorboards, growing louder and more insistent with each passing second.

"DELILAH? JASPER? Where the hell are you two?"

Scarlett. And she sounded exactly as frazzled as you'd expect from someone whose mother had just been magically abducted during a holiday feast.

Eps visibly tensed, several nearby cats mirroring his alarm. "Please don't tell her I'm here. She'd unmake me in a heartbeat. To her, I'm just leftover magical energy waiting to be recycled. But I'm rather attached to existing, you know? Even if existing means slowly turning into a crazy cat person."

"Cat gentleman," Jasper corrected, which earned him a genuine smile from the clone—the first expression that actually matched the real Zahir's.

"I SWEAR TO ALL THAT IS HOLY, DELILAH, IF YOU'RE MAKING OUT WITH THE ARCHIVIST WHILE MAMA IS MISSING . . ."

Delilah felt heat rush to her face. Truly, making out with the archivist had been occupying a distressing percentage of her mental real estate.

"You should go," Eps said quietly. "Your sister needs you. Just . . . please. Don't tell her about me. I'm not ready to go yet."

And there it was. A dilemma Delilah was absolutely not equipped to handle tonight—does a magical clone have a right to exist? Does it get to choose? The cats were watching her now, thirteen pairs of eyes somehow asking the same question. Thirteen pairs of eyes that existed because Eps was slowly but surely erasing himself to create them.

"What do you think? Do we protect them?" she asked Jasper softly.

He glanced from Eps to the cats, then back to her. "Pretty weird to meet someone who resembles someone I know, but who has no idea who I am," he said thoughtfully. "Makes me understand how it must feel for all of you when I . . ." He trailed off, but Delilah knew what he meant. "Anyway, it's your call," he concluded. "Until recently I thought magic only existed at children's birthday parties. I'm definitely not qualified to weigh in on the ethics here."

"C'mon, don't cop out on me. I'm asking for your opinion, so go ahead and have one."

"Well . . ." He folded his arms across his chest and tugged at his chin in thought. "Fundamentally, you're asking me, does Eps have free will? The magic of Oak Haven is yours to command, so inasmuch as Eps is simply magic in a different form, then no, he does not. On the other hand, he clearly has developed his own personality, separate from the Zahir we know, and has begun making his own decisions. So . . . maybe? Sorry that's not a more definitive answer. This is why I prefer history to philosophy."

Despite everything, despite the missing mother and the magician threat and the fact that Jasper Hopkins wouldn't even remember her name tomorrow, Delilah felt a rush of something dangerously close to adoration for this impossibly precise man who somehow understood that this wasn't about cats or clones. It was about choices. And about who gets to make them.

She turned back to Eps. "Your secret's safe with me for now. For as long as I'm able to keep it."

Relief washed over the clone's semi-transparent features. "Thank you."

"DELILAH MARIE MELROSE!" Scarlett's voice reached them from downstairs. Her pitch had reached that special timbre that suggested imminent catastrophe; the question was, was Scarlett trying to prevent it or cause it?

"We're coming! Don't come up here, you'll just trip over yet another box of Christmas ornaments," Delilah called back. "We'll figure this out, Eps. All of it. Just . . . maybe *stop* making cats for a bit? We need you to stay solid enough to, you know, exist."

Eps's smile was pure Zahir, full of the stubborn certainty that he knew best. "I make no promises. The Melrose Archive Protection Program continues unabated. Also they're cuddly and I love them."

Delilah and Jasper took a few steps down the stairwell when Jasper stopped suddenly. "Hang on," he told Delilah, and jogged back up. "Mr. Epsilon, one quick question. In all your scrabbling around up here, have you come across anything related to someone named Agnes?"

"Jasper! Would you stop it with the Agnes stuff?" *Gods, this man was cute but frustrating.* "We need to focus on my mother right now. Agnes died over two hundred years ago; she has absolutely nothing to offer on the magicians question, I promise."

"I'm sorry . . ." and he did look quite sorry, which really was adorable. ". . . but, Delilah, think about it. Agnes is significant in my life and in your life. That can't just be some kooky coincidence, can it?"

"It's very romantic," she assured him. "It's just not particularly helpful right now."

Scarlett's screech again. "DELILAH!"

Jasper sighed. "Right. Okay." But as he turned to go, Epsilon made a psst noise behind him.

"Hey," Epsilon whispered. "Hey you, Oak Haven's answer to Dr Jonathan Crane. I got lots about Agnes. I got Agnes for days up here. At the risk of sounding too conspiratorial, this is all about Agnes."

Delilah grabbed Jasper by the arm and pulled him down the stairs with her. As they went, she could feel the weight of the day settling on her heart. Her mother, vanished. Her powers, surrendered. Her home, under attack.

And yet.

As they made their way down the narrow staircase, Jasper rested his hand on the small of her back. And when they paused at the landing, his eyes met hers with an intensity that made her forget everything else.

"So," he said quietly, "you have a clone of your best friend living in your attic and making cats out of himself to protect your father's Christmas decorations."

"Just another day in Oak Haven," she replied, trying for lightness and missing by a mile.

His fingers brushed a strand of hair from her face. "We'll get your mom back . . . somehow. I don't know how yet, but we will."

"Promise?" The word slipped out before she could stop it, childish and vulnerable.

Instead of answering, Jasper leaned forward and kissed her. Not the desperate, clinging kiss they'd shared upstairs, but something softer. A promise in itself.

"DELILAH! I can hear you guys whispering! Get your butts down here!"

CHAPTER 19

THE MOST DANGEROUS
TIME OF THE YEAR

Scarlett descended the stairs two at a time, her curls bouncing with righteous fury. Meanwhile Delilah struggled to keep up. She was dragged down by a highly impractical velvet dress and the emotional whiplash of everything that had occurred in just the past hour. Her brain felt like an overheated cell phone running too many apps at once: *Mom missing. Town in danger. Magical clone in attic. Just kissed Jasper Hopkins. Mom MISSING.* Jasper followed at a safe distance behind the sisters with the careful precision of a man who'd wandered into a minefield and was trying very hard not take a wrong step.

". . . and I'm telling you," Scarlett was saying, "we're one hundred percent done taking crap from these Vegas rejects . . ."

Delilah sighed. This was classic Scarlett-in-crisis: all action, zero thought, and (all too frequently) maximum collateral damage. She'd been that way when they were kids, always ready to hex first and ask questions never.

"I'm serious, Del. They show up in our town, build their tacky casino, kidnap our mother? No. Hell no. Enough."

At the base of the stairs, Delilah grabbed her sister's arm, forcing her to halt. "Wait. Just stop for a second. Before we charge headlong into whatever half-baked revenge plan you've cooked up, what about Luna? Did you find her?"

"Oh!" Scarlett's battle-ready expression softened. "Yeah, actually. Good news on that front. Belinda Chatterjee's cousin's ex-wife Davika lives in Paramus—"

"Naturally." Delilah nodded. The concept of *six degrees of Kevin Bacon* was amateur hour among witches. No matter how obscure the connection, someone in your coven dated someone who hexed someone who knows what you did last summer.

"—and the Paramus coven has an exchange program with the one under Times Square," Scarlett continued, undeterred. "So they're getting an urgent message to Luna. And if she's already left the subway, they'll let us know where she headed next."

Jasper cleared his throat. "I'm sorry, did you just say there's a coven underneath Times Square?"

"Not now," Delilah mouthed at him.

"We can't wait for Luna," Scarlett announced. "We need to make a move."

Delilah felt her stomach clench. "And what move would that be, exactly?"

A triumphant grin spread across her sister's face. "*This.*" She flung open the double doors to the dining room.

The dining room turned banquet hall was largely empty now. Most of the guests had fled after witnessing their matriarch vanish in a puff of malevolent smoke. But gathered in the center of the room, standing in a loose semicircle that wouldn't have looked out of place at a particularly aggressive quilting bee, were about a dozen of Oak Haven's most formidable witches. They were armed to the teeth.

Jerusha clutched an antique sword that had probably last

seen action when tricorn hats were fashionable. Aphra was wielding a medieval hand loom that she'd converted into some kind of primitive crossbow, her normally gentle face set in a determined scowl. Polly from Spellbound Books had a chef's knife in one hand, a boning knife in the other, and at least half a dozen paring knives dangling from her belt. Beside Polly was her teenage daughter Violet, who was noodling around with nunchaku. But the most remarkable character had to be Belinda Chatterjee, who was cradling a ceramic gnome. A very angry-looking gnome, its ceramic body adorned with multiple grenades.

"Oh, come on," Delilah muttered, a headache blooming behind her eyes.

"Is that . . . gnome . . . wearing . . . bombs?" Jasper's breath was warm against her ear, sending a completely inappropriate shiver down her spine.

Get it together, Delilah, she scolded herself.

"Don't ask," she whispered back. "Just don't make any sudden movements. Belinda's gnomes are notoriously unstable, and I don't mean emotionally. Well, they're that too, but also unstable in the sense that nitroglycerin is unstable."

Delilah's gaze swept the room and landed on Zahir, who stood near the kitchen entrance, a pained expression on his face. "You let Polly steal your knives?" she called to him.

He threw his hands up in exasperation. "You expect me to argue? Belinda threatened to pull her gnome's pin if I didn't hand over my Wüsthofs."

"Ladies," Scarlett addressed the assembled witches, whose ages ranged from Violet's sixteen to Jerusha's near-immortal. "Tonight, we take the fight to the enemy. We may not have our magic yet, but we have something better. We have—"

"A suicide gnome . . ." Delilah muttered under her breath.

"—righteous anger and the element of surprise!" Scarlett continued. "Those magicians think we're just going to sit here and weep into our Saturnalia punch while they hold Mama hostage? Well, they've picked the wrong coven to mess with!"

The witches took their best shot at a battle cry but to Delilah it sounded less like a crew of fearsome warriors and more like a book club that had switched from chardonnay to tequila.

Jasper's hand found hers. His palm was warm, his grip surprisingly firm. Part of her wanted to apologize for dragging him into this mess. Another part wanted to drag him somewhere private and finish what they'd started on the stairs.

Not the time. But if not now, when? If Jasper left Oak Haven tomorrow, he'd forget her entirely. For a second time. Delilah shoved the thought out of her mind as hard as she could.

"Witches have not and will never lose a fight against magicians." Scarlett was really hitting her stride now. "Witches play to win all the time. In fact, I wouldn't give a hoot for a witch who lost and laughed. By the gods, I actually pity those poor magicians we're up against."

"This is George C. Scott," Jasper whispered. "She's literally doing the scene from *Patton*—is nobody going to point that out?"

Delilah shrugged. "Most of the witches aren't movie buffs, so I wager she gets away with it. Aphra probably caught her but she's too nice to say anything."

Scarlett whirled around to shush her sister before continuing. "My friends, it is highly likely that our mother is being held at that casino. And if she's not, someone at the casino *definitely* knows where she is. So we are going to march right up to that monstrosity, and we are going to go through them like crap through a goose!"

"You ladies realize this is a colossally idiotic idea, yes?"

The voice was male, bored, and vaguely European in a way that suggested its source had never actually been to Europe. Every head in the room turned toward a solitary figure seated at one of the few remaining banquet tables. Maximillian the Magnificent was methodically working his way through every leftover on the Saturnalia buffet, his tuxedo now polka-dotted with various sauces.

Delilah's first thought was, *Of course Max survived. Cockroaches and bad magicians, they live through anything.*

"What the hell is *he* doing here?" Scarlett glared at the magician with undisguised loathing. "Zahir, why are you sharing our leftovers with this mope?"

Zahir shrugged. "I went to the wine cellar looking for Kelly, just like you told me to do. Found him instead. And don't worry, I've got leftovers for days."

Scarlett rounded on the hungry magician. "You should've run," she said threateningly. "Why didn't you run when you had a chance?"

Maximillian sighed dramatically and set down a half-eaten turkey leg. "I thought that burgundy-clad harpy was taking me along for the ride. Instead, she transported me to your basement and left me there. Abandoned me among dusty bottles of—" he squinted at the label on the wine he'd apparently helped himself to "—Châteauneuf-du-Pape. Quite good, by the way."

"*Where did she take our mother?*" Scarlett was leaning in so close that Maximillian had to lean back to avoid ending up with a face full of angry witch.

"How the hell should I know?" He plonked down in a chair and slurped his stolen wine. "Why would I help you, even if I did?"

"Because if you don't help us, I will personally ensure that

231

your career path runs from 'mediocre magician' to 'mediocre magician who is also on fire.'"

Jasper's grip on Delilah's hand tightened. She glanced at him, surprised to see a small smile playing at the corners of his mouth. "Your sister is formidable," he whispered.

"That's one word for it," Delilah whispered back. "'Terrifying' and 'unhinged' are also acceptable." She ambled up beside Max to try a different approach. Good cop to Scarlett's pyromaniacal cop. "Do you remember us?"

He rolled his eyes. "I don't remember anything, remember? That's how you witches like it. Sure, *now* you want me to remember, but that's not—"

"No," Delilah interrupted. "Do you remember us from Las Vegas?"

Maximillian stared at the sisters, truly seeing them at last. His eyes widened with dawning recognition, then narrowed with outrage. "You!" he spluttered. "You tricked me! You stole my rabbit!"

"Rescued, more like. That poor rabbit had been stuffed into increasingly tiny hats for years. But yes. That was us."

"You want to see him?" Scarlett's smile turned predatory. "You want to see your little bunny Quentin again?"

"Wait, he's here?" Maximillian put down the wine. His face was suddenly alight with hope. "You still have him?"

"For the time being." Scarlett glanced over at Zahir, who had moved closer, his expression newly calculating. "Unless..."

"Yeah, the thing is," Zahir caught on immediately, "I was just about to whip up a little *lapin à la moutarde*. Rabbit with mustard sauce? Quite delicious, especially with some of that Châteauneuf-du-Pape you've been swilling."

"Don't you dare!" Maximillian half rose from his seat,

genuine panic in his eyes. "That rabbit is a trained professional! An artist!"

"What's it worth to ya?" Scarlett asked.

Maximillian slumped back down, defeated. "Fine. I'll tell you what I know. But keep in mind, I'm not very high up in the organization."

"Shocking," Scarlett deadpanned. "C'mon, out with it."

"Right, well. I understand that you witches all think magicians are nothing but card tricks and rabbits from hats. And yes, there are plenty of amateurs running around calling themselves magicians who don't know anything beyond basic sleight of hand. But that's just the beginning." He lowered his voice, forcing everyone to lean in closer. "Real magicians? Like that woman who took your mother? They're extremely powerful. Much more powerful than the average witch, I'll tell you that."

"Shut your filthy lying mouth!" hollered Jerusha.

"Hey, crone," Max shot back, "you want to hear this or not?"

"Enough," Delilah said before anyone else could interject. "Trust me, we've seen plenty of genuine magic from your people recently. No need to convince us of that. But what's their plan?"

Max confirmed what had already been suspected. The magicians were attempting to break the forgetting spell by introducing so much contradictory information that it would essentially blow a fuse. They wanted to turn Oak Haven into a tourist trap, just as Salem had become.

Scarlett shook her head in dissatisfaction. "None of this is new. You've all tried this game before."

He poured the last of his wine into his glass. "You know what they say, *if at first you don't succeed . . .*"

"Why, though?" Jasper interjected. His brows were drawn

together in rumination; it was an expression Delilah found distractingly attractive. "What do they gain from that?"

"For the money, honey?" Max suggested.

"No. No, that doesn't make sense." Jasper shook his head. "We met your bosses. They're not hurting for money."

Delilah felt a surge of warm appreciation for Jasper's cool head. Regardless of the chaos, his mind was still sharp. It was strangely comforting to have him there, applying his logic to their mess.

"He's right," she said, turning back to Max. "Any money they need, surely they can just conjure it."

"Not without power," Max replied, "which they are running out of. Sources of readily accessible pure magic are few and far between these days." He leaned forward. "The magicians want that grove of yours. And their thought is, if they destroy the town that protects it? Simplifies everything."

"I'm calling bullshit on that, too," Delilah said. "They have enough power to erect a fifty-story building overnight. They don't need our little grove. Why are they so determined to turn Oak Haven into just another stop on the Haunted New England tour circuit?"

"Oh who knows," Max said with a drunken shrug. "Maybe they just hate you people. Ever consider that? Simplest explanation is often the right one—isn't that what they say? If Occam's razor says *fuck you*, maybe it's as simple as that."

"Enough!" Scarlett slammed her hand on the table, making everyone jump. "*Why* doesn't matter now. The question is *where*. Namely, where is our mother? She's at the casino, isn't she? She must be."

Max sighed. "Well, yeah."

"I knew it!"

"But also no."

234

The witches exchanged confused glances.

"You witches like portals, yes? I'm presuming that's how you gals followed me to Vegas last year. You open a portal to one place, step through, and you exit the portal somewhere else. All well and good." Max gestured vaguely in the air. "But did you ever wonder what would happen if you stopped midway? What's between the portals?"

"Between?" Delilah repeated. Portals aren't hallways; they're doors. There's one side and the other side, there's no *between*. "That's absurd. There's no midway between portals . . . is there?" She turned to Jerusha, the eldest and arguably wisest of the group.

Jerusha frowned and shook her head as if to say, *No, that's not a thing*.

"Annnnnnnd that's why magicians are more powerful than witches," Max replied with a smug grin. "The space between the portals is exactly where your mother is being held. It's where the magicians hold anybody who crosses them."

The blood drained from Delilah's face. A space between portals? What did that even mean? How could Mama be somewhere that, by definition, didn't exist? Even the idea made her brain hurt.

"That can't be right," Belinda objected from across the room, hugging her armed gnome closer.

"And yet," Max said, "between every portal there is a space where you exist in both places and in neither. That's the space the magicians have learned to access and exploit."

Scarlett, never one to be deterred by mere metaphysical impossibility, straightened her shoulders. "Fine, whatever. So how do we get to them?"

"Impossible."

The temperature in the room seemed to drop several degrees as the witches all reacted to that dismissal.

"Nothing is impossible," Jerusha declared.

"Really?" Max laughed, but there was no humor in it. "Tell me this, witches. How many portals can you make? What's the total number?"

Delilah shrugged. "Infinite? I mean, any wall can be a portal to any wall somewhere else. So that's like asking how many walls there are. It's not a question with an answer . . ." Her voice trailed off as the implications hit her. "Oh gods."

Jasper's eyes widened as he followed the logic along with her. "If there are infinite portals . . . there are infinite spaces between."

"Yeah, now you get it." Max reached for his wine glass again. "You want to go on a hunt for your mother? That's not a needle in a haystack, ladies—it's a needle in the Milky Way."

Delilah felt the room tilt slightly, or maybe that was just her own sense of equilibrium failing. Jasper moved toward her, slipping his arm around her waist, the scent of him anchoring her to reality. She leaned against him without thinking, grateful for the support, for the quiet solidity of his body.

The assembled witches, moments ago so ready for battle, now looked stricken. Even Scarlett was momentarily at a loss for words.

Max studied their expressions and, surprisingly, took pity on them. "Okay, so that's the bad news, I guess. But the good news is, she's not in any physical danger. Magicians don't roll like that, their famous 'saw the lady in half' trick notwithstanding." He chuckled at his own joke, then sobered when no one joined in. "She's just being held there, in stasis. So stop freaking out, put the knives down, just take a breath. Because the reality is, you'll get your mother back when the magicians decide to give her back to you, and not a minute sooner." He took another glug of wine and added, "Can I see my goddamn rabbit now?"

The room fell into a stunned silence, broken only by the distant sound of the magical string quartet, which had somehow reverted to playing "Grandma Got Run Over by a Reindeer" despite no one being there to hear it.

Jasper was the first to speak. "Time," he said quietly, almost to himself.

"What?" Delilah turned to look at him, still hyper-aware of his arm around her waist, the heat of his body against hers.

"Time," he repeated. His eyes were bright with that spark of revelation she was beginning to recognize. "We've been thinking about this all wrong. If she's trapped between portals, she's trapped between moments. It's not a space problem. It's a time problem."

Max rolled his eyes. "Did you not hear what I just said? It's impossible—"

"Delilah," Jasper continued, ignoring him. "Didn't you say you had a time witch in town?"

"Louise? Ohh, I'm not sure that's a good idea."

"I'm just saying, if anyone would understand the problem of existing between moments, it would be her. Seems like someone worth consulting, no?"

Zahir took a step forward. "Dude, people who 'consult' with Louise have been known to get their brains scrambled."

"No no, Jasper's right," Scarlett said, perking up. "Louise is exactly who we need. She's been studying the nature of time since . . . well, since time was invented, if you believe the hype."

"Which we don't," Delilah added quickly for Jasper's benefit. "But she does know more about temporal magic than anyone else in town."

"Maybe she can help us understand what's happening to your mother," Jasper said, his eyes never leaving Delilah's. "And if we understand it, maybe we can undo it."

Max groaned dramatically. "Are you even listening to me? There's no undoing anything. Your mother is trapped in a pocket dimension between realities *until they decide* to release her." He set down his glass with exaggerated care. "Now, can we please focus on what's really important here? My rabbit? Quentin? Remember him?"

The witches began dispersing, their weapons lowered but their expressions still grim. Belinda carefully set her gnome down, murmuring soothing words as she tried to remember whether to disarm him with the blue wire or the red one.

"Jasper, listen." Scarlett stepped closer to him and Delilah. "Louise is a great idea. But Zahir isn't wrong, either— it's risky and she's unpredictable. But it's the best idea we've got at the moment. Del, you go with him. I'll deal with Max and make sure Belinda doesn't accidentally level the town with her gnomes. Just don't let Louise pitch you her timeshare scheme. It's not a real estate opportunity."

Jasper looked puzzled. "What is it, then?"

"She's trying to get people to literally *share time* with her. She'll take years off your life and add them to her own; it's a whole thing."

"Ohhhhkay. Right." From the sound of it, Jasper was starting to regret his super-clever idea.

As Scarlett continued lecturing Jasper on the dos and don'ts of dealing with time witches, Delilah found herself scanning the room. Something felt off. The witches were disbanding, their weapons reluctantly set aside, but there was a tension in the air that hadn't been there before.

That's when she spotted the movement in the far corner of

the banquet hall. A hip-looking young woman with pink hair—definitely not a witch, judging by her wide-eyed expression. She was edging her way toward the exit. In her hand was a phone, its screen still glowing.

Delilah felt her blood turn to ice. "Hey!" she called, already moving toward the stranger. "What are you doing?"

The young woman froze, stared at Delilah for a split second, then bolted for the door.

"You get back here!" Delilah shouted.

The tourist disappeared through the banquet hall doors, but Delilah was right behind her, heart pounding with a new kind of fear. "Stop! Stop right there!"

As she raced after the fleeing figure, one thought kept flashing through her mind: The forgetting spell was failing.

If that little influencer left Oak Haven with video? The magicians might not need to destroy Oak Haven after all. TikTok would do it for them.

CHAPTER 20
YOU'RE A MEAN ONE, MS. DEMAIN

As Jasper and Delilah walked hand in hand through town, it struck him that the festive atmosphere had taken a subtle turn for the worse. What had been kitschy and fun now seemed tense, bordering on militant. The decorations themselves were fine: magical garlands chased each other around lampposts; enchanted snowflakes fell in perfect geometric patterns; a quartet of gingerbread men performed holiday harmonies on the corner. But there was something forced about the level of cheer, something false. Like it had all been generated by a holiday-obsessed AI.

Beneath the surface, a sense of melancholy was everywhere.

"It's the magic," Delilah explained, catching his gaze as it followed an ornament that had detached itself from a tree to chase a squirrel. "Something's wrong, and even the enchantments feel it."

"Towns can't feel things," Jasper replied automatically, then regretted it. "I mean, normal towns can't. Obviously."

"Obviously. So anyway, back to Louise . . ."

Jasper realized the decorations weren't the only things

trying too hard: Delilah hadn't stopped talking since they'd left the inn, her words tumbling out in an anxious stream.

"Whatever you do, don't look her directly in the eyes. She'll take that as a challenge."

"Okay." Jasper nodded. *Seems straightforward enough.*

"But also, don't look at the floor. She'll take that as weakness."

"So . . . where should I look?"

"At her face, but slightly to the left. Maybe focus on her earlobe? She wears these complicated earrings . . . I think they're the crystallized tears of her enemies, maybe? Or that's what Scarlett told me. Anyway, they make a good focal point. And, trigger warning: never, ever mention Jacksonville. Long story. Also, don't compliment her outfit, but don't *not* compliment it either. Stay neutral on the outfit. And if she offers you tea, you should accept, but absolutely don't drink it."

As Delilah rattled off more warnings (don't sneeze, don't check your watch, don't think about the color orange), Jasper found his attention drifting to the graceful curve of her neck. He couldn't help wondering what it would be like to press his lips against that spot, to feel her pulse quicken under his touch.

Focus, Hopkins. The woman's mother has been kidnapped by evil magicians, and you're daydreaming about making out.

But his treacherous mind continued its wandering. Recent days had been a surreal blur: witch meetings, magical banquets, and that mind-melting kiss on the stairs. Now they were headed to consult a time witch who might help them rescue Kelly Melrose from a space that technically didn't exist . . . but somehow, all Jasper could think about was how beautiful Delilah looked with snowflakes in her hair.

". . . and that's why you should never, ever mention quantum entanglement theory unless you want to spend an hour listening to her rant about Schrödinger's fundamental misunderstanding of feline psychology."

"Delilah." Jasper stopped walking.

"What?" she asked, her eyes wide with concern.

They'd paused in front of All Who Wander, Oak Haven's travel agency, whose window dressing featured an elaborate scene of Santa's sleigh visiting the Seven Wonders of the World. Beside the entrance, an enchanted snowman was crooning "Every Year, Every Christmas" in a surprisingly accurate Luther Vandross voice.

"Did I forget something important? Oh no, did I mention her thing about shrimp cocktail? Because you absolutely cannot—"

Jasper reached out and gently brushed a snowflake from her cheek. Delilah's skin was soft beneath his fingertips, and he let his hand linger there longer than strictly necessary.

"You're worried," he said softly.

She gave a short, humorless laugh. "My mother's trapped in interdimensional limbo, magicians are trying to destroy my home, and I'm bringing a civilian to see a witch who once turned a mailman into a sundial for delivering too much junk mail. *Worried* doesn't cover it."

"I know." He moved closer until there was barely any space between them. "But we're going to figure this out. Together."

"You're very confident for someone who thought card tricks were the height of supernatural activity until a couple of days ago."

"What can I say? I'm a fast learner." Jasper leaned forward and kissed her. She tasted faintly of cinnamon and coffee. Delilah stiffened momentarily in surprise, then melted against him, her hands coming up to grip his lapels.

"Try not to worry so much," he murmured when they finally broke apart. "Everything is going to be okay."

"You haven't met Louise."

"True, but I've met you." He tucked a strand of hair behind her ear. "And I can't imagine anyone, be it witch, magician, or otherwise, getting one up on Delilah Melrose."

She laughed, a genuine bit of music better than any carol. "You're either very brave or very foolish."

"I've been called worse."

As he leaned in for another kiss, a thought suddenly occurred to him. Jasper pulled back, frowning slightly. "Wait a minute. What do I have to worry about? Witches gave up their powers for Saturnalia, right? So the worst Louise can do is be rude to me, which, frankly, is an occupational hazard at my office."

Delilah's expression shifted from dreamy to alarmed. "Oh no. No, no, no. The time witch does not participate in our town's tradition."

"Why not?"

She straightened her posture and adopted a deep, portentous tone that Jasper assumed was an impression of Louise. "'A surrender of my temporal powers would cause the past, present, and future to horrifically collapse into an ouroboros of catastrophic simultaneity.'"

"An ouroboros," he repeated.

"Of catastrophic simultaneity."

"Well, fuck."

"Exactly."

Despite this less-than-reassuring news, Jasper couldn't help but kiss her again. There was something addictive about how she responded to him, as if she'd been waiting for his touch as much as he'd been wanting to give it.

"*Excuse me!*" A sharp voice sliced through their moment. "Is this really the time for those shenanigans?"

They broke apart in time to see Jerusha pedaling past on a bicycle. "You have an important assignment to fulfill!" she called over her shoulder. "Stop frittering around and get on with it!"

As Jerusha disappeared around a corner, Jasper and Delilah exchanged sheepish glances. A grouchy witch on a bicycle immediately reminded him of *The Wizard of Oz*, and he murmured the Wicked Witch's theme.

"Very true." Delilah sighed. "But she's right. We should go and see Louise before I lose my nerve."

"Lead the way." Jasper offered his arm with a gallantry that felt both ridiculous and completely necessary.

As they continued down the street, Delilah leaned in close. "But just so you know, once we've sorted this all out? You and I definitely have some other things to get on with."

The look she gave him made his collar suddenly feel two sizes too small.

"Right," he managed. "Excellent. Looking forward to it."

"Me too," she said, and the promise in her smile carried him all the way to the clock shop.

Jasper's first indication that Louise Demain might be as terrifying as advertised was a six-foot-tall Krampus statue guarding the entrance to Tout le Temps. Unlike the cheerful snowmen dotted across Oak Haven, this horned, chain-wielding demon was humming Mozart's Requiem in a bass so deep it made Jasper's fillings vibrate. Its ruby eyes followed them as they approached the door.

"Huh," Jasper said, aiming at nonchalance and missing by miles. "That's not my favorite decoration in town."

Inside, Tout Le Temps was less 'quaint clock shop' and more 'dimly lit hoarder den,' home to everything from delicate pocket watches and sturdy chronographs to Ancient Greek water clocks and ceiling-high obelisks. And each told a slightly different time. Their off-beat ticking created a chaotic sonata that made Jasper's brain itch with the wrongness of it all.

But Jasper's mind really went into revolt when he stopped looking at specific details and took in the overall architecture of the place. The walls were parallel to one another but somehow also not at all, and they met the ceiling at nonsensical angles. "Something is seriously wrong with this room," he whispered. "It's … um … sort of … well…" He gave up. "What am I looking at?"

"Non-Euclidean architecture," Delilah said.

"Oh, sure. Of course. And what exactly am I smelling?" There was an odor of metal and incense and something else he couldn't quite identify, something unsettling.

"Eau de *Last Breath of a Dying Star*."

"Ah. Okay. You know, I think I'm just going to stop asking things."

On the far side of the room, Louise lounged in an antique chair, drinking tea and flipping through prehistoric scrolls with the privileged air of a bored housewife at her hairdresser. Simultaneously, and with no apparent effort, she was also engaged in repairing a massive grandfather clock sitting on the other side of the shop. The body of the clock hung open, and screwdrivers, pliers, and delicate gears floated in the air, dancing to her unspoken psychic instructions.

Delilah and Jasper stood there silently awhile, waiting for Louise to acknowledge them.

She did not.

Jasper shot Delilah a questioning look. She shrugged helplessly.

"Um, excuse me?" he ventured. "Ms. Demain?"

Louise's head snapped toward him. Her eyes were violet and ancient and as cold as the void between galaxies. They fixed on Jasper with predatory intensity.

"SILENCE, MEATSACK!"

The command boomed through the shop and rattled the timepieces. Jasper felt the words in his bones, as if Louise's voice had skipped his auditory system entirely and resonated directly with his skeleton.

"For what eldritch purpose do you breach the sanctity of my domain?" The air around her rippled with distortions, as if reality itself was struggling to contain her words. "Speak, you insignificant mote!"

Heart hammering in his chest, Jasper took an involuntary step backward. He tried to remember all the advice Delilah had given him. Don't look directly in her eyes, but don't look at the floor. Focus on the earlobe. An earlobe that was, as promised, adorned with jewel-like tears, shed over something unspeakable.

"Right. Hello. I'm Jasper Hopkins, county archivist, and this is Delilah Melrose."

"I am well acquainted with Melrose offspring." Her clockmaker's tools dropped to the floor with a clank, suggesting that her attention was now entirely focused on her visitors, whether they liked it or not. (They very much did not.) "The void whispers of your maternal progenitor, suspended in a

247

primordial abyss betwixt realities where time unspools as through the entrails of a gutted leviathan."

Jasper blinked rapidly while his fight-or-flight response landed solidly on the latter. He'd faced down angry county commissioners, he'd gone to war with budget committees. Nothing had prepared him for the walking existential dread that was Louise Demain.

"That's actually why we're here," Delilah said, and Jasper was relieved to note that her voice was impressively steady. Perhaps she'd get him out of here alive after all. "We were hoping you might have some insights about portal magic that could help us rescue my mother."

"And why would I deign to assist in such a futile endeavor? All space between portals is the dominion of nightmares beyond your comprehension, where loathsome unnameables feast upon the dreams of the unwary. Your mother is but one lost soul among uncountable others, trapped within gnashing maws of infinity."

"Sure . . ." Delilah said uncertainly. "I get that. But what do we do about it?"

"Nothing," Louise confirmed with a sadistic glee. "Magicians have claimed dominion over the spaces between. Much like the land upon which we stand at this very moment— once sacred hunting grounds of the proud Mashantucket people, before they were driven eastward by colonial avarice and the insatiable hunger of the pale-faced invaders."

She paused, eyeing her visitors with a challenging stare, as if daring them to contradict her.

Jasper cleared his throat. Despite his every instinct screaming at him to agree with whatever this terrifying woman said, his professional integrity couldn't allow such a mistake to go unchallenged.

"Actually," he began, his gaze fixed on Louise's ear, "these lands were historically occupied by the Schaghticoke. The Mashantucket lived along the Niantic River, a fair distance southeast of our current location."

"Oh, Jasper . . ." Delilah covered her face with both hands. "You just 'well actually'd' a time witch."

The temperature in the room plummeted, frost forming instantly on every surface. The ticking of the clocks became erratic, some speeding up while others slowed to an ominous crawl. A grandfather clock in one corner wept actual tears. Louise stood, her eyes now glowing with an inner light that cast violet shadows across her features. Her hair writhed like Medusa's snakes, and Jasper was suddenly, viscerally certain that if he looked directly into those eyes, he would be instantly transformed into something unnatural and eternally suffering.

"You foolish mortal!" Her enraged breath was visible in the now-freezing air. "You, whose lifespan is but a fleeting instant in the cosmic tapestry. You, whose consciousness is confined to a single timeline like a worm trapped in a narrow tunnel of dirt?"

"No offense intended, I just . . . I mean . . . history is kind of my thing, is all."

There was a terrible moment of silence during which Jasper genuinely believed he was about to discover what it felt like to be turned inside out while still alive. But then Louise's expression shifted. The glow in her eyes dimmed slightly, and she tilted her head in grudging appreciation.

"Fascinating," she said calmly, though the word still seemed to echo from multiple dimensions simultaneously. "Meatsack has a passing familiarity with his own unutterable history. How . . . refreshing."

The temperature began to normalize, frost receding from

the surfaces like in a time-lapse film. Louise snapped her fingers and two spindly chairs appeared out of the air. "Perhaps I shall entertain your queries after all. Approach and be seated, if you dare. But be warned—the knowledge you seek may unravel the very fabric of your sanity."

Delilah shot Jasper a look as they cautiously took the offered seats. The chair beneath him felt unnervingly warm, as if it had just been occupied by someone (or something) else.

"So," Louise said, her voice now almost conversational. "You seek knowledge of portal magic to liberate your mother. A noble yet ultimately doomed quest."

"She was kidnapped by magicians. They're holding her hostage until we agree to give them access to our grove. We need to get her back; *we just have to . . .*" Delilah's voice broke a little, although she was trying so hard to be strong. "Our family basically collapsed when we lost Papa. I can't imagine what would happen if—"

Louise cut off Delilah's speech with a single terrifyingly arched eyebrow. "And you believe I possess a solution to your picayune familial drama?"

"We were hoping," Jasper ventured, "that you might know something about the spaces between portals. Is there any way to . . . I don't know, to navigate them?"

Louise's eyes glittered with malicious amusement. "The modern witch's understanding of portal magic is pathetically limited. Protozoa attempting to comprehend Olympus. Portals were not always just doorways between two points. They were conduits of near-infinite power, capable of rending reality asunder and reshaping the cosmic order according to whim. Entire structures could be transported across the yawning abyss of space and time. Mountains could be moved. The very stars could be rearranged."

Delilah sat up straighter. "Wait . . . Entire structures? You mean we could potentially move something very large? Large as, say, a casino?"

Jasper turned to stare at Delilah with undisguised hunger in his eyes. *My God, she's so smart.*

"Theoretically," Louise conceded. "But such knowledge has been sealed away in the forbidden archives of antiquity, guarded by entities whose names would cause your tongue to wither and your eyes to liquefy should you attempt to speak them."

"But that's exactly what we need! If we could move the casino somewhere else, somewhere far away from Oak Haven, we could force the magicians to return my mother."

Louise laughed, if you could call it that. Better to say she emitted a sound like breaking glass and the distant screams of the damned. "You? Master bygone arts of grand portal magic? Impossible. Such knowledge died centuries ago, along with those wise enough to comprehend the terrifying implications of their power."

"Hold on . . ." Jasper felt a tingle of recognition at the back of his neck. "What about Agnes Bartlett? Would she have known these spells? I mean, I'm just spitballing obviously. But perhaps she might have documented this magic before it was lost?"

Louise's expression shifted subtly. Was that respect in those eyes? "Agnes Bartlett was the last to wield grand portal magic. But Bartlett has been naught but dust and echoes for centuries. Her secrets died with her, scattered to the winds of oblivion."

"Not necessarily," Delilah argued. "My mother found a letter of hers recently. Maybe there's other things squirreled away in the inn somewhere."

Jasper nodded encouragingly. "Epsilon said he found all sorts of things up in the attic. Perhaps we should see what he was referring to. Or maybe the town records would have something?"

Louise abruptly stood, and when she spoke, her voice once again reached a thunderous volume. "You have become tedious to me." She raised her hands, fingers splayed in an intricate pattern that somehow bent light into painful angles.

"Wait!" Jasper cried. "We're not finished—"

But it was too late. With a gesture resembling a conductor ending a particularly violent symphony, Louise sent Delilah and Jasper spinning into nothingness. His last sensation was a feeling of falling through infinite layers of reality, each one more eldritch than the last.

The last thing he heard was Louise's voice, oddly normal and almost appreciative: "Nice-looking fella."

Jasper's stomach lurched as reality reassembled itself around them. He stumbled forward, grabbing on to the nearest solid object, which turned out to be a tree trunk, to steady himself.

"What just—" he began, then stopped as he realized something was very wrong.

They were no longer downtown. In fact, they weren't in town at all. They stood in a small clearing surrounded by dense forest. No buildings, no streets, no enchanted decorations. Just trees stretching in every direction, their bare winter branches forming a complex lattice against the late afternoon sky.

Jasper turned in a slow circle, trying to orient himself. The only sounds were occasional chirps of brave winter birds and the soft whisper of the wind through the trees. Gone were the singing snowmen, the magical tinsel, and all traces of civilization.

"Where are we?" His voice felt unnaturally loud against the stillness. "Why would Louise teleport us to the middle of the woods?"

Delilah was staring at the angle of the sun, which hung low in the western sky, casting long shadows across the clearing. Her expression had gone from confusion to a sort of grim resignation. "Yeah no. That's not it."

"What do you mean? We're clearly in some forest. Did she send us to a whole different part of the county?" He gazed around again, searching for any landmark that might help him determine their location. "Well, wherever we are, I suppose we should try to make our way to some sort of civilization before dark."

Delilah just sighed and gave him a look that was equal parts pity and disbelief. "Jasper, listen to me. It's not a question of where we are. It's a question of when."

CHAPTER 21

BABY IT'S OLD OUTSIDE

Oak Haven had never been so wild.

The scent hit Delilah first. A sharp pine untainted by exhaust fumes and progress. The earthy richness of soil that had never once been turned, much less paved. The air filled her lungs with a purity that was almost painful. Where quaint colonial buildings should have stood, towering firs and maples reached toward the sky. Instead of cobblestone streets curved through town, deer paths wound between patches of wildflowers and berry bushes.

Delilah took it all in, mentally cataloging the differences between this primeval forest and the town she'd known her entire life. The geography was unmistakable. That sloping hill to the west would eventually become the road up to the oak grove. She could picture herself there, climbing that steep path up to the grove . . . but the path was who knows how many years away from being built.

Same place. Different time.

Beside her, Jasper turned in a slow circle, as if downtown Oak Haven would materialize if he just looked hard enough. "If we're in the same place, then where's the clock shop? Where's the town? Where are all those singing snowmen?"

"This is right where they'll be," Delilah gestured at the empty space around them. "Eventually. We're standing in exactly the same spot we were before. We've just been moved to a time before the shop. Before downtown. Long before Oak Haven existed at all. Or . . ." She paused, considering a darker possibility. "I suppose we could be here long *after* it all existed. Maybe some apocalypse wiped out civilization and it's all back to wild forest again." Seeing Jasper's eyes widen in horror, she quickly added, "But not even Louise would be that cruel. I mean. Probably."

"*She can do that?!*" Jasper's mind reeled with the implications. "Just casually alter our position in space-time?"

"We got off easy." Delilah straightened her coat, unfazed. "One time when we were kids, Scarlett broke one of Louise's pocket watches. Louise sent her back to the Cretaceous period, just out of spite. Scarlett was about to become lunch for a swarm of griffinflies when Mama tracked Louise down and forced her to bring Scarlett back. To this day, she still won't go near anything with more than four legs."

"Are you telling me—" Jasper's voice rose with each word "—that we're in the seventeenth century? Or even earlier than that?" He shook his watch violently. The device made a sad little rattling sound, and when he held it up, Delilah could see that the minute, hour, and second hands had all come loose from their moorings. Just bits of metal flopping around inside the casing.

"Oh God," he said, genuine panic overtaking him. "Should I be watching out for griffinflies? Or, or . . . God, I don't remember my prehistory suddenly. Saber-toothed tigers?"

Delilah tilted her head, miming intent listening. "No

buzzing so far. I think we're okay on the griffinfly front. And surely Connecticut has never been a home to tigers, saber-toothed or otherwise." She found his panic oddly endearing; sort of like watching a cat discover rain for the first time and not liking it one bit.

"You are taking this far too well for my taste."

She flopped down onto the grass and poked idly at a cluster of small purple wildflowers. They looked a bit like asters, but with more pronounced centers; a flower that hadn't been common in New England since colonial times. So this was definitely *pre*-Oak Haven. *Huh*, she thought suddenly. *Jerusha's tedious botanical history class finally paid off, after all.* "Remember, Jasper, I've been through this with the time witch before. Don't worry. Soon enough, Scarlett will notice we're missing. It won't take her long to figure out what happened. She'll go to the shop and demand Louise do whatever Louise does to reach through time and scoop us back up."

But Jasper wasn't listening. He stomped a few steps in one direction, apparently thought better of it, then stomped back and tried the opposite way. After three full circuits of indecision, he finally threw up his arms, glared accusingly at the sky, and plopped down on the grass beside Delilah.

"Nothing to be done," she assured him.

"Indeed, Estragon." He sighed. "I'm beginning to come around to that opinion."

Delilah grinned. "You know *Waiting for Godot*?"

"Historians can appreciate theater, you know."

"Well, aren't you full of surprises?" Delilah nudged him playfully, and she felt a little surge of excitement as a plan formed in her mind. "Speaking of surprises . . . I'm thinking my magic might work here. After all, we've traveled way, way, waaayyy before the point in time where I surrendered it for Saturnalia, so . . . I'm thinking . . ."

She reached into her jacket and pulled out her wand. With a flourish and a muttered incantation, a shimmering light bloomed around her. The familiar tingle of magic flowed through her fingertips, reassuring in its constancy; at least some things remained reliable, no matter when you were. When the light faded, their clearing had been transformed into a witch's interpretation of "glamping." A spacious tent made of silk stood nearby, its entrance tied back with silver cords. Inside were plush cushions, throws in jewel tones, and a low table set with two crystal glasses awaited. Outside, two comfortable-looking chairs sat beside a small fire pit where flames danced merrily, heating a pot that hung from an elaborate metal tripod. Fairy lights (from actual fairies, not the Christmas decoration kind) hovered in the trees, creating a romantic glow as dusk began to settle over the forest.

Delilah felt a little surge of pride at her handiwork. Luna could keep her yurts. *This* was how to travel.

Jasper stared at the transformation, mouth slightly agape. "You did all this . . . ?"

"Look, here's how I see it. We're deep in the past, which means no Stargazer Inn, and no missing Mama because Mama doesn't even exist yet. No magicians to fight . . . Nothing we can do but wait, frankly. So if we're gonna wait, we may as well wait in style, yes?" She walked over to the fire and lifted the lid of the pot, giving its contents a stir with a wooden spoon that materialized in her hand. Her face fell momentarily when she saw what she'd conjured. "Aw, man," she said, disappointed.

"What's wrong? And uh, is that . . . a cauldron?" Jasper approached cautiously. "Some sort of witch thing? Eye of newt, et cetera?"

"It's risotto, dummy. I was trying for lobster. This appears to be shrimp and scallop. But you know . . ." She grinned widely. "Nobody's nerfect, am I right? Check that case over there, would you? There should be some wine."

Jasper went to investigate a wooden case near one of the chairs. Inside, nestled in straw, were several bottles of wine. "A 1982 Château Lafite Rothschild," he read, impressed. "How did you—"

"Technically, I didn't steal it," Delilah said quickly. Mama would have her head if she thought Delilah was using magic for theft. "Everything will disappear once I stop maintaining the spell. So really, we're just borrowing it."

"That's remarkably specific magical ethics."

"Witches have rules too, you know. We're not barbarians like magicians are." Delilah winked as she expertly opened the bottle. The pop of the cork sent a small thrill through her. Papa had always made a ceremony of opening wine, teaching her the proper angle to hold the bottle, how to pull it just so. "Now, how about you sit down and relax? You'll quickly see that the distant past isn't entirely bad."

The sun began its descent beyond the tree line, painting the sky in strokes of pink. Delilah and Jasper sat side by side watching the spectacle while polishing off their impossibly expensive "borrowed" wine. Delilah felt a pleasant warmth that had nothing to do with the booze or the fire, and everything to do with the man beside her.

"So . . ." Jasper swirled the wine in his glass. "What was it like? Growing up in a town full of witches?"

Delilah tilted her head, considering. "Normal, I guess? I mean, I didn't know any different."

"But there must have been moments when you realized your life wasn't like other people's."

"Fair. Let me think . . ." She took a sip of wine as memories surfaced that she hadn't revisited in years. "Oh, man. I remember this one time, I was about six; Papa took me to the movies in Hartford. It was my first time outside Oak Haven, and I was so excited to see *Beauty and the Beast* in a real theater. Remember, I had these two super-annoying baby sisters at home, but on this trip I got to be special, just Papa and me.

"During the scene where all the dishes start dancing and singing? I got so caught up in the moment that I accidentally made my popcorn start dancing too. All these people started turning around, staring at us. Papa quickly pretended he'd spilled everything, and that's why the popcorn was, like, flying through the air. He bundled me up and hustled me out of there before I could make anything else move. He wasn't mad, though. He just laughed and said, 'My girl sure does love movies.'"

"He sounds like a great father."

"He was. Absolutely the best. When he died, all the color drained out of everything. Especially at Christmas. That was his favorite time of year." She hadn't meant to go there, to that raw place that still ached after all these years. But something about the golden light, the wine, the strange intimacy of being lost in time together made the words flow more easily.

"I'm really sorry you went through that," Jasper said, and there was something in his voice that made Delilah look at him in a different way.

"You've lost someone too," she realized.

He nodded. "My grandmother. I was sixteen. She practically

raised me because my parents were workaholic lunatics. In fact, she's the one who got me interested in history. She took me to every museum, historic home, and archaeological site within a hundred-mile radius."

"What happened to her?"

"Stroke. It was quick, at least." He took a long sip of wine. "At first I did the same thing you're doing: recoiled from everything that reminded me of her. I couldn't look at a museum brochure for two years."

"And yet you became a historian anyway."

"Eventually, I realized that avoiding things that reminded me of her meant that I was avoiding the things she loved most. All the things she'd given me. It was like losing her twice."

Delilah let that settle over her. How many Christmases had she ruined for herself? How many times had she refused to participate, saying it hurt too much, only to end up hurting anyway?

"When does it get easier?" Though she wasn't entirely sure she wanted to hear the answer.

"It doesn't, unfortunately. I mean, not exactly. It just . . . changes. The grief is still there, but it stops being the only thing you think about. The bad memories don't go away, so much as the good ones start to come back." He reached over and touched Delilah's hand. "For what it's worth, I think your father would be proud of you. Time-displaced glamping and all."

The comment surprised a genuine laugh out of her. "Oh, he would have thought this campsite was the coolest thing ever. Mama would be here complaining I was wasting my powers on nonsense and meanwhile he'd be roasting marshmallows for everyone."

They fell into silence, watching as the last rays of sun dipped below the horizon. Delilah found herself studying Jasper's profile in the firelight. It was uncanny how familiar he seemed. How necessary. This despite the fact that there was an obvious limit on how long he'd be around. He had a "hard out," as they say on television. And that would be that.

"Can I ask you something, Jasper?"

"Anything."

"Doesn't it bother you? Knowing that when this is all over, you'll forget all of this? Forget . . . um, forget me?"

He turned to face her fully. "It bothers me enormously."

"Then why stay? Why not just leave now and save yourself the trouble?"

"Because some things are worth experiencing *even if* they won't last," he said simply. "Heck, maybe *because* they won't last."

The answer caught her off guard with its sincerity. Delilah felt something shift inside her, as though a piece of herself that had been held rigid for a very long time had finally been allowed to relax.

"Hey," Jasper said suddenly, "let me ask *you* something: why don't the witches make exceptions to the forgetting spell? For romantic partners, I mean. You're all so powerful. Surely you could modify the spell to let certain trusted people keep their memories?"

"Ah, well. *And thereby hangs a tale*, as the Bard says. It used to be exactly as you suggest. For centuries, there was this special ritual they'd do for outsiders. A witch could vouch for her partner and bring them fully into the community, including gaining immunity from the forgetting spell."

"What changed?"

"Well, my friend, the year was 1908 . . ." She jokingly slipped into a storyteller voice that Papa always used when recounting Oak Haven history. "A witch named Eleanor Whitman fell

262

desperately in love with a charismatic magician named . . . oh, nuts, I always forget him. Alexander . . . Grey! Yeah, that's it. Alexander Grey. He swept Eleanor off her feet, apparently, and he offered to give up his entire life, just to be with the woman he loved. And remember, witches and magicians already didn't get along, even back then. So it was no simple thing. But Eleanor vouched for him, and eventually Alexander managed to win over the whole town. So the elders performed the exemption ritual. For a year or so, everything seemed perfect. Until . . ." Delilah leaned forward, the better to share this most scandalous tale. "'Twas a hot midsummer when Alexander revealed his true, dastardly intentions. He'd only used Eleanor to learn about Oak Haven's magical defenses. He and a group of fellow magicians launched an attack that nearly destroyed the town."

"What happened?"

"There was a magical battle so intense that it burned down half the forest surrounding the town. In the end, Alexander and his cohorts were defeated, but Eleanor . . ." Delilah trailed off. "She couldn't bear the betrayal. She walked into the oak grove on a snowy December night and never came out again."

"God, that's terrible," Jasper said quietly.

"After that, the rule became absolute: no exceptions to the forgetting spell. Ever. Not Nate, even. Nate was born in Oak Haven, but he isn't a witch, so he's in the same bind."

"You'd think being the thirteenth Earl would get him a little leeway."

"Nope." Delilah tried to sound matter-of-fact. "Which is why he and his friends have been doing their trivia training for over a year now."

"Trivia training?"

"Yeah, there's this theory that if they strengthen their memories, they might be able to resist the spell? But Scarlett told me they've had no luck so far. Nate can recite the batting averages of every Red Sox player since 1912, but it doesn't get him around the forgetting spell. Nobody gets around it."

The implication lingered in the air, a tacit acknowledgment of the one obstacle they'd never overcome.

"Well." Jasper set down his glass with deliberate care. "I suppose we should make the most of the time we have."

He reached out to her, his fingers gently tilting her chin up until their eyes met.

"What do you mean?" she asked, though she knew perfectly well.

"I mean that I'm here now. And so are you."

"That's an eminently practical approach to the issue, Mr. Hopkins."

His eyes twinkled. "You'll find me to be an eminently practical man, Ms. Melrose. And whatever happens next . . . whether we get around the spell or not . . . as of right now? I'm all in."

She leaned forward and kissed him. Not the frantic, adrenaline-fueled kiss they'd shared earlier, but something deeper, more deliberate. A kiss that acknowledged the precariousness of their situation while defying it all the same. His arms wrapped around her, pulling her closer until she was out of her chair and in his lap. She could feel the steady beat of his heart against her chest, the warmth of his hands on her back.

When they broke apart, breathless, the night had overtaken their encampment. The fairy lights in the trees had brightened in response, casting a silvery glow all around.

"I've wanted to do that properly since I saw you in that Saturnalia dress," Jasper confessed.

"What stopped you?"

"Oh, you know, evil magicians, time witches . . . all the usual rom-com obstacles."

Delilah laughed. "So predictable." She kissed him again, trying to pour everything she couldn't say into that moment. Then she climbed off his lap and tugged him toward the tent, with its soft blankets and pillows.

Inside, the cushions had transformed into a proper bed, covered in soft blankets that seemed to shimmer in the dim light. Jasper looked around, impressed.

"Your magic is very . . . accommodating."

"You have no idea." She pulled him down beside her on the bed and Jasper responded eagerly, his kisses growing more urgent, more intense. His hands were everywhere, roaming up her thighs and over her hips, as if he couldn't get enough of her either. Everywhere he touched, she lit up like a bonfire. She leaned into the sensation, refusing to think past this moment, past tonight. If this was all they'd have, they'd make sure it was enough to fill a lifetime.

The wind picked up outside, making the tent billow and flap ferociously.

Ignoring the racket, Jasper bent his head and began a languorous journey down her neck, planting tender kisses as he went. He lingered at the base of her throat, and the sensation made Delilah catch her breath. He moved lower, kissing the length of her collarbone, delicate and careful, savoring every moment.

Delilah moaned softly, and his lips trailed lower still, leaving a line of delicious heat in their wake.

"Jasper," she gasped, not sure if she was protesting or pleading for more.

The wind howled louder, more insistent now, sending disoriented fairies swirling around the tent. Then the ground began to shake. At first, it was just a slight tremor, easily ignored in the heat of the moment. But it quickly intensified, the earth beneath them rolling like a ship on stormy seas. A deep rumble, similar to thunder but from below rather than above, filled the air. Outside, trees were snapping and crashing down. Birds shrieked overhead, fleeing in panicked flocks. It felt as though something massive was approaching—something with the power to reshape the very landscape.

Jasper pulled away, bewildered. "What the hell is—"

Delilah was already on her feet, and she pulled him up with her. "Something's coming." With a swift gesture, she dissolved their glamping setup, the tent and fire and fairy lights vanishing as though they'd never been. They ran in the opposite direction of the falling trees, dodging branches and leaping over exposed roots. The ground beneath Delilah's feet continued to heave and roll, making each step treacherous. Her mind raced through magical possibilities; was this Louise coming to retrieve them, or some unforeseen consequence of time displacement? Or something else entirely?

Finally, they reached a massive oak tree. Delilah pulled Jasper behind it, both of them peering back at the clearing they'd just abandoned.

The air itself had begun to vibrate. Colors shifted and blurred at the edges, and a high-pitched screeching noise cut through the rumbling. It sounded like a hundred sets of bad car brakes being applied at once.

Delilah clapped her hands over her ears, but she couldn't block out the sound. She could feel the magic in the air. But not the familiar, controlled power of Oak Haven witchcraft, but something wilder, more primal. This was old magic, the kind that moved mountains and parted oceans. Then came a sonic boom—a wall of sound and pressure so powerful it knocked them both to the ground. Delilah felt the air being forced from her lungs, her vision going momentarily dark at the edges.

When she could breathe again, she pushed herself up on shaking elbows. The rumbling had stopped. The screeching was gone. An unnatural quiet had fallen over the forest.

She reached out for him. "Are you okay?"

He nodded, and they scrambled to their feet. Together, they peered around the trunk of the oak.

Where dozens of tall trees had stood just moments ago, now stood a barn.

A massive, sturdily built structure with distinctive curved braces reinforcing its corners. The roof was peaked steeply to shed snow, and a small cupola sat at its apex, topped with a weathervane in the shape of a crescent moon.

Delilah's breath caught in her throat. She knew this barn. Every witch in Oak Haven knew this barn, or rather, what it had become. "That's the original structure of the Stargazer Inn library," she whispered, awe overtaking her fear.

"I recognize those curved braces," nodded Jasper. "They're still visible in the library."

As they watched from behind the trees, the wide double doors of the barn swung open. Out stumbled a group of people dressed in somber Puritan clothing: men in dark coats and wide-brimmed hats, women in long dresses with white caps and aprons, children clinging to their parents' hands. They looked dazed, peering around at the forest and up at the night sky as if unsure where they were.

"One of my ancestors must be over there . . . Virigina Melrose. She was one of the founders. I wonder which one she is?"

An uncommonly tall woman emerged from the barn, her bearing regal despite her simple costume. In her hands, she clutched what appeared to be a large leather-bound book. For a moment, Delilah wondered if perhaps that was Virginia, but then the woman turned in a slow circle, surveying the area with a critical eye. When Delilah got a clear view of the woman's face, she gasped. The portrait from the inn's library had come to life before her eyes. Same stern features, same penetrating gaze. *Agnes Bartlett.*

Agnes held up one hand, and the murmuring crowd fell silent. "It is done." Her voice carried clearly through the night air. "We have escaped the trials of Salem. Here shall we build our haven, protected by oak and stone and magic unending."

The refugees gathered closer, their faces reflecting a mixture of fear and hope.

"The portal is closed," Agnes continued, "and with it, our connection to that place of death. But we are not without resources." She gestured to the barn behind her. "We have brought what we need to begin anew. Tomorrow, we build. Tonight, we give thanks."

As if on cue, the clouds above parted, revealing a sky blazing with more stars than Delilah had ever seen, untainted by centuries of light pollution. She felt Jasper's hand find hers in the darkness, their fingers intertwining. Her heart pounded with the realization of what they were witnessing. It was the moment that had set her family's destiny in motion.

They had just seen the birth of Oak Haven.

CHAPTER 22
TO CERTAIN POOR JASPERS

Jasper woke with a crick in his neck, an uncomfortable lump against his back, and an unfamiliar weight on his chest. He quickly realized the crick and the lump were explained by the fact that he'd been sleeping upright, propped against a tree. Then he looked down to find Delilah slumbering in his arms, her breathing deep and steady.

He didn't mind. Not in the slightest. It was without doubt the most pleasant crick he'd ever had.

They'd kept vigil out in the woods that night, watching the barn from a safe distance. But once the settlers retired inside, they didn't come back out, leaving nothing to observe but dim candlelight escaping the walls and the occasional bleat, cluck, or whinny of an unhappy farm animal inside. Eventually exhaustion had claimed them both. Delilah curled against him, her head tucked perfectly into the hollow of his shoulder as if the space had been designed for her.

Now, as dawn arrived, Jasper was able to take a moment and simply observe. The landscape was pristine and untouched by the "improvements" of humans. Dew glistened on wildflowers

269

that would be extinct by his time, while birdsong filled the air with melodies that had likely remained unchanged for thousands of years. The trees surrounding them weren't the carefully managed specimens of modern parks and nature preserves, but sovereign beings that had grown unchallenged for centuries.

Jasper found it bittersweet, that this wilderness would eventually give way to the cobblestone streets and buildings of Oak Haven. Progress always came at a price, he supposed. Of course, without those developments, there would be no history for him to preserve, no Stargazer Inn to welcome travelers, and no witches like the one currently drooling gently on his shirt.

Clearly, when this was all over, he was going to have a difficult choice to make: Delilah or the world. On the one hand there was magic, mystery, and this magnificent woman beside him, and on the other . . . what? Municipal records and fluorescent lighting? Didn't seem like much of a choice at all. *What if I just don't go home? Could I do that? Could I just stay?* The idea bloomed in his mind like a highly dangerous flower.

But before the fantasy could truly take shape, cold reality arrived. Who would he be, in this town of magic? A nebbishy archivist with no archives? Zahir seemed to be flourishing in Oak Haven without magic. But he's a chef; he has a genuine calling. Jasper had a calling, too, just not in Oak Haven. Without his job, who was he really? Just some guy with too-strong opinions on document storage.

No, Oak Haven was Delilah's world. Jasper knew deep down that ultimately he was just a tourist, just a stranger on the strangest vacation there ever was. And the thing about vacations is, they all end.

The thought left a hollow feeling in his chest, right beneath where Delilah laid her head.

His melancholy was interrupted by the sound of a door creaking open. Jasper tensed, peering around the massive oak trunk that had sheltered them through the night. The door to the barn swung wide, and a solitary figure emerged.

Agnes Bartlett.

Even from a distance, she was unmistakable—straight-backed, with the kind of purposeful movement indicating a woman who never wasted a single step. Her dress was simple but impeccably maintained, her hair tucked neatly beneath a linen cap. She carried a small book in one hand—perhaps a journal or a bible?—and moved with quiet determination toward the woods.

Jasper gently shook Delilah's shoulder. "Del," he whispered. "Time to wake up. She left the barn."

Delilah stirred. She sat up quickly, swiping at a bit of drool on her chin that Jasper pretended not to notice.

"Who? . . . Oh . . . you mean Agnes?" she asked, voice still rough with sleep.

"Heading into the woods alone. This might be our only chance."

Together, they rose and crept after the retreating figure, always keeping hidden among the trees. They caught up with Agnes beside a stream. She had settled herself on a large flat rock. Her book lay open in her lap, though she seemed more intent on watching the water flow past than on reading.

Delilah whispered to Jasper this waterway would eventually be called Bonfire Creek. "I can practically see the covered bridge that will span this someday. Luna fell in once and came up covered in pond scum—she looked like the Creature from the Black Lagoon. And one time Scarlett jumped off the roof of the bridge, but that's a *very* long story . . ." Delilah's expression

271

turned wistful. "It's so weird—my past is currently the distant future."

"What should we do?" Jasper asked uncertainly. "Do we approach her?" His historian's instinct warned against interfering with the past. What if they changed something crucial?

"*Of course* we approach her. She's the one person who can help us."

"But what about the timeline? What if we accidentally interfere somehow? Aren't we forbidden from talking to people in different time periods?"

"Forbidden by whom? H.G. Wells? Marty McFly?" She rolled her eyes. "Definitely don't say Doctor Who, because he interferes with different timelines in literally every episode. Or *she* does, depending on the series. Whatever, you know what I mean."

"Okay, but don't reveal anything that could change the future."

"Yeah yeah yeah . . ." Delilah stepped out of their hiding place and strode confidently toward Agnes. Jasper had no choice but to follow, feeling like a man walking into an exam three hundred years too early.

Agnes looked up, startled by their approach. Her hand immediately went to a small pouch at her waist—Jasper guessed it must contain some form of protective magic. Her eyes narrowed with suspicion.

"Good morrow," Delilah said. She stopped a respectful distance away and did her best to sound *historical*, whatever that meant. "Please, um, be not alarmed. My name hath be Delilah Melrose, and this—" she gestured toward Jasper, who was trying very hard not to hyperventilate "—is Jasper Hopkins. We, um, cometh from yon distant future."

Oh sure, just lead with that, Jasper thought. *Very subtle.*

Agnes's expression remained guarded, but she didn't immediately flee or attack, which seemed promising. "What manner of beings claim such impossible origins?" Her voice was clear and precise, with a hint of an accent that Jasper couldn't quite place—somewhere between English and something older.

"We're from Oak Haven," Delilah continued, "though in our time, it's centuries old. We were sent back by a time witch named Louise Demain."

"A time witch," Agnes repeated, her posture relaxing slightly. "I have heard tell of such practitioners, though I have not had the occasion to meet one. Their powers are said to be most unsettling."

"You said a mouthful, sister."

Meanwhile Jasper stood frozen, staring at Agnes Bartlett— *the* Agnes Bartlett!—with the helpless awe of a teenage boy unexpectedly meeting his favorite rock star. This was the woman whose portrait he saw every morning. The woman whose founding principles had shaped the entire county archive system, whose meticulous preservation techniques had saved countless documents from being lost to time. And here she was. In the flesh. Breathing the same ancient air as he.

Agnes turned her attention to Jasper, clearly noting his slack-jawed admiration. "Does thy companion speak, or is he afflicted in some manner?"

Delilah nudged him sharply with her elbow.

"I, um, yes, I speak," Jasper managed. "It's an honor to meet you, Goodwife Bartlett. Truly. I've—well, I've admired your work for a great many years. Or . . . I will admire it. I *will have* admired it?" He winced. "Grammar is, um, not my friend at the moment."

A flicker of amusement crossed Agnes's stern features.

"What work of mine hath earned such esteem from a man not yet born?"

"The county archives," Jasper blurted, unable to contain his enthusiasm. "You're its founder. Er, will be its founder. The organizational system you'll create is so effective that it's still in use hundreds of years later. Your preservation techniques saved countless historical records that would otherwise have been lost."

Delilah muttered, "I'm glad you're not revealing anything that could influence the future . . ."

"The archive building itself is remarkable. The load-bearing columns preserve the original eighteenth-century design while accommodating modern needs. Though, if I'm being completely honest, the electrical wiring is problematic. There's this horrible fluorescent lighting that buzzes constantly and makes everything look like it's underwater. I've submitted seven formal requests to have it updated, but apparently non-migraine-inducing lighting doesn't fit into the county budget."

Agnes blinked at him, clearly trying to process this babbling brook of information. "I know not what 'fluorescent' might be, but thy passion is most evident." A slight smile tugged at the corner of her mouth. "Though methinks it borders on unhealthy fervor."

Delilah snorted.

"Your portrait hangs in my office! I look at it every day. I mean . . . not in a weird way," he hastened to add. "Just with, you know, professional respect."

"That's enough, fan boy," Delilah muttered, patting his arm. "Let's not terrify the nice Puritan lady."

Agnes studied them both with shrewd eyes. "If thou truly art from days yet to come, tell me: will our efforts to establish a sanctuary bear fruit? Does Oak Haven endure?"

"Oh, we're still around," Delilah assured her. "Still hidden from the outside world, still home to witches. The Stargazer Inn, which is what your barn will become, has been in my family for generations."

Relief washed over Agnes's face. "These are most welcome tidings. We have sacrificed much to create this haven. And the poor souls we left behind . . . they weigh heavily upon my heart. Can you tell me what fate befell them?"

Jasper and Delilah glanced at one another, then down at their feet, uncertain what to say.

"Ah," Agnes said sadly. "I see the answer writ upon thy faces."

Jasper nodded reluctantly. "They um, they didn't make it."

Agnes closed her eyes briefly. "Lord, receive their innocent souls," she whispered, her voice barely audible. "Forgive us who fled while they remained." She opened her eyes. "So great a punishment for so small an offense."

"What offense?" Jasper asked. "Hang on, were they actually witches after all?" That would be quite a discovery.

"Nay." Agnes shook her head firmly. "Merely curious girls. They sought knowledge of magic, of spells, of the limits of our reality. That was their sin. Simple curiosity. Yet for that, they paid with their lives."

Jasper longed to press for more details; this firsthand account could rewrite the established narrative of the Salem trials. But Delilah took a step forward; it was obvious she had more pressing matters on her mind.

"Goodwife Bartlett, Oak Haven desperately needs your help," Delilah said, shifting the conversation. "The portal magic you used to bring the barn here? The witches have forgotten it over the centuries."

Agnes's expression brightened slightly. "That is well to hear.

I had resolved to destroy all knowledge of the spell, that it might die with my generation."

"But that's just it," Delilah pressed. "We need it again now. Your descendants need that spell to save our town." She quickly explained about the malevolent strangers and their attempt to expose Oak Haven to the outside world. "You were happy to hear Oak Haven still exists in our time, but without this spell to help us, it may not for much longer."

Agnes listened gravely but shook her head when Delilah finished. "The portal magic is too dangerous to be known widely. I will not enable such another exodus."

"But we're not trying to run away," Delilah argued. "We just need to move this . . . building . . ."

Jasper leaned in her ear. "Give her more details, maybe that'll help."

Delilah made a face. "You wanna explain a casino to this woman, be my guest." She turned back to Agnes. "I swear to you, we just want to defend our home, not abandon it."

Agnes was obviously unmoved. "I cannot risk such power falling into the wrong hands. The consequences could be catastrophic."

Jasper watched the exchange, desperately wanting to help but uncertain how. What could *he* possibly say to change her mind? He wasn't a witch or a magician. He was just a guy who liked old stuff and a new girl.

"They've taken my mother," Delilah said finally, her voice breaking slightly. "The magicians have her trapped in the space between portals. Without your spell, we can't save her."

That got Agnes's attention. Her head snapped up, eyes widening. "Trapped between? Such a fate is worse than death."

"I've heard," Delilah said softly. "That's why we need your help."

Agnes was silent for a long moment. She turned away, staring out at the creek.

Jasper opened his mouth to speak but Delilah laid a hand on his arm to quiet him. "Give her a second."

At last, Agnes turned back. "I cannot abide one of my descendants suffering such a fate." She fixed Delilah with a penetrating gaze. "I will help thee, but on one condition."

"Name it," Delilah said eagerly.

"I will not leave the spell to be found by just anyone," Agnes declared. "No witch, even one as seemingly virtuous as thyself, can be entirely trusted with such power."

Delilah began to argue, but Agnes silenced her with a raised hand.

"Instead, I shall conceal the spell beneath the archives of which thou spoke—the building where my likeness hangs. And thy hand alone shall be able to retrieve it."

"Me?" Jasper squeaked. "But I'm not even magical!"

"Precisely," Agnes nodded. "The magic shall respond only to the touch of one who cannot wield it for himself."

"That's ridiculous," Delilah argued. "Surely the spell should remain within Oak Haven, where we can protect it."

Agnes's expression hardened. "That is my condition. Accept it, or depart."

Before the argument could escalate further, a voice like thunder shook the trees around them.

"MEATSACKS!" Louise's disembodied voice boomed through the trees, startling them all. "I RETURN TO RECLAIM WHAT BELONGS TO THE PRESENT!"

"But wait!" Delilah shouted to the sky. "We need more time!"

"I HAVE ALL TIME—YOU HAVE NONE!"

A brilliant light engulfed them, the ground shaking beneath

277

their feet. Jasper reached for Delilah instinctively, his fingers barely brushing hers before reality itself seemed to tear open around them.

The last thing he saw was Agnes Bartlett's face, serene despite the chaos. Her lips moved in what might have been a blessing or a final instruction, but it was impossible to hear over the roar.

And then they were falling, tumbling through a kaleidoscope of fragmenting moments, until—

THUD.

They landed in an ungraceful heap in the center of Oak Haven's town green.

Jasper blinked, disoriented by the sudden transition and the assault of garish colors and loud sounds. The tasteful buildings of Oak Haven's downtown were shrouded in gaudy signs and displays. "AUTHENTIC WITCH SOUVENIRS!" screamed one sign in neon. "HAUNTED WALKING TOURS EVERY HOUR!" proclaimed another.

Tourists swarmed like ants across an open jar of honey, snapping photos with their phones. Many wore loud-colored T-shirts emblazoned with cartoonish witch silhouettes and slogans like: "I GOT MY HEX ON IN OAK HAVEN!" and "MY PARENTS WENT TO WITCHTOWN AND ALL I GOT WAS THIS STUPID T-SHIRT." Across the street, a banner announced the grand opening of the "WITCH HISTORY WAX MUSEUM," promising a "*terrifying torture dungeon experience!*" in the basement.

Jasper and Delilah gaped at their surroundings, the same dark thought occurring to them both at the same exact moment.

Are we too late?

CHAPTER 23
HOLLY HASHTAG CHRISTMAS

Moments ago, Delilah had witnessed the mystical birth of her hometown. Now, she was staring dead-eyed at its potential end.

Her stomach lurched with a fresh wave of nausea that had nothing to do with temporal displacement. Oak Haven's quaint gazebo, where she and her sisters had spent countless summer evenings—where Papa had taught them constellation names while they licked ice-cream cones dripping sticky trails down their fingers—was now wrapped in purple twinkle lights and draped with fake cobwebs. A banner announced the gazebo as "YE OLDE WITCH TRIAL SELFIE STATION," where tourists could pose with their heads and hands locked in stocks while fake flames "burned" them at the stake.

"You have *got* to be kidding me." Delilah struggled to her feet. "That's *wildly* offensive."

Jasper hoisted himself to standing beside her. "And historically inaccurate."

"Good grief, Jasper. Inaccuracy is just the rancid cherry on top of this shit sundae of awful."

She could feel her blood pressure rising with every tacky

sign. This wasn't just cultural appropriation. It was *familial* appropriation. Her family. Her home. Her hand slipped automatically into her pocket, fingers closing around her wand. She'd vaporize that booth, for starters. Just a quick spell, nothing too flashy—

Nothing happened, of course. She felt for that familiar tingle, the electric buzz that ran from her fingertips up her arm when she cast. Delilah stared at her wand like it had personally betrayed her but, of course, she knew it wasn't the wand's fault. It was Saturnalia. "Still no magic in town." She sighed. "And there I was, really enjoying having it again."

"Does Saturnalia end soon?"

"Depends on *when* we are."

A hunched figure in a pointy black hat and flowing robes rushed past, clutching what appeared to be a cauldron full of glitter-infused "potion bottles." Delilah caught a glimpse of the woman's face and felt her blood freeze.

"*Aphra?*"

The figure stopped short, head whipping around. Indeed, beneath the Halloween-store costume was Aphra. Elegant, dignified Aphra, now looking for all the world like Margaret Hamilton's understudy.

"Delilah?" Her eyes darted nervously around the crowded square. "Oh my gods, where have you been? Quick, come with me."

Before Delilah could respond, Aphra grabbed her arm and dragged her out of the park, across the road, and into a narrow alley between buildings. Jasper hurried after them, nearly colliding with a walking tour led by a witch whose costume had clearly been ordered from the "Slutty Salem" section of a catalog.

Once they were hidden from view, Aphra pulled off her

pointy hat and ran a hand through her flattened hair. "You've been gone for days. When did you get back? Scarlett's been losing her mind trying to track you down."

"We just returned, literally minutes ago," Delilah said. "Louise sent us to witness the founding of Oak Haven, if you can believe it. We actually met Agnes Bartlett and she— Wait, you said *days*? What's happened? And why are you dressed like an extra from *Hocus Pocus*?"

Aphra's face darkened. "Everything's gone to absolute shit, is why. Remember that tourist girl you chased out of the inn? She was a social media influencer with *millions* of followers. She posted videos and photos of Oak Haven, those went viral, and suddenly we were flooded with visitors. The magicians saw their opportunity and took it."

"And the forgetting spell?" Jasper asked.

"Faltering, clearly. The girl's photos and videos never should have been visible, much less shareable. Now, all kinds of visitors are finding their way to Oak Haven *on purpose*. That's never happened before. We've always had tourists occasionally, but they were like you, Jasper. They stumbled into us. They didn't come here deliberately. Now, though? Lots of people are talking about us, lots of people are *posting about us* . . ." Aphra glanced around nervously. "On the upside, the tourists complain a lot about experiencing memory glitches. That's our only saving grace at the moment. They come here but then they can't remember precisely what happened. So that means we aren't one hundred percent fucked yet. But people certainly remember enough to keep coming back, so the shit we are in is pretty deep."

Delilah had known Aphra their whole lives and never heard her curse this much. A troubling sign, no doubt. "When does Saturnalia end, so we can fix this mess?"

"That's the thing, Saturnalia should've ended days ago! Del, tomorrow is Christmas Eve! Can you imagine, Christmas arriving at last, and we're *still* stuck in the middle of this shit? Trouble is, the magicians erected wards around the grove, like the ones protecting their casino, but stronger. We can't get through." Aphra's voice cracked slightly. "And without access to the grove . . ."

"We can't end Saturnalia and get our magic back," Delilah finished grimly. "Well, I'll go take a look at the wards. Maybe if Scarlett and I put our heads together, maybe we can—"

"No! Belinda already tried that with her exploding gnomes, and we haven't seen her since. Same with a few others who confronted the magicians. They vanish."

"Just like Mama."

Aphra nodded. "Scarlett's organized what resistance she can. They meet in the basement of the Stargazer. Rather, what used to be the Stargazer. It's called Hex Marks the Spot now."

"Yuck. And you? What's with the get-up? You working for the magicians?" Delilah couldn't quite keep the edge out of her voice.

"No! Not the way you mean. Everyone who resists too openly gets 'disappeared,' Del. The rest of us are just playing along while we try to figure something out. And I need to get back. I'm leading the 'Enchanted Yarn Experience' at two, and if I'm late, they get suspicious. She jammed the pointy hat back on her head, her eyes hard with resolve. "Go to the inn. Basement entrance through the old coal chute. The password is 'Quentin.' Don't ask, it was Scarlett's idea." With that, she swept past them, transforming back into a hunched crone as she returned to the street, cackling dramatically for the benefit of passersby.

Delilah and Jasper exchanged looks. "Should we head over to the inn?" he asked.

"I have a different idea, actually. Tell me what you think of this. Louise clearly sent us back so we could run into Agnes. Right? *Which means . . . ?*" She paused, to let Jasper catch up. But he just looked confused. "Which means . . . she can send us wherever she likes. So! If she sends us back to right before Saturnalia, I can warn everyone about what's coming. And I can convince the witches not to give up their magic in the first place. Then, we won't be helpless."

"Decent plan, but shouldn't we really be focused on how I can get my hands on the spell Agnes talked about?"

Delilah knew what that plan would mean: Jasper leaving town. Her entire being revolted against the idea.

"If I can get back in time to stop us from giving up our power, we won't need it. But first, I *seriously* need caffeine," Delilah said, rubbing her temples. "My brain feels like a ricer, trying to process the three hundred years we just skipped over."

The only coffee shop in town, Hexpresso Yourself, was near the town green and, fortunately, mostly empty at the moment. Out-of-towners apparently preferred exploring the more obviously "witchy" attractions to sitting down for a latte. Managing barista duties was Milo, who'd been doling out coffee drinks since the Melrose sisters were in high school. They cracked a relieved smile upon seeing Delilah. "Heyyyy," Milo sang out, "a familiar face at last! And one not wearing a pointy hat. What can I get you kids? The usual?"

"Please. And whatever he'd like too." She nodded toward Jasper.

"Just black coffee," Jasper said, then added, "You know, in Rome, they considered coffee drinkers suspicious." At Delilah's raised eyebrow, he shrugged. "I figured historically relevant coffee trivia was fair game."

Despite everything, she found herself smiling. "Valid. Grab us that table in the corner while I pay?"

Milo shook their head. "Melroses don't pay, come on. Go sit, I'll bring it right over."

Once Delilah and Jasper had settled into their seats—as far as possible from the handful of tourists taking selfies with their "Magic Mocha Potions"—she pulled out her phone for the first time since they'd returned.

"*Melroses don't pay*," Jasper repeated, eyes twinkling. "Gosh, I keep forgetting I'm running around with a town celebrity."

"Oh hush, Milo's just—" She gasped suddenly. Her eyes went wide staring at her screen. "Holy hellfire. Thirty-seven missed calls from Scarlett, sixteen voicemails, and . . . oh no."

"What?" Jasper leaned forward, concern etching his features.

"Look." She turned her phone toward him, displaying her social media notifications. The tiny red bubble showed a number so high the app had given up counting and simply displayed "999+."

"That can't be good," Jasper said, pulling out his own phone.

"Oh my gods . . ."

The hashtag #OakHavenWitches was trending, accompanied by #MemoryTown and #WitchTok. Delilah's fingers hovered over the screen, a morbid curiosity compelling her to tap on the first video. It was a teenage girl with perfect winged eyeliner and a pentagram drawn on her forehead.

"So I just got back from the COOLEST place, you guys!" The girl's enthusiastic chirping hurt Delilah's ears. "It's this little town called Oak Haven where ACTUAL WITCHES live! And like, they TOTALLY do magic but only if you catch them before noon because that's when their powers are strongest due to the lunar cycles!"

"What in the holy hells is she talking about . . ."

"So I, like, bought this AUTHENTIC witch potion—" the girl held up a small bottle filled with what looked suspiciously like maple syrup with glitter in it "—and the witch who sold it to me said it was made with herbs picked under a full moon and can make your crush text you back! I'm going to try it tonight, so like follow for an update!"

"Who is selling fake love potions around town?" Delilah closed the app with a pained expression. "Jerusha would never."

"Probably the magicians cashing in," Jasper suggested.

Milo brought their drinks over, and Delilah wrapped her hands gratefully around the warm mug. "So, Milo, tell us. How bad is it out there?"

They glanced around to make sure no tourists were listening. "It's a nightmare. I've had to make up fake 'witch coffee rituals' all week. Some guy yesterday wanted me to 'enchant' his latte for an extra twenty bucks."

"Well, I hope you took the cash," Delilah said.

Milo looked a little embarrassed. "I just put the shape of a star in his foam and mumbled some Latin I remembered from high school."

"Smart." Delilah nodded appreciatively.

"Anyway, I should get back to the counter. The Resistance meets at—"

"The inn, I know. Aphra filled us in."

Milo nodded and headed back to the counter where a woman in a "BASIC WITCH" T-shirt was demanding to know if the oat milk was "moon-blessed."

Jasper held out his phone. "Check this one out. Nearly three million views."

A stand-up comedian in a dark club was mid-routine: "So my buddy went to this place called Oak Haven last weekend, right? He comes back and I ask him how it was, and he goes 'I don't really remember.' I'm like, what do you mean you don't remember? Did you party that hard? And he's all 'No man, I just . . . I remember being there, but I can't tell you a single thing about it.' So I said, 'Oh, so it's like Vegas?' And he goes, 'No, because with Vegas, you remember the hotel and the casinos and THEN you black out from drinking. With Oak Haven, you black out FROM JUST BEING THERE!'"

"Great," Delilah huffed. "We're a punchline now."

"At least it sounds like the forgetting spell still works somewhat."

"Small comfort. Oh, let's check out this one: relationship drama, from the look of it." She tapped on a video of a tearful young woman sitting in her car.

"Storytime: I think my boyfriend CHEATED on me in Oak Haven!" she began, dabbing carefully at her eyes to preserve her immaculate eyeliner. "We went there last weekend, and now he claims he doesn't even REMEMBER going! But I found THIS—" she dramatically held up a lipstick tube "—in his jacket pocket, and it's NOT MINE! He says he has no idea where it came from because we 'never went to any witch town' and now I'm like, did the witches erase his memory to COVER HIS TRACKS?"

"Great, so now we're breaking up couples," Delilah groaned. "The divorce attorneys of New England send their thanks."

Jasper had gone quiet, staring at his borrowed phone with the look of a man witnessing a slow-motion car crash.

"What?" Delilah asked. "What could possibly be worse than —oh."

It was a famous meme. A wild-eyed, disheveled man stood in front of a conspiracy board covered in photos, papers, and red string connecting everything. But someone had photoshopped "OAK HAVEN TRUTH" across the top, and added witch hats to some of the photos. The caption read: "Me trying to remember literally ANYTHING about my trip to Oak Haven after leaving town."

"That'll be me soon," Jasper said softly. "Down in my basement, losing my mind as I try to piece together what the hell happened to me here."

Delilah couldn't even begin to imagine what to say. She laid her hand atop his and squeezed. "Let's not give up quite yet." But as she set her mug down, her coffee suddenly tasted like ash.

A group of tourists entered the café, laughing loudly and taking photos of the plastic cauldrons hanging from the ceiling.

"We need to see Louise." Delilah pulled her hand away reluctantly. "Now. Before #WitchTok turns into #ActualWitchesExposed."

As if on cue, her phone lit up with another notification. "Louise's shop is down that way. If she can send us back to the day before Saturnalia, this whole mess would never happen. Let's just hope she's in a helping mood."

"And not a turning-people-into-sundials mood?" Jasper stood up too.

"To be honest, I'm not aware of another moment where Louise has ever *helped* anyone? I guess that makes us a little bit special, come to think of it. I just hope she hasn't died from the shock."

CHAPTER 24
FROSTY THE NO, MAN

The bell above Louise's shop door jingled with inappropriate cheerfulness. The time witch's usually peaceful domain now resembled a carnival midway, with tourists clustered around, soaking up the strangeness. In the center of it all stood Louise, her violet eyes blazing with barely contained rage as she dealt with a line of customers.

"No, this bauble shall not reverse the irreversible decay of your mortal flesh," she was saying to a middle-aged woman in a fanny pack. "It merely marks the ceaseless march toward your inevitable oblivion. Nothing more."

"But the sign says 'Turn Back Time,'" the woman insisted.

"Such is the deceitful tongue of commerce. A linguistic snare crafted to extract currency from the perpetually gullible masses that swarm like mindless larvae across this realm."

The woman huffed. "Well, there's no need to be rude!"

"Rudeness is but one of the infinite horrors at my disposal." Louise snapped her fingers, and the woman vanished with a small *pop*.

A horrified murmur ran through the remaining customers.

"Uh, what just . . . I mean, where'd she go?" bumbled a man in a "GOT HEXED IN OAK HAVEN" T-shirt.

"She dwells now in what your historians call the Middle Ages," Louise said with an unnatural smile. "Where she may commune with the pustulant harbingers of plague, witness the exquisite spectacle of public dismemberment, and experience the olfactory symphony that is human existence without sanitation. Who among you yearns to be next?"

The shop emptied with astonishing speed.

As the last tourist fled, Louise turned her gaze on Delilah and Jasper. "Ah I see, you've returned. Very well . . ." She made a vague little wave with her hands. "Get on with it, then."

Delilah and Jasper glanced at each other, then back at Louise. "Get on with what?" Delilah asked.

"Well, I can only assume you've come to prostrate yourselves at my feet, expressing infinite gratitude for how I dragged your pitiful forms across the vast temporal abyss."

"Ah. Uh, right. Yes, we are supremely grateful . . ."

Louise nodded. "Of course. Prostrate away."

"Sure, right," Delilah said hesitantly. "Actually, though, we're here because we need your help again."

Louise went terrifyingly silent, fixing her gaze directly into Delilah's soul. "You what?"

"If you could send me back to before Saturnalia . . ."

"You dare petition me for *what* abomination against the cosmic order?"

"Oh, nothing as big as an abomination, surely. Just a few days, a week maybe? See, then I can warn everyone not to surrender their magic. And none of this would have happened."

Clocks slowed, stopped, and began to run backward. Louise seemed to grow taller, her shadow stretching impossibly across the floor and up the walls. Delilah feared her anger but the face

290

of the time witch held an expression that was far more terrifying than rage.

She looked . . . disappointed.

"I bestowed upon you a boon beyond mortal comprehension," Louise said miserably. "I parted the veil between epochs and guided your insignificant forms to the natal moments of your wretched settlement. *You fetus*, do you not see that I provided you with greater assistance than I have provided any human in a thousand years?! *I helped!* I never help, but I helped you!"

"You did! You totally did, Louise!" Delilah could feel the conversation going deliriously wrong, but she didn't know how to reverse course. "And that was really great, Louise. So great. It's just that—"

"Yet my generosity has failed to slake your thirst?" Her voice was an anguished mix of shock and grief. The tone of a creature who'd never had her feelings hurt before. Of a creature who hadn't realized she possessed any feelings in the first place. "You are saying . . . I am . . . insufficient?"

"Oh no, that's not what Delilah means at all!" Jasper leaped in to try and help. "You've been enormously helpful. It's just, we have this new idea about how to fix Oak Haven's problem. And we just thought—"

Somewhere in the shop, a pocket watch exploded into a pile of gears and springs. "The arcane manipulations of chronological fabric do not exist to rectify every trivial disbenefit your kind inflicts upon itself!" A cuckoo clock began to melt before their eyes.

"But this isn't some trivial disbenefit," Delilah argued. "This is the fate of our entire town, our way of life!"

The time witch threw back her head, releasing a laugh like the death rattle of a thousand condemned souls. "You

291

mewling specks, do you not see? Your 'entire town' is but a momentary aberration in the cosmic horror that is Time itself. You would have me unravel the fabric of reality because your pitiful holiday ritual yielded undesirable consequences?"

"But—"

"BEGONE FROM MY SIGHT!" Louise thundered, her voice seeming to come from everywhere and nowhere at once. "Lest I cast you into the gaping maw of the universe to witness the final extinction of your species. An event I have joyfully observed countless times across infinite timelines!"

The bell above the door jingled again. A balding man in cargo shorts stepped in, cradling a broken pocket watch. "Excuse me, is this the clock repair shop? My grandfather's watch stopped working and—"

Louise's rage evaporated instantly, replaced by a predatory gleam. "Yes. Enter, temporal pilgrim, and let us see what I might do to you. I mean, for you. Have you ever given any thought to the many benefits of timeshares?"

Jasper seized the opportunity to pull Delilah outside, half dragging her down the street before she could protest further.

"She sent that woman to the Middle Ages for literally no reason at all!" Delilah complained. "But she won't help us fix this very serious problem?"

"I got the impression that Louise considers human problems beneath her notice. Like asking Stephen Hawking to balance a checkbook."

She sighed. "Okay, I surrender. Let's go to the inn. Maybe Scarlett has a plan that doesn't involve Ms. Temporal Superiority Complex back there."

"There's always the Agnes plan . . ." Jasper reminded her.

"Shut up," she suggested.

Together, they started down the street toward the inn, as the shadows lengthened behind them like an omen.

Getting to the Stargazer—or what had been the Stargazer—was like navigating a witch-themed Pinterest obstacle course. And when they arrived, they found the inn was in the same shape. It was a nightmare of fake cobwebs, plastic cauldrons, and animatronic black cats that meowed the theme from *Bewitched*. This wasn't her home anymore.

"Listen, Delilah," Jasper said carefully as they strode toward the inn, "I have a thought, if you don't mind hearing it?"

"I am made of ears at the moment. What's your thought?"

"Well, Aphra said the forgetting spell was getting shaky, right? So, maybe we can use that to our advantage here. Maybe I could actually get to my office, find the portal spell, and get back here, then back there without a problem."

Delilah stopped short. "Why are you so eager to leave all of a sudden!" Her voice came out sharper than she intended, that old defensive edge back in full force.

"No no," he said gently. "Not eager at all. Just practical. I mean . . . I want to save the town, Delilah. Don't you?"

"I want to save *us*, Jasper. Don't you?" Her vision went a bit swimmy as her eyes filled with tears. She knew she shouldn't be taking this out on him. It wasn't Jasper's fault the town was in shambles. All he'd wanted was to help out. But the thought of him walking away, forgetting her . . . it clawed at her insides like a mouse trapped in her chest.

Delilah and Jasper stood there on the sidewalk, facing each other, caught between the past and future, trapped in a present neither one of them wanted. He reached out and gently stroked her cheek, then pulled her toward him, pressing his lips to hers.

She took hold of his face with both hands and looked at him —really looked at him. His rumpled shirt from their wilderness adventure, the slight stubble along his jaw, those worried eyes behind smudged glasses. Her chest ached with the absurd, impossible wanting of a future she clearly couldn't have. She'd spent so long avoiding attachments only to find herself desperate to keep one. "Last resort," she said finally. "Agnes is our last. Damn. Resort."

"Agreed."

Locating the old coal chute required circling to the back of the building, where thankfully few outsiders ventured. The rusted metal door yielded to Delilah's push, revealing a narrow, dusty slide into darkness.

"Ladies first?" Jasper suggested weakly.

"Chivalry really is dead," Delilah muttered, but she went ahead anyway, sliding down into the musty darkness below.

She landed with a thud on a pile of cushions, Jasper following seconds later with considerably less grace. Before they could orient themselves, a familiar voice called out: "Password?"

"Quentin," Delilah replied.

"Del?" Scarlett emerged from the shadows, her hair wild and her eyes ringed with exhaustion. "Holy shit, you're back!" She flung herself at Delilah with enough force to nearly knock her over, hugging her fiercely. "I went to see Louise and demand she send you back . . . I nearly ended up in the Jurassic period myself!"

Delilah hugged her back, surprised at how good it felt. "We met Agnes Bartlett. It's a long story."

"Save it for the others," Scarlett said, pulling back to

examine her sister. "You look . . . Something has . . . Wait, did something happen between you two?" Her eyes darted suspiciously between Delilah and Jasper.

"Focus, Scar," Delilah said, feeling heat rise in her cheeks. "Aphra said you've been organizing resistance?"

"Trying to." Scarlett led them into the darkness, deeper into the basement. "It's been . . . challenging." She opened a creaky wooden door to the old root cellar, dimly lit by battery-powered lanterns. Maps of Oak Haven were pinned to the walls, with red X's marking magician checkpoints. A few familiar faces looked up as they entered: Zahir, handing out sandwiches; the four Earls, cleaning an alarming array of antique weapons; and a handful of other witches Delilah recognized from around town.

"Jasper!" Zahir abandoned his work and rushed over, pulling his new pal into a bear hug. "Thank God you're all right. We've all been worried sick since Louise zapped you away."

"It's good to see you too," Jasper replied. "I wish the circumstances were better."

"No shit." Zahir lowered his voice. "Listen, whatever happens next, I want you to know that I get it. I get what you're facing. Moses and I—our whole situation . . . I remember very well what it's like. The thing is, I don't regret it. Not for a second. Even if it couldn't last, it was worth it when we had it."

Jasper nodded. "I hear you. Still hoping it won't come to that, but . . . Anyway. Thanks."

Delilah pretended not to hear this exchange, though her stomach clenched painfully at the implication. Zahir understood what they were facing better than anyone because he'd been through it himself. The realization broke her heart a little—she remembered when Moses had left, and she remembered how terribly *que será, será* she and her sisters had been in response to Zahir's misery. They hadn't understood back then. But boy did she understand now.

"So what's the plan?" she asked Scarlett, forcing her attention back to the crisis.

"I was hoping you'd come back with one," Scarlett admitted. "We've tried everything to break through those wards. And we keep sending out messages for Luna. She never gave up her powers for Saturnalia, so she might be our best hope. But no luck so far."

"Well," Delilah said, "Jasper and I might have found something we can work with." She quickly explained what they'd learned from Agnes: the portal spell that could potentially move the entire casino, and the magicians with it.

As she spoke, excitement spread through the group. Faces that had been bleak with desperation began to light up with hope. By the time she finished, the basement was buzzing with energy.

"That's brilliant!" Scarlett exclaimed. "If we can get that spell—"

"There's a complication," Jasper interrupted quietly. "Agnes hid the spell somewhere only I can retrieve it."

He didn't need to finish. Everyone understood what came next.

"Ah." Scarlett's excitement dimmed slightly. "Well, that's . . . unfortunate."

"Is there another way?" Zahir asked, glancing between Delilah and Jasper with obvious concern. "Did Agnes literally say that only Jasper could get it?"

"Not necessarily," Delilah quickly replied.

"Delilah . . ." Jasper shook his head. "You know she did."

"Maybe that's not what she meant. She said it was where

none with magic may find it. There's a lot of people out there with no magic."

"That's most people," noted Eleven. "Maybe the boys and I can go fetch it. How about that?"

"Hey," Scarlett said brightly. "Maybe Nate and I can go. Perhaps I'll get my heist after all."

Jasper frowned. "I fear Delilah is being overly optimistic here."

"Am not," she shot back. "That's exactly what Agnes said. None with magic can find it."

"She was looking at me. Straight down the barrel at me."

"Doesn't mean anything."

"Listen, you two," Scarlett interrupted. "Who gets the spell is really a side issue."

Delilah had expected the other witches to react that way. Hearing it from her sister was an open-handed smack across the face. "A side issue! How can you say that to me?"

"Del, the entire town is at stake. Let's have some priorities here. What we do with the spell once we have it, that's the real question. For now, let's work with what we know. If we get this spell, we can send the casino—where, exactly? Some place where the magicians will definitely want to negotiate terms, so we can get Mama and the rest back home. The Grand Canyon? Or Mars? Can we open a portal to Mars?"

"Pittsburgh," suggested Jerusha.

Everyone turned to stare at her.

"What?" the witch said defensively. "A lot of people don't like Pittsburgh."

The group began debating potential destinations, strategies, and contingency plans. Weapons were examined. Maps were consulted. Everyone had at least one opinion; most had several.

Through it all, Delilah stood silent, watching as her

relationship with Jasper was reduced to less than an asterisk to the struggle to save Oak Haven. Even Scarlett clearly regarded Jasper as an acceptable casualty. And yes, logically speaking, Delilah understood. The fate of their home, of generations of witches, of their entire way of life, had to outweigh one man.

Logic, however, had very little to do with the cold weight settling in her chest.

Across the room, Jasper met her gaze. In his eyes, she saw understanding, resignation, and something else. Determination. He was going to do this, she sensed. No matter what she said.

Around them, the planning continued, voices rising and falling with the cadence of impending battle. But Delilah and Jasper remained locked in their silent communion, alone together in a room full of people, while the others debated what to do with the spell that could destroy their relationship.

CHAPTER 25

THE SEASON OF GIVING (UP)

Jasper had been missing from his own life for nearly a week. The perplexing bit was that he couldn't bring himself to care very much.

Somewhere in the real world, Jasper's apartment was gathering dust. His mail was piling up. His plants were dying. Did anyone even notice he was gone? Toby, perhaps . . . but if he did notice, did he mind? Most of his coworkers viewed Jasper as a rather uptight irritant. Jasper could picture his boss, Nancy, sighing with relief at the sudden absence of demands for better lighting in the archives. The others were probably delighted that the basement was empty; they could toss all their paperwork on his desk and flee back upstairs before he had a chance to correct their spelling.

Instead of showing up for work, Jasper was sitting in the dimly lit basement of the Stargazer Inn, watching as the eldest Earl brothers prepared for their mission to retrieve the portal spell. Ten and Nine—Nate's great-grandfather and great-great-grandfather, respectively—were strapping on what appeared to be vintage pirate gear: eye patches, leather vests, and an assortment of antique weapons that belonged in a museum rather than on an octogenarian's hip.

"You sure this is necessary?" Jasper asked. "It's a county clerk's office, not a Spanish galleon."

"Never hurts to be prepared." Nine tested the edge of a dagger against his thumb. "You've never seen that scalawag Toby in a bad mood."

Jasper couldn't help but chuckle. Nine had never even met his colleague Toby. But Jasper had, in fact, seen Toby in many different moods, none of which demanded the presence of medieval weaponry. But he kept this observation to himself. Nine and Ten were nervous enough already.

After a flurry of final instructions—"ask Toby about the Patriots, they're his favorite team and he's easily distracted by sports talk"—Jasper watched them depart through the coal chute, climbing with surprising agility for men their age.

"Do you think they'll find it?" Delilah asked, settling beside him on an overturned crate.

Jasper studied her face in the dim light, considering how to answer. Hope and dread battled in his chest. "I'm sure they'll try their best," he replied, which wasn't really an answer.

"So," she said after a moment, "I've been wondering something. It's two days before Christmas. What are you missing out on right now? Any family gatherings? Office parties with bad eggnog?"

The question caught Jasper off guard. "Missing?" He laughed softly. "Believe me, I'm not missing a thing."

"Come on," she pressed. "There must be something. Some Hopkins family tradition? Matching pajamas, maybe?"

Jasper shook his head. "My parents always treated Christmas like a military operation. Precise schedule, specific gifts from a pre-approved list, dinner at exactly 3 p.m. The whole thing was about as spontaneous as tax season. My grandmother was the only one who made it bearable. She'd sneak me out for impromptu sledding or slip me a mug of hot chocolate when no one was looking. Called it our 'Christmas jailbreak.' But once she passed, the magic was gone."

"Yeah." Delilah nodded. "I hear that, trust me. So nobody's expecting you to show up with a fruitcake this year?"

"My parents are on a cruise. We exchange gift cards via email."

"I see, well that's horrible. I suppose I've accidentally rescued you from a depressing solo microwave dinner and a night of PBS documentaries."

"You've done me a huge favor." Jasper smiled despite the situation. "A magical town under siege by power-hungry magicians is a significant upgrade from my usual holiday plans. Don't worry, there's nowhere else I'd rather be."

Their eyes met, and Jasper felt that now-familiar spark between them. It was a bit terrifying, how quickly she'd become essential, how the thought of forgetting her felt like losing a limb. But before he could say anything more, the coal chute rattled, announcing the Earls' return. Far, far too soon.

They tumbled in, looking disheveled and defeated.

"That Toby's a crafty one," Nine grumbled, removing his eye patch.

"We started off okay," said Ten. "I asked about the Patriots, just like you suggested, Jasper. But then Toby asked what we thought about Brady's chances against the Buffalo Bills next week. And this old codger—" he nodded toward Nine "—went completely sideways."

"He's the one brought up Buffalo Bill!" Nine cried indignantly. "I told him that no-good son-of-a-bitch swindler still owes me twenty dollars from a poker game in '03!"

"2003?" Jasper asked, confused.

"*1903.*"

Nate groaned, sinking his head into his hands. "Double-great grandpa, the Buffalo Bills are a football team. From *this* century."

"Well, how was I supposed to know that?" Nine threw his hands up. "In my day, we named things after what they were, not Wild West showmen who cheat at cards!"

"It got worse," Ten continued. "When Toby tried to explain that Tom Brady was a quarterback, Nine said, 'Quarterback? I'll tell you what, I want a whole lot more than a quarterback from Buffalo Bill. Damn him and damn his nancy-boy pal Tom Brady, too!'"

"Oh no, Nine!" Scarlett said, barely holding back a laugh. "You called Tom Brady a 'nancy boy'? And then what happened?"

"We uh, we made a tactical retreat," he replied with as much dignity as he could muster. "Let's just leave it at that."

"You're lucky you made it out alive, frankly." Jasper sighed, trying not to let his disappointment show. "It's okay. We've got other options."

Earls Eleven and Twelve were already gearing up for their attempt. This time, they'd sneak in through a back door, avoiding Toby entirely. Jasper spent the next fifteen minutes explaining the layout of the building, drawing diagrams, and emphasizing all the places they should avoid.

"Remember, my office is in the basement, across from the boiler room. The portrait of Agnes Bartlett hangs on the north wall. Seems like the best place to start the search."

"Basement, boiler room, portrait, north wall," Eleven repeated. "Got it."

An hour later, Nate's phone buzzed. His father was calling from the archives of the Schoharie County Historical Society. "The directions were very specific about the building," Twelve complained, "but less so about which county it was in."

Jasper winced, realizing he'd assumed too much. "I'm sorry," he said, "I didn't think—"

"Well," Scarlett said, "we shouldn't wait for them to get back. Who's going next?"

The third pair of volunteers were Jerusha and Belinda's husband Sam Chatterjee. This seemed to have more potential. Sam was highly motivated, given the fact that Belinda was among the disappeared, and he'd had a lot more experience with the real world than the Earls. This time Jasper provided them with explicit directions, both to the clerk's office and where to go once inside. "Remember, be casual. Don't mention anything magical. Just say you're looking for historical records of property deeds or something."

"I understand," Jerusha said sternly. "I was navigating the world while you were nothing but a dirty thought in your father's mind."

"Uh, right . . . Yeah, I wasn't suggesting otherwise," Jasper said quickly. "Just, you know, as a reminder."

Less than an hour later, Priti Chatterjee received a phone call from the Pleasant Valley Senior Center. She listened intently, saying little beyond: "Uh-huh . . . uh-huh . . . yes, I understand." And finally: "I'll be right over."

"What happened?" Delilah asked when Priti got off the call.

"According to the nurse I just spoke to, Jerusha marched up

to Toby and announced, 'Hark, mortal! I am a witch of great power, temporarily bereft of my magical abilities due to seasonal obligations. We have arrived to retrieve an ancient spell hidden by Agnes Bartlett, she of the stern countenance and impeccable record-keeping.'"

"Great . . ." Jasper dropped his head into his hands. "I'm sure Toby wasn't freaked out by that at all. What about Sam?"

"Apparently my dad was nodding along, adding helpful details like, 'I'm here to touch the document, since witches can't.' Toby decided the two of them must have wandered away from the old folks' home and he had them picked up." Sighing, Priti grabbed her medical bag and headed out to retrieve them. "They're likely enjoying Jell-O and *Murder, She Wrote* right now."

Jasper's hope flickered anew when Zahir and Aphra volunteered to make the next attempt. They seemed the most level-headed of the group, not to mention the most familiar with the world outside Oak Haven. "You've got this," he told them. "Just be casual. If anyone asks, you're researchers interested in county history."

"Researchers. History. Got it," Zahir agreed. "But, um, can we borrow Nate's car? The old folks keep taking our cars and not coming back."

Aphra nudged Zahir. "You mean Jasper. It's Jasper's car."

"Right, sorry! I'm a little tired. Jasper, can we borrow your car?"

The wait for Zahir and Aphra's return stretched Jasper's nerves to the breaking point, and not because of the borrowed car. He paced the basement, acutely aware of Delilah watching him, her own anxiety evident in the way she kept rearranging the emergency supplies.

When Zahir and Aphra finally returned, they looked like they'd narrowly escaped a disaster.

"We were so close . . ." Zahir collapsed onto a crate, exhausted. "Made it all the way to the basement!"

"Went brilliantly at first," Aphra said. "Got past Toby without a hitch. I explained how we were doing research on New England architectural preservation . . . He got so bored halfway through my explanation, he just waved us through."

Jasper nodded. "That's my Toby."

"We found your office," Zahir continued. "Everything was going according to plan. We located Agnes's portrait and were examining it when we heard voices upstairs."

"Turns out," Aphra said grimly, "Toby was giving a tour to two police officers who were there about a missing person case."

Jasper's stomach dropped. "About me?"

"Yes, about you!" Zahir exclaimed. "You haven't shown up for work or called in sick. They were concerned."

"We overheard them talking about checking the basement," Aphra continued. "And James Bond over here lost his shit."

"I lost no such thing," Zahir protested.

"Oh really? When the officers called out, 'Anyone down there?' This genius yells, 'No one, Officer!'"

Jasper stared at them, momentarily speechless.

"In my defense," Zahir said, "I'm a chef, not a spy."

"We had to make a run for it," Aphra concluded. "Out the emergency exit. The alarm went off."

"Which was actually helpful," Zahir added, "because it masked the sound of us knocking over a shelf of county tax records from 1973. But look at the upside: people do actually miss you at work."

Aphra nodded but added, "On the down side, we are definitely on a watchlist now."

Delilah laid a comforting hand on Jasper's arm. "We've still got Scarlett and Nate."

Indeed, Scarlett had insisted on making the final attempt, dragging a reluctant Nate along. "If anyone can pull off a heist, it's me," she'd declared. "I've been training for this my whole life."

"Repeat viewings of the *Ocean's Eleven* series doesn't count as training."

"Oh ye of little faith. Sit tight, folks. Nate and I have got this."

The waiting stretched out, minutes bleeding into hours. The basement grew quieter. Through narrow windows near the ceiling, everyone could see the sun going down. The day was nearly over, and the clerk's office would be closing soon.

Jasper found himself staring at Delilah's profile. Her pointy chin, the slight furrow between her brows, the way her hair curled against her neck. He was memorizing her, he realized. For all the good it would do.

The coal chute rattled, interrupting his thoughts. Scarlett slid down first, her face flushed with excitement that quickly turned to disappointment when she saw their expectant faces.

"We almost had it," she announced.

Nate followed, his hands wrapped in what appeared to be improvised bandages made from his own shirt. "Sorry, Jasper. Really sorry."

"We were brilliant," Scarlett began. "First, we ditched your car two blocks away and approached on foot."

"Clever," Jasper admitted.

"Then we noticed the police were still there," Nate continued, "so Scarlett created a distraction."

"What kind of distraction?" Delilah asked suspiciously.

"I may have broken a window, which set off some sort of alarm." Scarlett shrugged. "But it was for the greater good. While everyone rushed over to see what set off the alarm, we slipped in through the back door. Found your office exactly where you said it would be. Agnes's creepy old portrait was right there on the wall. I swear, Jasper, she was watching us. Her eyes followed us around the room."

"That's just a trick of the paint," Jasper said, though he'd made the same observation many times.

"So Nate checked behind the portrait," Scarlett said, "and there it was! A secret compartment with an old parchment inside."

Jasper leaned forward. "You found it? The spell?"

"The parchment is behind Agnes's portrait, just like you thought it might be," Scarlett explained. "But when Nate tried to take it, it . . . rejected him."

"Painfully," Nate added. "He unwrapped one hand to reveal angry red burns across his palm. "When I tried to touch it, this happened. It was like trying to grab a hot coal. I tried with my gloves on, too, but my gloves just caught fire. I'm definitely not allowed to touch that thing."

Jasper hadn't felt so ashamed in a long time. "God, Nate, I'm so sorry. I hate that you got hurt over this."

"I'll be all right—don't you worry about it. Sorry I couldn't grab it for you."

The group fell silent. There was no way around it. The spell wouldn't allow itself to be retrieved by just anyone.

"It has to be me," Jasper said quietly. "It can only be me."

"Yep." Nine nodded. "The sentient coat rack has point."

"*Hey*, Nine," Delilah said sharply. "I don't care if you are a billion-year-old pirate, don't talk about him like that."

Jasper smiled sadly. "It's okay, Delilah. And thanks for trying, everybody. I can't even express how much I appreciate it. But I'll go to the office tomorrow, first thing. The clerk's office opens at nine."

"Hold on a sec," Nate said suddenly. "He can't go alone. By the time he gets to his office, he'll have forgotten what he's doing there."

The group fell silent as they all simultaneously (and unsuccessfully) tried not to look in Delilah's direction.

Scarlett raised her hand. "I'll do it." Her usually snarky tone was replaced by something different, something protective and kind. "Me and the radiator will go get the spell—it's no problem. Right, Jasper?"

Before he could agree, Delilah wrapped one arm tightly around his. Her voice was barely above a whisper. "I'll take him."

Jasper turned to her. "Delilah . . . maybe it's better if—"

"No, it should be us. We found Agnes together; she told us about the spell together . . . we should finish it together."

Scarlett shook her head. "No, no, don't either of you put yourselves through that. I can take him out there, get the spell, bring it back. Del, you shouldn't have to watch it happen. You don't have to do every shitty job, you know."

"I don't," she agreed. "But I do have to do this one."

"Hey, guys," Zahir said, desperately trying to change the mood. "We've all noticed the forgetting spell being a bit funky, right? We wouldn't be glutted with tourists otherwise. So . . . you know . . . maybe it won't be as bad as we think."

"Oh I agree," Jasper lied. "I'm sure it'll all work out."

"Well, uh . . ." Zahir cleared his throat. "It's Christmas

karaoke tonight. I know we're not exactly in a karaoke headspace right now, but the whole town is expected to participate. So, shall we head over?"

"I'm sorry, did you say *karaoke*?" Jasper asked. "Now? With all this going on?"

"It's a tradition, every year on the night before the night before Christmas," Delilah explained. "Usually, the witches use their magic to enhance their performances. Special effects, perfect-pitch spells, that sort of thing. But this year . . ."

"This year we'll be singing au naturel," Scarlett finished. "It's going to be a beautiful disaster. Plus, Zahir's right: it'll look majorly suspicious if we don't show up. Plus, we could all use a break from this basement, don't we agree?"

Nate rolled his eyes. "You just want to hear Polly butcher 'O Holy Night' without magic."

As the others made plans, Jasper settled beside Delilah on the basement steps, both seeking a moment of privacy.

"So, karaoke," he said, trying to sound casual. "Are you going to sing?"

"Without magic?" she said with a grimace. "That sounds like a terrifying idea."

"I bet you're not that bad."

"Trust me, I am. What about you? Will you serenade us all with a Christmas classic?"

"I was thinking something less seasonal," Jasper replied, surprising himself. "Maybe something from the Eighties."

"You're full of surprises, Hopkins." Delilah gave him a sidelong look. "A closet karaoke enthusiast?"

"I wouldn't go that far. But it seems like a perfectly reasonable first date."

"A date?" Her eyebrows rose. "You're asking me on a date to a Christmas karaoke contest?"

"I am." He adjusted his glasses. "What do you say?"

"Our first-slash-last date . . ." She was quiet for a moment, then nodded. "Well then, we better make it count."

"I was thinking the same thing," Jasper said, reaching over to tuck a strand of hair behind her ear. "And afterward . . ." He took a breath, suddenly nervous. "Afterward, we'll have the best night of our lives. Something worth remembering, even if I can't."

"I'll remember for both of us," Delilah promised, her voice catching.

Jasper pulled her close, breathing in the scent of her hair, committing it to whatever part of memory might survive the forgetting spell. The steady beat of her heart against his chest, the warmth of her breath on his neck, the curve of her body fitting perfectly against his. These sensations felt more real than the entire life waiting for him back in the "real world."

Tomorrow, he would retrieve the spell and set in motion the events that would save Oak Haven and, in all likelihood, separate him from Delilah forever.

But tonight . . . tonight they still had time. And Jasper intended to make every second count.

CHAPTER 26
IF THE FATES ALLOW

It was Christmas Eve-eve in Oak Haven, and the old folks said son, she won't see another one. And so they sang some songs, rare old holiday tunes. They turned their eyes away . . . and dreamed about winning the annual Christmas Karaoke Cup.

Delilah nursed her mulled wine at a corner table in Double, Double Boil and Trouble, watching as Earl Nine and Ten took stood up to introduce the next performer. The pub was packed with witches and non-witches alike, all apparently determined to pretend everything was normal, despite the influencer invasion and the conspicuous absence of Kelly Melrose, Belinda Chatterjee, and several other Oak Haven witches.

"Next up," announced Nine, squinting at a handwritten note, "is Sam Chatterjee with his rendition of 'Jingle Bell Rock'!"

Jasper leaned closer, and Delilah could feel his warm breath against her ear. "Is it weird that he's so cheerful?" He nodded at Sam, who bounded onto the stage with alarming enthusiasm. "What with his wife missing and all?"

"It's weird for him to be so cheerful when she's not

missing," Delilah replied, frowning. "Mr. Chatterjee's not a cheerful guy in general."

And yet, Sam grabbed the microphone with the confidence of a Vegas headliner. With a deep breath, he sent the opening notes of the holiday classic echoing through the pub. What followed was a performance that could only be described as aggressively joyful, complete with TikTok-inspired dance moves.

"Who wants to rock around the Christmas tree with me later?" Sam called out during the bridge, which earned him shocked looks from longtime residents.

"His wife is literally trapped in trans-dimensional limbo," Delilah whispered to Jasper. "What is he doing?"

Jasper's expression turned grave. "He's forgotten."

"Forgotten? No, that's not—" But Delilah's protest died as Sam took a theatrical bow, his face showing not a single hint of worry or grief.

"You know what," Delilah said, "I'm sure he's just putting on a brave face. He knows everyone is thinking about Belinda having been taken. He just doesn't want people to worry about him." Delilah watched as Sam rejoined his friends, accepting high fives and backslaps as if he were celebrating a promotion rather than enduring his wife's unexplained absence.

"Thank you, thank you!" Sam called as he left the stage. "Merry Christmas to all! Best holiday ever!"

Jasper turned to Delilah, one eyebrow arched. "That's pretty damn brave."

She shook her head. "It's fine." Jasper might be right, but Delilah wasn't ready to admit what that would mean. Because if the forgetting spell was breaking down, it meant their time was running out. Not just for retrieving Agnes's spell, but for herself and Jasper, too.

Still, where others saw failure in their various attempts to get Agnes's spell, Delilah saw progress. They knew exactly where the spell was hidden now. Behind Agnes's portrait in Jasper's office. They just needed to figure out how to retrieve it without losing him along the way.

"You know," she began, "I'm thinking . . . Maybe we could—"

But Jasper's attention had shifted to the stage, where Aphra was now setting up for her performance.

Dayo appeared at their table, sliding another round of drinks in front of them. "On the house," she said with a wink, and she slid into the empty seat beside them. "Thought you might need fortification for what's coming. You guys were drinking scotch, right?"

Delilah and Jasper glanced at one another. They were absolutely not drinking scotch, but who's going to complain about a free round? *After all*, Delilah thought to herself, *it wasn't like Dayo could be expected to remember every drink order, right?*

But inside, she knew. Dayo absolutely could be expected to remember every drink order. Usually, Dayo could remember who had ordered what *last week*. Not tonight, though. The forgetting spell was never supposed to impact people who stayed within the town limits, but now it was spreading like a virus.

"Much appreciated!" Jasper forced as much cheer into his voice as he could. "But is Aphra going to be that bad? Like, *double-scotch, neat* bad?"

"Without her magic? Catastrophic," Dayo confirmed. "But we love her anyway."

Delilah had always appreciated Dayo's calm amusement at Oak Haven's perpetual chaos. As a non-witch who'd voluntarily chosen to stay in town, Dayo was living proof that some connections were worth sacrificing for.

"How do you do it?" Delilah blurted out, surprising herself.

"Do what, hon?" Dayo asked.

"Choose to leave your old life. Knowing you could never go back."

Dayo's warm smile turned thoughtful. She glanced over at Aphra, who was nervously adjusting the microphone. "When you know where you belong, it's not about leaving. It's about coming home."

Jasper's hand found Delilah's under the table. Could it really be that simple? To just choose each other, consequences be damned?

Aphra's rendition of "Silent Night" was anything but. Her untrained voice wavered painfully on the high notes, causing undisguised wincing in the audience. Still, Delilah felt a surge of unexpected hope. Maybe they didn't need perfection. Maybe being together, broken spells and all, was enough.

"It doesn't have to be you," she whispered to Jasper.

"What?"

"The spell. Maybe Agnes was wrong, or maybe we're interpreting her words wrong. We could try again, get someone else to—"

"The Earls tried," Jasper reminded her. "Your friends tried. Nate has burns on his hands because he tried to do something that I should have done from the beginning. I think we have to accept that Agnes meant what she said."

"Maybe, maybe not. Anyway, the forgetting spell is clearly breaking down," Delilah argued, keeping her voice low. "Maybe it wouldn't affect you anymore."

"Well yeah, that would be good. But there's only one way we're going to find out. Which is, I have to go."

The evening progressed with each performance more entertainingly terrible than the last. Jerusha, who'd been sprung from the senior center, delivered a spoken-word interpretation of "Frosty the Snowman," turning that cheerful tale into an existential meditation on impermanence. Then came Zahir's turn, clutching the microphone with the determination of a man facing execution.

"On the first day of Christmas, my true love gave to me . . ." he began confidently enough, but then his expression clouded. "One pound of butter, unsalted." The audience tittered as he continued. "On the second day of Christmas, my true love gave to me . . . two cups of flour, and one pound of butter, unsalted." Before long he was listing: "Seven sprigs of rosemary, six cloves of garlic . . . fiiiiiive golden egg yolks." Dayo was wiping tears of laughter from her eyes, and Aphra had her face buried in her hands.

"He forgot the lyrics," Jasper whispered.

"Oh come on," Delilah objected. "That's a joke. He was clearly doing a bit."

"What about when Nine introduced him as 'whatshisname, that tall fellow'? Was that comedy, too?"

"Maybe they're just drunk. Nine is an old pirate, and this is a party . . . What do you expect?" But Delilah had to admit, something was off. The forgetting seemed to be accelerating, even among people like Zahir, who'd lived in Oak Haven his whole life. Small lapses cascading into larger ones as the night wore on.

But why is this my damn problem to fix? Resentment sparked up in Delilah's chest. After all, Scarlett had ended up living as a bird for an entire year because it fell to her to save the town. Now Delilah had to give up Jasper? *Why was it always a Melrose who had to sacrifice? Why couldn't someone else take the hit this time?*

"I believe our next performer is . . ." Ten squinted at his card, then looked up with a triumphant smile. "Jasper Hopkins! Come on up, young man!"

Delilah's head whipped around. "You signed up?"

Jasper adjusted his glasses nervously. "I may have. When in Rome, right?"

"What are you going to sing?"

"You'll see," he said with surprising confidence. He gave her hand a quick squeeze before making his way to the stage.

Jasper cleared his throat, looking slightly terrified as he faced the crowd. "So, I'm not much of a singer," he began, "and I'm definitely not a fan of Christmas music."

A good-natured boo rippled through the audience.

"But," he continued, "sometimes you meet someone who changes how you feel about . . . well, everything." His eyes found Delilah's across the dim pub. "This is for you."

The oddly mournful opening notes of "Have Yourself a Merry Little Christmas" filled the room, and Jasper began to sing. His voice wasn't spectacular. A little thin, a little "pitchy," as they say at singing competitions. But his earnestness mattered more than the notes. When he reached the part about all of us being together that strongly implied we would never be together again, Delilah felt tears pricking at her eyes.

When Jasper finished, the applause was genuine and warm. Jasper made his way back to their table, his face flushed with embarrassment.

"That was . . ." Delilah began, but found herself unable to finish the thought.

"Terrible?" he suggested.

"Perfect," she corrected, and kissed him, not caring who was watching.

The kiss deepened, and suddenly the pub felt too crowded, too noisy. With no discussion, they both stood, offered some flimsy excuses to Scarlett and Nate, and headed for the door.

The winter air hit them like a shock as they stepped outside, stars glittering overhead in a clear December sky. Oak Haven at Christmas had always been beautiful, even with its kitschy magic and over-the-top decorations. Now, with tacky tourist traps lining the streets and the ominous silhouette of the casino looming in the distance, it was a study in contrasts: the beautiful and the grotesque side by side.

"Your room or mine?" Jasper asked, his breath visible in the cold.

Delilah smiled. "Mine has a better view."

They walked quickly through the town center, hand in hand, stealing kisses in the shadows between streetlights. Once, they had to duck into an alley to avoid a tour group being led by a witch in an outrageously pointed hat. But even that couldn't dampen the electricity between them.

By the time they reached the Stargazer—or, Hex Marks the Spot, according to a garish new sign outside—Delilah's heart was racing with a mixture of desire and a fierce, protective ache. This man, with his precise mind and surprising courage, had somehow become essential to her in just a matter of days.

Her room was mercifully unaffected by the tourist takeover, a sanctuary of familiar comfort. When the door closed behind them, Jasper pulled her into his arms, his kiss deep and urgent. His glasses fogged slightly from the temperature difference, making her laugh softly against his mouth.

"Something funny?" he murmured.

"Just you," she said, gently removing his glasses and setting them aside. "All of this. Us."

"Is that a good thing?"

"The best thing." Delilah's fingers worked at the buttons of his shirt, revealing pale skin beneath. "I never expected you, Jasper Hopkins."

He caught her hands, his expression suddenly serious. "Delilah, before we go any further, I need you to know something. Whatever happens tomorrow . . . whether I remember you or not? This is real. You are real to me. The most real thing I've ever known."

She felt tears threatening again and blinked them away. "Don't. Don't talk about tomorrow."

"Okay," he agreed, kissing her forehead, her cheeks, the corner of her mouth. "Just tonight, then."

Their clothes fell away piece by piece, a gradual unveiling. Jasper's hands were gentle but confident as they explored her body, finding places that made her gasp and arch against him. There was an urgency to their movements, a desperation born of limited time. Jasper moved with deliberate care, his eyes never leaving hers, as if memorizing every expression, every sigh. She watched him watching her, both of them fully present in this moment that would have to last forever, somehow.

Later, tangled in sheets and each other, they talked in the hushed tones of new lovers sharing secrets. Jasper told her about his childhood obsession with historical markers, how he'd make his parents stop at every bronze plaque they passed. Delilah confessed to a brief career as a teenage troublemaker, using minor spells to rearrange items in the general store. "Troublemaking was always my sister's department. My attempts to keep up with Scarlett were always a little pathetic."

"I would've liked to know you then."

"You know me now," she reminded him.

"I do." He pulled her closer, his heartbeat strong and steady against her cheek. "And I'll know you tomorrow, too. Even if I don't remember."

The words were a knife twist, but Delilah said nothing, letting the rhythm of his breathing lull her into sleep. Whatever tomorrow brought, they had this night. It would have to be enough.

Morning dawned clear and crisp, sunlight streaming through the window to paint golden stripes across the rumpled bed. Delilah woke to discover Jasper was already awake, watching her with that same intensity she'd seen last night.

"Creepy," she murmured, but she was smiling.

"Beautiful," he countered. He reached out to brush her hair back from her face.

Neither made a move to get up. Instead, Jasper pulled her closer, his arms wrapping around her as if he could somehow stop time if he held on tight enough.

"We should probably . . ." Delilah began, but let her words trail off.

"Probably," Jasper agreed, pressing a kiss to her forehead. "But not yet."

As they lay there in silence, she tried to memorize the feel of him, the rhythm of his breathing, the way the light looked against his skin. She stored these details away like treasures: the small scar above his eyebrow from a childhood fall, the way his fingers traced patterns on her skin as if mapping territory he intended to revisit.

"I wish we had more time," she whispered finally.

Eventually, Delilah's sense of responsibility became too heavy a weight. They dressed, stealing kisses between buttons and zippers, reluctant to break the spell of the night before.

The inn's dining room was serving a tourist-friendly breakfast buffet, complete with pancakes shaped like witch hats and orange juice labeled "Magic Potion." Scarlett and Nate were already at a table, heads bent together in hushed conversation that stopped abruptly when they spotted Delilah and Jasper.

"Well, well, well," Scarlett drawled, her eyes dancing with mischief. "Look who's here."

"Morning," Delilah replied, sliding into a chair with as much dignity as she could muster. But a flush rose to her cheeks.

"Sleep well?" Nate asked, his expression perfectly innocent except for the slight twitch at the corner of his mouth.

"Or at all?" Scarlett asked, mock-innocently.

Delilah reached for the pot of coffee at the center of the table, desperate for caffeine and a change of subject. As she poured, she noticed an old lamp on the sideboard behind Scarlett, one she didn't recognize from the inn's usual decor. It was ornate, made of tarnished brass with a dusty shade that had certainly seen better days.

"What's that?" she asked, nodding toward it. "More additions to the 'authentic witch experience'?"

Scarlett glanced back. "No idea. It was here when we came down."

Curious, Delilah rose and went to examine it. "Since when did we have oil lamps in the dining room?" She reached to turn it on, but nothing happened. "Great, another thing in this place that's broken."

She gave the lamp a little shake. "Typical. Everything's

falling apart, and we're stuck having breakfast surrounded by plastic cauldrons and—"

The lamp shuddered in her hands, growing suddenly warm, then hot. Delilah dropped it with a yelp, jumping back as it began to twist and stretch, the brass melting and reforming into limbs, the shade collapsing into long, dark hair.

In seconds, where the lamp had been, a woman now stood —lanky, with wild hair and wide, delighted eyes.

"Surprise!" she announced, throwing her arms wide.

"*Luna*!" Delilah and Scarlett shrieked in unison.

"In the flesh. Finally." Luna grimaced, rolling her shoulders as if working out a cramp. "Do you have any idea how uncomfortable it is to be a lamp for three hours? I think I've got a crick in my . . . well, everything."

Delilah launched herself at her younger sister, nearly knocking them both over with the force of her embrace. Scarlett was right behind her, turning it into a three-way hug that threatened to topple them all to the floor.

"You're here! You actually came!" Delilah cried.

"Of course I came," Luna said, squeezing them back. "Sorry it took me a while to get all your messages. Karpathos isn't exactly known for great communications."

"Karpathos?" Scarlett pulled back to look at her sister. "What, like the Greek island? What were you doing there?"

"Studying with a coven that worships Proteus," Luna explained, as if it were obvious. "Actually, you'd really have enjoyed it, Del. Proteus was a god who hated talking to strangers so much he used to shapeshift so they couldn't find him. He'd become a lion, or a tree, or water, even. Just to avoid humans and their stupid questions."

Delilah grinned. "Sounds like my kind of guy."

"The Proteans were teaching me shapeshifting, but I had to

321

come here before I finished my lessons. So I'm not exactly great at it yet. Which you might have noticed when I got stuck as a lamp."

"A lamp," Jasper repeated faintly from the table, looking like he was seriously questioning his sanity. "The sister was a lamp."

Luna's attention snapped to him, her eyes narrowing with interest. "And who might this be?"

"Jasper Hopkins," Delilah said, suddenly feeling shy. "He's the county archivist. And, um . . . my . . ."

"Boyfriend," Jasper supplied helpfully, rising to shake Luna's hand. "It's nice to meet you. I've heard a lot about you."

"Boyfriend!" Luna's eyebrows shot up, her gaze darting between Jasper and Delilah with undisguised delight. "Well, well, well. Looks like I missed quite a lot."

"You have no idea," Nate said dryly, the only one at the table who seemed entirely unfazed by a woman transforming from a lamp. "Pull up a chair, Luna. We've got apocalypse scenarios to discuss."

As they settled around the table, Luna was quickly brought up to speed on Jasper's involvement in their predicament, though she claimed to have gathered most of the details about the magicians and Kelly's kidnapping while in her lamp form.

"So you've been eavesdropping," Scarlett accused.

"I prefer the term 'passive reconnaissance,'" Luna replied. "And it's a good thing I did, or I'd be completely lost now." She turned to Jasper with a sympathetic expression. "I take it you're the only one who can get us the spell we need. And when you do . . ."

"Well, it's located out of town," he said. "So . . . yeah."

Luna's romantic heart was clearly visible in her pained

expression. "There has to be another way. I wonder if I could shapeshift into a version of Jasper. Would that—"

"Are you able to become a perfect copy of another person?" Scarlett interrupted.

"Uh," Luna sighed. "I'm not able to become a perfect copy of a lamp. So no."

"I wish there was any other way, but I just—" Scarlett took Delilah's hand, but then she abruptly paused, and her face went blank. "I'm . . . um . . . sorry, what was your name again? I'm sure I know you, but I can't seem to . . ."

"Scarlett," Delilah whispered, her heart sinking. "I'm Delilah. Your sister."

Recognition flickered across Scarlett's face, then solidified. "Right! Delilah! Sorry, I don't know what's wrong with me today."

But the damage was done. The implications hung in the air, too awful to ignore.

"Oh, man," Nate said quietly. "That's so much worse than last night. You okay, Scar?"

Scarlett gave her head a little shake, like she had water trapped in her ears. "What just happened?"

Nate put his arm around her. "It's okay, babe. You're okay. You just forgot something for a second."

"No no, that's not possible," Luna said, although she'd just seen it with her own eyes. "We're witches. We're immune."

"The breakdown is accelerating," Jasper said. "We saw a lot of evidence last night, at the um . . . you know, the place we were at. With the singing." He sighed. "Oh shit. Me, too."

"But that means . . ." Delilah began, unable to finish the thought.

"It means we're out of time," Nate finished for her.

"Mama," Scarlett said suddenly. "Where's Mama? Shouldn't she be down for breakfast by now?"

"She's been kidnapped by the magicians," Delilah said gently. "Remember?"

Delilah and Luna exchanged stricken looks. "It's happening to witches," Luna said, horrified. "The forgetting should never, ever happen to witches."

In that moment, Delilah knew there was no more delaying, no more hoping for another solution. The forgetting spell was collapsing around them, and with it, any chance of saving Oak Haven without sacrifice.

"We have to go," she said quietly, taking Jasper's hand. "To the county clerk's office. Now."

Jasper nodded, squeezing her hand. "I know."

"I'll go with you," Luna offered. "Maybe between the three of us—"

"No." Delilah shook her head. "Stay here with Scarlett. If we have any chance against the magicians, we have to all get our powers back. That means putting an end to Saturnalia, which means breaking the magician wards up at the oak grove. You figure that bit out, and organize everyone for what comes next. We'll handle this."

Luna looked like she wanted to argue, but something in Delilah's expression stopped her. Instead, she simply nodded, reaching out to hug her sister again. "Be careful," she whispered.

"I will," Delilah promised. They both knew the danger wasn't physical.

As they prepared to leave, gathering coats and car keys, Jasper pulled Delilah aside, his expression solemn. "It's going to be okay." He kissed her then, soft and sweet and full of promises they both knew he couldn't keep. "Let's go."

CHAPTER 27
A CHRISTMAS TO FORGET

Driving out of Oak Haven, Jasper kept both hands at ten and two on the steering wheel. His allegiance to driver's ed guidelines had never left him. Also, having something to hang on to felt both right and necessary at the moment. He glanced at Delilah in the passenger seat. "So once we get the spell, you'll need to figure out exactly how to use it. Agnes wasn't exactly forthcoming with details."

"I'm assuming it will all be clear from the parchment," Delilah replied, her voice tight. She hadn't stopped fidgeting since they'd left town. "There'll be some sort of instructions."

"Like IKEA furniture, with fewer leftover screws. Hey, so, you remember your cover story, right?" Jasper had taken great pains to invent a story that his future self would deem at least glancingly plausible. "It may not be easy to get me to do what you want."

She smiled, a bit weakly. "I remember. Don't worry, I'll get you to take me to your office."

I don't know, he thought suddenly. *Seems awfully risky to drive to my office right now. Why are we even doing this? Something about a document?* He frowned, trying to sort through the fog that seemed to be settling in his mind. He shook his head slightly, hoping that might dislodge the growing confusion.

"Jasper? Are you okay?"

"Fine," he muttered, though he wasn't. His thoughts were like papers scattered by a strong wind, and he was frantically trying to gather them before they blew away entirely.

They passed the Lost Fox Inn, then the local veterinary hospital, then the combination convenience store and gas station. Familiar landmarks, certainly. Yet somehow everything looked slightly wrong. Did he even know this place?

"We were talking about the spell," Delilah prompted. "From Agnes Bartlett's hiding place."

"Oh sure, Agnes Bartlett." He knew that name well; her portrait hung near the stairs that led to his office. But any context had disappeared from his mind. The *who* was clear enough, but the *why* . . . that was fading fast. "Agnes, yes, of course."

He noticed Delilah watching him closely, her eyes filled with an emotion he couldn't quite place. Worry? Sadness? *Oh dear,* he thought, *why does she look so sad? What's troubling her so much?*

And more importantly . . .

Who is this person?

The question struck him with such force that he instinctively hit the brakes and pulled the car sharply onto the shoulder. His tires crunched on gravel as Jasper put it in park. His heart hammered in his chest.

"Jasper?" The strange woman reached for him.

He recoiled, pressing himself against the driver's door. "I'm sorry, but I don't . . . Who are you? What are you doing in my car?"

Her face crumpled for a split second, then recovered. "You don't remember me."

It wasn't a question.

"Should I?" He adjusted his glasses nervously. *Get it together, Jasper. People don't just materialize in cars! Clearly you invited her in.* "I mean, obviously I should, since you're in my car, but I . . . I'm drawing a blank here."

She took a deep breath. "My name is Delilah Melrose. I'm an archivist specializing in document preservation. You called me about a very unusual find."

"I did?" This sounded plausible. He did occasionally consult with other archivists.

"Yes. Someone filed a liquor license for J&J, Incorporated at 278 West 113th Street. You were quite puzzled by it."

Jasper blinked rapidly. The liquor license. Yes, that was real. He remembered seeing it, remembered being perplexed by the impossible address. But he definitely didn't remember calling this woman. *Clearly I must've, though.*

"That's right," he said cautiously. "The address can't exist."

"Exactly. And when you drove out to investigate, you found some unusual things. You contacted me because of my expertise in historical document authentication."

Oh yes, something was coming back. He could picture himself driving away from work, hoping to avoid the office Christmas party. But everything after that was a total blank. *God, how embarrassing.*

"And now we're going to your office," she continued gently, "because you believe you've found a historical document that might explain the discrepancy."

"I see." He didn't, not really . . . but admitting total confusion seemed far worse than playing along. When one discovers a beautiful woman in one's car, one tries one's best to avoid looking like a complete idiot. "And this document is . . ."

"Behind Agnes Bartlett's portrait. You noticed something unusual about the frame yesterday and wanted me to take a look."

She was so specific, so confident. And she knew about the liquor license, which wasn't something a random stranger would ever guess. Still, the gaping maw in his memory was unsettling.

"I'm sorry," he said, restarting the car. "I must have hit my head or something. Things are a bit . . . fuzzy."

"Everything's okay, Jasper." Her voice held a kindness that seemed excessive for whatever professional relationship this (presumably) was. "Let's just get to your office."

As he eased his car back onto the road, Jasper couldn't shake a strange feeling that something profoundly odd was happening. He stole glances at the woman beside him—Delilah Melrose, she said. She kept stealing glances at him too, which only increased his discomfort. Each time their eyes met, she quickly looked away, as if he'd caught her out somehow.

By the time they pulled into the county clerk's office parking lot, Jasper's discomfort had taken the form of a tight knot in his stomach. Had they had a conversation yesterday that he'd completely forgotten? Was he losing his mind? Dementia at thirty-five seemed extreme, but what other explanation could there be?

"Ready?" Delilah asked as he cut the engine.

No, he thought. *Not remotely*. But he nodded anyway, committed to seeing this bizarre situation through.

Toby was at his usual post behind the reception desk when they walked in, his eyes widening comically at the sight of Jasper.

"Holy shit!" Toby exclaimed, jumping to his feet. "You're alive!"

"Uh, yup," Jasper said, confused. "Was there some notion I might not be?"

"You joking?! Everyone's been going crazy, looking for you. The boss filed a missing persons report! Goddamn cops came by to interrogate everybody, for Christ's sake!"

"Police?" Jasper repeated weakly.

"Yeah, that's what happens when you disappear for over a week!"

A week? Jasper felt the floor tilt beneath him. Not just a few hours, not just a day. More than a week was missing. "I, um . . . I don't really know . . ."

"He had an accident," Delilah interjected smoothly. "A fall. He hit his head pretty badly."

"You had. A fall," Toby's skepticism dripped from every syllable.

"Yes. I took him to the hospital. The doctor said to expect some temporary memory issues but assured us he'll be fine in a few days."

Toby's eyes darted between them, a slow, leering smile spreading across his face. "A fall," he repeated, this time exaggerated air quotes. "Did he fall on you, sweetheart?"

"That's very rude. Jasper is a colleague of mine. I'm a document preservation specialist."

"Oh ho, I bet you are." Toby's grin widened as he leaned toward Jasper. "Listen, Jas. Next time you pick up a little stranger? Just call in sick like a normal person, okay? The boss is seriously pissed. So are the clerks in the other departments, even that anonymous benefactor of yours called. He's pissed off, too. Everybody's pissed off, dude."

"We really need to get to the archives," Delilah said firmly.

"Sure, sure." Toby waved them through. "Hey and uh, Merry Christmas."

Their walk to the basement felt interminable, with Jasper's mind desperately trying and failing to fill an impossible gap in his memories. Over a week, Toby said. He'd lost over a week.

"This way . . ." Jasper ushered Delilah down the basement stairs. He was overwhelmed with gratitude to be on familiar ground. The archives were his domain, the place where everything made sense.

"The portrait you mentioned is right at the bottom there." The stern-faced woman gazed down at them with the same judgmental expression she'd worn for centuries.

"Perfect," Delilah said. "Can you take it down? We need to look behind it."

Jasper balked. "Take it down? It's very fragile! We can't just—"

"Please, Jasper. It's important."

Something in her voice, an inexplicable note of desperation, made him hesitate. This was clearly important to her, though he couldn't fathom why. Despite his reservations, he gently, gently lifted the portrait from its hook. It was heavier than he remembered, with the ornate wooden frame adding considerable weight.

"Now what?" he asked, holding it awkwardly.

"Check in the back. There should be something there."

Jasper turned the portrait around, expecting to find nothing but dust and perhaps some faded label. Instead, a piece of yellowed parchment, its edges crumbling with age, was attached to the back. How had he never noticed this before? He'd personally rescued Agnes's portrait from a dumpster; surely he would have seen this before.

With careful hands, he extracted the parchment and

returned Agnes's portrait to the wall. "This is remarkable," he breathed, his historian soul momentarily overriding his confusion. "The parchment itself looks to be late seventeenth century, possibly early eighteenth? But I have no idea what language this is."

"Yes, it's exactly what we're looking for," Delilah said, reaching for it. "I should take this with me . . . for . . . um . . . proper preservation."

Jasper instinctively pulled it back. "I'm sorry. I can't just let you take this. It could be of significant historical value. There are protocols, procedures for handling artifacts of this age."

"Jasper." Delilah's voice was gentle but firm. "That's exactly why you called me, don't you remember? My expertise is in document preservation. This is precisely why *you asked me* to be here."

He hesitated, looking from the parchment to Delilah and back again. Her story was plausible, more or less. And yet . . .

"I don't remember calling you," he admitted. "I don't remember this parchment. I don't remember the past week at all."

Her expression softened. "The doctor said memory loss was normal after a concussion. It'll come back eventually."

Would it, though? Jasper wasn't convinced. But he also couldn't think of a better explanation for what was happening. And if he had specifically reached out to this specialist for help, refusing her now would be quite the dick move. Reluctantly, he handed over the parchment.

"Thank you," Delilah said, carefully placing it in the inside pocket of her coat. "This means more than you know."

She lingered, looking at him with an expression that made him deeply uncomfortable. Studying him, almost.

"Was there something else?" he asked when the silence stretched too long.

Delilah blinked rapidly. To Jasper's horror, he realized there were tears in her eyes.

"I just want you to know," she said, her voice barely above a whisper, "that the time we spent together was . . . important to me."

Jasper stood frozen, utterly at a loss. *What in hell am I supposed to say to that?* "Time we spent . . . What, in the car?"

A small, sad smile. "Yes. In the car."

"I'm sorry," he said inadequately. "I wish I could remember more."

"It's okay." She straightened her shoulders, visibly composing herself. "I should go."

"Do you need a ride somewhere? I could—"

"No." The word came out sharper than either of them expected. "No, thank you. I'll manage."

Before he could respond, she was gone, her footsteps echoing up the stairs, leaving Jasper alone in his office with a gaping hole in his memory and a week's worth of unfiled paperwork on his desk. He gazed at the catastrophe his unattended office had become and let out a deep sigh. "Merry Christmas to me."

Delilah made it exactly three-tenths of a mile from the county clerk's office before sobs overwhelmed her. She leaned against a maple tree, its bare branches offering no shelter from the winter sky.

He didn't know her. After everything they'd shared—the

kisses, the conversations, the night wrapped in each other's arms—Jasper had looked at her with nothing but confusion and embarrassment.

Of course, she'd known this would happen from the moment she'd understood Agnes's plan. No, much earlier. From the moment he'd first smiled at her, she'd known. But the knowing hadn't prepared her for the reality. That blank look in his eyes, the careful politeness of a man dealing with a stranger's inexplicable emotional outburst.

"Such a damn cliché . . ." She wiped angrily at her tears. "Crying by the side of the road like I'm in some goddamn Nicholas Sparks novel."

Making things even worse? She had no ride back to town. In their rush to secure the spell, they hadn't bothered to think through the logistics. Now she was stranded. Magicless, miles from home, with no way back except her own feet.

She pushed off from the tree, determined to at least start walking. Maybe some physical exertion would help distract from the ache in her chest. One foot in front of the other. Left, right, left, right. Basic stuff, really. Even a heartbroken witch could manage that much.

A crackle of energy in the air made her pause. A familiar shimmer of a portal materializing rippled the winter air, and then Luna stepped through, her wild hair catching the light.

"Del!" Luna rushed forward, enveloping her big sister in a fierce hug. "Oh God, you're crying . . ."

Delilah collapsed into her embrace, letting Luna hold her up as her own strength failed. "I got the spell," she managed between sobs. "But he's gone, Luna. When he looked at me, there was nothing in his eyes at all."

"I'm so sorry, Del . . ." Luna stroked her hair, a gesture so reminiscent of their mother that it only made Delilah cry harder. "It's not fair. None of this is fair."

Delilah took a few deep breaths and wiped her face with her sleeve. "Okay . . . okay, sorry. Pulling it together, I promise . . . How did you find me, anyway?"

"Locator spell. Scarlett realized that you'd left in Jasper's car and that you'd need help getting back to town. Some of the witches are waiting for us just outside the grove. I'm going to try to bust up those magician wards. I hate to rush you, but we probably should get going."

Delilah nodded, drawing another deep breath to steady herself. "Let's roll. Believe me, I want this to work more than anyone."

"Hey . . ." Luna wrapped her big sister in one more hug. "I truly am sorry everything turned out like this. I know you fell hard for that bookmark with legs."

"Oh my gods . . . You've been home for about ten seconds and you're *already* spending too much time with Scarlett."

Luna opened another portal back to Oak Haven. Before stepping through, Delilah glanced back toward the county clerk's office, barely visible in the distance.

"Goodbye, Jasper . . ." She turned away, following her sister into the shimmering light.

CHAPTER 28
DO YOU WANNA BUILD A CLONE MAN?

The witches gathered just beyond the perimeter of the grove in a fretful clump. Above and beyond towered the massive oaks, with their gnarled roots and whispering leaves. For centuries, the grove had been the wellspring of the witches' power. The beating heart of their town. Now, it was as unreachable as the moon.

The magicians had encircled the area with an intricate web of formidable wards, far surpassing those that safeguarded their bustling casino. These wards created an impenetrable barrier, preventing anyone (witch or otherwise) from stepping foot into the sacred grove without the magicians' say-so. The witches could sense the wards from a hundred yards away: an unnatural, imposing blockade that made their skin itch and their stomachs go sour. There was nothing they could do except linger at the bottom of the hill, staring helplessly up at their stolen birthright.

When Delilah stepped out of Luna's portal, she couldn't help but notice how pathetic the witches looked. Quite the sorry little battalion, armed with nothing but hope and, thanks to her sacrifice, an ancient parchment.

Delilah said a silent prayer that the key to their victory lay in Agnes's old spell. *It has to*, she thought. *It has to be worth it.*

"You got it," Scarlett said eagerly when Delilah approached with the parchment in hand. "The portal spell."

"The very same," Delilah confirmed. "Although, what language this is, I have no clue. Hopefully it contains an incantation for moving entire structures across vast distances."

Jerusha peered at the text, her wrinkled face scrunching in concentration. "I can read it, clear as day. The incantation is complex but not impossible."

"Only one problem." Aphra expressed what they all knew but didn't want to say. "We've got no magic to power it."

The ritual to end Saturnalia was as important as the one that began it. Without proper closure, the witches' powers remained locked in the oak grove's crystalline trees. Inaccessible and dormant.

"I ought to be able to fix that," Luna said. "I'll break through."

Delilah and Scarlett gazed at their baby sister with a bubbly mixture of pride and doubt. Luna was powerful, sure . . . but would it be enough?

"First off, let's try something straightforward." Luna rolled up her sleeves. "The wind-bending technique I learned in Mongolia."

She positioned herself at the edge of the wards, her arms moving in fluid, circular motions. The winter air responded, swirling around her in a miniature cyclone that grew more and more intense, with leaves and small branches caught in its vortex. With a powerful thrust, Luna directed the whirlwind against the invisible barrier. The air crashed against the wards like water against stone: impressive to witness, but ineffective. The barrier didn't even ripple.

"Okay, Plan B," Luna muttered, shaking out her hands. "Let's try the Warlpiri method."

This time, Luna crouched low to the ground, pressing her palms against the frozen earth. Delilah recognized the Australian telekinesis Luna had been so excited about during their travels. A tremor ran through the ground, small at first, then building in intensity until small rocks and clumps of earth began to rise, hovering a few inches above the ground.

With a grunt of effort, Luna sent the debris hurling toward the barrier. Each stone and clod hit the invisible wall with a dull thud before falling harmlessly to the ground.

"Well, shit." She brushed the dirt from her hands. "Let's try something a bit more . . . creative."

Over the next hour, Luna worked her way through a National Geographic–level compilation of obscure spells. If David Attenborough had ever done a BBC series on magic, it would have looked roughly like this. She tried the shapeshifting techniques of the Greek Proteans, transforming herself into mist to slip through the barrier. She attempted the death-defying illusions she'd learned from trickster spirits in Haiti. She tried a technique from the mountains of Armenia that involved aggressive throat singing.

Nothing worked. The wards would not be smashed, or tricked, or sung into submission.

Finally, Luna sat heavily on a fallen log, sweat beading her forehead despite the winter chill. "I'm out of ideas," she admitted. "I keep thinking there's one more thing . . . or maybe two? But I can't remember now. Everything I *can* remember, I tried . . . But it's not enough."

Delilah plonked down beside her sister, the weight of their

failure pressing down on them both. "So that's it, then. We're stuck in a perfect trap."

Scarlett joined them on the log. "We need magic to break the wards, but we can't get our magic back until we break the wards."

"Catch-22." Luna sighed.

Jerusha nodded grimly. "And without our magic, we don't have enough power to use the portal spell to move the . . . you know, the thing. The big thing."

"Casino," Luna whispered gently.

"Right, right . . ."

"I can't believe this," Delilah said bitterly. "I gave up Jasper for nothing. I sent him away, and we're no better off than before."

No one argued. What could they say? It was the truth, plain and simple. The portal spell had been their last, best hope; a huge sacrifice had been made to obtain it, and it may as well have been an onion dip recipe.

"Maybe we could try again tomorrow," Aphra suggested without much conviction. "Luna could rest, recharge . . ."

"It won't make a difference," Luna said, shaking her head. "The wards are too strong, too complex. This isn't the work of a few stage magicians playing at real power. This is old magic, the kind that reshapes reality."

The same kind of magic Agnes Bartlett had used to move an entire barn across space and time, Delilah thought. The kind of magic that had created Oak Haven in the first place. "It's weird, isn't it," she said aloud. "Our whole lives everybody told us that the magicians were a joke. Turns out they aren't that much different from us."

"They are *hugely* different!" Jerusha said fiercely. "Don't you ever speak like that again. We would never treat them this way. We'd never treat anyone this way."

"Anyway, we're screwed." Scarlett stood up, brushing off the back of her coat. "Mama's trapped in some interdimensional limbo, we're powerless, and the town is being turned into an increasingly tacky tourist trap with every minute that ticks by. I don't know about you guys, but I could use a drink. Or twelve."

No one argued with that assessment either.

The pub was mercifully empty of tourists in the late afternoon. Dayo, bless her, took one look at their faces and immediately started lining up shots.

"That bad, huh?" she asked, sliding glasses across the bar.

"And then some," Scarlett replied. "We're officially out of options."

"Did something happen with . . . you know?" Dayo's eyes flickered to Delilah.

"It's done," Delilah said flatly. "He's gone. And it was for nothing."

The liquor burned as it went down her throat, a welcome distraction from the hollow feeling in her chest. She pushed her glass forward for a refill.

"I'm really sorry," Dayo said, pouring generously. "About all of it."

"That makes all of us."

The witches claimed a table in the corner, away from the windows where tourists occasionally peered in with camera phones at the ready. The afternoon stretched into early evening, marked by rounds of drinks and increasingly despondent conversation.

"You know what I don't understand?" Luna said, gesturing with her glass. "How the magicians got so powerful. All of a sudden, they've got magic that rivals what our ancestors could do?"

"They've been planning this for years," Aphra pointed out. "Ever since their last attempt failed."

"But where did they learn it?" Luna pressed. "That kind of power doesn't just appear overnight. I've traveled all over, studied with some of the most powerful magical practitioners in the world. Even they couldn't pull off what these magicians are doing."

"Maybe they found a wellspring," Jerusha suggested. "An untapped source of magic."

"Or maybe they're channeling power from somewhere else," Scarlett added, her eyes unfocused as she contemplated her drink. "Like, siphoning it off."

"From where, though?" Delilah asked. "Their headquarters in Vegas? Come on."

The conversation circled uselessly, theories rising and falling like the level of liquid in their glasses. By the time Zahir arrived, lugging bags of groceries for the pub's kitchen, they had exhausted both their ideas and most of their hope.

"Ladies!" Zahir called cheerfully as he bustled past their table. "You all look terrible. Day drinking on a Tuesday? Kelly Melrose would never approve."

"Well, I'll tell ya what, Z," Scarlett said, slurring a bit. "I'd give anything to have my mother come storming into the pub to give us a dressing-down for getting drunk before dinner. Seriously, anything."

"Did you get the . . ." Zahir made a vague gesture with his hand. "The thing?"

"The spell? Yes." Delilah shrugged. "For all the good it does us."

Zahir paused, setting down his bags. "No luck at the grove, I take it?"

"The wards are impenetrable," Luna confirmed. "Even with my powers intact, I couldn't make a dent."

"Damn." Zahir's cheerful demeanor faltered. "I was really counting on you folks to save the day."

"So were we," Aphra said grimly.

Zahir disappeared into the kitchen, the sounds of unpacking and preparations drifting out to them. Soon, he emerged with a tray of food.

"On the house," he announced, setting down plates piled with pub-food masterpieces. "Can't save the world on an empty stomach."

"Zahir, you angel." Scarlett reached for a scotch egg. "How do you always know exactly what we need?"

"You're a magic man, Zahir," Jerusha agreed, digging into a plate of nachos with surprising gusto. "Pure magic."

"I wish." Zahir laughed. "If I had even a fraction of your powers, I'd have this place cleaned up and the prep work done in seconds. Alas, I'm just a simple chef trying to keep you witches fed and functioning. A magic man I am not."

Not magic.

The words echoed in Delilah's mind, triggering a memory. Another Zahir, semi-transparent, surrounded by cats.

"Holy shit." She stood up so suddenly she nearly knocked over her glass.

"What?" Scarlett asked, alarmed. "What just happened?"

341

"Epsilon," Delilah said, heart racing. "Eps. The clone in the attic."

"The what now?" Luna looked confused.

"There is some magic left. Scarlett's failed kitchen doppelgängers."

Understanding dawned on Scarlett's face. "You're right, Del. They were literally made of magic. Too bad I got rid of them all."

"But you didn't, though. The, um, let's see, the fifth one. Epsilon. He has been hiding in the attic."

"What?! That little bastard!"

Zahir looked deeply concerned. "Hang on . . . *Who*?"

"I'm clearly missing something important here," Luna said, looking between her sisters. "There's a clone of Zahir in our attic?"

Scarlett nodded. "Zahir was working so hard, trying to run two kitchens at once, so I tried to conjure multiple Zahirs to help out."

Luna gasped. "Oh my gods, Scar . . . That's way too advanced. No offense but you aren't experienced enough to do a spell like that."

"Yeah, no shit. Wish you'd been here to tell me that at the time. It was a huge mess to mop up and apparently I didn't even get it all."

For the first time since leaving Jasper at the county clerk's office, Delilah felt a flicker of genuine hope. She grabbed her sister excitedly. "What do you think, Luna? Would that give us enough power, do you think?"

"I have no idea. I've been all over the world and I've literally never heard of anything like this."

"Well, what do you say, little sis?" Scarlett nudged Luna playfully. "You wanna meet a clone?"

CHAPTER 29
FATHER CHRISTMAS (GIVE US SOME MAGIC)

Delilah stood at the bottom of the attic stairs, clenching the parchment and staring up into the dark attic. The stairwell felt impossibly narrow and somehow like it was getting narrower still, like a nightmare where the walls kept closing in. Or that garbage compactor scene in *Star Wars*. That's about right, she thought. The garbage monster is coming for us all.

Behind her, Scarlett was doing her patented stress-pacing: three steps left, pivot, three steps right. She'd worn through the carpet in her bedroom doing that all through high school. Annoyed the hell out of Mama.

Ugh. Del instantly wished she hadn't thought about her mother. Would this absurd plan even work? Was Mama okay? Was she hurt? Would they ever see her again?

This was a spectacularly bad line of inquiry.

At the back of their little witch delegation, Luna and Jerusha huddled together whispering ideas back and forth. Beside them, Aphra leaned against the wall, methodically cracking her knuckles, an anxiety tell Delilah hadn't seen since childhood.

The stress is getting to us. We're all devolving.

"We need to get our story straight before we go up there," Delilah told them. "And quietly. The last thing we need is Eps overhearing us debate his sacrifice like we're discussing a dim sum order."

"Wait." Aphra gazed at Delilah, utter bafflement written all over her. "Who is Eps? I don't know anyone named Eps."

Luna leaned over and whispered in Aphra's ear. "Eps is the clone we're hoping to use as a source of magic."

"Oh right. Sorry, I . . . I don't know why I just forgot that. How could I have forgotten that?"

Luna gave Aphra's shoulder a friendly squeeze. "Don't feel bad. It's happening to everyone."

"Anyway, as I was saying . . ." Delilah was desperate to keep the conversation on track. Who knows how long they had before the forgetting had washed them all away. "We can't just waltz in and tell him we need to use him as a magical battery and, oh by the way, erase his entire existence."

"He has no 'existence,'" Scarlett replied sharply. "He's not a person. He's magic that's been put into a particular shape, that's all. And hey, I'm glad my magic enjoyed playing human for a while. But sorry, fun's over."

"We need to decide on the best approach," Luna interjected. "Do we use Eps to attack the wards around the grove or do we cut to the chase and use him to power the portal spell and move the casino?"

"Isn't it obvious?" Scarlett threw up her hands. "We go after the casino. Once the magicians are gone, their wards aren't an issue."

"Now hang on." Delilah was already envisioning all the ways this could go catastrophically wrong. Scarlett's plans had a tendency to be as solid as a chocolate teapot. "All we have to go on is the promise of a three-hundred-plus-year-old spell.

What if it doesn't work? We'll have wasted Eps and have nothing to show for it."

"It will work," Jerusha cut in. Her arthritic fingers traced the symbols on the parchment with a reverence that bordered on creepy. "The spell requires tremendous power, but between Luna's magic and what's contained in the clone, we probably have enough to move the entire structure."

"See?" Scarlett's smug expression made Delilah's palm itch with the phantom sensation of a slap spell she couldn't currently cast. "Go big or go home—that's what they say."

Delilah pinched the bridge of her nose, feeling the beginnings of a tension headache. "She said *probably*, Scar. We could expend all that magic and still fail."

Which would leave them where, exactly? Eps gone, no backup plan, Mama still trapped in dimensional limbo, and Delilah haunted by the memory of Jasper looking at her like she was a complete stranger. The thought of him created a queasy sensation in her chest.

"Respectfully, Jerusha," Aphra offered carefully, "it's not only a question of power. Eps has to participate willingly, or the magic might not work at all."

"*Willingly*?!" Scarlett's voice ricocheted off the walls. "Eps has no will. My gods, how many times do I have to explain it? He's a magical construct in the shape of Zahir."

Delilah rolled her eyes. "He had enough *will* to get himself up to the attic."

"He's a battery with feet," Scarlett insisted.

"He's been hiding up here for months and you had no idea. So maybe Eps *is* nothing but a battery. He still outsmarted the hell out of *you*."

Luna stepped between them, hands raised like she was directing traffic. "This isn't helping. We need to—"

The attic door swung open.

They all froze like teenagers caught sneaking cigarettes behind the gym. Eps stood in the doorway, arms crossed, wearing an expression that hovered somewhere between annoyance and resignation. Behind him, a fuzzy parliament of cats peered down at them with identical judgment in their mismatched eyes.

"I'll do it," he said flatly. "If for no other reason than to shut you people up."

Jasper Hopkins had spent a lot of Christmas Eves alone in his office. His parents traditionally took off for a Caribbean cruise— their annual escape from both familial obligations and the New England winter. He had no siblings nearby, no significant other, and a remarkably small circle of friends, most of whom were spending the holiday with their own families. His grandmother, the only person who'd ever made Christmas feel special, had been gone for decades.

Still, he generally found the experience of working on holidays to be not only satisfactory, but actually desirable. The building took on a peaceful quality when it was empty. No phones ringing, no doors slamming . . . The companiable silence usually allowed him to sink into the meditative rhythm of proper archival work.

Tonight was different.

He sat there at his desk, surrounded by a week's worth of paperwork: tax rolls, business licenses, birth certificates, and deed transfers, all demanding his immediate attention. But he found himself unable to focus on any of it. His eyes kept drifting to Agnes Bartlett's portrait, searching for . . . what, exactly? Some clue to explain his missing time? A hint about that strange woman who'd appeared and disappeared?

"This is ridiculous." He turned away from Agnes's intense stare and clicked on the small radio tucked on his bookshelf. A Christmas carol spilled out: Bing Crosby's velvet voice crooning about the sort of weather he most desired for the holiday. Jasper waited for his usual reflexive annoyance at holiday music to kick in, but instead found himself humming along.

What in the actual hell?

"I'm losing it," he said aloud, the words echoing in the empty basement. "Completely losing it."

The radio DJ announced the next song, "I'll Be Home for Christmas," as recorded by the Carpenters. Jasper felt an unexpected lump form in his throat. The melody washed over him, achingly familiar, and for a moment he could have sworn he heard another voice, not Karen Carpenter, but someone else. Someone far less polished but just as earnest . . .

He switched the radio off, blinking away the ridiculous moisture that had gathered in his eyes.

"Get a grip, Hopkins. It's a stupid song."

But it wasn't really the song. It was everything. The missing time, the strange woman, the way his colleagues looked at him with that mixture of pity and suspicion.

His eyes landed on the liquor license that had started this whole mess. J&J, Incorporated, 278 West 113th Street. As far as Jasper knew, there was no such address in the county.

Before he could talk himself out of it, Jasper grabbed his coat and keys. The paperwork could wait. What he wanted was answers.

The massive casino loomed against the darkening winter sky, its garish neon lights cutting through the twilight. Delilah stood with her sisters, and Jerusha, Aphra, and Eps at the edge of the parking lot, far enough from the entrance to avoid drawing attention but close enough to see the steady stream of tourists and gamblers making their way in and out of the revolving doors.

Eps looked more solid than he had in the attic, perhaps due to being outdoors or perhaps due to Luna's magical assistance. But he retained that unsettling translucence that marked him as not quite real. A small tabby cat curled around his ankles, one of several feline creations that had insisted on following him out of the attic.

Jerusha had spread the parchment across the hood of Nate's truck, tracing the symbols as she muttered translations under her breath. The others huddled around to hear whatever wisdom the aged witch might offer.

"This incantation is complex," Jerusha said, "but manageable. Agnes Bartlett was a meticulous record-keeper. Every step is clearly outlined."

"But can we do it?" Luna asked, eyes scanning the unfamiliar script. "This spell moved a barn, which is cool, but we're trying to move an entire high-rise."

"Actually, size isn't our primary challenge," Jerusha replied. "It's the people. Moving living beings requires significantly more power and precision than inanimate objects."

Scarlett frowned. "There must be hundreds of people in there."

"At least," Jerusha confirmed grimly.

"So where are we sending them?" Aphra asked, voicing the question they'd all been avoiding. "We need a destination."

Yet another argument broke out, with suggestions ranging from "the bottom of the ocean" (Scarlett) to "the Kalahari Desert" (Luna) to "Macao, because who'll notice" (Aphra).

Delilah was still wrestling with the ethics of what they were about to do. She pulled Eps aside. "You don't have to do this, you know. We can find another way."

Eps's semi-transparent features arranged themselves into an expression remarkably like Zahir's when he was being patient with a particularly difficult customer. "No, you can't. And that's okay."

"It's not, though. We're asking you to—"

"To serve the purpose I was created for," he interrupted. "Look, when Scarlett tried to unmake me the last time, she was just doing it to clean up a mistake she'd made. But this?" He gestured toward the casino. "This is worth it."

"Are you sure? Because an hour ago, my sister was calling you a 'magical battery with legs,' and I don't want you to think that—"

"That I'm sacrificing myself because your bickering annoyed me into oblivion?" His mouth quirked in a very Zahir-like smirk. "I'm not. I am magic given form, Del. Assuming my original form to save Oak Haven is obviously correct."

The tabby cat at his feet meowed plaintively, and Eps reached down to scratch behind her ears. "I do have one request, though."

"Name it."

"The cats. I know your mother will hate them, but—"

"She'll understand," Delilah said firmly. "After what you're doing for us, she'll welcome an entire clowder of cats."

"A clowder?"

"Group of cats. Luna taught me that one."

"Huh." He smiled faintly. "I've been calling them a 'catastrophe.'"

Despite everything, Delilah smiled. "That works."

"Delilah!" Scarlett called, waving them back over. "We need to get started."

"So start." She shrugged. "I'm useless here anyway."

Jerusha shook her head. "No, you can still join us reciting the incantation. Come stand over here. And Eps, you're with Luna."

Eps gave the cat one final scritch along her chin. "Meow," he told her.

As they rejoined the group, Delilah couldn't shake the feeling that they were making a terrible mistake. Not because of Eps—he'd made his choice—but because the power of the spell, the destination, the very nature of what they were attempting felt reckless in a way that went beyond even Scarlett's usual impulsivity. But on the other hand, what choice did they have?

"Where did we decide to send it?" Delilah asked as the group gathered their supplies.

"The Mojave Desert," Luna answered. "Isolated enough to minimize collateral damage, but not as challenging to reach as the Kalahari. And not immediately fatal to the occupants, unlike . . . uh . . ." Luna's eyes flicked at Scarlett ". . . some of the other suggestions."

Scarlett rolled her eyes. "*Whatever*. You guys are too nice."

"Here." Jerusha handed Delilah a slip of paper with her section of the incantation written out phonetically. "You'll be at the northern point. Luna east, Scarlett south, me west. Aphra and Eps will anchor the center."

Delilah looked down at the words, strange syllables that felt like they might burn her tongue when spoken. Then she looked up at the casino, its gaudy facade an insult to everything Oak Haven stood for. She thought of Papa, how he'd given up everything to start a totally new life with Mama, here among the witches. *This is for you too,* she told him silently.

It was time.

Jasper drove with the windows cracked despite the winter weather. He needed some sharp winter air to keep his thoughts clear. The radio played Christmas carols, and he found himself turning up the volume rather than switching it off. Each familiar tune seemed to tug at something buried deep in his memory, like trying to recall a dream upon waking.

He'd been driving aimlessly for nearly an hour when he spotted it: a massive structure rising above the tree line, completely incongruous with the surrounding landscape. It looked like someone had airlifted a Vegas casino and dropped it in the middle of rural Connecticut.

"That has to be it," he muttered, following the access road that wound toward the blinking lights.

As he approached, Jasper rehearsed what he would say to the management. Something professional but firm about improper paperwork and county regulations. He'd demand explanations about the impossible address and the mysterious J&J, Incorporated.

The parking lot was surprisingly full for Christmas Eve, cars with license plates from all over New England packed into neat rows. Jasper found a spot near the back, locked his car, and began walking toward the entrance, his breath fogging in the cold air.

He was about fifty yards away when something made him stop. A feeling, not quite déjà vu but similar, washed over him. He'd been here before. No, that wasn't right. He'd been somewhere like here. With someone. Someone important.

Jasper looked up at the casino, its neon signs casting multicolored shadows across the parking lot. For a moment, he thought he saw movement around the perimeter of the building. But when he blinked, there was nothing there.

He took another step forward, then another, drawn by some inexplicable compulsion. This place held answers, he was certain of it. Perhaps he should go inside?

A strange thrumming filled the air, like overburdened power lines. No—deeper, more resonant than that. The hairs on Jasper's arms stood on end. The ground beneath his feet began to vibrate subtly. Then not so subtly.

"What the—"

He gazed up at the casino and saw it sort of wobble, as if he was viewing it through rippling water. The edges of the building became indistinct, blurring into the night sky. Then all the lights flickered once, twice, three times . . . then stabilized in a way that seemed fundamentally wrong, as if they existed in a slightly different reality than everything around. The terrified shouts of hundreds of people echoed across the parking lot. And then, between one heartbeat and the next, the casino was gone.

Jasper stood frozen, staring at the empty space where, seconds before, a fifty-story building had towered over the treetops. Nothing remained. As if the casino had never existed at all.

"Right," Jasper said to empty air, his voice unreasonably

steady given the circumstances. "Okay. Fair enough. I am losing my mind."

Behind him, his little car waited in a parking lot that now served nothing at all. Above him, stars twinkled in a clear winter sky. And inside him, a strange grief blossomed. Not for the building, which was appallingly ugly and absolutely deserved to go wherever the hell it had gone. No, the grief was for something else. Something he couldn't name but knew, with absolute certainty, that he had lost.

CHAPTER 30

CHRISTMAS (BABY PLEASE GO HOME)

Once the incantation began, the air grew thick and foul, the consistency of milk left to expire in the sun. Delilah felt a surge of untamed magic writhe across her skin, far more powerful than anything she'd felt before. More savage, even alien. Ancient words poured from Jerusha's mouth like they'd been waiting centuries for this precise moment, each syllable carrying the weight of Oak Haven's very foundation.

Luna had planted herself facing east, her eyes glowing with borrowed magic as she channeled Eps's power through her own formidable abilities. Scarlett faced south, her voice steady despite the trembling of her hands. Jerusha commanded the west with a sort of timeworn resolve. And Delilah was turned toward north, feeling strangely calm as she completed the diamond of their spell-casting. In the center stood Eps. He was only barely visible now, a ghostly smear of color and fabric.

"Walls between shall crumble," Jerusha thundered, her voice carrying despite her age.

"Earth shall yield its grip," Luna responded.

"Structure shall be unmoored," Scarlett added.

"And what was here shall be elsewhere," Delilah completed.

The casino began to shimmer, its edges blurring like air rising from a summer pavement. Gaudy neon signs flickered, their lurid colors bleeding into the night air. The top hats stopped rotating, frozen in time.

It's working, Delilah thought with a mixture of exhilaration and disbelief. *It's actually working!*

"The next verse is . . ." Jerusha's voice faltered, her eyes going wide with panic. "The next verse is . . ."

Delilah's heart seized. *The spell can't be interrupted. Not now.*

"Mountains bow, waters part," Luna whispered urgently.

The old witch's face cleared. "Mountains bow, waters part," she continued, her voice gaining strength again.

Okay, back on track. Delilah felt sweat trickle down her back. *If Jerusha can just get through this incantation, everything should be fine. Except, wait . . . no!*

Somehow, she saw the next catastrophe coming without forming a coherent thought about it. Instead, an old nursery rhyme popped, unbidden, into Delilah's head:

This is the church, this is the steeple . . . but in this casino, too many damn people.

Some of them would be swept away with the building; perhaps *most* of them would. But without sufficient magic, some would be left behind. Maybe on the twenty-ninth floor, or the thirty-seventh floor, or the forty-second . . . There would suddenly be no floor underneath them at all.

Luna understood the situation, too, but her hands were occupied with casting. "Delilah!" she shouted. "You'll have to catch them! Remember the Walpiri!"

"The Walpiri taught me to move *a rock*," Delilah hollered back. "One rock, *singular*."

Naturally her other sister had to weigh in. "You caught Nate, though! Remember? By the Christmas tree?"

"Again," Del shouted, "singular."

"Principle's the same," Luna argued. "Use the wand, maybe that'll help!"

As she took the wand out of her coat, Delilah groaned at the thought of Mama learning she'd needed it in order to do her job as a witch. *Alas, I do, in fact, need my wand in order to do this job.* And then a worse thought: *Oh shit, I also need magic.* "Luna! How do you expect me to do this? I don't have any magic, remember?"

"Look down!"

Snowball, Eps's fluffy white cat with the mismatched eyes, was pawing at her ankle.

"She was forged from Eps, which means she's made from magic too."

"Aw, c'mon . . . you want me to use her for power?" Delilah said. "Poor Snowball!"

But if she didn't try, all those unsuspecting visitors, innocent folks from Woonsocket or Nashua or Brookline, who'd all been drawn to that trendy witch casino they'd seen on TikTok . . . They'd all tumble about six hundred feet and splatter across a frozen New England ground.

Snowball gazed up at her, meowing impatiently. Delilah picked her up and tucked her inside her coat. "Is this gonna work?" she asked the cat. She just meowed again, which wasn't helpful, so Del posed the same question to her far-more powerful sister.

"Damned if I know!" Luna's voice was cracking from exertion. "But this casino has about ten seconds before it's swallowed by the uh . . . by the big thing . . . you know. Anyway, chop chop."

"Okay." Delilah sighed heavily. She kissed the top of Snowball's head and whispered, "Good kitty. You're the best little gal ever." Then she lifted her wand. She squeezed her eyes tight, envisioning herself standing in the Great Sandy Desert. She tried to remember the smell of the sand, and how the sun felt on her skin. And after several deep, cleansing breaths, Delilah stretched out her arm and . . .

She caught them all. Forty-seven people, each one grasped by an invisible power. It was like conducting the world's strangest symphony. Every gesture of her wand controlled the descent of panicked humans who'd suddenly found themselves suspended in mid-air. With every life saved, the cat's purr against her chest surged, acknowledging and even approving this wild, unorthodox wielding of forbidden magic.

"Holy shit," Scarlett breathed, momentarily breaking her part of the incantation to watch her Grinchy sister saving Christmas tourists. "That's some Big Mary-Poppins Energy right there."

"Focus, ladies!" Jerusha's orders sliced through the chaos. "The spell is destabilizing!"

They refocused, and the spell flowed from their lips with renewed urgency. As the casino dissolved like sugar in hot tea, a sound like the unholy offspring of a thunderclap and a vacuum cleaner echoed across the sky. After a final, thunderous surge of power, the structure vanished entirely, leaving behind nothing but shocked tourists and a handful of profoundly confused casino employees who happened to be outside. Luna collapsed from the effort, landing on the frozen ground like a marionette with cut strings. Epsilon had disappeared entirely, as had Snowball.

But the other cats had survived; they were curled up on the pavement, grooming one another as if not a single interesting thing had occurred in the past hundred years. Delilah smiled down at them. *Don't you worry, kitties,* she thought, *I'll convince Mama to let us keep you around. Oak Haven could use a few cats ... and Epsilon deserves a furry memorial.*

"Holy mother of—" Scarlett stumbled backward, tripping over her own feet and landing hard on her butt. "Did we just ... did that actually work?"

Delilah stared, her mind struggling to process what her eyes were seeing. Or rather, what they weren't seeing. No tacky architecture. No rotating top hats. No magicians. "I think we did it," she managed, the words feeling inadequate for the sheer magnitude of what just took place. "We just . . . fixed the skyline."

Jerusha hobbled over to help Luna to her feet. "Breathe, child. The magic takes a heavy toll."

Luna's face was tuberculosis pale, her normally wild hair hanging limp with sweat. "That was ... intense," she wheezed. "Like trying to fit the entire Pacific Ocean through a drinking straw."

Meanwhile, rescued tourists and stray employees milled about, their expressions ranging from stunned disbelief to outright panic. One woman in a sparkly "WITCH PLEASE" T-shirt kept taking photos of the sky, as if her phone would reveal something her eyes couldn't see.

"Um, guys?" Scarlett gestured toward the increasingly agitated crowd. "What do we do with ... them?"

Aphra stepped forward, her expression resolute. "I'll handle it. I spent the last week pretending to be a 'genuine witch tour guide,' so I can certainly manage these folks." She straightened her shoulders and strode toward the confused group. "Ladies and gentlemen!" she called out, summoning the same theatrical presence she'd used during her Enchanted Yarn Experience. "On behalf of Oak Haven, I want to thank you for participating in our annual Holiday Illusion Spectacular!"

The tourists blinked at her in confusion.

"What you just experienced was a masterful example of mass hypnosis and state-of-the-art holographic projection," Aphra continued smoothly. "We hope you enjoyed this unique entertainment experience! Click like and subscribe for more."

"That's only for videos," Delilah called out. "Not real life."

"But I don't understand," a man in a plaid jacket protested. "I was up fifty bucks at blackjack!"

"All part of our famous immersive simulation," Aphra assured him. "Now I suggest you let me lead you back to your cars. It's Christmas Eve, after all. Surely you have families to visit." Amazingly, the crowd began to follow her, their confusion giving way to a sort of bemused acceptance. One woman was already telling her companion, "I told you those slot machines couldn't possibly be real. They were paying out way too much!"

"Aphra is a goddamn genius," Scarlett whispered. "Think they'll actually believe that whole 'Holiday Illusion' garbage?"

"They believed a casino materialized in the woods overnight," Delilah pointed out. "Safe bet they'll believe anything at this point."

The witches stood in stunned silence for a long moment, staring at an empty space where, seconds before, a garish monument to the great humbug had dominated the landscape. The afterimage was still burned into Delilah's retinas, like a ghost hovering in the cold night.

"Did we just kill a bunch of gamblers?" Scarlett asked suddenly, that thought clearly just occurring to her. "Like, the tourists and stuff?"

"The Mojave isn't exactly the surface of the sun," Luna

360

replied, still sounding winded. "They're probably just improperly dressed and super confused."

"So what's next?" Delilah asked. "We need to get to the oak grove, right? Finish Saturnalia and get our powers?"

Before anyone could answer, the air began to shimmer, coalescing into a rectangle of light. Within the rectangle appeared an enraged figure they recognized all too well: Ramona, the burgundy-suited magician who had taken Kelly.

Scarlett folded her arms across her chest and grinned wickedly. "What's next, you ask? Next, we get our people back."

CHAPTER 31
RUN, RAMONA, RUN

The air crackled with a sudden violence as a portal appeared, looking more hastily torn open than carefully crafted. Ramona emerged, looking distinctly unprepared for this particular battle. Her silver hair was disheveled, and the faint echo of other voices clung to the air around her, as if she'd been yanked suddenly away from some other (no doubt equally nefarious) task.

"What. Have. You. DONE?!" Ramona's face contorted with fury, and her power radiated outward like heat from a furnace, distorting space all around. "Do you have ANY idea of the punishments that will rain down on you?"

Scarlett stepped forward, chin lifted defiantly as she positioned herself between Ramona and her sisters. Delilah could see the slight tremor in her sister's hands. *That's not fear,* Del thought. *That's Scar restraining her own anger.*

"We did what we had to." Scarlett's voice was steady despite the dangerous electricity in the air. "That monstrosity was really bringing down property values."

Ramona's eyes narrowed dangerously, pupils contracting to

363

pinpoints of pure hatred. "You dare jest with me?" Each word left her lips like shards of ice. "What have you done to my people?"

Delilah felt a moment of genuine doubt flutter in her chest. *Did we go too far here?* But then she remembered her mother's absence, and her resolve hardened like frost on a windowpane.

"That's exactly what we're here to discuss." Scarlett rocked back and forth on her heels. "You want your people back? Give us ours."

"Where is our mother?" Delilah stepped forward to stand beside her sister, and she was pleased to hear her own voice coming out steadier than expected. "And Belinda, and the others you took."

Ramona's lip curled into a sneer, revealing teeth that seemed too white, too perfect. "You are in no position to make demands." But there was a flicker of something in her eyes. Calculation, perhaps, or the first seedlings of doubt.

Luna joined her sisters, positioning herself on Delilah's other side. "We just yeeted your entire operation to Location Unknown. I'd say that puts us in an *excellent* position to make demands."

"As for where they are now . . ." Scarlett said with exaggerated casualness, "I voted for dropping the whole mess in the bottom of the Mariana Trench. You guys have diving suits in the casino supply closet?"

Ramona's anger literally lifted her several inches off the ground, her luxurious boots hovering in the icy air. The air around her shimmered with heat distortion, despite the season. "You wouldn't dare!"

Luna tilted her head, looking at Scarlett with mock concern. "Oh, Scar . . . I don't know if they'll have time for diving suits." She turned to face their adversary. "The pressure at the bottom of the Trench is quite intense. They're probably pancaked already, no?"

Delilah bit back a smile. Luna had never been one for confrontation, but when she *did* join the fray, she always brought her A-game.

Ramona's face flushed an alarming shade of crimson. A pulse of energy emanated from her, strong enough to send dead leaves skittering across the ground at their feet. She looked to be one twitch away from a full-blown aneurysm.

"You will return our property and staff to their original location immediately," she commanded, and her voice resonated with a sort of material power that pressed against Delilah's eardrums.

"Sorry, no can do." Scarlett shrugged with exaggerated nonchalance, though Delilah noticed her sister shifting her weight subtly into a more defensive stance. "One-way trip, I'm afraid." She took a half-step forward, her expression hardening. "But here's what we can do: you release our mother and the others, and we'll give you the location. And don't worry, I didn't win the argument about the trench. They're not dead . . . yet."

A beat of silence stretched between them, broken only by the distant honk of some poor tourist who couldn't seem to find his way back to the main road. Behind the magician, the glowing rectangle reappeared. Delilah caught glimpses of ornate furnishings and the shifting movements of other figures through the shimmering doorway.

"You're bluffing," the magician's words practically vibrated. "You witches don't have the ability to open a portal that large."

"Umm, those fifty missing stories behind you suggest otherwise." Delilah gestured at a gaping void where the casino had stood. The starlight caught on her fingers, highlighting a tiny tremor of fear that she couldn't quite control. "You magicians should really pay closer attention to your real estate holdings, if you don't want to lose them. Wanna test what else we can do?"

Ramona's eyes flicked from sister to sister, assessing them all. Delilah felt the weight of her gaze like a bad touch, cold and invasive. The magician rolled her eyes and vanished into the rectangle of light.

Indistinct murmurings drifted through the portal, suggesting she was conferring with others. Delilah caught fragments—"impossible," "consequences," "retrieval"—but couldn't piece together the whole conversation. She exchanged glances with her sisters, raising her eyebrows in silent question. Luna shrugged minutely while Scarlett made a little thumbs-up gesture.

When the magician reappeared, her expression was marginally less murderous, though the air around her still shimmered with barely contained power.

"Very well. A trade. Your witches for our casino."

"It's not really a trade," Scarlett corrected, "so much as it is a hostage negotiation. And you're the ones who need to pay up."

The magician's nostrils flared, and for a moment, Delilah thought she might actually breathe fire. Instead, she pressed her lips into a bloodless line before responding. "Fine. They will be returned."

"That's just item one," Luna said firmly. She gestured toward the hill where the oak grove stood, its silhouette just visible. "The wards have to be removed."

"And we want all that tourist crap cleaned up immediately," Delilah added, feeling bolder with each passing moment. "And fix the forgetting spell you tried so hard to break."

Ramona's face twisted with contempt. "If witches had any

366

real skill," she said haughtily, "you could have solved all those issues easily."

A look passed between the sisters, a silent communication born from a lifetime of shared mischief. Luna cocked her head to one side, her expression suddenly innocent in a way that made Delilah brace herself.

"You know how my sister mentioned the Mariana Trench?" Luna's voice was light, conversational. "Well, that was far from the only idea we kicked around. Me, I'm known as the whimsical one, so my big idea was sending your casino to the surface of the moon." She tapped her chin thoughtfully, eyes wide with mock concern. "How good are magicians at holding their breath? Do you know, Del?"

"I think David Blaine does that pretty well . . ."

"Oh gosh, that's right!" Luna snapped her fingers in exaggerated realization. "So, what do you say, Magician Lady? Wanna find out which one we chose?"

Ramona's face went from red to white during this exchange, color draining away like water down a drain. A muscle twitched violently at the corner of her eye. Through the portal behind her, Delilah could see other figures moving with increasing agitation.

"All right," said the magician through gritted teeth. Each word seemed physically painful to pronounce. "You win."

Delilah felt a rush of triumph so intense it made her light-headed. "Fix it now," she added. "Not eventually, not tomorrow. Right now."

Another sudden disappearance, more conferring inside the light. Delilah caught sight of an older man with a silver-streaked beard gesturing emphatically, his face twisted with anger. After a moment, the magician reappeared again, her face twisted as if she'd just bitten into something rotten. Delilah could almost taste the woman's defeat in the air—bitter and metallic.

"Oh no," Delilah said without an ounce of sympathy. "Did we get you in trouble with your boss?"

"Shut up," snapped Ramona. "And step back."

The sisters exchanged glances, then took three synchronized steps backward. Aphra and Jerusha followed their lead.

A second portal appeared beside the first, this one darker, its edges ragged. Through it, Delilah could see a barren landscape stretching into what looked like infinite darkness. A void between realities that made her stomach lurch just looking at it. After a moment that felt like a lifetime, Kelly, Belinda, and three other Oak Haven witches stumbled through, blinking at the sudden change of scenery.

"Mama!" The word tore from Delilah's throat before she could stop it, raw with emotion she hadn't allowed herself to feel until now. She and her sisters rushed forward as one, colliding with their mother in a tangle of arms and relief so profound it felt like physical pain.

Kelly smelled like home: cinnamon and woodsmoke and that indefinable scent that had meant safety for Delilah's entire life. She clung to her mother, face pressed against her shoulder, suddenly a child again despite everything.

"It's all right, my darlings . . ." Kelly murmured, her hand cradling the back of Delilah's head. "I'm here now."

She looked remarkably unruffled for someone who'd been trapped in interdimensional limbo. Her silver-streaked hair was perfectly coiffed, her clothes unwrinkled as if she'd just stepped out for a moment rather than being held hostage in some non-Euclidean nightmare space. But when Kelly pulled back from the group hug, Delilah saw the dangerous gleam in her eyes as she glared at the magician.

"Ramona." Kelly's voice carried the chill of every New England winter at once. "I see your hospitality hasn't improved since our last encounter." Kelly straightened her already-straight jacket with a precise movement that Delilah recognized as her mother tamping down fury.

"This isn't over, Kelly," Ramona spat, her face contorted with the special hatred reserved for old enemies. "Not by a long shot."

"Oh, but I think it is." Kelly's voice was smooth as river stones and just as implacable. She stepped forward, positioning herself slightly in front of her daughters, still protecting them, even now. "You've lost, my dear. Yet again. Take your second-rate illusions and crawl back to wherever it is failed magicians go to lick their wounds."

Ramona's face twisted with rage so pure it was almost beautiful. "*Where are my people?*"

Luna nodded, her expression carefully neutral though Delilah could see the triumph in her eyes. "We've sent them to 35.0110° N, 115.4734° W. The Mojave, not Mariana. Go now, get them. And don't you ever come back."

"You'll regret this. All of you." Ramona's gaze swept over them, landing finally on Luna. Her eyes narrowed, focusing with predatory intensity. "Especially *you*."

The portal snapped shut with a sound like a thunderclap, leaving behind only a faint smell of ozone and the echo of Ramona's threat. For a moment, no one moved, as if afraid that the wrong words might somehow undo their victory.

Scarlett, naturally, found her voice first. "Why'd she single out Luna? I'm just as scary as Luna!"

Delilah had to laugh. "You so aren't."

"Hey!"

"Girls!" Kelly brushed some nonexistent dust from her sleeves. "No bickering, please. We've had one hell of a day."

"Mama." Delilah launched herself into another hug, burying her face against her mother's shoulder like she hadn't done since she was a child. Her voice came out muffled against Kelly's coat. "Are you okay? What did they do to you? Where were you?"

Kelly's arms came around her, strong and steady as always. "All excellent questions, darling. But perhaps better discussed somewhere warmer? And with a martini?"

"Two for me," Belinda Chatterjee called out. "I need one for each hand."

"Oak grove first," Jerusha insisted, and her voice carried a heavy authority. "We need to complete the Saturnalia ritual and reclaim our magic. No cocktail is more important than that."

Belinda harrumphed. "Says the woman who *hasn't* been sitting in a void for—oh wait! How long have we been gone? I hope we didn't miss the pageant?"

Scarlett went to Belinda and wrapped her in a warm hug. "We waited on the pageant. No pageant without you, Mrs. Chatterjee."

"Ladies, let's get back to town." Kelly was suddenly all business, and she gathered her dignity around her like a warm winter coat. "It's time to end Saturnalia properly."

The grove seemed to know they were coming. As the witches of Oak Haven approached, the trees swayed despite the absence of wind, their bare branches reaching toward the star-strewn sky as if in welcome. The crystalline frost that had encased the trees since the beginning of Saturnalia glittered in the moonlight, like thousands of tiny diamonds waiting to be reclaimed.

Most importantly, the magicians' wards were gone, vanished along with the casino and its operators. The witches moved freely up the hill, their breath visible in the cold air, their faces upturned toward the magic that awaited them.

Delilah walked between her sisters. For the first time in a very long while, she felt something like peace settling over her. They'd done it. They'd saved the town, rescued their mother, and sent the magicians packing. It was a victory by any measure.

So why did she still feel that hollow ache in her chest?

Because some victories come with sacrifices, a voice whispered in her mind. *And yours was Jasper.*

She pushed the thought away, focusing instead on the task.

The ritual to reclaim their magic mirrored the one that had begun Saturnalia. They encircled the largest oak, hands joined, words spoken in languages that predated Oak Haven itself. Kelly took her place at the head of the circle, her presence commanding attention without effort. "Sisters," she addressed the assembled witches, "we gather to reclaim what is rightfully ours. To take back the power we willingly surrendered, now enhanced by its temporary separation from our mortal forms."

The witches joined hands, forming a circle that pulsed with anticipation.

"As we come to the close of Saturnalia," Kelly continued, "we honor what we have learned in our time without magic. Strength of community. Ingenuity born of necessity. Resilience that defines us, not as witches, but as women. Now, we reclaim what is ours." Her voice grew stronger, filling the grove. "Not as a privilege, but as a responsibility. To protect our home. To preserve our history. To ensure our future."

As Kelly began the incantation, the frost clinging to the trees began to shimmer more intensely, pulsing in time with her words. The other witches joined in, their voices weaving together. Soon, Delilah felt a familiar tingle of magic stirring within her, a warmth that started in her core and radiated outward.

The crystalline frost melted into streams of golden light, flowing from the trees. Delilah watched in awe as the magic returned to its rightful vessels, filling each witch with reinvigorated power. She felt her own magic flood back, a homecoming so profound it brought tears to her eyes.

As the last of the light dissolved into the circle, a collective sigh swept through the grove. They were whole again. They were witches once more.

Kelly lowered her arms, her smile warm with satisfaction. "Saturnalia is ended. Our magic returns, stronger for its rest."

Cheers erupted from the assembled witches, hugs and laughter spreading through the group like wildfire. Families reunited, friends celebrated, and for a moment, all was right in Oak Haven.

Or, most of the women felt that way.

As the others began making their way back down the hill, toward homes and hearths and well-deserved holiday festivities, Delilah lingered. She found a quiet spot at the edge of the grove, perching on a fallen log that offered a view of the distant town. Oak Haven sparkled below, Christmas lights twinkling in the darkness. But as perfect as it all looked, there was something missing that she couldn't deny.

Jasper.

With her magic finally restored, Delilah couldn't help but think about how she might use it. After all, what's the point of having magic at all, if you don't use it to solve your problems?

Why not just take this wand Mama hates so much and straighten it all out? Maybe she could create a remembering spell, to counter the forgetting. A spell to bring him to her side. A spell to bind him to Oak Haven forever.

Yeah, she thought. *I could totally do that.*

But she wouldn't.

In her letter, Agnes Bartlett had written that magic wasn't a dress pattern to be adjusted for better fit. Some things couldn't —shouldn't—be "fixed," no matter how much you wanted to.

Jasper deserved a life unencumbered by the complications of loving a witch. A normal life, with a normal partner, in a normal town that didn't disappear from his memory every time he went to work. She should let him go find that.

"You okay?" Scarlett's voice came from behind her, unusually gentle.

"Yeah, Del," Luna said kindly. "Are you all right?"

"Not really." Delilah didn't turn around; her eyes remained fixed on the town below. "But I will be."

Her sisters settled beside her on the log, one on each side, and they all sat in companionable (not to mention unusual) silence for a long moment. Eventually Scarlett broke the mood with a deep sigh. "You know, Del, for what it's worth? I think you're making a mistake."

"Oh?"

"Yeah. I mean, look at Nate and me. We're making it work, even with the whole forgetting thing."

Del turned to look at her. "You told me he literally won't propose to you because of the forgetting spell. That's not exactly great."

Her sister shrugged. "Okay, you got me. It's not. But I mean . . . we're happy, though. A wedding would be cool but it's hardly the main point. The main point is obviously the fucking."

Luna covered her face with her hands. "Scarlett, oh my gods!"

"It is my job as middle sister to speak the truth," Scarlett declaimed. "Come what may. That's a double entendre, you know, *come what may*."

"I am begging you to stop," Delilah said with a chuckle. "Anyway, it's different for you guys. Nate grew up here, he has a hundred ex-pirate relatives in town. He's part of the fabric of Oak Haven. But Jasper's whole life is out there."

"So? Dayo moved here to be with Aphra, didn't she? Priti Chatterjee found herself a hot guy and talked him into moving to Oak Haven. It happens sometimes—it's not that weird."

"It happened to Papa," Luna offered quietly. "He had a different life before he and Mama met. But he chose her."

Of course Luna was right. Their father had been an outsider, a normal man just like Jasper, who'd stumbled into their magical world and chosen to stay, despite the costs. "It's not the same," she insisted, but suddenly her voice lacked conviction.

Scarlett shook her head. "No, I think Luna has a great point. My thought is, when you figure out the right spell, you cast it, consequences be damned."

Delilah snorted. "That's terrible advice, Scar. Advice like that is exactly what has gotten you into so many scrapes over the years."

"Maybe. But things have worked out pretty well for me, if you didn't notice." She nudged her shoulder against Delilah's. "What do you say, Luna? Should she go after Jasper or let him go?"

"Ohhhh I just got here. I met him for about two seconds."

"Come on," Scarlett urged. "This is the hour of sisterly advice. Let's have it."

"Well . . ." Luna leaned her head back and looked up at the

stars for a long time. "I've never been in love. So I can't say what I *would* do, much less what anybody else *should* do. But, I will say—" she broke away from gazing at the stars to lean her head on Delilah's shoulder "—I think it's lovely that you care enough about Jasper to let him go, if that's what he needs."

"Oh my gods," Scarlett groaned. "Your advice *sucks*, Luna."

In the valley below, Jasper finally got back into his car and drove away, his taillights disappearing around a bend in the road.

"Come on." Scarlett stood, offering her hand. "Let's go home. Zahir's cooking up a feast, and I want to get home before Belinda has chugged every martini in Oak Haven."

Delilah let herself be pulled to her feet, knowing that home, with all its chaos and complications, was exactly where she needed to be right now.

As the sisters walked down the hill, arm in arm in arm toward the twinkling lights, Delilah felt the pain of the past few days settling into something manageable. They had won. They had survived. That would have to be enough.

CHAPTER 32
CHRISTMAS TIME IS HERE

Christmas came upon a morning clear in Oak Haven, sunshine glinting off snow that had fallen overnight. The town looked like something from a holiday card: picturesque buildings with smoke curling from chimneys, evergreen wreaths on doors. And the magician had been as good as her word: not a tacky tourist trap in sight.

The Melrose family gathered for their traditional Christmas breakfast. Kelly presided over the dining room, which had been returned to its normal dimensions but was no less impressive for it. An enchanted string quartet played proper Christmas music for once, and the ornaments on the massive tree bickered away good-naturedly.

"More pancakes, darling?" Kelly offered the plate to Luna, who was already on her third stack. "Assuming you have room in there?"

"I'm still replenishing my reserves," Luna explained around a mouthful of syrup. "Portal magic takes it out of you."

"I'm just glad to have you girls home." Kelly's expression was uncharacteristically soft this morning. "All of you."

"Even me?" Scarlett asked with a cheeky grin.

"Especially you, though I'm still not entirely convinced you didn't start this whole mess."

"Hey!" Scarlett protested, flicking a blueberry at her sister. "I take minor offense to that."

"Only minor?" Luna teased.

"Well, she's not wrong."

The kitchen door swung open, and Zahir entered carrying a tray laden with fresh scones. "The Injaberes send their thanks," he announced, "along with some good news. Apparently the forgetting spell is healing nicely. They tested it by sending Uncle Joseph to the grocery store in the next town over. Then they picked him up an hour later. He had no memory of Oak Haven beyond a strange craving for gingerbread."

"Excellent." Kelly nodded approvingly. "And the tourists?"

"Gone, as far as we can tell. The gift shops have transformed back into proper Oak Haven businesses overnight." Zahir set down the tray and pulled up a chair. "Although Jerusha is put out that her 'Hex Marks the Spot' T-shirts are now just blank fabric."

"She'll get over it." Kelly waved dismissively. "More importantly, has anyone seen my Christmas star? The old one, with half the lights burned out?"

"Attic," Delilah said quietly. "Eps found it and thought I might want to keep it. For . . . reasons."

Kelly's eyes softened. "Your father would be pleased. He always insisted that star was lucky."

"I know." Delilah smiled, the memory of Papa no longer quite so painful. "I thought maybe we could put it on the tree this year. For old times' sake."

"I think that's a wonderful idea." Kelly reached over to

squeeze her daughter's hand. "Edward always said that old star would guide you all home, no matter how far you strayed."

Delilah fetched the star from the attic, where the surviving cats were making a holiday meal of the remaining attic mice. As she carried the star down to the lobby, Delilah studied its beautiful imperfection. As a kid, she'd demanded to know why Papa didn't just buy a new star, or have Mama conjure something fancier. Now, so many years later, she was finally beginning to understand.

"Would you like to do the honors?" Kelly asked when Delilah brought her the star. "I assume you can manage this much *without* a wand, yes?"

Delilah bristled. "Mama, I saved forty-seven lives with that wand."

Scarlett and Luna both groaned mockingly. "Oh ancient gods, hear my cry," hollered Scarlett at the ceiling, "please make Delilah stop bragging about the forty-seven lives!"

Kelly grinned. "Teasing, Del, I'm just teasing. Go on, put the star up for us. I hear a rumor that you mastered telekinesis on your travels. So . . ." She nodded toward the top of the tree. "Let's see what you've got, kiddo."

Delilah exhaled deeply, concentrating her powers on the star. The family heirloom rose slowly toward the treetop and settled gently atop the highest branch. The working bulbs flickered to life, casting a warm, uneven glow across the lobby.

"Perfect," Kelly declared. "Now, who's ready for presents?"

As they settled around the tree, Delilah felt a sense of peace she hadn't experienced in years. Oak Haven was safe. Her family was together. And if there was still an ache in her heart where Jasper should be, well, maybe that was the price of victory. Outside, soft flakes of snow began to fall again, drifting past the windows. Oak Haven was healing, returning to itself. And so, perhaps, was she.

The star shone above them, its wonky light a testament to the enduring magic of the season. Not the false perfection of some corny Christmas movie, but the real one: a little complicated, a little busted, but always there for you when you needed it most.

Papa would have approved.

By late afternoon, the dining room of the Stargazer Inn had undergone yet another transformation. Kelly had outdone herself, reshaping the space into an elementary school auditorium so convincing that Delilah could swear she caught that distinctive blend of construction paper, paste, and nervous child sweat that defined every school performance she'd ever attended.

A makeshift stage had been erected at one end of the room, the curtain fashioned from repurposed tablecloths. Rows of folding chairs filled the floor space, and awkward paper snowflakes dangled precariously from the ceiling.

The people of Oak Haven trickled in, and Delilah positioned herself near the entrance to help direct the flow of traffic. She watched as Aphra and Dayo arrived arm in arm, their heads tilted together in private conversation. The love between them was palpable; it surrounded them like an aura.

Next came the recently reunited Belinda and Sam Chatterjee. Sam hadn't let go of his wife's hand since her return, as if afraid she might vanish again. They found seats near the front, whispering and giggling like teenagers on a first date rather than a couple who'd been married longer than the performers had been alive.

"They're gross," Scarlett commented, appearing at Delilah's side.

"They're in love."

"That's what I said. Gross." But a moment later, Scarlett's glowing smile betrayed her words. She waved crazily across the room to Nate, who was helping some of the smaller children adjust their costumes. He caught her eye and pulled a face that made her laugh out loud.

"You okay, Del?" Luna asked, materializing on her other side. "Your aura just went all muddy."

"I'm fine," Delilah lied. "Just . . . you know . . . holiday feelings."

Luna's expression was sympathetic but mercifully free of pity. "Want me to turn you into a lamp for a while? Very peaceful. Zero emotional processing required."

Despite herself, Delilah smiled. "Rain check on that."

A small commotion from the side of the makeshift stage caught her attention. A little girl in an oversized deer mask was sobbing uncontrollably, her tiny shoulders heaving beneath the weight of stage fright.

"I got this one," Delilah said, and swiftly made her way through the crowd.

The child, Delilah realized as she got closer, was Ava Chatterjee, one of Belinda and Sam's precious grandchildren. She'd backed herself into a corner, her deer mask askew. Tears poured down her face as she tried to remove the cumbersome headpiece.

"Hey there," Delilah said, crouching down to eye level, and helped the little girl free herself from the deer head. "What's going on, buddy?"

"I c-c-can't," Ava hiccupped. "It's too scary."

"The mask?" Delilah gently daubed away her tears. "Or the audience?"

"All of it! Everyone's gonna look at me!"

"Well, yeah. That's kind of the point of a performance. People look at you while you do cool stuff, and they all secretly wish they could do it too."

"But what if I mess up?"

Delilah considered this. "You know what my father used to tell me, when I was scared of messing up? He said that everyone's so busy worrying about their own mistakes, they hardly ever notice anyone else's."

"Really?"

"Really. And besides—" Delilah lowered her voice to a conspiratorial whisper "—with this big ole mask on your head, nobody will know which deer you are. If you mess up? Just blame your younger sister. It's always worked for me."

Ava gave this idea the kind of profoundly serious consideration that only an eight-year-old can. "Daisy *is* sort of a klutz..."

"There you go! Perfect fall guy. So what do you say?" She held out the mask.

With a deep breath, the little girl accepted the deer head back from Delilah. "Okay. I can do it."

"That's the spirit." Delilah gave her shoulder a gentle squeeze. "Go get 'em, Bambi."

As Ava trotted off to join the other children, Delilah felt a lightness in her chest. It wasn't happiness, exactly—the Jasper-shaped hole was still there—but it was at least happiness *adjacent*. A sense of purpose, maybe. She made her way back to where her sisters had saved her a seat, squeezed between them like the filling in a witch sandwich.

"Crisis averted?" Luna asked.

"Indeed. The show will go on."

The lights dimmed and a hush fell over the audience. From somewhere behind the curtain, music began to play, a haunting melody that spoke of primeval forests and deeper magics than even witches typically wielded.

The curtains parted to reveal a winter woodland scene, complete with enchanted paper snowflakes that actually fell and paper trees that swayed in a nonexistent breeze. At the center of the stage stood two enormous puppets, each at least eight feet tall: the Holly King and the Oak King.

The Holly King was a magnificent creature, draped in red robes with a wild crown of holly berries and dark green leaves sprouting from his head. His beard was white as the snow outside, and his eyes—enchanted to blink and move—glowed with an eerie blue light. Beside him, the Oak King wore robes of green and gold, his massive head crowned with oak leaves and acorns. His face was youthful and vibrant, a stark contrast to the weary wisdom etched into the Holly King's features.

"They get better every year," Scarlett whispered, clearly impressed.

Delilah nodded. "That pageant committee fights like cats and dogs but they always pull it together in the end."

The music swelled, and from the sides of the stage, the children emerged, half in the green and gold of the Oak King's followers, the rest in the red and white of the Holly King's. They wore oversized masks of woodland creatures, sprites, and forest spirits. Ava pranced out with surprising grace, her deer mask now adorned with actual twinkling lights for antlers.

"Is she supposed to have light-up antlers?" Luna murmured.

"Whatever works," Del said, grinning.

The pageant unfolded in a series of somewhat awkward but

utterly charming dances, the children circling their respective kings while singing a song that told the tale of the seasonal battle. The lyrics, which Delilah had known since childhood, spoke of the eternal cycle: the Holly King's reign over the dark half of the year, the Oak King's dominion over the light.

"*The Holly King stands tall and proud,*" the children sang, their voices thin but enthusiastic. "*His winter kingdom cold and still. But as the wheel begins to turn, the Oak King rises with a will!*"

The puppet kings began to move independently, their enormous limbs animated by magic as old as Oak Haven itself. They circled each other like boxers in a ring, and their little followers mimicked their movements in a choreographed battle that was both comedic and strangely moving.

"Remember when you were the lead deer?" Luna whispered, nudging Delilah.

"God, don't remind me," Delilah groaned. "I tripped over my own hooves and knocked over three sprites."

"Best pageant ever," Scarlett said with a grin. "Papa laughed so hard he cried. And Luna peed herself."

"I was only three—good grief!"

On stage, the battle reached its climax. The Holly King, who had ruled throughout the dark winter months, began to falter as the Oak King's strength grew. The children playing the Holly King's followers dramatically collapsed to the ground, while the Oak King's court danced with increasing vigor.

"The wheel must turn, the light return," sang the children, their voices growing stronger. "The Oak King rises, now we see! The days grow long, the earth renews, and all the world feels young and free!"

The Holly King gave one final, magnificent bow, acknowledging his defeat with grace. Then, to the delight of the audience, he removed his crown of holly and placed it at the feet of the Oak King before retreating to the back of the stage, where he would wait until the summer solstice brought his turn to rule once again.

The audience erupted in applause as the children took their bows, their oversized masks bobbing precariously. Ava, her antlers still twinkling, caught Delilah's eye and gave an excited wave.

After the show, the audience milled around the not-really-a-school-auditorium, congratulating the children and helping to dismantle the set. There was syrupy fruit punch and cookies on offer at the back, so naturally the sisters gathered there.

"So, Luna." Delilah fixed her youngest sister with a pointed look. "How long are you sticking around this time?"

Luna shifted uncomfortably. "Well, I should really get back to Karpathos. I'm only partway through my lessons with the Protean witches."

"Oh come on," Scarlett said. "You can learn to be a shapeshifting blob some other time. We just saved the town from disaster. Doesn't that earn us a little Luna time?"

"If I remember rightly," Delilah added, "you literally got stuck in the shape of a lamp just the other day. Maybe take a beat before diving back into advanced transfiguration?"

Luna's resistance was already crumbling. "I guess I could stay through New Year's . . ."

"Perfect!" Scarlett slung an arm around each of her sisters. "The three Melrose witches, back together again. Nothing can stop us now."

Across the room, Kelly was supervising the magical dismantling of the stage, her silver-streaked hair perfectly coiffed as always. She caught Delilah's eye and beckoned her over.

"Uh-oh, Mama wants you." Scarlett wiggled her eyebrows.

"Probably gonna hand the inn's keys back to you. And not a minute too soon, in my opinion. Filling in for you this year has been more than enough. I am so ready for retirement."

Delilah's stomach dropped. Was that all that was waiting for her? After all her travels with Luna, winning another battle against the magicians, finding and losing Jasper . . . Was she just going back to the reservation desk she'd been chained to for a decade? *That's all there is?*

"So, Mama . . ." She decided to just rip off the damn band-aid. "I imagine you're eager to have someone competent running the inn again."

Kelly's eyebrows arched. "Am I?"

"Well, I'm home now, so I can take over from Scarlett. God knows what kind of mess she's made of the reservations system."

"Absolute catastrophe," Kelly agreed, her tone carefully neutral. "But I was thinking of asking Luna to help out for a while. She seems to need a home base between her adventures. And I think all you girls should understand how to run the family business."

Delilah blinked. "Luna? Running the inn? She'd enchant all the furniture to turn into wildlife at the stroke of midnight."

"Perhaps," Kelly conceded. "Might be entertaining, though."

"But . . ." Delilah floundered. "What about me? What am I supposed to do?"

Kelly regarded her eldest daughter with a meaningful expression, but what *specific* meaning it held, Delilah couldn't tell. "What do you want to do, Delilah?"

The question caught her off guard. What did she want? She'd spent so long doing what was expected that she'd almost forgotten how to want for herself. Well, except for Jasper, and look how *that* worked out. "I don't know. I'm not exactly qualified for much beyond hotel management."

"Nonsense," Kelly scoffed. "You're a powerful witch with a talent for organization and a keen eye for detail. I can think of several paths that might suit you."

"Like what?" Delilah asked, her voice small. "Working at Nate's hardware store? Helping Aphra with her yarn? I can't cook well enough for Zahir to hire me, and with everyone's magic restored, it's not like the witches of Oak Haven need much assistance with anything."

A slow, knowing smile spread across Kelly's face. "Actually, I have something rather different in mind."

"What are you talking about?" Delilah's frustration boiled over. "Gods, Mama! Why is everything a riddle with you?"

Kelly patted her daughter's cheek affectionately. "Patience, darling. All will be revealed." She glanced past Delilah and her smile faltered. "Oh dear. Jerusha is trying to enchant the punch bowl again. I'd better intervene before we have a repeat of the Sangria Incident of '03."

And with that, Kelly swept away, leaving Delilah standing alone, utterly confused and but also a little intrigued. *What's the old lady up to?*

Outside, snow continued to fall, blanketing Oak Haven in a fresh layer of possibility. Tomorrow was another day. And maybe, just maybe, it would bring something completely unexpected.

CHAPTER 33
WHAT ARE YOU DOING NEW YEAR'S EVE?

Jasper's office chair had always been perfectly adjusted to his liking . . . until today, when it felt like a medieval torture device designed specifically to complement his boss's verbal flogging. Nancy sat at the far side of his desk, her post-vacation tan forming an ironic contrast to the storm clouds gathering on her face.

"So let me get this straight." Her skepticism was so intense it was almost material, like Jasper should offer it its own chair. "You disappeared for a week. Nobody had a clue where you were.."

"I was conducting essential historical research," Jasper replied, the words sounding hollow even to his own ears. What research? Where? His memory offered nothing but a strange collage of feelings: excitement, fear, and something else he couldn't quite place. Something that felt like . . . loss?

Nancy's eyebrow arched so high it threatened to detach from her face entirely. "Historical research. I see. And what exactly were you researching that was so important you couldn't be bothered to tell anyone where you were?"

Jasper opened his mouth, then closed it. Then opened it again. "I was investigating an anomaly. In the county records." He adjusted his glasses, stalling. "A liquor license for an address that doesn't exist."

"A liquor license." Nancy's mouth flattened to a horizontal line.

"Yes. For J&J, Incorporated. At 278 West 113th Street, which as you know is impossible."

"And this required you to vanish without a trace for over a week? It didn't occur to you to, I don't know, make a phone call? Send a text? Release a carrier pigeon?"

Jasper swallowed. The truth was, he had no idea where he'd been or what he'd done. The days were a blank slate, yet somehow he felt changed, as if he'd lived a lifetime in that lost period.

"I'm sorry," he said, because what else could he say?

Nancy sighed, the kind of bone-deep exhalation that suggested she was recalculating her retirement timeline. "Jasper, do you know what your job is?"

"Historical archiving and preservation—"

"Filing," she interrupted. "Your job is filing. And retrieving files when needed. You can call yourself the Grand Pooh-bah of Historical Paperwork if it makes you feel better, but at the end of the day, you're a file clerk with delusions of grandeur."

Each word landed like a poison dart. Not because they were cruel, although they sort of were . . . but because they were true. His scholarly pretensions didn't change the fact that his primary function was to make sure the right papers ended up in the right folders.

"Now," Nancy continued, "your little side project . . . the one where you actually get to be a historian? You already know

390

that's not even funded by the taxpayers. That comes from a private grant. A very generous grant from a donor who, coincidentally, wants to speak with you."

Jasper's stomach dropped. "The donor wants to speak with me?"

"Yes. The donor is just as unhappy with you as I am. Nay, more unhappy. You can expect a phone call shortly. I suggest you have a better explanation ready than the one you just gave me." Nancy turned on her spiky heel and headed for the stairs. "Jasper? Whatever's happening with you? Fix it."

He crumpled, laying his head on his desk like an exhausted student after a painful test. The familiar smell of his office—old paper, older wood, and a bit of something organic that Jasper swore was not mildew but definitely was—now felt oppressive, rather than comforting. When he sat back up, Agnes Bartlett was glaring down at him from her portrait, her stern expression somehow more accusatory than usual.

"Don't look at me like that," he muttered. "You don't know what I've been through."

Neither do you, a small voice in his head responded.

Jasper slumped into his chair, surveying his domain. Perfectly ordinary records of births, marriages, property transfers, and business licenses. The mundane machinery of county government, waiting to be filed by the county's most reliable employee. An employee who, apparently, had experienced some kind of unfortunate psychotic break.

That had to be it, right? Otherwise, how could he explain his behavior? What could have possibly pulled him away from his responsibilities? More importantly, how could he promise it wouldn't happen again, if he didn't understand why it had happened in the first place? Something else nagged at him too: a persistent ache, a sort of internal phantom limb. As if he'd lost something important but couldn't remember what.

The phone rang, startling him from his reverie. He stared at it for a moment, then squared his shoulders and picked up the receiver.

"Archives Department, Jasper Hopkins speaking."

"Mr. Hopkins," said a woman's voice that was somehow both warm and terrifying in equal measure. "This is Kelly Melrose."

"Uh, okay? And you are?"

"I am the anonymous patron."

Jasper nearly dropped the phone. He'd been searching fruitlessly for this individual for years and now she was just . . . calling him. "Wow, I . . . I don't know what to say. It's so nice to hear from you. Thank you so much for—"

"I understand you've been absent from your post recently."

He swallowed hard. "Yes, ma'am. I apologize for that. It won't happen again."

"Mr. Hopkins, I devote considerable time, energy, and personal funds to a wide variety of philanthropic efforts. One of these is the preservation of the history of the northwest corner of our state."

"It's a fascinating region," Jasper offered weakly.

"I am deeply committed to these projects, and I only work with people who are equally committed. People I can rely on."

"I am committed," Jasper insisted. "What happened was . . . an anomaly. I've never missed a day of work before this."

"Hmm." The sound was neither agreement nor disagreement. "That's as may be. Nevertheless, I believe it would be prudent to implement some safeguards."

"Safeguards?"

"Yes. You will take on an assistant. Someone you can train to maintain the archives in your absence, should you decide to *wander off* again."

Jasper's heart sank. An assistant. Someone strange in his carefully curated workspace. Someone talking, breathing, *existing* in his private sanctuary. He loathed those moments when other clerks stopped by for *five minutes*; how was he going to share this space all day every day? "Is that really necessary?" He tried to keep the desperation from his voice.

"It is. The arrangements have been made. Your new assistant will arrive shortly."

Jasper wanted to argue. He truly, desperately wanted to argue. But what could he say? Kelly Melrose was the only one who made it possible for him to do the work he adored so much.

"I understand," he said finally.

"Good." There was a pause, then she added, "Don't fuck this up, Hopkins."

The line went dead.

Jasper just sat there, staring at the receiver as if it might somehow spring to life and explain what the hell had just happened. His mysterious, uncompromising patron was forcing Jasper to take on an assistant. Presumably it was a form of punishment for his unexplained absence.

This was a nightmare. *An assistant.* Someone invading his space, disrupting his routine. What if they were chatty? What if they were messy? What if they ate tuna sandwiches at their desk or played the radio or, God forbid, wanted to discuss *sports*? A horror movie of potential scenarios flashed through Jasper's mind: sticky notes plastered everywhere, pens without caps, coffee rings on historical documents. Someone asking him question after question, forcing him to explain and re-explain processes that should be as natural as breathing. Someone watching him, judging him . . .

Someone reporting back to Kelly freaking Melrose.

The sound of the door opening at the top of the stairs made him freeze. Already? The nightmare begins today?

"Hello?" A voice drifted down. Female, with a slight huskiness that stirred something in Jasper's memory.

He stood up, straightening his tie and brushing imaginary lint from his sweater vest. Professional. He needed to be professional.

Footsteps descended the stairs, and then she appeared: a woman in a crisp blazer, with dark hair cut in a sharp bob. Her eyes found his immediately. "I'm Delilah Melrose. Your new assistant. We drove here together once . . . Do you remember that?"

"We've met?"

"Yes, you brought me here to inspect a document you found. Inside that portrait of Agnes Bartlett."

Ohhh. Yes. That part was coming back now. She'd been with him, right at the conclusion of his Lost Week. This woman, this achingly beautiful woman, had somehow appeared in his car. And they'd driven here, and Toby had made rude comments . . . and then she'd left, just as mysteriously as she'd arrived. "Hang on, do you . . . by any chance . . . know what happened to me recently? I had a concussion or something and . . . You were there. Weren't you? I think you were there."

A small smile played at the corners of her mouth. "I, um . . . Gosh, I'm not sure how to respond to that one. I don't want to get ahead of myself. How about this—" She extended her hand. "It's a pleasure to meet you. I'm looking forward to working together."

He accepted her handshake, and the moment their skin

touched, Jasper felt a jolt of . . . something. Recognition? Déjà vu? Or just static electricity from the carpet? "Welcome to the archives, Ms. Melrose."

"Please." Her grip was confident and firm. "Call me Delilah."

As he looked into her dark, soulful eyes, Jasper had the strangest thought: *Maybe an assistant won't be so bad after all.*

ACKNOWLEDGMENTS

Christmas is first and foremost a matter of faith. That faith may take the form of religious observance, or it may be faith in the potential for peace on Earth, the generosity of Santa Claus, or that the turkey won't come out dry this year. And of course the holidays are also very much an invitation to joy. So I want to acknowledge the many people who provided me with generous helpings of both faith and joy as I went through the process of creating *Jingle Spells*.

First, endless gratitude to my editor Amy Baxter, whose thoughtful insights are matched only by her utterly infectious enthusiasm. Amy has the rare gift of making even a grumpy, professionally self-doubting author believe that maybe she knows what she's doing. *Maybe. Sometimes.*

To the entire editorial and sales teams at Avon, you are such a joy to work with that I sometimes forget this is meant to be a business. Thanks for being ridiculously good at your jobs.

My agent, Courtney Miller-Callihan, continues to be the reason I exist as a writer at all. As I say too often and yet somehow not enough, Courtney is a superhero disguised as a literary agent, and I remain grateful to her every single day.

Speaking of people who are vital to my continued existence: my family, Mark and Jonah. Thank you for understanding why I spent months muttering about portal magic and time travel. You are my favorite people in any century.

A quick note for readers who enjoy bookish Easter eggs (er . .

.Christmas eggs?). Every chapter title in this book is a pun on a classic Christmas song. If you're looking for ideas for your holiday playlist, I hope you'll seek out these musical inspirations. In my opinion, it just ain't Christmas without Shane MacGowan's snarl to remind us that love is complicated, beautiful, and occasionally requires bail money.

Finally, my thanks to every reader who believes in magic, whether it's the spell-casting kind or the everyday miracles of connection and forgiveness. May your holidays—however you might celebrate—be filled with joy and faith and a bit of wonder, too.

E.G.

THE SISTERS WILL BE BACK WITH LUNA'S STORY IN 2026!

Loved *Jingle Spells*? Go back to where it all began with *Impractical Magic*. . .

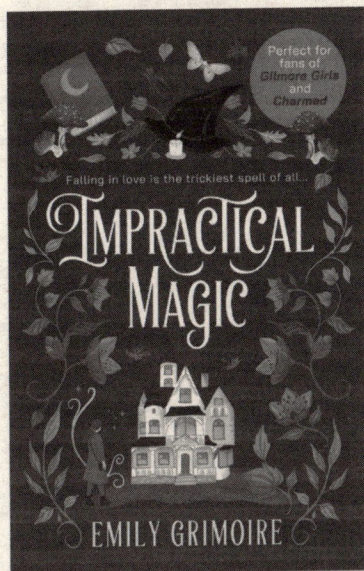

Gilmore Girls meets *Charmed* in this cosy, small-town, second-chance witchy romance.

Available now in paperback and eBook!